FATAL WOMEN

FATAL WOMEN

The Esther Garber Novellas

Tanith Lee
writing as
Esther Garber

With an Afterword by
Mavis Haut

First edition published in 2004 by Egerton House.
This revised edition published in 2013 by Lethe Press, Inc.
118 Heritage Avenue • Maple Shade, NJ 08052-3018 USA
www.lethepressbooks.com • lethepress@aol.com
ISBN: 978-1-59021-310-0 / 1-59021-310-6
e-ISBN: 978-1-59021-073-4 / 1-59021-073-5

This is a work of fiction. Names, characters, places, and incidents are products of the author's imagination or are used fictitiously.

Set in Garamond, Desdemona, & Harrington.
Cover art: David Gilmore.
Cover and interior design: Alex Jeffers.

Cataloging-in-Publication Data available from the Library of Congress.

TABLE OF CONTENTS

To Anna and to Judas, and for Mme Sade K.

Esther Garber

Women are creatures of night

Anna Garber,
Various Philosophies

Rherlotte

They fell in love—and lay stunned, and staring at each other, their bodies and hearts already broken, from the hardness of love's floor and the height from which they had crashed down.

Various Philosophies,
Anna Garber

CHAPTER ONE

 This is the story of how I died.

CHAPTER TWO

Because I don't remember my father, all men have a look of him, for me. Even young men, since he was once also young. Old men, too, although he was never very old. Little boys in sailor suits—once he may have been a little boy in a little sailor suit, his mother wiping an orange ice from his chin. Babies in perambulators. Therefore, Armand looks like my father. He is thirty-three years old (Christ's death age), and handsome. A dark brown head of hair and darker moustache, bright, shoe-polish eyes, tawny, rosy complexion. He has the build of someone who played cricket at an English school, and who rides horses in the chestnut woods at Petignot, which he did and does. He is well-dressed, too, his top hat like a black mirror. A silk tie in claret red, a rose in the buttonhole. The elegant gloves tossed aside the way he tosses things aside. Armand Blos.

"Drink your champagne," he says to me.

I smile, and raise my glass. Sip.

"We'll have those little birds, with the sauce. Do you like those?"

I smile once more. I hate them, actually, or would rather have them twittering on the trees, than have their bones crunching between my teeth. But I intend to please Armand Blos. A lovely pliable, admiring supper companion, which is what he expects.

"Your eyes are quite green," he says to me.

"Yes?"

"Quite, quite green. Like young gooseberries. That's strange. When we met, I thought they were blue. But through that veil… How provocative." He laughs, having liked being provoked, as I meant him to.

"What about this fish? Do we fancy it? Perhaps the dish of chops. But you women, you always must have the sweet things, mustn't you? Eat nothing, and only want the sugary trifle or the strawberries in chocolate."

I smile. Armand knows everything about women, and he has good reason to. He's studied them such a lot.

I say, lowering my gooseberry eyes—Lilas compared them to jade, the last time they were compared to anything—"Perhaps to kiss is the sweetest."

His heat comes all across the table, across the embroidered cloth; white on white, from Sèvres, where we only thought they made china.

"My little darling. You know I can't wait. But we'll eat first. You must eat. There is nothing of you. I could snap that little waist with my hands."

I flutter. Briefly. Fluttering isn't really what I am best at. Even an Armand might just see through it.

He refills my glass. It's so lucky I have my grandmother's head for alcohol. Maybe more of her than that. More than she'll ever know.

The private room is perfect, and I'm aware he'll have used it often before. He is known at this discreet and expensive restaurant.

Long ago, revolutionaries dined here, he says, Danton, perhaps, Robespierre. The decor has changed somewhat. The red velvet swags and the thick lace curtains, the gas-lamps above the cheer-ful fireplace with its heap of coals. The candles on the table, that don't smell as good as candles at my grandmother's, but then she has beeswax put into them. She's a bitch. A queen bee.

I'm bored with the room, its good taste just slightly, accom-modatingly garish, the almost but not exactly naughty classical painting of Leda, twined with a puffed-out, ugly and penial swan. I'm bored, oddly, with Armand, as if I really had come to dine with him, and afterwards let him screw me, probably on that velvet couch over there, just behind the Chinese screen.

How peculiar.

I find my mind slipping away already to my own flat on the street that I will call rue Bucher. To my own fireplace and the monstrous electric kettle, my cup and saucer, the Russian tea caddy, my slippers, my cigarettes in their box, the bowl of apples. I don't think there's a sweet thing to eat in my flat. Even the apples are sharp and acid, as I like them to be. I refused from the age of five to have sugar in my coffee.

When the waiter comes in, despite my wandering mind, I turn my face away, under the heavy sweep of reddish hair I have arranged just so. Perhaps I have a husband I'm betraying. Maybe he simply thinks, poor, lowly waiter-worm that he is, that I disdain him utterly. Only an Armand Blos is good enough for me.

Outside it's raining, silver beads heavy on the panes behind the lace. Carriages in the street. The throaty sound of the city, and the mumbled swish of wheels stumbling weightless through the water.

Autumn dissolves in tears. New, fluid, clean and gleaming in the rain. I, in my pale blue silk, my hat with violets, and veil of blue lace. In my wig of red hair that Lilas loaned me. She said, "Don't tell me. *Don't*. Hush. Not a word." Of course, I'm still dressed for the afternoon, discreetly obscured. This evening I was caught in the rain—my fiction. I went innocently into that notorious café to save myself from a wetting. But seeing Armand—who could resist Armand?

The waiter's gone. The dishes are all set out under their covers. There's more champagne. The man opened it and was sent packing with a robust tip.

Armand puts one finger on my right hand.

"Won't you take off your hat?"

Oh, he likes my hair!

I look into his eyes. It's safe, he only sees shiny gooseberries. "Soon."

Where I was first brought up, they fetched the milk warm to the door every morning, and the gossip with it.

Constance, my rich grandmother, had made herself such a niche that, in front of her, they pretended she was gentry.

Of course, when I say brought up, I was only there off and on, when my mother was too engaged or dismayed to have me.

The plain fact was, my grandmother, and my mother, both of them, were whores. Mind you, whores of a valuable sort. The *cared-for* sort. Courtesans, perhaps. My grandmother being very adept, and my mother a complete fool, who fell in love with her protectors, or with young servant men. I remember her always in tears, always in the rainy autumn of an affair, or the winter following its death. I despised her, and feared Constance. I suppose I have something of them both. Well, yes, I have to say I have, although, then, I would not have seen it.

Anne Blos wrote to me on a piece of palest mauve paper, in a deep blue ink. She didn't use my name, addressed me only as *Mademoiselle*. She said she had been a friend of Lilas Dûle, and that she wished very much to get my advice.

When I received this letter, assuming at once it was what it turned out to be, I didn't know quite what I felt. I'd been living the life of a sloth, or a wealthy old woman's life, almost. My flat had everything I wanted. The meals, when I desired, were sent up from the restaurant across the way. Strolls I took in the park among the statues, or up the Bois, in the green summer sunshine. I needed only a small dog on a leash, but—not needing one at all—had none. I rose when I wished. Slept when I wanted. Sometimes I paid a visit, here or there. Was I happy? God knows. Contented, smug, I think. How well I ran my life. Everything in its place.

I took a carriage to the address Anne Blos had sent me, knowing it would be her very own house, and so it was. I mean to say, not her house, *his,* Armand's, where she lived and had her being as his wife.

"Who shall I say?" asked the fussy maid.

"A friend of Mademoiselle Dûle."

The room was big and polished, with lace on the chairs. It led into a conservatory, a glassy indoor city garden. A palm dominated the vista, crowding up to the crystal roof, and all the pots of flowers crouched in its shade, turning pale.

Anne Blos got up to greet me. She was herself extremely white. She looked as if someone had died that morning, which was curious or not, depending on one's taste. After she'd sent the maid for coffee, she offered me a chair. I passed a mirror on the wall, and in between the gilt cupids, glimpsed myself. But then I knew myself very well. I didn't merit a second glance.

She however went directly to the mirror, as if to check up on me by means of some sorcerous left-over of my reflection remaining there. In fact she was seeing to herself, patting her hair, pinching her cheeks for color—no one, apparently, had told her about rouge.

She settled on another chair, folding the wings of her dress. Sat staring at me.

She said, "Lucette will be back in a moment. We'd better wait."

I looked at her coolly, and thought, *She sounds like a lover.* But I could never have been tempted. Anne was a big-boned woman, her hair dark and piled high with some help from a bad hairdresser. Her face was that of a bug—large popping eyes, small features but for the long, thin mouth. He had married her for her money, and so got her money, but she had not got him in exchange.

It wasn't really what I'd anticipated. But then, it had only happened once, almost twice, before. In the other instances there had been beauty and motives of passion. Yet wasn't this also passion, bubbling under her anaemic skin?

The coffee came in an incised silver pot, with wafers that had cherry paste, and a dish of chocolate creams. Women liked sweet things, didn't they? Did she want them, or think I would? Neither of us touched a mouthful, and the coffee mostly went cold.

She was one of those women who are foolish over their children, trying to turn a boy into a tiny, nearly sexless husband, or a girl into an adventurous version of themselves. But I understood Anne had no children. Nor any pets to console her. She had had to face up to destiny unbuffered by anything but wealth. And banknotes make poor cushions in the end. Money does bring happiness, but it can't send away certain miseries: illness, death, unrequited love. And anyway, the money was now all his.

She explained to me about the money, hesitantly. The small income she had now, and what he did with the rest. Of course, he treated his friends, went deeply into ridiculous business ventures and failed, gambled and lost. But mostly he spent on women. Other women.

"May I—may I call you Phèdre?" She misinterpreted my gaze. "Not if you don't wish."

"Please."

"It's such—a classical name."

"My mother was fascinated by the theatre."

In her true life, Anne Blos would never have stopped to speak to me, let alone speak about my whore-courtesan of a mother who had died of a broken heart when an Italian pastry cook, fifteen years her junior, had told her they were done. Promises of love are like pie-crusts, and so, seemingly, are hearts.

When my mother died, I was about fourteen. I had had a random schooling, strange country schools, and tutors in Paris, one a thick-bearded German, who, rather than teach me his execrable language, liked to sing me mournful German songs, hammering the while on my mother's piano.

After the funeral, Constance, a corseted stone stem in black, topped by a cartwheel hat that had more plumes than the horses, took me aside. She told me I was to go to another school, farther south. She said I could learn the things I required, music, etiquette, other tongues, how to draw. Probably she was instinctively training me to be the perfect expensive whore, or gentleman's companion.

I stayed at the school for years, doing very little. You paid for your daughters or granddaughters or nieces to do little, there. I never mastered anything, except how to play pieces of music from memory, even one piece of Liszt—my show-piece, as they said. I would never acquire the ability to read music. I was eventually the oldest pupil left abandoned there.

Constance had married before my mother died. At forty-five, she had borne two more daughters. These girls, my aunts, were younger than I by some eight years, while the husband was dead of apoplexy.

She allowed me to come to her house at O—, for a visit of a few weeks, then sent me to find an apartment with the help of an agent. The flat was found, and the agent swore he was in love with me. I was nineteen. When I told him, standing there amid those bare rooms, to go away, he said he would drown himself in the river. But I think he didn't.

Constance, at her country house, had given me one last lesson, which rendered mirrors, thereafter, mainly redundant. Standing me naked, but for my chemise, before the long cheval glass, Constance told me what I was.

"You're very beautiful, Phèdre. You can even carry the silly name she gave you. You have quite a calm air of piquance, the mysterious. What do you want from life?"

"I don't know, Grandmother."

"How strange that sounds. Well, there's no need for you to do anything at all. I've settled an income on you, as you know. I don't expect thanks."

"Thank you, Grandmother."

"Use rose-vinegar to bring out the highlights in this black hair. Bathe your eyes at least once a week. Shed a few tears every day, if you're able, it clears the ducts. Use no cheap eye-black. I'll give you the address of the ones who make my charcoal powder. A touch of rouge for the lips. Never corset too tightly. You have a small waist, but may need to do it when you're older. Believe me, it isn't to be wished for." She drew back. "Have you had a man?"

"No, Grandmother."

"Have you ever wanted a man?"

"I don't know."

"That means, of course, you haven't. They're filthy brutes. But you're not a nun. When the time comes you want to, be careful. Do all the things I told you. I fell pregnant only twice, and that in itself is a miracle. I think those two demon girls lay in wait for years inside me. My penalty for all those escapes."

She leaned forward and laid her lined dry face against mine. Her features had broadened, but she had good bones, and her complexion, though powdered and papery, is unblemished, and once like petals, or so they were said to have said. Her eyes—are like vipers.

"Youth and Age," said Constance, my grandmother. "What color are your eyes?"

Outside, in the garden of O—, I could hear the demon daughters shrieking as they climbed trees after birds.

"Grey."

"No, quite wrong. They're hazel. Wet the charcoal and apply it to your lashes with the brush I shall give you. Don't blink until it dries."

Armand eats heartily, now I've taken off my hat. I had to take off the wig too. Lilas got it for me through her theatrical connections, and although it would look convincing on the stage, close to, without the hat, there can be no doubt it's false. My black hair cascaded, down my back, over my shoulders. He watched in delight. "But *why*—dear girl—when you have such hair?"

"My secret," I said. "I'll tell you…later." I've had a few mouthfuls of things, and when he presses me, I say I'm a little nervous. And he concludes I am waiting for the crystallized fruits and ginger tarts.

Anne Blos had smoked cigarette after cigarette. She explained to me that Armand hated to see women smoke, and she whitened her fingers with lemon juice and egg-white to hide the stains.

"I suppose you think I've been an utter fool," she said. I said nothing. She said, "I don't know Mademoiselle Dûle very well. But one day she came here—some sort of charity she does, or pretends to do, for the families of dead actors. I burst into tears. She'd seen a mark on my face, you see. Oh, he hadn't hit me, but it was what she thought. Of course, after her own—I told her that I truly had cut my cheek on the edge of the dressing-table.

But it was because I was so upset that it happened. I was stupid, too, with something I'd had to take. My head hurt so much."

I finished my cigarette. Hers were not so good as my own, or at least, I preferred my own.

"Yes?"

"It was what he said to me. From the very first, he's taken everything from me that he can. He even took my mother's rubies—he said, Can I take them, dear? I need some money quickly. I was so scared of his disapproval, the way he looked whenever I said no to anything. So I said, Oh, yes. If you have to have them. And he kissed my cheek, and took them. And now some Jew woman is wearing them all over the Champs Elarnes. Well, there you are. But so long as I've let him have his way, and never said anything about his women, he's been kind to me."

Poor pathetic creature. She put down her lids over her locust eyes. Her lashes were pale. She'd never heard, either, of charcoal powder.

"The women," she repeated. "I can't begin…"

"There's really no need."

"Well," she said, "I have to tell you this. There are always women, but also, there's one. *One* woman. He thinks of *her,* I believe, as he would a wife. Not me, *oh,* no. But her. She's supposed to be lovely, but she remains faithful to him and winks at all the others, and he goes back to her. She has a house he bought her on the Boulevard Strauss. Maybe he helped pay for it with my mother's rubies." She looked up and straight at me suddenly. "If Papa had lived, he'd have shot Armand."

"Yes, perhaps."

"He would. I've had no one to guide me."

And obviously had not been able to guide herself.

She said, "It was—I made the mistake—of mentioning this woman. His *mistress.* A Mademoiselle de Gillan. He'd been extraordinarily extravagant; he wanted me to get some money from a particular trust, all I have left. I flashed out, If you're so desperate, couldn't she do something? Eh, he said, who d'you mean? I mean, I said, Mademoiselle de Gillan. At that he ruffled up. He looked furious, as if I'd insulted, yes, his *wife*. I. I who am his wife."

"Most trying," I said She expected something, the way the hungry seal in the Zoological Gardens expects a fish at feeding time. She received it the same way, snapping her jaws.

"He said I wasn't to mention *her*. There was nothing immodest. She was only his friend. The only woman friend he'd ever had, since women were generally so ignorant and foolish. I said, And so am I, I believe, for putting up with all this. Oh, I'd never said anything like that to him before. You should have seen him. He swelled up. He strode up to me. I thought he would strike me. He shouted into my face. I can't repeat what he said. I'll never forget it. It goes round and round and round in my brain. That I was slow-witted. That I was—I was so hideous I made him physically sick. He told me—oh, he told me even the smell of me made him—vomit—I can't, oh, I can't…"

"It's all right, madame, there's no need to say any more."

"Never has anyone been so cruel. Oh, I *know* God never blessed me with any looks. But I've done my best. I've tried to make up for it. And this, my reward."

"Please don't upset yourself."

"Upset—I've wept every night until my pillows are wringing wet. It isn't my fault I'm ugly! How could he—how could he—he's had everything. There's no one to protect me. He went straight out and left me there, he went to *her,* this *bitch* de Gillan."

Anne Blos stood up, flaming, rouged now with rage and pain. It did not improve her and her eyes and nose were red, too. It showed the measure of her desperate grief, that word she'd used, which a woman of her "refinement" should not have let past her lips. That word, and sending for me.

With Lilas, it had been quite the other way.
I had seen her act, I think it was Racine. She had a very small part. But she was achingly pretty. Then, a year later, I met her in the street.

I met her because she was standing in the street, holding on to a blossoming almond tree with her gloved hand. Properly dressed, immaculate, she was fainting, and no one had noticed.

It seemed I was drawn to her on runners, something pulled me right up to her. I said, "Excuse me, mademoiselle, are you quite all right?"

She turned up two swimming azure eyes, and instantly leaned against me, her head on my shoulder. I held her up, she was very light. She said, "Oh God." And presently, "Is anyone looking at me?"

"Not at all."

Of course, a few people were, but she hadn't fallen down. I'd opened my parasol too. We might have been sharing a joke, under the almond blossom, two elegant women friends, fashion-plates, with our lace jabots and shady hats.

After a moment I said, "My flat is just across the courtyard. Can you walk a few steps?"

"Yes, if you don't let me go."

Rather odd. Lucky, or not.

By then, at twenty, I'd had a few encounters. Indeed, there had been at the eccentric school, with its Swiss and Italian mistresses, a pair of girls with whom I had sat, on the old swing, up in the green woods. I remember so well the slender leg of Marie-E. in its black stocking, the neat shoe rustling the fallen papers of another year's leaves. Putting my hand upon the ankle. *Oh, you feel just like a snake!* And my snake tongue in her wild raspberry flavored mouth. Later the stockings were peach-colored, with embroidery. Her garters had roses. There were also small roses on her breasts that I liked particularly, gently, to bite. Sweets, after all.

I helped Lilas into my apartment, let her into the armchair with carved arms, and started up the kettle. The flat has electricity, a wonder to some. (Constance frowns upon it. She quotes the novel *Frankenstein*; galvanics create monsters.)

"How idiotic. I've never fainted."

"You didn't quite faint."

"If you hadn't rescued me, mademoiselle, I would have done."
She sighed. "What a lovely sitting room. Do you live alone? I
thought so. There's nothing masculine. How very restful."

Her pale color was coming back. I gave her a brandy made at
O—. She stretched in the dark green chair, and unpinned her
hat. She had a fine mass of light brown hair, some of it tumbling
down.

"It was the pain," she said.

"Are you ill?" I think I may have been alarmed. It wasn't in me
much, to become involved with such things. My mother perhaps
made me fearful of and impatient with illness and tears.

"No, no. But—someone—no, I mustn't burden you, mademoiselle."

I told her my name. She exclaimed at Phèdre. "But I played
Phèdre once! Oh, not in the city, not here. No, it was a little
seaside town. But I was very *good.*"

I told her I'd seen her act, forgotten which play, but remembered her. She blushed. I think she can, as some can, blush at a
wish. She did it to thank me for the compliment, and thanked
I was.

We drank Russian tea and ate slices of orange. We smoked my
cigarettes, for which she used an ivory holder. Finally she told me,
very fast, very simply, "I'm the property of a man, a jealous man
who beats me. He gave me such a blow on the side this morning—the bruise is black. My maid put on a poultice and bound
me up. I felt better, and came out—but suddenly, I thought I'd
be sick, and then all the trees turned into a big pink cloud."

She smiled at me with blue, cat's eyes. "You came out of the
cloud and held me up. It was very kind."

During the afternoon we talked about her life. Her stage career which ended when The Man—she called him at first only
Jean—took a fancy to her. He didn't like her to act. He said it was
a whore's profession.

Gradually, as the evening shadows gathered, his shadow gathered too over the room. She had no one to talk to but her maid,
and a couple of feckless friends who were envious of her "luck."

"Being kept," they called it, and didn't want to hear anything serious.

Jean Viktor Pascet had some money. He worked in an office of banking. He was, she said, tall and grotesque but very strong, hirsute—exciting, she had initially found him. But with his primal appearance came the primitive lusts of a cave man. He was rough in bed and vicious out of it. Although he refused to marry her, which at first, she said, she might have liked, he wanted her to be "loyal." "I mean," said Lilas indignantly, "I've had only two tiny affairs since I've known him. He never guessed. It's such crazy things he takes against." He accused her of bedding the butcher's boy because she had said he had nice curly hair. The first beating came after a party among the actors, to which she'd gone, and taken him at his urging. He'd flirted with all the girls, but since she kissed her former manager on the lips, Jean Viktor Pascet, once home, knocked her across the room. "My head caught something, the fender, I think, and bled. He got upset anti picked me up, promising he'd never hit me again if only I was *good*."

But Jean Viktor had moods, just, said Lilas, like a woman before her courses or in the middle years. He was unreasonable.

Only once she tried to leave him. He indefatigably followed her as far as Versailles and there, in a grove of the famous gardens, blacked her eyes and loosened one of her teeth.

Early on, when she guessed he had another woman, she begged him to leave *her*. Then he beat her worse. The latest assault had been because she had said she wished to visit her actress friend, Minou. Jean Viktor accused Minou of poncing for the manager again. When Lilas explained this manager had died, Jean Viktor grew violent. Probably, I thought, he had cracked one of her ribs, and urged her to see a doctor. "Oh, I did see someone. He said that a corset was the best thing for it. And then, you see, if *he* finds I've gone to a doctor, Jean will say I'm interested in him, though he's a man of sixty."

Finally it was late, and she went home. She said he wouldn't be there. There was a prostitute he now sometimes attended on the rue Bac, especially after they had, as he put it, had a tiff. He would be gone for two or three nights in a row, to show his displeasure.

She wrote to me the following day.

All is well. But already I miss you. May I come and bring you a little present for your kindness?

The little present was a pearl pin. She said it had been her mother's, but it was modern, and quite valuable. She was already wooing and deceiving me. Days passed, and in her eyes there was a look I had seen in the eyes of all my Maries. Presently she stumbled upon some invisible thing—her bruise was quite gone by then—we fell together and I kissed her. It turned out she too had had her "little pleasures," as she called them, among the actress dressing-rooms, two or three excited women crowded together in a small space, damp with scented sweat, chalkily powdered, dressing and undressing. Lilas had painted toenails and a smooth interior, which, plumbing it with two of my fingers, I found made her into a maenad. Her hair tossed, full of feathers from a punctured cushion, she was holding up her breasts in her hands like lovely ripe fruits, giving high screams, kicking, until she fell back dazed and laughing.

She liked deceiving the cave man too, so safely. He was convinced, she said, women could do nothing for each other. If they said they could, it was a ploy to get a man "at the job."

"You know," he says, "I'd like to discover a bit about you. Won't you tell me anything?"

The third bottle of champagne is open. He wanted to send for more, but I said, No, no, wait a little. He guessed correctly, I don't want the waiters to see me without hat and wig.

"So little to tell," I say. I take his hand, large, well-manicured, male, a blush of hair at the bases of the fingers. What is obviously a marriage ring. "And you?"

"Let's both be secret then," he says.

I drop my gaze. "I've been—am being—very indiscreet."

"I'm glad. I'll take care of you, my pretty little girl"

It's strange to me, the way men see me. Always the little, the pretty, this fragile, snappable, slender wisp. Strengthless and

yielding. Whatever do I do to them, or do they do it to themselves, to cover their eyes with the lenses that make me, if not the
world, into a rosy rose. There are thorns, of course, but all women
are untrustworthy.

"Do you think you can give a little of yourself to me, my dear?"
asks Armand, "*you,* if not your history."

"Yes."

He beckons me. I get up and go and sit down beside him. He
puts his hand around my waist, another to my chin. He leans to
me and kisses me. The eating kiss. He tastes of tobacco and wine.
Smells of some cologne. I clutch him, and as I do so, clutch with
my hand at his glass, as if not knowing what I do, careful not to
upset a drop.

"What is it? Do you want a drink? Here, here's my glass…"

"No, no more. I can't. I haven't a good head for wine."

"One sip…" coaxing. But to this he won't coax me.

"I feel rather dizzy. I must…" I stand up.

Alarmed, perhaps even annoyed—will I puke or swoon and
spoil his fun—he swigs off his champagne and pours himself
some more.

I go back to my own side of the table, to get the furniture
between us.

"Dearest monsieur, I want to give myself to you. So much. But
you see…"

"What?" Yes, he's impatient. He'd thought my going over to
him, kissing him, that was it. It was, obviously. Not what he
expects, however.

And now he mustn't, whatever happens, *kiss me again.*

My grandmother, Constance, gave me a great many useful things. The charcoal powder, a special rouge, a bottle
of scent made uniquely for her when she was young, called *Palis-
sandre,* which was no longer quite fresh enough to be put on, but
which smelled wonderful sprinkled on my fire. Also, things came
to me from my mother's enormous hoard of clutter, in her dark
apartment that looked towards the river. I spent hours in that
sombre yellow light, the blinds down at the windows for death.

Sorting through the drawers and closets. She seemed to have kept everything. Old letters about nothing, and a few that were improper, empty powder boxes, blouses crumpled into heaps because they were no longer fashionable, or were impossible to clean, two or three of Indian silk, or lace. She kept cards of invitation, dead dry roses given by admirers, slips from the theatre, tokens of the railway, bits of wool, ancient novels, combs, broken earrings, stockings with holes, and worn out coins, unknown keys, a lucky rabbit's foot that hadn't worked.

There was very little from her childhood, however. She'd left her toys, and part of her soul, at O——, in Constance's mansion that was called locally the Château, despite being a mere house. It dominated the top of the village street, its garden tumbling behind it down and up, to the woods and fields, and to a carriage-way down which quite a few aristocrats had scrambled for the coast in order to avoid the guillotine. In my mother's day, sometimes sheep fell into Constance's garden from the one particular field that stood above the terraces. They were never hurt, but their bleating would fetch an old woman and a boy from the kitchen, beating pans, to drive them back up the sloping returning way they had been too sheep-like to notice for themselves.

The house had come to Constance from a powerful man, when she was in her thirties. She later took her apoplectic husband there in her forties, and killed him off with my shrieking, insane child-aunts, the local cream and butter, the ghosts of my mother and the sheep and all her illustrious previous men.

She had thought herself past the age for children, she boldly told me. When she fell for Sophie and Susie, she hadn't had her courses for a year. What was God playing at? But Constance didn't believe in God, and never set foot in the village church. Her absence, as she said, sat there for her.

"Grandmother, what's this?"

"That? It was among your mother's things?"

"Yes. I thought it was scent, but it doesn't smell."

"Let me see."

This conversation occurred just before she packed me off south, at fourteen, to that school with swings and Marie E.

She took the small bottle, uncorked it, sniffed.

Then she stared at the bottle.

"Where was this?"

"In the drawer by her bed."

"Oh, my God," coldly said Constance, who did not believe in God. "But no. Surely not. The stupid little simpleton. And I gave her this!"

My mother had, after the Italian cook-boy, sobbed herself into a dreadful cold, and taken to her bed. There she seemed to grow smaller and smaller, shrinking away. On the very evening the letter I had written to Constance reached the Château, I walked into her blind-yellow bedroom and found my mother had crumpled in like a dead flower. She'd wanted to die. Said it over and over. And there she was, her goal accomplished.

Broken hearts would of course kill if they truly broke. Ah, but they do break, they do.

At fourteen, Constance took the mysterious bottle away from me, but about five years later, she gave it back.

After Anne had told me about Armand's ill-treatment of her, she wept for a long time. Her big, spare body, that the corseting hadn't quite made to look like a woman's, shook. I waited. Eventually, she said, "Do I presume Mademoiselle Dûle—Lilas... She said you helped her."

"Did she?"

"Yes."

"In what way?"

Anne Blos blew her nose yet again into the lace handkerchief. What joy all the laundresses have.

"I'll give you anything I can. There is a little money left, although it won't last much longer. I could sell this house—I hate it now. I don't need so many rooms. What ever you want. Not to have to look at him. Not to have to know it's there, that mouth, that said those things to me."

That day I call, in retrospect, The Day I Stole My Servant's Hat. It has the sound of a modern play. Something frivolous and smart, perhaps by Foline. Or, I suppose, maybe a short story by Chekhov.

The sequence began with Lilas coming to see me for a luncheon of grapes, pears, and new bread with Normandy butter. She'd powdered the bruise on her cheek and arranged a curl over it. I said nothing. I never did say anything, she would always tell me. Generally now, too, he beat her on the body, although never, through some curious code, on the breasts. "He'll say, Turn around you slut, I don't want to hit you there. He likes me to thank him after, for being so careful with me." *That* was on the day her back was black from one shoulder to the slim, almost-not-there buttocks.

We sipped Muscat, and she said, not how he'd hit her, but, "I can't stand any more, Phèdre. I'm going to run away again."

"But you always say, he'll catch up to you and beat you worse."

"I know. But—oh Phèdre, will you help me?"

"What can I do?" Did I mean, I would do anything, only tell me what? Or did I mean: Don't involve me in this, please?

Lilas wept and drank her Muscat. Tears and wine and the dew on the pears. Charming, like a painting. *Weeping Girl with Fruit*, an illustration from The Day I Stole My Servant's Hat.

"*I* don't know. I won't ask. No. I'll think of something."

We drank more. She cheered up. About three, she delved into her handbag, and brought out a package.

"It's a present. But for both of us. Oh, you'll never guess. Maybe you'll be shocked."

She said Minou had been given it by an admirer who purchased it at Karikal in India. Minou had been too afraid to use it. Just looking at it, Minou said, made her skin prickle and blush. But Lilas said she had used it, now and then, alone. Alone? I didn't believe her. But there are always taps with water and wash bowls, even bathrooms, now, in Paris.

The thing was almost shaped like a flattened crescent moon. Not quite. It was ivory, she said, and whitish, very smooth, like silk to the touch. In the middle was a little bulge that might be anything, rather like a slender napkin ring. From this, the two smooth, round-topped horns went up. They were only the width around I could make between finger and thumb. A toy, not for virgins, but for young girls, or those who wished always to be surprised by well-made men.

Having sloughed all her outer garments, the frilly knickers and petticoat and corset, and lying there on my sofa in her ribboned, transparent chemise, she slipped one of the horns into herself, to show me. Then she wriggled a little, giggling.

I wasn't a virgin. It was a woman who had taken that, with her strong pianist's hands, two years before.

"Let me do it," Lilas said as I kneeled astride her.

She pierced me with great care, but having seen so much of her, I was already trembling and prepared.

Lilas sat up against me. I grasped her under the arms, the little fawn hairs there like rough tinsel. Her breasts swam up and down from the chemise-top. She put her arms around my neck. As we kissed, trying to suck out each other's tongues, the two little ivory phalluses worked away busily against the itching inner mound of Venus which is called the womb, and the dear little napkin ring rubbed us.

Lilas pulled her head aside. She gasped she could feel my tongue deep inside her, tickling her vagina, although she used words both coarser and more euphemistic.

My crisis came like claps of thunder. Lilas shrieked, dying in my arms, her arched back offering her breasts as I died on them in turn.

"Isn't it a lovely present?" whispered Lilas. She insisted that we mustn't move, but lie there, myself burying her beneath me. She said she wished everyone were as light in weight. Of course, quite soon, we began to itch again, the clever ivory moving about at every breath. She screamed so loudly this time I was glad some of the other tenants in the building were deaf.

Because the cave man would be off at the rue Bac, or, as Lilas said, picking up some harlot from the alleys at St. Germain, Lilas stayed with me until nine o'clock. She went home in a carriage, sore and smiling.

I was woken in the morning by my cleaning woman, who seemed to have no name, but whom my grandmother had christened Brunhilde.

She regarded me, in my dressing-gown. Then came in as if by right. I suppose she had one.

The concierge had arranged for Brunhilde to do my cleaning when she learned I hadn't a proper servant. Brunhilde "did" for two others in the building. She cleaned very well, and, once every month, dusted all my books in the five bookcases in my study. Everything, but for three things, was always replaced in perfect order. The three things were: a stone egg that lay on my blotter, which she put on the windowsill, a picture in the sitting room of a meadow with poppies, which she always tilted to the left. And a dictionary, which she put back once a month upside down.

In winter, Brunhilde had sometimes made me, over my fire, a garlicky, thick cabbage soup, bringing all the ingredients, ready cut up, herself. It was served with sour cream and was good. She refused payment for this additional task.

As she cleaned the sitting room and study, I sat in my bedroom brushing my hair. The door was ajar, and outside, on the table beneath the hall mirror, lay Brunhilde's dark hat, quite small and unfashionable, with one cabbage-like red rose. Roses weren't suited to Brunhilde. She was big and brown, with a bush of grey hair held fast by a thousand pins. Her wedding ring was sunk so far into the flesh of her finger she boasted a thief would need to cut off the finger entire to get it. Although she seldom spoke, it was often in startlements. I had gathered too that her husband was long dead, killed by a train at Paisse-sur-mer.

Perhaps the hat had been young then.

Now I studied it, and saw for the first time that it was the hat of a prostitute of several years ago. Only its dinginess disguised it.

Brunhilde had made coffee, but before I went to drink it, I picked up the hat of my slave and put it into the bottom of an ornate wardrobe from O—, under a pile of old dresses meant one day for charity.

Did I know what I did, and why? Yes, surely. I can't remember, but they tell us now, that the mind does things, and causes us to do things, that we don't always understand, but which have a true meaning in our inner awareness.

When Anne had cried herself to a standstill, she apologised to me. She added, "But you see how it is, Mademoiselle Phèdre. You see what's been done to me."

I stood up.

She too jumped to her feet. "Don't go…"

"It's better that I do. I want you to write to me and tell me where I can meet him, where he goes to find these better-class women you speak of, that you say he likes."

"To incriminate me," she said. She squared her square shoulders. "Why not. Very well. But do you mean—you will?"

"We haven't spoken, madame. Do what? We're friends of Lilas Dûle, and have been speaking of the actors' benefit."

He's becoming elated. I mean, Armand. He has stood up, and he's telling me all about the things he wants and intends for his future. He keeps veering away from talking of one particular woman, because he still wishes to possess me, and she's a favourite, probably that one Anne Blos made a special mention of: Mademoiselle de Gillan. Even so, his enthusiasm sparkles. And rain like harsh gravel is flung at the window.

Yes, he's sweating, too. I'm careful, smiling, agreeing, keeping my distance. Sometimes he takes a turn around the table, needing to move about now, his heart beating fast with energy and decision. He tried to snatch a kiss, but I turned my head. "Just give me a moment, dear monsieur. Let me look at you. How I love the sound of your voice."

Far gone enough now, he accepts this. Flaunts himself. His colour is red and his eyes brilliant. I can see he would be thought handsome.

He's thirsty, but I left him all the champagne.

Then his heart flutters, apparently. He touches his breast, looks surprised. Laughs it off. Continues to harangue me, now with a Greek poem, which he rightly thinks I can't translate.

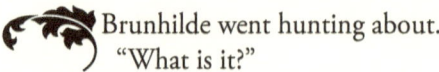Brunhilde went hunting about.

"What is it?"

"I can't find my hat."

"Oh, but I thought—how strange."

We hunted together, and obviously didn't find it. "Look, there's one of mine. Why don't you take it? The hat will turn up somewhere. Perhaps I moved it without realizing."

"I can't take your hat, mademoiselle."

"Yes. Look. This is plain and respectable. And see, it has a red rose."

She took my once fashionable hat, examined it. She knew she would not look her best—that *is,* her worst, her most dowdy and sensible, her most iron and clay self, in it. But needs must.

"It's kind of you. I'll bring it back. Perhaps, if you find my hat, you'd send it on. To the Post Office on rue St. Michel."

"Of course. I'll look thoroughly this afternoon." (She would never see it again.)

"My uncle used to say," said Brunhilde, "things vanish away. Goblins take them. He vanished just like that. He walked into a shop that sold cigars, and never came out. They never saw him in the shop, either."

With this, a tale told often in different forms, but one I'd never heard from her before, she left me. Her uncle was my omen, in his way.

That evening, clad in one of the charity dresses, and in my cleaning lady's hat, I went out and took the omnibus to the rue Bac that lies some twisted way behind the church of St. Germain. I had powdered my face very much, rouged my cheeks. I kept my eyes down, and the better women shrank away from me.

Demonstrably, I might have missed him. But I knew he'd probably be going there, and how he went first to drink, and then came swaggering through the streets about this hour.

It was dusk. A lamp stood on the corner, sickly near-green as a bad duck's egg. Jean Viktor Pascet came from the shadows of non-existence, the wings of life, out on to the stage.

I couldn't miss him. He was just as she'd described. They always have been. Women who are so terrified and angry, remember well and paint vividly. If she says to you, And he has one leg one inch shorter than the other, or one hair that grows awry in his moustache, you can be sure it's so. It is love that's blind.

When he was close, I accosted him.

"Pardon me, monsieur. I was looking for the church."

He looked right at me. Although the lamp was behind him, I saw his face was squashed and dark and sodden. He had terrible small eyes that never stretched the skin around them. His eyebrows met. An unlined face, that of an evil child. For certain, a cave man.

"Church, eh? Sure of that, are you?"

I gave the low coarse laugh Lilas had long ago taught me, her own in unguarded moments. "Well, it's church, if there's nothing better."

"Like a drink would you, lovely?"

"I've got my own. Do you like brandy, monsieur?"

"Oh, yes, I'm partial to a brandy. What'll it all cost?" I told him a low whore's price. He nodded approvingly. "That's a bit high."

I put my arm through his. "Maybe I'll take a little less, monsieur. I think you can please me. I like your kind of gentleman."

And where, you ask, did I learn these nauseous acting skills? Oh, but women always act. And I'd been to the theatre, hadn't I. And the school where they told you, incidentally, how to behave with a man. What a lady does. And that means, by the way, what any woman does. Constance once said, "Almost any man will believe you want him. The ones who don't—beware of them." But Jean Viktor believed. He saw the twinkle in my eye.

We walked, and he asked if I had anywhere to go. I said there might be a room we could have at an hotel I knew. By then we were in the darkness of the alleys, and he was drinking the brandy fast. He felt me as he did so, with his hairy hands, my breast, and my central parts, through my skirts. "Or we could do it here," he said. I said, No, I wasn't used to that, primly. He said that was good. He liked to see I didn't expect him to lean me on a wall, although a moment before, he would have done exactly that.

I wasn't sure, of course, how long I'd have to spin all this out. I didn't know precisely how it would work. But I could see he was getting very excited, and sweating, and he was drinking now for thirst. When he offered me the brandy I turned my head away with it, pretending to drink, all prim again. And when he tried to kiss me, I said, Not here, not here. It wasn't safe. Some ruffian might try to take advantage of us. And he approved of my common sense.

He started to tell me I was a lovely girl, and better than his regular girl in the rue Bac. He might just set me up, if I suited him. And I clung to his arm, so when he staggered, I was pulled about, and I laughed as if it was such a joke. Which it was, naturally.

I had no second of fear. I never have, in those situations. And I wasn't afraid with Armand Blos, not even when he lurched away from the fireplace and clutched the table, glaring at me, the sweat thick as syrup on his forehead, his brown hair black with it.

"What the deuce is the matter with me?"

Did they both say that? Probably the first one, Jean Viktor, spoke more coarsely. *What the fuck's up with me?*

I moved away from the table, and Armand crashed down on his chair. He pulled at his silk tie and sprung his collar open.

"Can't breathe. Open the window—"

I didn't bother with it. Next minute a gush of saliva came out of his mouth.

Jean Viktor's eyes were bulging. He reeled away from me, hit the wall and slipped down. The brandy went with a smash. He clutched his throat, belly.

"What have you done to me?"

Did either of them say that? Probably neither. What was I, after all, an easy, willing woman, found in one case on the street, in the other fluttering her lashes from a momentarily raised blue veil, in a café where plenty of bored or loose women went to display themselves.

Armand did give a choked cry of pain. But the rain on the windows was loud by now, and a carriage galloping by. Then his throat closed. He collapsed across the table.

I didn't watch, with either, the death spasms. Jean Viktor lost control of his bowels, but Armand, for some reason, did not. The mixture in Constance's bottle, which she gave my mother for her protection, a compound perhaps of opium and strychnine and some other tincture, unnamed, has variable effects. If my mother took it, she died quietly, for example, and no one save Constance suspected a thing.

When Jean settled into the muck and night on the alley's floor, I walked briskly away. I went up by the old Odeon, and came out at last against the river, which holds this city together like the hooked-up seam of a gown.

No one had seen me then. And, with Armand, they saw only what they had seen so often, a slender, well-enough dressed female creature, red-haired, and veiled to protect herself.

I put on again my disguise. There was a useful mirror above the hearth, and a back stair from the restaurant, of course. I took the stair, leaving Anne's husband also, dead as a doornail, all over the tablecloth from Sèvres.

CHAPTER THREE

There is a passage in a Greek play—Euripides, possibly, I'm not definite. The hero laments that, on the morning he inadvertently committed a terrible sin against nature and the gods, Apollo had "Dressed the land in gold, set crowns upon the mountain tops." Surely they might instead have warned him to be careful, by an influx of ominous darkness, tempests, lightning.

This day was overcast and crystallized by a cold like white sugar. The chestnut trees were already dropping dead black leaves, and the almonds in the street were dusted white, as if by a thin snow.

The letter was white with black ink, simple. It said:

Dear Mademoiselle,

May I trouble you to meet me at the cemetery of St. Luc, about three this afternoon? I think that we should speak.

I remain, in appreciation of your acceptance,

Mme R. de G.

My first thought was, the great network of women's whispers, sighs, hisses, screams, had caught in my name yet another one who needed me. But I was reluctant. Even though I didn't know, not having bothered to inquire, that le Jardin de St. Luc had been the place of Armand Blos' burial, not eight days before.

Whether to go? What should I do?

I ate my warm roll with white butter, and drank my bitter coffee.

Gradually the sugariness faded from the almonds, and the street bustled.

She knew my address, after all, Madame R. de G. If I failed her, might she seek me here? Would that be any better?

I found her name irritating. It's secrecy. Also some notion it evoked of awkwardness.

In the early afternoon I found myself dressing to go out. I put on a dark green tailored costume. I was elegant. I would after all arrive at the place, look for her, spy, slip away if unimpressed or uneasy.

Mme R. de G.

The lid of the sky hung low, lined with silver towards the river and the cathedral. The carriage jolted me. Were there bones lying on the ground?

Near Les Invalides, a dead carriage horse lay in the road, with two cabmen shouting above it.

Indeed, I had my omens; I won't complain.

So many gravel paths lead to a small chapel. Dark trees bend over the gravestones. Here and there are the monuments. A Virgin with stone roses gathered in her veil. Such things.

I walked slowly. I was ready to pretend to be interested in some particular grave. It was, by the big old clock, fifteen minutes past the hour of three.

Some false note of weather had drawn out a clump of pale yellow narcissi. Looking across from them, I saw a woman standing alone, quite near the chapel. She wore black. Mourning, obviously. If this were she, and she wanted my skills as an assassin, did she have vengeance in mind?

But this might not, after all, be the one.

I went up slowly, stealthily, as if only searching out a special marker. During this, I studied the woman covertly. She was quite tall, slender, curved at the bosom. The dark hat tilted, allowing a glimpse of hair that looked now quite deep in tone, now lighter. Was it red?

Pausing. I gazed down raptly and read the words: *You are taken from me to God.* Death, the arch-lover, snatching away. Betrayals of all sorts.

"Mademoiselle…pardon me," her voice was soft, yet it carried. When I heard her voice, it was as if a hand had passed over me, or some shadow. I've heard them say: *A step on my grave.* But there were graves everywhere, and none was mine.

I straightened, as if vague, my mind elsewhere.

"Can it be, mademoiselle, that, like myself, you came searching for Armand Blos? He's here."

I straightened and looked directly at her.

"Blos?" I asked. "No, not at all."

"But you're the one they call Phèdre," she said.

I stared at her coldly, and hard. My grandmother has perfected this look, and I'd learnt it long ago. It quells servants, women. I'd never dare it with a man, who must always seem the superior. But this one might have been a man, for all the giving way it produced in her. She stared me down, and I stared her down. At last, as if merely exasperated, she shrugged one shoulder, turned a little, pliant in her black clothes. She pointed to the mound at her feet with the ferule of an umbrella. "He died recently. He was found dead. In a private room of a restaurant, but then you know, don't you, Mademoiselle Phèdre."

I said, as remotely as I could, "If you want me for something, you'd better explain. Are you the one who wrote to me, *R. de G.*?"

She turned abruptly back to me. "My name, mademoiselle, is Rherlotte de Gillan. I've heard you called only Phèdre. I believe some families do lack a second name."

"And who told you all this about me?"

"Why, mademoiselle, women hear these things murmured, and murmur to others. You're common property, with some."

My heart was hammering. I was flustered, perhaps frightened. At the grave I didn't glance. It might not be his. And her strange name, which might not even be real.

"I ask again, *Madame*—so you styled yourself, I believe—do you want something from me?"

"Yes," she said. She said, "I know what you did to him. Ah, don't be alarmed. The police are utterly in ignorance, as so often in these cases. And of course, I have no proof. But mademoiselle, I wish you to know, not all the world rejoiced at Armand Blos' death."

She was the mistress Anne had ranted against. Of course, *de Gillan*. I'd been told. She didn't care what she did; loved him. And he had treated this one as a wife.

"I regret your loss," I said. "It seems to have upset your mind a little."

Her face *flamed* white. Her eyes—*burned*. For a moment, she couldn't speak. Then she said, "Don't talk this rubbish. I know you killed him. Was it poison? Yes, the woman's weapon. I'll tell you now, I'll bring you down. I'll make you pay for what you've done. Consider me mad, if you like, if it helps you. You won't escape me."

I said. "Madame, I might in my turn go to the police. I haven't done a thing, and your unhinged threats make me think you'd be better taken care of."

She left his grave. She strode in her straight skirt up to me. She stood tall almost against me.

"Do what you want," she said, "*think* what you want. You'll never be free of me. I'll make you give it back in your blood, your heart's blood. You've spilt mine."

"You loved him," I said. I was, I thought, trembling, but I didn't show it. My voice—trained in the theatre of the world—was firm. "But from the very little I ever heard, he was a poor specimen. He's dead then. Well, well."

She was so near, her breath met my lips, pure but alien.

"Some of us," she said, "do love. I don't care what he was, never cared. I loved him, you're correct. He was all my life was worth. But now, I have another purpose. Now I have you to hunt down, Phèdre."

I smiled. I thought she would lift her gloved hand to hit me and I would catch it.

But she was already walking away, she was on one of the gravel paths. The shadow of a black tree fell on her blackness, and as she came out from it, her fiery hair gleamed in the paleness of the afternoon, like something in a famous, recent, clever painting.

I watched until she reached the gate, and went out. A carriage came up. She was gone.

Then I did look at the grave, and there it was, this new mound, the marker not even set there yet. But someone had laid violets— How? It was autumn…oh, some florist's hothouse.

This had never happened before. If there had been any mourners for Jean Viktor I never learned. For the other girl, she had recanted and called me off.

I had been the hunter.

What had I better do? I went over to a seat, and sat on it. Countless women no doubt had done exactly that, shaking and not quite able to catch their breath.

She might try to kill me in turn. Had she been promising that? But if so, why not here, a sop for the dead, just as in the Greek and Roman myth. A dagger, a glass of vitriol—what a fool I'd been to chance this meeting.

I walked down from the cemetery, and lost my way in a maze of streets, and finally found a cab. But I gave the address of Lilas' apartment, then changed it to the apartment of Elise. Did I think Rherlotte de Gillan was following me? Why should she? She had already got hold of my address.

After I killed Jean Viktor, Lilas became afraid to be my lover. Was she afraid of him—or of me? Although I didn't tell her what I'd done, she knew, of course. He had been found dead, and in a strange morgue she had had to see him, and when she fainted, it was reckoned quite proper. They had said they thought a woman had poisoned him, some jealous whore of St. Germain.

I could see her afterwards, not avoiding my eyes, but staring straight through them. As if to find the true Phèdre at their backs. She would make excuses. Then, if we coupled, either reach a tremendous crisis, or writhe uneasily, incapable of pleasing herself or me.

Once she began to avoid me, I soon found others. One meets women so easily in this city. It's all so innocent, at first. There was a little waitress who would put her pink feet on my shoulders and say in rapture, "Oh, as good as chocolate!" Or the financier's wife I met once in the park, who turned very passionate in the carriage, urging me on, until, by the time we had reached the rue Bucher, she was violently gaspingly finished, worn out, had a headache, and wanted to go home at once. I had only seen an inch of thigh, and touched her breast through all the ruffles. A week later, she wrote me a pitiable letter, begging me never to tell a soul about our *misunderstanding*. I sensed there had been many of these, both letters and misunderstandings.

I liked especially the girl I found in a bookshop. She was just seventeen, and had been in love with all the heroines in all the books, and made me into each in turn. Now a cold priestess, now a hot-blooded princess riding astride a horse, now a great singer. Even sometimes she wanted a little game, where she would lie in her chemise on the bed, her hands clasped on her bosom, eyes closed and lids flickering, and I would have to "wake" her, which I always did with great interest.

But I'm listing here my triumphs. They're redundant in the face of what I have to tell. Let me desist.

Elise had been available to me some while. She was a slimly plump, ash-blonde young woman of nineteen, who lived with her mother near the church of St. Sulpice, whose bells we heard sometimes at odd moments. The mother was a milliner, and absent from seven in the morning until seven or eight at night. Elise, who painted, and sold her pictures, stayed at home. She did the housework, and in the evening prepared their supper. I had met the exhausted mother only once, when she had come home most unusually a little early. Elise and I had been saying our goodbyes, and were utterly decorous. I paid my dues by purchasing on the spot a small picture of a spaniel, which, at my flat, lay in a drawer, except on those rare occasional days when Elise came over the river to visit me.

Although Lilas and I remained "on friendly terms" we had seldom had possession of each other for more than a year. Besides, she had passed on to others her secret, of which she refused to talk, ever, with me. She saw sometimes too, a handsome lawyer, who, she said, often threatened to make her his wife. She was useful in the matter of loaning me the red theatrical wig—I'd wished to inculpate her, under the circumstances. I had even returned the wig to her. She had thrust the box away at once.

Despite or because of these things, now it seemed more sensible to have come to the apartment of Elise.

Elise was my slave. I think she liked to be. Her mother, from the position of her own servitude, had somehow instilled in her the wish to wait on others.

From her startled "Phèdre—oh is it really you? How pale you look. Your hands are ice. Oh, come in," to the goblet of cognac, kept only for medicinal aid—"I'll tell Mama I had one of my headaches—" she fluttered warmly over me. At another time, I would have been stirred by her attentions, her scent of lavender, charcoal, painted paper. Not now.

Was I at all clear? I suspect I wasn't. I immediately said to her, "Will you do me a favour, Elise?"

"Anything—anything at all, darling."

"A man's been pestering me."

"Wretched brute."

"Here's some money. Would you take the cab outside and go over to my flat? Make sure no one's loitering."

Elise sprang up at once. Seldom going out, except for slow tired walks with her mother on Sundays, she yearned for action. She had on her hat and wrap and was gone in five minutes.

But how stupid of me. She would be looking out for some hulking male figure. Not for the terrible svelte figure of "Madame" de Gillan.

Patently, I made Elise go so that, under cover and in a different room, I could consider alone what had befallen me.

And what was it? Did I even know?

De Gillan had no proof, she said so. She could do nothing, because she had wanted to do something and not found what it was she would do. Although she'd had the opportunity to murder or disfigure me, these things she was too fastidious perhaps to attempt.

The threat was all she had, her declared vow of revenge on me. Revenge she would never get.

She was beneath my contempt. To have loved such a creature as an *Armand*. To parade her distress at the loss of an *Armand*. What a dunce she must be.

I drank the cognac down. I sat back in the battered, comfortable chair where Mama sunk her creaking bones and weary stitch-pricked fingers every night.

Shutting my eyes, I felt myself fall a thousand feet into something that wasn't sleep—for I was conscious. A kind of trance. Beset by moments of dreams, knit together by apparently rational thoughts.

I was back at the gate of the Jardin de St. Luc. I was going in. It seemed I had to play over again that scene. As if, playing it for the first time, I'd missed so much. But what had I missed? An encounter with this ordinary, well-dressed, bourgeois, cool—yet obviously hysterical—woman, who had loved Armand Blos.

There she is on the path up near the little chapel. Why not turn back, now; avoid her. I should have done so then. Yes, I was as much a fool as she, risking the interview.

But on I go. Along the graves, to meet again, yet properly for the first, Rherlotte de Gillan…

She's wearing black—mourning for whom? (It was Armand. I know it, now.) Yes, she had vengeance in mind. Upon Phèdre.

Something at that moment seems to check me, but I take no notice. I move up slowly, stealthily. During this, covertly, I study her. Tall, almost my height, surely. Slender, but curved at the bosom, blossoming there. The dark hat tilted, allowing a glimpse of hair. It's red.

Pausing. I gaze down. Words on a grave…*gone from me to God*. I've never thought of death that way. The taker, the taken. My mother all crumpled up in that bed. Meaning nothing. One more object to be tidied.

"Mademoiselle. I beg your pardon." Her voice, this woman's voice, is sweet, soft, yet carries. A hand passes over me, a shadow.

I straighten, vague, and interrupted.

She says, "Can it be you are also searching for the grave of Armand Blos? It is here."

She has, now I look at it, the face of a statue. Not the white Virgin near the gate, with her veil of roses. Rather something classical. The antiquity of Rome, the proud daughter of some noble house, the Flavians, the Caesars. But in the white and classical Roman face, these two eyes, somewhere between jewel-blue and jewel-green, level, unblinking, flashing light like steel, under the graceful, hand-carved brows.

"Blos? No, not at all."

"But you're Phèdre," she says.

My name in her mouth. My name sounds changed and new.

I stare at her, with my grandmother's cold, hard look, but she, this one, gives it back. Not jewels then, the eyes, but turquoise mirrors. She stares me down. I stare her down. Do I give way first? I think…I may have. And she shrugs, and turns her shoulder. Tiny waist. But the shoulders quite wide, very straight, not tired by supporting the sumptuous breasts. Flame runs over the coils of hair under the hat. She points her sword—for a moment, a sword it is—but now—an umbrella—at the mound before her feet.

One can just see Armand lying inside it. He laughs. And is gone. She says, "He died only recently. Was found in a restaurant. But you know."

I say, "You'd better explain. Are you this woman, *R. de G.*?"

With the movement of a fencer, she spins back at me. Her chin is up. A rounded chin, such as a statue would have. The eyes flash again. So cool, so brilliant, adamantine—only soft with, flooded with, *colour.*

"*I* am Rherlotte de Gillan."

I stare. This name. Have I heard it ever? I must have heard it. I know it. Anne must have said. She did. But not the first name. *Rherlotte.*

She insults me, without raising her voice. She never has.

"Your family, I believe, has no second name."

Who told her this?

"Women murmur about you," she says. What's she saying now? Not only am I a bastard, but also an "unnatural" woman. A woman who prefers women to men. *Is* she saying this?

My heart, hammering. Flustered and shaky, frightened perhaps. Her strange familiar name. It might not be real. It's outlandish.

"What do you want?"

Her skin is white as the marble statue she was before some magic—the kiss of Armand?—brought her alive. Her lips are perfectly shaped, the upper arched, the bottom lip rounded as if for biting. The tint of rosy amber. Is it rouge? They look, her lips, her mouth, warm to touch. She says, "I know what you did to him. Don't be alarmed. The police are as usual in ignorance. And of course I have no proof. But I want you to know, Phèdre, not all the world rejoiced at his death."

He had treated her as his wife. Not Anne, who was, but this one.

I say to her face that she's unhinged.

Her *face flames* white. Her eyes—*burn*.

That red, shaped mouth says to me, "Rubbish. I know you killed him. I'll bring you down, I'll make you pay for what you've done. You won't escape me."

I say I will go to the police, and tell them I've been threatened by a madwoman.

She leaves his grave and strides to me. She stands so close, almost against me. Is she an inch shorter than I am? But the power of her fills up the space, and she towers. Her eyes belong to the caracal, the lynx, set in the luminous marble face. Her lashes are the colour of shavings of bronze. The arched brows like long, combed, tawny feathers. The lids of her eyes are, seemingly artlessly, a little dark, and burnished. I can smell the faint ambrous musk of her hair. She's cleaner than the inside of an apple.

I imagine her eating apples, biting them. Drinking white milk, so her throat ripples, the wonderful mechanism under the drum of smooth skin. Her teeth are *white* as milk. I see their biting edges.

She says: "Do and think what you want. You'll never be free of me. I'll make you give it back in your heart's blood. You've spilt mine."

A shudder passes up my back. Every bone of my spine quivers. What has she said? Is it some spell?

I won't show her that I tremble. That would be most unwise. The years of controlling my voice before my harsh grandmother, my weak mother. To men who came into my mother's apartment in Paris. That makes me able to say, flat and firm, "You loved a poor specimen, from what I've heard."

She turns her head then, as if she can no longer breathe the same air that Phèdre breathes. Her profile—yes, the goddess Diane on an ancient silver coin. The straight nose, rounded chin, the huge, moulded eyes, the lips that are pure and forbiddingly chaste, yet sexually cruel, voluptuous with saying No. Did she tease him to her feet? Did he lie helpless under her strength? He's there now, on his back in the ground, but why does he laugh at me? I killed you, Armand. It was I who won.

The face of the moon goddess Diane strikes back at me.

"He was all my life was worth. But I have you now."

She is the huntress, not I. She rides them down, the fleet deer in the forest, even the tigress she rides down, and casts into them her moonlit spears.

If she raises her hand, I'll catch it. I'll crush the bones until blueness appears about her lips, until she screams and falls against me.

But she's also too fastidious to strike me with more than the angle of her face, her eyes. Her spears.

In any other place or world—she *would* have killed me. A dagger through my heart.

She's walking away. Her hair, flames, fades, flames.

She's left him violets. Shall I tread on them, mash them? There had been violets on the hat that I wore for Armand, as I wore Brunhilde's roses for Jean.

In the cab—is she following me? Or has she gone the other way, to wait at my door.

Rherlotte de Gillan. Diane of the marble flaming moon.

FATAL WOMEN —

Let me run to earth.

But the last net of dreams shows me death standing in the road, above a fallen carriage horse. Under the hood, Death has a red mouth. Is it myself I see, or her?

When I extricated myself from Elise, reminding her that her mother would be coming home—it was almost six—I returned to my flat. No one, according to Elise, was anywhere about. She had even, as I'd found at the door, inquired of my concierge if anyone had left a message. No one had.

But when I entered the building, I saw the envelope addressed to me.

A pang went through my side. An actual pain.

I took up the envelope. It was pale mauve, with blue ink. Inside was an instruction, where I might receive quite a large sum of money.

Anne Blos added, in her prim way, *I am so grateful to have had your help in this enterprise.* She had incriminated herself with idiotic honourableness. The night of his death, playing Bezique with friends. Only I could bring her down.

I didn't need the money. Would write to tell her so. Instead I must pack my bag. The night train was not so pleasant, but I would take it. And tomorrow be at O—.

CHAPTER FOUR

The house at the top of the street is large enough, I had no thought Constance would be put out by my unannounced manifestation. She has countless servants. All in terror of her. The only drawback was my aunts.

At the gate, *they* were both waiting, as if they knew.

Perhaps they did.

"Why are you here?" said Sophie at once.

"To visit you," I said.

Susie, also staring at me, said, "We don't need you."

They have such big, unblinking eyes, which sometimes they narrow, a sort of yellowish blue. White, small, sharp teeth, in small, soft *shut* mouths. Cascades of hair, which in Susie is quite dark, more tortoiseshell in Sophie. Sophie is plumper, too. Otherwise, almost identical.

These, the demon children who lay in wait in Constance's womb, for her to be careless in her forties.

They were thirteen. An unlucky number.

With little polished nails, Sophie pawed at my two bags. Georges-of-the-Station had got down from the trap, and was preparing to carry my luggage to the house door. I thanked him, tipped him, and took the bags. They weren't heavy.

Susie's white dress was stained with garden things, fallen leaves, bark, moss. Sophie had a spot of something pink on her blue blouse.

"Are you coming in?"

"Of course, what else."

"It's very early," said Susie.

"We've been up since dawn."

"We always are."

With difficulty I got by them, as they plucked my tailored jacket, wove around me, and up to the door, which stood open.

In the flagged stone passage, a maid was hurrying towards me.

"Oh, mademoiselle. Mistress isn't waked yet. Shall I tell her— I don't like to—"

"It's perfectly all right. I'll see her after breakfast. Would a cup of coffee be possible?"

Constance anyway called me in to breakfast with her. My aunts came too, but she sent them out.

When they loitered in the doorway, she threw a slipper at them, and they vanished.

"They'll listen at the door."

"Perhaps. But they're soon bored. Then they'll go away."

I said, boldly, because Constance hadn't been, herself, very polite to me ("Good God, isn't there enough for you to do in Paris?"), "Are they mad?"

"I expect they are. Children of old age. He was almost sixty-five, and I, as you recall, was not young."

She had a country breakfast, two eggs in their shells, a plate of bread, dishes of butter, jams, apples, a bowl of cream. She drank strong tea, and tossed back an inch of some white spirit, maybe the local brandy.

To me she offered only bread and butter.

"I know you don't eat."

"I'm tired. I was travelling all night. A maniac with an accordion or hurdy-gurdy, I'm not sure which, went on and on in the carriage. It snowed at Petignot." I had been troubled by that at the time. The train jerking over the crossing with its little house of one yellow window, the flakes drifting on the wind to mingle with our cinders. Armand Blos had ridden his horses in the woods there. Anne had had a farm in the neighbourhood. She had it again now, and the horses wouldn't feel his impatient and perhaps inhumane hands ever again.

"Snow. There's no snow until November. Don't you remember? You always hated it as a child."

"Yes. I hate snow. I don't know why."

"A gypsy told me snow was your enemy. Or ice. That was a long time ago. Another said men would be the enemies of your mother. Is that why you're here?"

"I don't understand."

"You do. Because of a man."

I'd have to tell her something. I had made something up on the train, altered it, fiddled with it, as the hurdy-gurdy churned round and round in the back of my nose and ears.

"In a way. A woman of my acquaintance became envious. She thinks her husband has an interest in me."

"Does he?"

"Nothing less likely."

"I thought not." She began on her second egg. "By which I mean, Phèdre, you wouldn't be interested at all in him."

"He wasn't appealing, no."

"No, I'm sure." She ate, swallowed. She drank her tea. "Your mother put you off, didn't she? What you saw. So much sobbing and wringing of the hands."

"She had an unhappy time."

"You despised her." I said nothing. Constance said, "So did I. You, I. We're not fashioned from the same clay as your mother. Then again, you're not like me. We'll say no more. How long will you stay?"

"I don't know. A few days, if you'll allow me to."

"And then this matter will have blown over?"

Would it? I was without thought, the hurdy-gurdy had eaten my cunning. I must wait for it to grow back.

"I expect it will."

"She's so very angry."

"Mortally so." It was out before I could stop it. I visualised myself and Rherlotte de Gillan fighting over the favours of Armand. This made me laugh.

My grandmother frowned. "Is it a law suit?"

"It—might be. I don't think she'll bring herself to that. She's very...abstemious, I think."

"Was he worth it?"

"I said, I had nothing to do with him."

"Very well." She peeled an apple. Belatedly offered the bowl to me. I took one of the fruits. It was russet, red, the smooth colour of a mouth. I held it in my hands as she dismissed me to the upper room that had always, in this house, been mine.

Little blue checks on the curtains and brown flowers. The wallpaper sallow damask, patched with a hint of damp near the ceiling. Ivy grows over the window. Sometimes they cut it back, but this time they had let it alone for some while.

There's a memory always of lying sidelong to this window, on the pillows of goose-feathers, with the dark mahogany posts and back of the bed all gathered into shadow, and that window, green as jade outside from the ivy leaves, and inside from the old fern that grew in a pot.

What was I, as a child? It doesn't matter now. Someone else.

I couldn't sleep, tossing and turning, too cold at first despite the stone bottle filled with hot water, then too hot, throwing off the old fashioned quilt that smelled of dried roses.

Then I dozed. Rherlotte stood on a huge monument above the tomb of Armand. She was made of marble, all but eyes and hair. She drew back her marble arm and hurled the spear at me.

I woke up with it in my breast.

What had happened?

Sophie and Susie were at the bed's foot.

"Will you take us to Paris?"

"No."

"We want to go."

"Tell Constance."

"Constance says no."

"Run away. Hide on a train."

They looked at me scathingly. They had thought of it perhaps, realized that it wouldn't work.

Why weren't they at school? Would a school refuse to have them?

They stood in the window now, and their shadows crossed the bed like two bars. I should have locked the door, but had forgotten.

"Go away, I want to sleep."

"You had a nasty dream."

"Yes."

"What was it?"

"I dreamed I woke up and you were in my room."

One of the maids knocked, came in and told my aunts that my grandmother wanted them for their lessons, so explaining the mystery of their presence in the house. They went quite eagerly, but only, I was sure, to do some mischief.

For a while I did sleep then. I dreamed of the usual inane things one does. And then a dream of making love to Lilas, she screaming with joy, but not myself experiencing anything at all. As if those parts of me had turned to stone.

In the afternoon, after our huge country midday dinner of roasted chicken pieces, rice and vegetables, the house lay torpid. In my grandmother's room, the old stove chugged. She often said it was a wonder she'd never been asphyxiated, but then, there were so many cracks and tiny holes in the house, and the windows rattled loosely at the softest breath of wind.

Sophie and Susie slept curled together on their blue eiderdown. They shared a double bed. I had once considered if they did anything surprising together, but they seemed sexless to me, probably not. They'd rather catch butterflies and eat them alive, which I had seen. Or sit on the highest front wall, throwing small stones at passers-by on the street. There had been many complaints to Constance. But such was the spurious power the village had given her; she was able to dismiss them all with little presents.

Once the house slept, I went up to the attic. The ceiling was low enough it touched my head, although Constance could walk upright. Had she shrunk?

I found at once the enormous trunk with the broken lock. Reaching far down inside it, among old mothy clothes and ribbon-bound masses of crumbling paper, I inserted the poison bottle. She had given it back to me when I took the flat in Paris. She said it was for my protection. I'd said, But my mother had had it, and maybe used it in on herself. Constance said briskly, "Then the more fool she. But she didn't. That was a silly woman's fancy I had."

I accepted the bottle from curiosity. Sometimes I would take it out, uncork it, sniff. It had the same dead aroma of nothing, as before.

Still, it had had a taste of life—or death—with me. Jean had sampled it. And, of course, Armand.

As I let it go among the contents of the trunk, I felt no relief, no lightening of my burden. But really, I hadn't expected to.

When I left the trunk, standing up, I looked a moment around me. The attic was full of terrible things. A stuffed snake from India that perhaps belonged to Constance's husband. A set of antlers from a stag, and a whole box of bones and fossils out of the hills around. In a chest lay embroidered, spangled clothes falling to pieces; some might have come from the eighteenth century. There were paintings of men on horses, and women with faces like masks, so tight-lipped and empty eyed. Everything was being spun together into a thick dough of cobwebs. One shouldn't come in here at all to disturb it.

Below in my room again, I gazed through the jade plates of the ivy. A light rain was sprinkling down. The elderly fig tree looked as if made of metals, iron, copper. They had already stripped the figs, which ripened early here. Up on the slopes the fields blew with tasseled stalks. Elsewhere you saw them, men and women walking with their scythes. Cutting everything down. It might have been the Middle Ages. They'd moved the sheep, Constance had said.

I picked up the apple from breakfast. Although I'd only played with the hearty lunch, I was unable to bite at this fruit that was the colour of the mouth of Rherlotte.

What was she doing? Evolving some plan? Or had she stormed and wept herself out at last, now in the grey limbo which is called healing, but is only the realization that one can do nothing, nothing will ever improve.

How had she loved him so? *She.* I had only been able to look at her properly in memory, but then I saw what she was. I couldn't understand it. I pictured Constance saying sternly to me, "How would you ever know what was attractive or not, in a *man*?" Very true. Very true.

Days passed. Nights passed.

There seemed to be too many meals and not enough of anything else.

I went for walks about the village, where ancient villagers, brown as the autumn leaves, took off hats, or sometimes bowed to me. Once a woman came to her door leading her two fat, smiling children. The girl ran up and handed me a posy of crocuses already fading. Another time, a crone came and put a huge egg, honey-coloured and still warm, into my hand. "To make your cheeks bloom."

Laughable and embarrassing though it all was, I found something also sinister. I had been a child here. Had they then pitied or mocked me? I was in some sense their prisoner even now, because they had watched stages of my early life, seen me after my mother's death, and when I returned from the southern school.

At night, I heard the wind grind and whine round the house. There was a full moon, and the dogs for miles about bayed at it for hours. Owls yelled as they swooped across the fields. So much noise. So much life.

Although I locked my door, my aunts had found a way to pick the lock. Twice I came back to find all my few clothes, my hair brush, pins, powder box, scattered on the floor or bed. Why twice? I'd added nothing. Perhaps they'd forgotten their first foray. Both had a poor memory, except for slights or particular pleasures. The woman who brought the milk, the postman, were *bad*—they'd both once shouted at the sisters, one could guess a hundred reasons why. That jam was *good*, this one *nasty*.

Constance seemed to make no attempt to control them. Although she had conceived, carried and borne them, she never thought of them as being hers. They were two tricks played on her. And in just this way they went on. However, they'd never crossed her. She was the only one.

I asked what lessons she taught them. She said, very little, they wouldn't sit still, or if they did they fell asleep. She had brought them tutors, but the tutors ran away.

One day Constance would die, and would I then inherit my aunts? Perhaps I should have retained the poison bottle.

After six days, I was desperate to leave. Rain fell heavily and glutinously now as glycerin. The trees were almost bare. It was very cold. Constance accused me of bringing this forward winter from Paris.

"Then I'd better go back."

"High time," she said.

When I packed my bags again, Constance sent a boy for Georges-of-the-Station, and the trap. It would be a morning train now. I would reach the city by night.

My grandmother sat in her drawing room, upright in a carved black chair. She had put on her rings, for my departure.

Do I have any actual appearance of Constance? Her hair is lavish, worn folded in a snood behind her skull, a style at odds with everything. Deliberately, I expect. Long jet earrings. She keeps to touches of black, a proper wealthy country widow, this well-heeled whore.

I can see nothing of me in her, or her in me. But she's there.

"Take this," she said.

"What is it?"

Had she given me some memento?

"Unwrap it, if you like."

I undid the plain and withered paper. Inside, the bottle of poison.

What could I do? I stood there holding it. She said not a word, and so finally neither did I.

I got wet in the trap despite the large umbrella Georges put up over me. He and his brown horse steamed in the rain, sometimes shaking their heads.

I fell asleep at last in the train, and had no dreams I recollect. I might have been dead, unless the dead do dream. One hopes not. In death one hopes to escape from everything.

CHAPTER FIVE

Paris by night, dry with gas lamps and dull, warm windows. Above, the web of stars. The sound of the city, which grumbles.

I seemed to have been away a year. It had been a mistake. I had no one to assist me, no one who loved or wished to protect me. (I could hardly count servile little Elise, who would probably run errands for a street porter.)

Who, anyway did I need? What had I to fear? Some maddened lover, a fool who had loved a fool. By now she doubtless wished she had never accosted me.

Even so, stepping into the building, a catch at my heart. But no one had left anything for me. And if anyone had come, they'd left no trace.

I'd thrown the softening apple away on my journey. There was nothing to eat. I didn't want a thing. There had been too much food. Some wine, one narrow glass. A water biscuit dipped into it. Then my bathroom—there were no such luxuries at O—. And my harsh, horrible, amazing electric light. My Frankenstein kettle to make a cup of tea.

I lay in bed, warmed from the bath, drinking the black tea.

It seemed I'd fall back into the nourishing dreamless sleep of the train.

At first I did. At three or thereabouts, I woke again. Wide, wide awake, as if I'd been shaken.

In the darkness, I *smelled* her. Was it in fact a dream? That amber musk, her fresh skin and breath. She might have been bending over me, the dagger poised.

I jumped up and put on my light.

No one was there. I searched to be sure. Outside the outer door only city silence made a noise like the sea.

Damn the bitch, she'd been waiting all the time, here in my own refuge, to smother me. Or was I going quite mad. It might only be that.

They were small but elegant, these houses. This one was washed with palest oyster pink, and had dark green shutters, like something from the far south. Behind the railings prickled along a box hedge. A tall linden grew in the courtyard, stripped of leaves and already in the grip of early winter. A giant child of bones.

The ride hadn't been long. Across the city in the afternoon. The river shone with its different, winter light.

The Boulevard Strauss was perfectly easy to find, and alighting from the cab, at once, as if it were meant, a maid came down a path with a letter in her hand.

I'd thought anyway I should be able to make out the house. It would be a house of mourning, its blinds down, even black crepe hung about. Of course, it was nothing of the sort.

The maid looked at me as I stood before her, waiting, my pre-destined messenger. "A Madame de Gillan lives in this street, I believe?"

"Oh, yes, mademoiselle. That house down there." She had pointed it out carefully, so I couldn't go wrong at all.

Armand, according to his wife, had bought his mistress this house. Had it already been in these colours, or had some celebra-tory mode in her caused her to repaint it? To celebrate him, even. I could just see him arriving; quite drunk, very late, beholding the lamp left burning for him in the hallway, and the one seductive rosy upper window of her bedroom. I hesitated by the gate. Then pushed it open and walked around the tub that held only green shrubbery. Up the steps to her door. It was not a modern street. No electricity at all. The knocker was of well-polished brass, a fine hand from the seventeenth century holding a slender scroll.

Without any choice, I took a deep, uneven breath. I felt very cold. I rapped the knocker decisively.

The maid came, dainty and neat, not a hair out of place.

"Good day, madame."

"Is Madame de Gillan at Home?"

"Yes, madame." No preamble. No feinting, to make sure I was welcome. Did the bitch *expect* me? Or some other woman— "Who may I say?"

"Say *Phèdre.*"

Not one flicker of query.

"Very well, madame. If you would follow me."

She led me straight upstairs. The treads were polished with a rich olive runner. The banister post was a woman like a caryatid. This seemed compatible. De Gillan was just such a being.

An upper room opened before me, with glass doors, shut. Irises of stained glass framed in clasps of purple: the image of her, already there, before me, and I wasn't ready, so half turned myself away. I gazed back down the stair, holding to the caryatid at the top.

But the neat maid had trotted to the doors, opened them, then gone through. An iris-coloured curtain drawn aside. A Persian rug across the floor. Everything immaculate, burnished, wiped, dusted, kept faithful to its most lovely hue. And there. Herself. She. *Rherlotte.*

She was standing now, by the desk where she had been sitting writing.

I must look at her.

I turned back, lazy, as if I had only been more interested in something else.

My God. Oh my God.

What is this feeling, of falling, of panic, of heat, of ice? Am I truly so utterly terrified of her? All the way here, my hands trembling, shivering, a sickness lying under my breastbone.

The light was behind her from a long window. She seemed to float, her feet not quite on the floor. She wore not black, but the darkest grey. Her hair was loosely done, drooping in heavy, silken loops and ropes. The colour of her hair. There never was such a colour. It wasn't *red.* How could I have thought it was red? It was the colour of marigolds that are almost pink.

I hated her face. I'd slap it. I'd walk up to her and strike her as she'd have liked to do, but was too bourgeois to attempt, with me.

"Thank you, Marthe."

The maid went by me. Left us, closing us both up in a glass cage between the crystal window and the glassy iris doors.

Could I speak? It seemed I had to. Or she'd smother me, like the half-dream when her ghostly soul leaned over me the night before.

"I hope you're well, madame," I said. No one would know, would they? Did she know I couldn't breathe?

She said, remotely, idly, "Quite well, thank you. Yourself?"

What an exchange.

"No, madame," I said. Inspiration appeared. "I'm vexed. It's been very trying for me. So I've come to see you."

"What's vexed you, then?" she said. Her bizarre politeness hadn't extended to inviting me to sit. I paced up and down, once, twice. I'd had to move. Everything else seemed moving. But when I stopped, all things stopped. My heart had been thudding wildly, now it too was stilled. I couldn't feel my flesh at all. I hung in the air, as she did, feet off the floor.

"Your accusations, Madame de Gillan, upset me very much. Another woman would have sought a lawyer. I've come to confront you, as you saw fit to confront me."

"Oh," she said. She seemed nearly listless. She went drifting off down the room towards her fireplace. A cozy fire burned there. On the mantelpiece was a Louis XVI clock, or what looked as if it were. "There wasn't any need to come here," she said. "I told you the facts. There's nothing more to say."

I shouted then, stagily throwing my voice as Lilas taught me by doing it herself. "How dare you, madame. How *dare* you. To accuse me of a crime. To threaten me. Your very actions prove you know me to be innocent."

She half turned. She had a little sad, humorous smile just creasing her cheek. "And how is that?" she asked.

"For God's sake, if I was such a villain—a murderess—didn't you fear for your own life in accosting me?"

"That," she said. She sighed. The world was leaden on her today. She looked into the fire that made her hair pale and ordinary. "I must explain, Phèdre, I don't care about my life. Not anymore. Once he was dead, my concern in living left me. To go on—is just a show."

"You said to get vengeance on me gave you a purpose." There were tears in my eyes. How astonishing. As if she actually had distressed me by her false verdict. She'd spoken my name. I could still hear it ringing round and round, making my head spin.

In my handbag, the bottle. Yes, brought with me. I could go to her, force open her mouth, force in the edge of the bottle. One sip, one choked swallow. If she resisted, I could throw her down. Though she was tall, she was less strong than I, this I could sense.

She remarked, "I said many things to you. Yes, if I'm able to destroy you, I shall. But you see how it is with me. How weary I am." Again she sighed. She leaned her arm on the mantelpiece, rested her head upon her hand. Her back was to me. How easily I could attack her.

But she didn't care. No longer the huntress. Or, if she was, she was lost in the great wood of the world. As I now felt myself to be.

I sat in a chair unasked. About her eyes I'd seen fine lines. She was older than I.

She straightened up suddenly and turned around and looked at me. When she did it, my blood seemed to drain out of me, straight into the floor.

"You're in a bad way," she said. "Have I scared you?"

"I told you you had, by your lies." (She had seen.)

She was brighter. Her eyes, sparkling.

"Yes, you do me good," she said. "I like it, to dismay you. After what you did to me."

I would need to get up. She was moving towards me now, along the carpet. Before she reached me, I should be on my feet. Too late.

She leaned right over me. Everything swirled, my sight occluded. The ceiling seemed to swim down. She had put her hand on my face. It was a gentle hand, warm after all, not marble.

"How satisfying to find you're only made of flesh," she startlingly said. "So vulnerable."

I wrenched my head away, and rose against her. For a second my body brushed over hers. It was like an electric shock. It threw us both back from each other.

Then again I saw her warrior's face. She showed her teeth at me. Her eyes were blades. So much for having no fear of death at my hands.

"You're insane," I said. I had to speak her name. I got it out as if it were made of rocks and briars. "*Rherlotte de Gillan.*"

She raised her chin at the battle-note of her title. We were still close enough, I could feel the warmth that came from her, the scent of her, some perfume, brought out by the fire.

"Are you going?" She seemed genuinely amused now. She gave a little light laugh. "I should like to see you from time to time."

"Should you? You fucking bitch, you can rot."

Her eyes widened at the words. Her lips pressed together. She was affronted, not by my violence, but by my uncouth phrases. Worse than Anne Blos. Little bourgeoisie. Had she ever known a moment's pain, until her buffoon of a lover was shoveled into the ground?

I said, "Never come near me again. If you do anything, I'll have you put away. You swore your own oath to me. I swear this to you. Damn you to hell."

Turning to go, I lost her. I couldn't see her. Then, she came towards me again, her refection, in the iris doors. She stood immobile. Her red mouth lay upon a petal of an iris. I could have smashed the glass with my hand, but before I did it, I saw the blood, the shards, the mess on her neat and pretty room. And I didn't want to, didn't want to.

I opened the doors and went out. Down to the street, I suppose. Into the street. Away.

CHAPTER SIX

We went to the funeral in a carriage, my mother and I. Is it only a memory again, the yellow blinds, half down at the carriage windows. Death, then, always dressed for me in yellow. It was my father who had died. Was I about four? One of my earliest recollections. I believe he was in his late thirties. Perhaps a little older. My mother must have been something like twenty-four years old. She sat crying under her veil. She kept saying, I'm sure she did, "What shall I do without him?" although I never recall he had been there. And, "He was so fond of you, Phèdre." But did I ever see him for more than a few seconds? He's absent from my mind except in the words of others.

He must have been wealthy. He left her something. But we shouldn't have been at the burial, that was most improper. And she went in a spirit of utter abnegation. It wasn't any passionate protest or display. It was, in an awful way, her total *respectability*.

The cemetery was full—with the dead, but also with the living. Where was it? I can't think at all. The day was overcast, or was that only the mood of death and my mother's continual weeping? She stifled this as we stood at the back of the crowd, where actual sightseers, a charwoman, a road-sweeper, two gallants on their way home from an all-night binge, had accumulated to stare, cross themselves, or mock.

I kept waiting for us to do something, go forward, look at the grave, as, even then, I'd been told people did. I didn't relish it, but couldn't grasp why we didn't have to. There must have been a priest, at least. He too, a casualty of my memory.

Then I wanted it to be all over. I was tired and very bored.

One of the gallants came up to us. He started to play with my long black hair, and I pulled away.

"What a pretty little girl, madame."

My mother raised her tear-soaked face. "The dead man was her father," atrociously she said.

The gallant sussed her at once. Not so difficult. She was well-dressed, yet stood at the back of the crowd, had no place in it. He said, "If you'd allow me, I could take your child for a little walk. This must be very sad for her."

But then his friend came up and hoisted him away. "For Christ's sake, Philippe. Not that young, you stinker."

If my mother knew what went on, if she'd have let him have me for an hour, to feel over and probably worse, God knows. She only went on crying. And finally the funeral concluded, and then, when all the other mourners had gone, she went and stood over his grave, that they were waiting to fill in.

The first flung clod was on the coffin, which was a handsome one of mahogany, with silver handles. Some flowers were there too. Incense still spiced the air.

"What shall we do?" said my mother.

No one answered, and we went home.

The current maid—we were always losing and replacing them—gave me blancmange and cake. But I wasn't upset. For my mother, the maid had, naturally, only the most resentful contempt. She muttered something about her sister, whose husband had been taken from a brawl, not of his making, dying, with his arm pulled off. "Ten kids to feed and clothe, and never a tear in public. It's them with the time to grieve as mourns."

The sound of my mother sobbing was so constant in my ears, I sometimes still hear it. This isn't quite madness. Little noises of the street, the wind under a latch, rain that drips down, these can be mistaken. Do I feel sorry for her now? I feel sorry for no one, not even myself. I have few tears and none for loss, even my own. What does that make me? What do I care?

A day or so after my visit to the Boulevard Strauss, Lilas came unexpectedly to see me.

I say unexpectedly, because no longer did she ever call on me. When I went to her, it was in order to get hold of some necessity—the address of a bookseller. A red theatrical wig…

"Oh, Phèdre, darling love. I never see you now. You do neglect me so."

She acted as if we were women friends in the conventional way. But I knew her. There was a certain light in her eyes. As I poured out the tea she'd requested, she kept touching my hand with little, fluttering pecks. At last she said, "Are you quite all right, Phèdre?"

"Yes, quite."

"You look so beautiful—almost not *here*. Transparent. *Glacial.*"

On the bureau behind me lay the letter she'd handed me on her way in: "It was in the birdcage."

This is where the letters were left below. On the round table at the common entrance, stood an empty birdcage, courtesy of the concierge. In this cage the letters lay, sleeping birds. Dead birds.

This bird was white with fine black writing.

I'd put it aside. Lilas said, "Won't you open it?" Nosy and pained at once. She would always rush to receive her post. "No, it's nothing. Perhaps the glove woman's bill."

Now the letter sat behind me. Crouched there. If it were a bird, would it fly up, and settle suddenly on my neck, tearing with its claws and red beak?

Yet there were others in the city who wrote with black ink on white paper. I couldn't recognize the writing so soon. The writing of Rherlotte.

But Lilas said, "Can't I sit beside you?"

"Why not."

"Are you putting me off? Oh dear. You know, my sweet, I think I'll have to marry that young man. My lawyer. He's so insistent. And he's two years younger than me. But his old father—bless him—well, I charmed the old man. At first he was dead against it all. But now he says nothing matters, I have a *goodness* in nature. Of course, there's only supposed to have been one indiscretion.

That was—that was *Jean.* I said I'd been frightened of him, which I was. They know he came to a bad end."

I said nothing. Lilas said, slowly, "I know I'm quite safe in your hands."

"Yes, you know."

"The other one. Oh—Phèdre, Phèdre—" suddenly she flung her arms about me, laid her head, with its floss of fawn hair, on my breasts. "How are you so brave? You're like a knight. The knight who fights the dragon. And rescues us."

"Am I?"

"You hate me now," she said. She played with a false button on my blouse, as if knowing this one couldn't come undone. "Ever since—you've put me off. Did I revolt you, poor weak Lilas, unable to help herself."

"I think you've been the one who stayed away."

"Let's change that. Oh, it will be lovely. I'll have a beautiful apartment near the Louvre, looking out to the Tuileries. The old man's promised. And dearest Edouard will be away such a lot, sometimes all night, on his cases. And he just isn't the sort of man who'd suspect a thing, even if he found us in bed together. And if he did," she looked up at me laughing, her breath fragrant with a cachou she was sucking, "do you know, I think he'd leap in beside us."

"And I should leap out."

"Oh, Phèdre. Haven't you ever felt anything for a man? I can't believe you haven't."

"Where are you going with this?" I asked her. "Do you want him to marry both of us, in case I testify against you, or blackmail you in some way. Rest assured, Lilas. All that's forgotten. I'd never trouble you with it. You're the one who speaks about it in drawing rooms. And doubtless receives a tip."

"*I?* What are you saying?"

"Anne Blos," I said, "approached me. How else do you think— You'd told, her, she said, how I helped you. I expect that was worth a few sous."

"I only said that you'd been kind when I was desperately unhappy. She jumped to a conclusion because she wanted to."

Lilas pretended to be affronted. I wished to slap her pretty face, put her out, kick her down the stairs.

"Let's say no more about it," I said.

"You hate me. And I still love you, Phèdre. I've had my little pleasures with women. But oh Phèdre, Phèdre. With you—I thought I'd die of it sometimes. I don't mean *that*! I mean needing you. And you so cold. You only wanted me for that. You felt nothing."

"All right."

She got up. She picked up my cup—not hers, mine—of white porcelain painted with little flowers, and deliberately threw it into the fireplace, where it smashed.

Calmly, disgusted, I compared this petty, mean upheaval with my session at the house of Rherlotte.

"Perhaps you should go, Lilas."

She was in tears. Had she really never learned tears don't move me, or only the tears and weeping sounds of lust.

I stood up, and she backed away. She said my name. Then snatching up her hat rammed it hard on her head, sticking in the pin as if to skewer her brain.

She ran for the door and was gone.

As I gathered up the bits of the cup, I smelled her perfume over everything. The oriental scent her betrothed had found her: *Frankincense*, it was called. The heady aromatic of churches, funerals—

I spent some time putting the pieces of the cup into a linen napkin. I don't know why. A souvenir?

Then I tidied up the tea things.

Then I went and took hold of the white and black letter.

I walked about the room with it. Adjusted a picture, straightened a cushion. Into my study I went. I poised at my desk, running my eye over this and that. The sinister egg on the blotter. Books.

Eventually I sat down, tore open the envelope. Spread the letter before me.

No idea remains to me of how long I sat there, reading the letter over and over again. It grew dark. Then I rose and drew the curtains.

In my sitting room the fire was low, I stirred it and put on some more coal. My hands were nearly numb, and the letter somehow still stuck to one or the other of them.

Dear Mademoiselle Phèdre—so Rherlotte addressed me. Then, *I said I should like to see you. I can't resist seeing you. It's quite frantic with me. Perhaps you'd meet me in the White Room at Les Épices, for one of their lunches. With so many honest, mundane people all about us, we should be safe enough from each other, do you think? I wonder if you will come again to meet me. Shall we say noon, tomorrow?*

Inevitably now, I considered her quite mad. I lay awake two thirds of the night, thinking this. In the morning I bathed, used a powder with the scent of crushed honeysuckle. I dressed myself in a blue silk dress. The dress I'd worn—that night. (The night I'd poisoned her lover.) Demonstrably I should have burnt it. Long ago, I'd disposed of Brunhilde's hat, first the dress, in bits, on my fire. It took me some while, scissors, sparks careering dangerously up the chimney. The hat from the dinner with Armand, even that, I'd seen to, snipping it to pieces and feeding it away into the flames.

I had another hat, more suitable, a pastel sky of silk, with one long green feather.

I chose green gloves.

Blue and green. Her eyes?

The White Room, like Les Épices itself, was once an English experiment that dared to open in the city. Now it was in the hands of the French, but faded, not very popular.

The door was opened for me by a lackey in black and red.

What could be more ordinary, two bored, well-to-do women of the smart, but not extravagant order, taking a little lunch, while they discussed fashion, children, men. What else do real women discuss or do? Real women, the kind men have invented.

What did I feel, all that time. What does one suppose? I had had to take a brandy before leaving the flat. I dropped my key. In the carriage, I was giddy, longing to make it turn about and take me back.

When I got out, again that sensation of having no feet, floating. Everyone was a puppet, a ghost. Nobody had any solidity at all, least of all myself.

I wouldn't have been surprised if she'd got hold of a pistol and shot me dead as I crossed the threshold. What worth did her words have—the honest, mundane about us. They didn't have any part in this. It was only she and I.

I saw her at once. She was already there. Sitting at a white table in the room that was like a sculpted confection of meringue. The unlit chandelier wafted in space behind her, lit to lights by the windows shining in its prisms. She wore a mauve costume, still the colour of mourning, of course. In her hat was a spray of feathers, cinnamon in colour, like the combed feathers of her brows.

She was just the same. All things change with memory but not Rherlotte. She was identical to her recollected image. Was she beautiful? Something. She was something that had no logical adjective to describe it. One might say, fire sat there, or sun in winter ice.

I was at the table before I knew what I was doing. She watched me all the way, and the ground seemed to tumble off under my feet which didn't touch it.

"How nice that you could come," she said. The waiter was at her shoulder.

"It was kind of you to ask me to meet you."

"Oh, not at all. We're such old friends."

Laughter danced behind her eyes. She was all amber, white-amber, amber-amber. Her eyes were blue amber with green amber stars.

I sat down.

The waiter was decorous. Two such charming young women. And wealthy. (Had she forgotten my coarse language to her previously? But I hadn't smashed the door.)

She was choosing things. She was asking me if I would like this, or this. Like a clockwork toy, Phèdre was saying, yes, that would be just right. She could have offered me a dish of woodchips in arsenic. Perhaps she had. What, after all, had I given *him*?

When the waiter went away, she looked at me. Her eyes held mine. She drew in a little breath and said, "I wondered."

"What?"

"If you would come here. After so much rage."

"Yes," I said, stupidly.

Rherlotte drew off her kidskin gloves. Her hands were pale, with tapering fingers. Her nails had been polished into sea pearls. She wore no rings, despite her masquerade as "Madame."

"We have both," she said, "been brave. And here's some wine for us to drink to each other's courage."

The waiter saw to us protectively and patronizingly. We were women. But she had chosen something luminous from the north, with a golden look and faint taste of strawberries. I can't remember what it was. Sometimes, even now, I lie awake again, trying to recall such details. I saw it, drank it, heard it spoken of. But no, it's gone forever. As they say, forever and a day.

We drank.

"Don't be frightened," she said to me. "I haven't forgiven you."

"Do you want to talk of all that again?" I said. The wine, after the cold ride, perhaps the brandy, had gone to my head more than I was used to.

"No, I don't want to talk about the past. Not now. I'll say only this, Phèdre. You're all I have left of Armand. All I have left."

Blood or wine thundered in my brain.

They were putting a dish of something before me. What was *that*? I can't, I can't remember. But, you see, I was looking only at her. Devouring her. That meal tastes of her, is scented by her. I ate her flesh and sipped her soul. Rherlotte.

Well, you knew. Why must I lie? I didn't know it then. No, I was simply curiously happy, there in the middle of this madness, breaking bread with my enemy. I almost laughed, and she, she did laugh. She stretched across and put a delicate leaf of some herb on to my plate. "Eat this, then drink the wine. Yes, like that."

I did so. I recollect a flavour of strange elements. Pleasing. I said, "Did you put something on it?"

"Ah, no," she said. "No, Phèdre. I couldn't do that to another, even to you."

The last course was a lemon water-ice. We toyed with it with tiny silver spoons.

All around, the honest and mundane, most of them of the male species, eating, rumbling at each other. There had been many eyes for us. She'd say, "Look at that one," or, "He wishes we weren't quite so proper."

The luncheon had only been her. She said, "You eat very little. Were you kept hungry as a child?"

"Yes. But not for food."

And then she said, "How beautiful you are, Phèdre." Almost what Lilas, what others, had said.

When I looked into her eyes now, I dropped again, miles down. Struggling I put up my head out of these oceans.

"Why do you say such a thing?"

"I'm puzzled. How could you *do* such a thing?"

Was I drunk? I'd never been so. A couple—three—glasses of this unusual wine. A brandy. Some liqueur that was bitter. "But I haven't done anything," I said, "I'm under your spell."

"Are you?" she said softly. "Then you would have to tell the truth."

"I'd tell you what you wanted to hear. If you want me to say I killed your lover, then I'll say it. I didn't, of course."

"Of course you did." Then she said, "I seem to have known you since I was a girl. Is this what happens? The murder has made us intimates."

I began to see her throat, the white column with the moving wonder behind it that throbbed as she spoke. Her lips were a moment moist with liqueur, then matt. The lobes of her ears were translucent, and from each hung a tiny raindrop of opal.

"What shall we do about it all?" I said.

"There's nothing to be done."

Soon after, the lunch was over. We'd finished. Didn't linger over coffee or petit fours. We got up. We walked separately together to the doors and glided through.

I said her first name. It came easily to me now. Much too easily.

She turned and looked at me, her eyes just an inch below my own. "Goodbye, my dear," she said. "What a pity it all is. Never mind. Goodbye. Until we meet again."

What had we talked about? I must have been asked about my childhood—for I'd told her something of it. The "Château," my grandmother. But I diluted her strengths and said nothing about her calling. In my mother's case, too, I was reticent, or think I was. I seem to recall I presented her only as an indolent and rather unhappy woman. I tried not to show my irritation (but must have done?). Did I want to make a favourable impression—*on Rherlotte*?

The lunch had been a craziness. For hours after, despite what she'd said, I thought she must have poisoned me. I awaited a burning sensation, nausea, death. And all the while I sat or moved about in the blue silk dress.

Why hadn't I offered her, instead of those tamed vignettes of my life, the knowledge that this was the dress I wore when I killed Armand Blos, and watched him die in front of me?

Had she guessed?

Had she told me *anything* about herself, beyond only the unutterable yet uttered fact of her lover's murder? I seemed to remember a sentence here or there, lilies floating on the surface of the phantom, fairy lunch. She was once a shop-girl—could I believe such a thing? Or that she had, like me, relatives in the country, a small house or a farm, but it had been sold. She had in childhood swung in a swing suspended from an oak tree. But then, wasn't I only confusing this with my memory of the swing at the school, where I had sat rocking with Marie-E.

Did I entirely confuse her, Rherlotte, in some peculiar and unsuitable manner—with *myself*?

I wasn't even sure really that we'd spoken to each other. Everything had been anyway a conversation. Her lifting of the glass of wine. My hand upon a spoon or knife. The herbal leaf she passed me which could have been deadly aconite.

I took off the dress at last and laid it on the bed with the hat and gloves. I looked at the things. They were my witnesses, but couldn't speak. None of them carried a mark. I sniffed them. They smelled only of Phèdre and her scent. Had I imagined everything?

Before, I had sworn I'd never go near her again. Told her so. But I'd gone without a thought, or only thinking she was insane and it didn't matter.

Did I sleep that night? I don't know. This begins a time when there's nothing of me, except when I'm with her. I think there was a dream. Of her, obviously. She was bending over a pool and feeding white creatures, perhaps swans. Something she may have told me from her youth, or some children's tale. The Little Goose Girl, the Swan Princess.

Her notes came. I'd find them in the birdcage, or fallen on to the table. Once the postman handed me her letter. He seemed suddenly rimmed with terrifying gold in the cold grey street. It was always the same. Would I come to lunch with her at Les Épices, or some other old-fashioned place, or take tea with her at the Café Flor? I wasn't invited to her house. I knew she wouldn't come to my flat. Always neutral—safe?—ground.

The second note, I remember that. And how I sat down at once and penned a reply, sternly... *Since you don't believe what I've said to you, I can't credit that you truly wish to see me.*

But she assured me that this was the very reason. I was the last of him—all she "had left."

I tore up my note, and hers, and the next day I met her. This was five or six days after the first lunch. In elegant gilt chairs we nibbled lettuce sandwiches and drank tea flavoured with bergamot.

From this point all conversation between us becomes one long conversation that circles about itself, always repeating the same things, altering them subtly, developing upon them, like the movement of a symphony, or variations on a theme.

I see her with the slice of lemon, held by a silver implement, like a tiny round of stained glass. She wears a grey hat, the velvet trim, something white fluttering, white lace at her throat, a little cameo brooch from the Roman, a girl with the same alabaster face as her own.

"The winter is so long. Too long. Already it's begun. Spring seems to vanish in a flash and summer soaks away. But the cold. Is it a premonition of something?"

"Death," I say, "do you mean?"

"Do I mean that? What do you think I mean, Phèdre?"

"I imagine you to be a good Catholic," I say. "What have you to fear?"

"If I were, everything. But I don't believe in God. A God would be merciful and kind to us. There'd be no pain."

"God, allegedly invented pain, to try us."

"I defy Him, if so," she said. "That wouldn't be a God, Phèdre, but the Devil."

"You're a Cathar," I say, and then, always pausing before I speak it, "Rherlotte."

"Perhaps. They believed the Devil made the world to deceive and hurt us. Oh, yes. I could think that."

And I see her in the White Room again, mixing a drink for us—I'm sanguine now, she won't kill me here—something lucent, something like strawberry syrup.

"All these minor actions, Phèdre, with which to fill our days. We wake, we get up, we put on our clothes and go about, turning over knives and forks, swallowing tea, writing in our journals, until it's time to go to bed again and pointlessly, stupidly, dream."

"Dreams…" is all I say.

Rherlotte says, handing me the silvery pink drink, "I dream of Armand. But even when he takes me in his arms, I know that he's dead. There's a sound in the dream, like a low pessimistic drone. From that I know."

Do I say to Rherlotte, I dream of you. You feed the birds, and swing on your swing, or ride on a red horse over the meadows.

I've seen you as Jehane d'Arc, and they were tying you to the pyre. Lighting the first of the wood. Your proud, cool face, your raised chin. You wore mail at the stake, but your hair was put up just as now, with these two full ropes of marigold covering the tips of your white shells of ears. You wouldn't give in. You never do.

"When I was a child," she said once, "I used to think one had only to be good. That it was easy."

"I think it would be easy," I said, "but the mind outwits it."

She put her hands together. "Ah, Phèdre. You're right. How clever you are. Like an arrow, straight to the point."

And a tight hot wave passes up through me. Is it a blush of pleasure at this inane little accolade?

Ah Phèdre, the mind. But there is the body too. All this while I hide her from myself, myself from myself, myself from her. That she fascinates me I must accept. That I would, if *everything* were different, and she inclined, like to make love to her; this I can't be so imbecilic as to refuse to see.

But when I first look at her, each time, this sensation of falling, falling down, but into an abyss which has no floor. Even when I think of her, quite often, when the image of her comes into my inner eye, and she is physically distant across the city in her pink house of green shutters, the naked linden tapping its bones in her yard, even these sightings throw me off from the precipice of falling.

If I fall, to where do I fall? Shall I reach the bottom of the chasm? Will it kill me, this fall? Or is it only flight, the sole form of flight of which I am capable?

Rherlotte…
    Rherlotte.

And now, our fifth luncheon. It was to be special, but I didn't know this. One thinks, when a pattern is established, it will continue for a while at least. Until some new thing comes to disrupt it. She and I, sitting and talking out our variations on a theme of her loss, the unadmitted development of my murder. What could change or dislodge us? I should admit the truth, or she find some other interest? We would quarrel, as at the first, the second, time of meeting. Although *quarrel,* of course, is not the proper word. Even then each of us spoke like some musical instrument, sounding across the panoply of a whispering orchestra. First this phrase, and then the responding phrase. Hers harsh, then dainty. Mine obscure—then violent.

There was still the violence. I choked it back. I saw it now as lust, which must be held away from her, since perhaps she knew, as she seemed to indicate the second time, what Phèdre is.

And yet, she must keep seeing me, it was she who wrote, it was she who asked me always, begged me, to come to her. She said, "You saw him last alive." I answered, "Only in your fantasy, madame. I was nowhere near Armand Blos when he died. Wherever he was."

I wait for her notes. I look for them, going endlessly up and down stairs. If something white is in the birdcage, I pull it out. Even if not white—perhaps she's changed her writing paper. But the notes are always the same, black upon white. Her hand is well-trained but not exactly careful. At the end of her gracefully-formed sentences, sometimes a coil or dash of the pen. Her name is signed small, yet there's a flight from the final *e.* Away, away it goes, a stroke of darkness, towards the future.

And now, here's the note speaking of lunch. Just like all the others, the seven or eight notes from Rherlotte. Tomorrow. Now there's a tomorrow.

I've burnt that dress. The blue one. Cut it up and fed it to the fire. In the depth of a drawer, the little bottle. I should throw it away, but someone might find it.

In the dusk, the frosty stars come out above the city. The street lamps shimmer in the icy air.

I dream, that night before the special lunch, that Rherlotte is in a boat on the river. She sits there quietly, trailing one hand in the green, luminous dusk water. Who steers the boat? I can't see. Perhaps, after all, I do. At the Café Flor, then, they set aside an area "for ladies," and fat pigeons of waitresses attended to one. I had been there several times recently, with Rherlotte, and was greeted: "Good day, madame."

Rherlotte hadn't yet arrived. I sat down at the table, shook out a napkin, drank from the water glass which had now been filled.

"Such a cold day, madame. Will you have something to warm you?"

Rherlotte would warm me. "No, thank you."

Did I really admit it to myself? Perhaps not.

I looked about. The walls were painted with almost-innocent terracotta frolics, girls of the eighteenth century with stemmed waists and pushing breasts, carrying panniers of flowers and fruit, young men in culottes, with powdered hair and hunting dogs. Here and there a satyr playing a syrinx. Cherubs at the corners. After half an hour, the waitress returned.

"Madame's friend is so late today! Can I get you anything while you are waiting?"

I came out of my daze, my dream. I looked at a clock. Rherlotte had never been late. Normally she was there before me, or if I was early, she would come in on the very hour.

I picked up my glove and put it down.

Would the pigeon waitress go down and ask if any message had come round for me?

She did so. Returned again, she seemed humble. "No message, madame."

I waited, drinking water, playing with the napkin, the glass. Looking at the pictures on the walls, trying to explain for myself some story behind them. This young man wanted that young woman, but the satyr would have her first.

All about, the other women ate their lunch, chattering. It sounded like a nest of disturbed starlings. Rherlotte did not have this sort of voice. Hers was low, and sweet. If she sang, she would be, perhaps, a light contralto. And there was a trace of accent, wasn't there? What could it be? From Marseilles, Normandy? I'd wondered at her name, but never asked her. It was like an antique name. It didn't quite belong here.

Now it was after two. They were clearing the tables. The velvet cord was lifted away for me by a bowing waiter from the "men's side," as I went out.

In the foyer I stood at a loss. Was she ill? Should I go to her house—no, no, surely not. Had there been some accident on the icy road, a horse slipping, wheels sliding—

Outside the windows of the Café Flor, the city was set in glass-grey twilight. The winter sun already westered, in a court of clouds, scorched but without colour.

Why was I being such a fool? Of course, she simply hadn't come. Hadn't wished to. Maybe even in the moment of pinning on her hat, taking up her umbrella or her handbag, she had thought distinctly, What am I doing? Go there, to *her*? But *why*?

And she hadn't come to me. She had realized at last the height of her folly. I would never see her again.

I drank a glass of white Voule, and smoked two or three cigarettes. I played English Patience at my table, and couldn't get the game ever to come out.

After sunset, the evening passed. Once I heard a sound, as it seemed, at my door. I went to see, but no one was there, and so I went down to the birdcage table. There were three letters, but none for Phèdre.

About ten o'clock I sent for some chocolate from the neighboring restaurant, something I seldom drink. I didn't like it, had only a few sips.

I slept at first, then woke. Every time I woke I seem to have heard someone calling me, urgently. I wasn't so fanciful as to think this a communication of the mind from her to me. Near dawn, I began to sleep quite deeply. There was a sensation of dropping deeper and deeper, as though into sand. After which…oblivion.

We were in the carriage, and the yellow blinds were down. Everything was very dark. I looked at my mother sitting there, a shadow, in her black. We were going to my father's funeral.

But I wasn't a child. This seemed wrong. Surely I was too old to be here?

I glanced at my mother again. She sat very upright, her hands folded in dark kidskin gloves. Under the blackness of the hat, her red-marigold hair gleamed like metal in the sub-fuse.

She smelled fragrant. I couldn't identify the scent.

Then the carriage stopped. We got out, and there was the cemetery, miles of it, sweeping away and away between the chestnut trees that were not green but coppery. The grass was high and stiff with frost like icing sugar.

I walked behind her. There were no others there. We came to a grave. A tall white marble marker rose, with a carved satyr on top.

She stood looking down, and I stood beside her. Finally she said, "He was of no importance, Phèdre. Now I have you."

When she said this, a tide of warmth, of heat, went through me. I felt lifted up. I reached to take her arm, but now we were in another place, high up on the marble balcony of a château, with a vast darkened window at our backs, a window with many panes, and below a park with enormous trees where a full moon, pale, opaque yellow, was rising like a night flower from the ground.

Our clothes had changed. I liked these better. She wore a white dress with a tight waist, a full, swinging skirt. Her breasts, mounted upon the bodice, flushed with colour against the white silk. Her hair was loose, her marigold hair, streaming down over her shoulders. She pushed it back with a laugh.

"Well, here we are," she said. "Now where is your heart?"

"In the usual place, I suppose," I said.

"Oh, there?"

She put out her left hand and laid it over my left breast. I wore the same sort of old-fashioned gown, mine a yellow like the moon's, and my hair loose as it was in childhood, and on that other night.

"But I can't feel your heart," she said, "haven't you got one, Phèdre?" I said nothing. She said, "Or have I taken it?"

We walked down a long, curving stair, the kind one might see at Versailles, some palace. The lawns were clipped and plush, and the moon stood now on the turrets of the château, which hadn't one light, garlanded below by the huge green trees. There was a lake, stepping stones. I ventured out only on these, but Rherlotte slipped into the water like a swan, in her white dress, and swam a little way.

The moonlight was warm as a fine spring day. It shone down through the water. At the bottom were strange bony plants without leaves. But then Rherlotte swam back to me. She raised her head. Her hair was like amber now, but wet over her shoulders, darker, like water weeds.

"There's a fish in the lake," she said. "Look down. There it is."

I looked and saw there was a golden fish swimming about. It had the wings of a dragon-fly which beat slowly, glittering, under the water.

"Come with me," she said. "Come with me, my dear."

She came up out of the water and left her dress in the lake. She was naked, and white as snow. On her round breasts the buds of her nipples were a rosy fawn. The rose of hair between her legs, the gossamer in her armpits, these were rosy gold.

Her hair now looked gold too, until it reached her shoulders, and, wet, seemed dark as my own.

She took my hand. We were under the trees.

The grass was warm, so real, so real. Did I know I was dreaming?

I kissed her body. I began at her eyelids, her mouth, her chin. Her neck I kissed. Her arms, her palms. Her breasts and belly. Her rosy fleece. All down her legs, her bare white feet with little polished toenails shaped exactly like ten gems for a necklace. The smell of her dry hair was like fresh narcissus. Where it was wet from the lake with winged fish, it had the aroma of marzipan.

So much, I wanted to bring her to pleasure. She lay smiling, calm, relaxed. Not repulsing me, not averse to me. I kissed her mouth again, delving into the velvet heat between her lips. I suckled her breasts until the nipples rose firm and hard. I kissed her lower mouth, the crisp silk of her sunset hair. The valley of her loins received me, rich with her secret perfume, like cinnamon, pepper, myrrh. She spread herself for me. She made no sound. Her heart, which I felt beating in her womb, was regular and not fast.

All at once she had sat up. She held my face in her hands. Her eyes in the moonlight were grey. "Lie back, Phèdre."

I had lain back. I too was naked. I felt the grass shiver under me, so real. She was pressing me down. She bent over me. Her hair fell round us like a tent of amber silk with the moon caught like a lily. The wet tips of hair shivered over me like water snakes. Her eyes wouldn't let go. I hung from her eyes, helpless. I saw the edges of her white teeth.

A long roller, almost the crisis of sex itself, coursed through me. She said, "Now I will subdue you."

In terror I gave way beneath her. All of me opening. I felt her fire on every surface. I gave myself up and screamed in agony, torture and delight. Until my screams brought down the moon, which fell into the château, lighting it from attics to cellars.

CHAPTER SEVEN

"Why, Phèdre—darling—oh what a strange thing you should call just now." Elise stared at me as if I were something very odd, a dog in a frock, a talking armadillo.

"Then this isn't the time for me to visit you? I'm sorry."

"Don't be offended, dear Phèdre. There's no reason at all you shouldn't be here. Mama knows you are my friend. I've told her you bought three of my pictures. Of course, I sold them to others," she added, disapprovingly. "I know your flat's too small, and one of *my* silly little works was more than enough."

She was wearing a pale pink, unsuitable springtime chiffon dress, with a ribboned sash, that, because it had never been in fashion, never could be. Elise prided herself on being, as an artist, beyond such things. She was.

"But you see, dearest, before they come—and they'll be here at any moment—I'll have to confess to you."

"Confess?" I asked idly.

Outside an icy wind funneled down the narrow streets. The church of St. Sulpice had seemed to crouch, dowdy with stone snow already.

Why I'd come here was out of a sort of habit, possibly. I'd expected my accustomed welcome, an Elise with the grey overall over her blouse, rushing to make me tea.

"Well, you see, Phèdre, I'm—" it burst out in an excited rush— "to be engaged, yes, I truly am. Oh, it's all been so sudden. But he's quite a forceful man. He came to buy a picture, one evening when Mama was at home, because he said it was more proper. He'd heard of my work, and then he spent ages looking at everything I'd done. He was very complimentary, and made a few criticisms which were most astute. Actually, he didn't buy a picture. But then there was a little note. Would Mama and I take tea with him. Finally, he most decorously asked if he could see me alone. I should have told you before. It's been a whirlwind. Are you glad for me, dearest?"

"If it's what you want."

"Isn't it what all women want? A husband. A little home. Eventually a family…"

I felt my eyebrows lift. I should have known from the romping kittens and tender spaniels. Her slavishness. I said, before I meant to, "And what about our affair, Elise. Have you told him about that?"

Elise blushed, her colour at odds with the pink of her dress. "Phèdre, *no*. Of *course* not. *That* doesn't matter. I mean, it was a little game we played, wasn't it? And you're very precious to me. But in the end, we settle down, don't we. And here's my chance. We'll still be the *best* of friends."

Obviously, I should have left at once, but then the engagement party arrived, in a ringing of doorbell, with mountains of cake, sweeping through like a tidal wave, carrying all before it.

The cakes came from the patisserie across the way, and were very, very lush, full of creams, decorated with alcoholic fruits. And there was a lot of a sweet Italian wine the shade of urine, which I declined, along with the cakes.

Elise, radiant, took me presently to meet her intended betrothed. The mother, also radiant, perhaps seeing now a life for herself free of millinery, although I doubted it, spoke his name to me in a reverent voice, and all the other guests—about twenty of them crushed into two small rooms—applauded, as if a prize had been announced.

"Monsieur Leprince!"

Moliére couldn't have done it better, with such a name. The prince was a few inches taller than Elise, and portly, the shape of an egg that finally divided in two legs. If he had a neck it was carefully hidden, and his hair was plastered staunchly sideways, oiled, and not thick. He had a small moustache with some contrasting ginger in it. His little oval eyes were dark, and also oiled, and so, very bright. He took my hand and shook it in a way that a man shakes a woman's hand who knows women are fragile, incomprehensible, marvelous, expendable creatures. The handshake said it all. Also the putting of the neckless head to the right side, the *twinkle.* "I've heard your name with awe, mademoiselle. What a bold stroke!"

Elise said, "It's from the theatre. From the play."

"Of course it is, my dove. I've read the play, in the original Greek. But oh, that was some years ago. I'd stumble with it now, I fear. Mustn't stumble with the name!"

He smiled, always he smiled. His teeth leaned a little. He wasn't quite young enough, and yet you couldn't take exception. A young woman may marry an older man. The reverse—God forbid!

He patted and pinched Elise, liking her flesh, apparently. He pressed cake upon me, which again I refused.

"But Phèdre must have a glass of wine! So passionate a name, and so abstemious!"

They said he was a wit, and recounted many funny things he had done and uttered, as for example when the carriage had run over a dog and he said the bump was like riding on a camel. (I thought Elise's sentiment might struggle with this, but she only laughed.) Or when he described his superior in some firm or other, as the Great Conundrum, with a mixture, I could hear at once, of groveling respect, and what he himself saw as dashing, daring cheek.

He stood smiling and smiling by, tickling Elise's elbows. The guests fluttered round like moths. Old women of the mother's acquaintance, an admiring old aunt of his, a couple of comrades from his office, the concierge and some neighbors.

Whenever I spoke of going, it was Monsieur Leprince who would stop me, calling them up in battalions to block off my escape. "Now, I've only just met her, this charming friend of my dear Elise. Just think what the Great Conundrum will say, when I tell him I have met an actual *Phèdre.*"

In the end I drank a few mouthfuls of the wine, and was immediately dizzy from the horrible stuff. I thought I was in hell, where I belonged. Everything had become a punishment, if not here, then somewhere else. And so I stayed.

How long had it been since the special luncheon to which Rherlotte did not come, since the dream by which I knew I had given myself over to her? Do others find love such a terrible state? No. All the world loves a lover and loves to love. But for me—it was like illness. More so, I must think, because I was alone in it. And alone indeed.

After one week, I needed to corset less in order that my clothes, growing too large, should fit me. My wrists seemed transparent. My eyes. Did I even know what I did?

As with this, now, this awful thing in which I had been caught up. Elise's friend. Her "best of friends," and Monsieur Leprince now *paddling* my hand, as Shakespeare puts it, perhaps eager to make another bonus conquest.

Oh *God*. We walked along the road against the winter wind, with Elise on one of his arms, I on the other. Her mother, slightly put out, waddled behind, her corns stuffed into small blue shoes.

The restaurant was just a street or two away, to take a carriage wasn't necessary—so the generous Monsieur Leprince informed us.

And then these awful long, white tables, with their dire festive flowers from the hothouse, looking now like the dreadful "Immortal" flowers that have been burnt and dried, mummified and dead, with injections of unlikely colour. And he must have Elise on his right, and he must have *Phèdre,* the passionate, dramatic woman, on his left. (The poor mother's face fell like a bad dough.)

And this I allowed, having no reason left to me.

Elise seemed very glad. She told me clever male things he had done, and told him lovely feminine things I'd done. That she'd had toothache, for example, and I'd brought her a tincture of cloves, which cured it. And he basked between us, and, when he had had some of the cheap champagne, called us his Two Beauties. (Presumably not knowing the slang.)

The aunt was displeased. Mama was displeased. Yet recklessly I remained. I thought of standing up and calling for a toast. "I've had the virginity of your wife, Monsieur Leprince, which doubtless she thinks to conceal from you by squealing and being arid from disgust. And now she hopes she and I, behind your egg-shaped back, will carry on just the same. Do you know, Monsieur, there's a certain place at the side of her neck, and on the inside of her thigh, and if you play there with your tongue, she dissolves. No, you'll never learn. I can imagine you. Up like the lark, but lacking all song. Down like a shutter."

I ached. What tincture of cloves for this toothache of the heart?

Damn them, let the meal be poison.

"I hope," says Monsieur aside to me, sportively, licentiously, "when you are married, dear Phèdre, your husband won't have a son!"

"Ah, monsieur," I say. "Good husbands are rare."

He takes it as a compliment.

If I had that *bottle* would I tip it in his wine? Rid the world of this nincompoop.

What have I drunk? I've eaten nothing.

Why am I here.

Where should I be?

Musicians come. Were they hired? Zigeuner music, hot and full of malice. Their eyes blaze on us. We, idiotic, full of drink.

It's dark now in the street.

When I get up, Monsieur catches my arm. "But *Phèdre*!"

"You must excuse me for just a moment, Monsieur."

But he won't. At last, Elise and I. Oh. A room with mirrors. Elise powdering her face and neck, touching her lips with red.

"Isn't he a fine man, Phèdre? You won't be angry. You *like* him."

"Oh, enormously. Yes. You were made in heaven for each other."

"And you'll come to the theatre? It's only us, and Mama, and his Aunt Claude. You said you would. It's a very clever play. And I shan't understand it. But *you* will."

A play now? I've said I'll go too? Someone must have dropped out. When will this evil end?

The play. I see it in snatches. I've drunk their foul wines. I'm drunk. Drink doesn't do any of this to me. But I'm poisoned. Poisoned.

Oh, won't you come, my love, won't you lead me away. Let me lie down beside you. I won't touch. Your warmth. Your cool, kind hand upon my head.

Rherlotte.

What am I thinking of?

I don't know what the play was, but it was interminable. And then, there came in it, a masked ball.

Columns soared, flimsy plaster that probably shook a little as dancers cavorted over the stage. Orange lamps hung down in the garden of a château. Huge trees on the backdrop…

There are baboons, and maidens from the seventeen hundreds. There was an elephant, and a soldier. And then Death came down the steps, in a black cloak, Death whose face was not to be seen.

Elise gasped, and put her hand to her throat. Monsieur Leprince patted her. Why do I remember that?

The footlights shone on them, the revelers caught out by Death. But now Death comes again, another Death.

There are two of them.

Each clad in black. Their faces hidden.

The lights drop low.

Which is myself? Which death am I? And which is she? Which is *Rherlotte*.

I wait for the two deaths to fling off their cloaks. One a young woman with black hair, one a naked woman with hair of pink marigolds.

But they don't throw away their cloaks and the scene relapses into a muddy twilight as the curtains close.

CHAPTER EIGHT

Wandering along by the river, an old man came up to me and took my arm.

I said instantly, "You're mistaken, monsieur. I'm not for sale."

"Dear child, I didn't think you were. But it's such a cold night. And the river. How horribly cold that must be. Just look at it. So cold and black and heavy, and do you know how dirty it is? Someone caught a fish there, ate the fish and died. You wouldn't like it, mademoiselle. Trust me, no."

I realized he thought I'd been meaning to throw myself into the Seine, as have countless others. It hadn't occurred to me, but at his instigation, it did. Then I considered it. It was a fact, the water looked very black, thick yet empty. To go down would be easy. The shock of the cold, stunning at once. But then, how could one be sure. There might be a mistake, a rescue, or worse, death be an actual place, where one would have to go on, with no escape at all.

"I was only walking, monsieur."

"Very well. But let me take you home."

I glanced at him. He was tall but stooped, with a fine, grey beard. His clothes were flawless. On his head, the top hat of the Opera, the theatre.

I'd been at the theatre, hadn't I. And afterwards, Monsieur Leprince had promised us all oysters, but at such a cheap restaurant, I was certain, by then, they'd all die of intestinal inflammations.

I said I must go. He pressed my hand. Elise, drunk on pure stupidity, clung to his arm.

"No, no, our Phèdre. Phèdre must have oysters."

"Ah, monsieur. They make me sick."

Aggrieved, frowning, such a little thing; I had at length so simply put him off. I went away. I walked into the city.

A woman mustn't walk city streets unaccompanied, by night. I knew as much. And yet, there was about me some circle of protection. As on the night I courted Jean Viktor Pascet. The evening when I put myself in the path of Armand Blos. None else came to me.

There were trees in a dance of bare branches about the lamps. A fine rain falling. Will there be another spring? Perhaps not.

I, the huntress. But I walk in fear. Any man might cage me. One has. But not through himself.

And in the end, the shining river, and the old gentleman come from some play, that was I'm certain far more erudite than the drama Elise's amour had chosen for us.

The old man turned to me mildly, and indicated his carriage.

"I know it isn't quite right, mademoiselle. But you seem.. at a loss. Will you allow me the honour of taking you to your home? You've nothing to fear. Alas. Twenty years ago, I would have offered you some danger. But not tonight. An old man, dear girl. If you won't, I'll fret, and it isn't good for me. I'll lie awake, wondering what became of you."

What did I care? This man. His kindness some further act of the play, which he was now performing for himself.

"I haven't far to go."

"Nevertheless."

The carriage stood black on the black night, wet with the rain. The horses, sleek with water, looked like a funeral team for the chariot of the hearse. Perhaps he was lying.

He guided me towards the vehicle.

"Come now. Get in."

Probably hanging about like this would give him rheumatism. It served the old fool right.

I thought of her suddenly. Rherlotte. That she would flirt with him just a little, reminding him of his youth, showing that she, at least, was not unaware that beneath his crocodile skin and cobweb beard, once he had been young. She would put her hand warmly on his arm, thank him, and mount into the carriage.

I found I had done so.

We sat. He a decorous length from me.

The carriage started.

It came to me, I'd given him, as my address, the house on the Boulevard Strauss.

Now why was that?

"Yes, I know it. A pretty street."

Am I Rherlotte, then? Is this *my* theatre? Playing her part, since she has vanished in the wings.

Well, he'll drop me there, and I'll wait until he's gone. No lights will be in her windows. There's no Armand for her to be await- ing. It's late. As the château was in the dream, every pane will be black.

As we turn into the street, an asphyxiating pain roams through me. I know what it will be like to die, alone or among strangers.

But he says, "See, there you are. And the light is burning for you."

I look. It *is* her house. It positively exists. Grey by night, the shutters black. The bare tall tree. But in the pane above the door, a globe of palest reddish blue. And above, up there, that rosy window. The window of her watch-lamp, left burning for her beloved. For him. For Armand.

"Now, what is it? Shall I come to the door with you?" says the old man.

I brush away two lines of tears that aren't mine. I stare at him. He blinks and gazes into space, astonished by my look. My grandmother's look. After all used on a man.

"Thank you, monsieur."

When I'm out of the carriage it goes off at once. Can it be he finally saw he had taken a serpent into his bosom?

Standing on the street, and looking up. I expect the light of the upper window to go out.

Did Armand stand here? No, he strode straight to the door. No doubt he had the key. No doubt he entered and she came out, standing on the stair, her face lit by the lamp in the hall, her hair gilded by the lamp above.

What's she done to me? The night is so cold, and I'm outside. That horrible betrothal party. Am I drunk still? No, sober as if rinsed in a river. I'm quite sure of this.

When I find myself rapping at the knocker, the hand with the scroll, I can't think what I've done. What will become of me? Who am I? I don't know who I am, to have done such a thing. I hang by a thread from the stars of the rain. And as they fall, they let me go.

It was midnight, thereabouts. The maid, Marthe, came to answer my knock in a bundled dressing-gown.

"Mademoiselle—"

"Tell her, Phèdre."

"But mademoiselle."

From above, the voice. Her voice.

"Yes. Very well, Marthe."

Her voice pulled me up the stairs. They were in a half-dark, and the caryatids, standing like wardresses, blank-eyed and wooden.

Where am I going? The iris doors stand open, and inside is the room. It's here the lamp burns, after all. I can see it. An oil lamp with a white bowl painted with roses. The curtain drawn a little back from the thick lace.

The other lamps are low, and the whole room itself a smoky rose, lit by glints of firelight.

Near the fire, a small table with an old-fashioned chestnut-coloured cloth of frilled chenille. Two chairs upholstered in pale lemon silk. There are candles on the table, not lit. Two places set, with two light green flutes for drinking bubbly wine.

The Louis clock says six minutes to twelve.

There's a kettle on a hook over the fire, a contrivance like the one I have at my flat. The kettle makes a faint buzzing, like a contented bee. Two tea cups and a pot stand on a lacquer tray by the hearth. The caddy, the sugar bowl.

All these things mesmerize me,

Rherlotte appears from the room's farthest end, out of the rose shadows. Everything dims, retreats from her flaming centre.

She wasn't wearing mourning. Not tonight. She was dressed for a dinner, in a gown of darkest green velvet, cut low at the bosom, and leaving her arms and shoulders almost bare. Her hair was piled up high, with a comb in it. She had two silver ear-drops, and on her wrist a silver bracelet from which hung a little silver heart.

I said, "I'm sorry. You won't want me here. I'll go in a moment."

She said, "It's all right. Come to the fire."

There was a chair, and she indicated I should sit in it. I did so. Thoughtlessly I unpinned my hat. I took it off and put it by, and then, for a reason unknown to me, I undid my hair.

She was bending to the kettle by then, but she turned. She smiled. "What wonderful hair, Phèdre."

I closed my eyes, but there was movement in the room, swinging and turning. I opened them again.

She was pouring the hot water into the pot. From the tea came a smell of fruit.

"But you've had guests," I said.

"Oh, no. Not at all. I always do this in the evenings. I've done it for so long."

I remembered the table set for two. I said, "In case Armand should be free to come here."

"Yes."

"Every night."

"Not every night, of course. But I put things ready. There'd be some cold supper. Some wine. In case he might come."

"And when he didn't come?"

"Why then," she glanced at me seriously, quietly, explaining. "I'd go to bed."

"Alone."

She looked away from me into the fire.

"When Armand visited me, Phèdre, it wasn't always for my bed. You must recall, he was married. Generally he went home between one and two or three, to his wife. Often we'd sit and talk. We'd known each other some years."

I said, "Was he worth it? All this? Your waiting. Your dressing for him. The cold supper. You remind me—of Penelope waiting for Odysseus. And she promised she'd remarry when her husband's shroud was finished, and unpicked the weaving every night, so no one else could have her. While he whored with all the sorceresses and goddesses and nymphs of the islands."

Rherlotte smiled at me again. "How lovely, Phèdre. I never thought of that. That I might resemble Penelope. I like the image very much."

"You were as blindly faithful and he as licentiously profligate."

"I don't see Armand as an Odysseus. No. Now and then, there was a woman. He was easily fired."

"You forgave him," I said harshly. "Over and over."

"Forgave him for what? It wasn't a sin. He didn't do it from a desire to hurt or harm. It was natural to Armand. Why would I mind it? He came back to me."

I spoke a curse of the streets. On this occasion she had no reaction to it. She poured the tea into one of the cups, the cup left waiting for the remembrance of Armand, and gave it to me, with the sugar bowl.

"How curious you should come tonight," she said. Almost what Elise had said.

"I've intruded on you."

"No, Phèdre. No. I was lonely tonight."

Without adding sugar, I sipped the tea. It had a taste of smoke, and something acidulous, like oranges.

"But you must often have been lonely."

"Sometimes, perhaps. That is, since his death."

I stared at her. She looked into the fire. Her skin was flushed from its clustered light.

"Yet I killed him, you say. How can you want me here?"

She looked at me, only for a moment. She still knelt by the fire. Her fleeting eyes, starred with the flames.

"Oh, Phèdre. But you weren't what I expected. A girl. What had I imagined you'd be before I met you? A Gorgon. A monster."

"You remembered that. On the day you were to meet me at the Café Flor. You remembered I was a monster, and so you didn't come."

She said slowly, thoughtfully, still not looking at me, "I had indulged myself too much. That was what I remembered."

"Indulged—with what?"

"Indulged myself with you, Phèdre. And it was time to stop. High time."

There were some white flowers in a vase. The candles were held by one of Odysseus' nymphs in yellow enamel. The wicks were blackened. Perhaps they had last burned when Armand was here.

"Shall I go at once?" I blurted.

She said, "Yes, my dear. Soon you must."

"And after that—"

She said, "After that, then what, Phèdre?"

"I must avoid you."

She sighed. She turned her head and looked up at me. Her face—was the sweetest, most living thing I ever saw. I wanted to frame it in my hands, as she did with me in my dream. I wanted only to hold her, look at her. Surely nothing else…

"It would be best, wouldn't it," she said. "If we avoid each other."

"You hate me so."

"Do I? Yes, but I must hate you, mustn't I?"

"Because I killed the man you loved. That ridiculous, crude, posturing boor. Oh, yes. How he was with me—would you have recognized him? Strutting, bragging. Stuffing me with food and champagne so that he could push me over on my back. He was as hot as a furnace. He wanted to feel me, crush me. He was as ready as any lecher. And that room, they knew him so well there. How many had he taken in there, got drunk, and screwed? God knows. It reeked of him, that room. His cologne. His *need*."

I stopped. I realized what I had told her. A cold rushing went through me, then a singing heat.

"You see, I'm confessing to you—Rherlotte—if I mustn't ever see you again, better get it done with now. Yes, yes. I murdered him. I did it. There was no difficulty. It was poison. Quite quick. I don't think he suffered greatly. Except for the last few seconds."

She too, standing up now. She was, in that rose room, white. Deathly marble white as I'd first seen her.

"Do you know what you're saying?" she said. "That finally you've let it out?"

"Of course I know. What do you think? Did he teach you, your lover, to be as stupid as he was? I *know*. I *know*. And now you know. What will you do? Run to the police. Do it, Rherlotte. Give me to them. I'll go with you. Or do you want to kill me yourself? Look, here's a sharp knife on the table you laid for his ghost."

She shuddered.

"I couldn't put violent hands on you."

This definitive statement infuriated me. "Not even to finish me off? But wouldn't it be worth it? You loved him so much."

"Oh yes," she said, "I loved him." Her head went back. Her eyes were black. "You don't understand me, do you? Let me tell you. My life ended when you killed him, but I didn't even know he was dead. How could I? To whom could I go, to ask, when all at once he didn't ever come to me?"

"You might have thought he'd tired of you," I said. I wanted so much to hurt her. Why? All I wanted was to hold her.

"No, I didn't think that," she said. She drew in a long breath, and her beautiful breasts moved above the scoop of the velvet bodice. I could see her heart beating, not so fast, but in hard, hard strokes. "In the end, Marthe went for me. She found out from the Blos' maid. That he'd been discovered in a restaurant." The fire flashed in her eyes. "Don't you see? Don't you *see*, Phèdre? I didn't even see him, dead. She buried him, his wife. How could I? And so he isn't dead for me, physically, and he should be. But how can he be? Had I been his wife, I'd have said some sort of farewell. But he was alive—and then there was that mound of turf in the cemetery of St. Luc. Sometimes, when I'm half mad, I think perhaps everyone has lied to me. Even about you, this plot. That he isn't dead but was taken away a prisoner. Doubtless you find that bizarre. I do, myself. But you have no idea, Phèdre, what love will do. What it puts on me."

"Yes," I said. "I know. Of course I know."

"How can you *know*?" she said bitterly. "Look at you. Phèdre, made of this cold, cold snow, with her black hair. Phèdre, impervious to all. How could you know anything about love?"

"I love *you*." I said it without any heat, and all at once all of myself seemed poured out of me. I was a shell and felt nothing at all. I saw her face from a long way off, a beautiful thing that I didn't recognize. Either she wasn't human, or I was no longer human, or never had been. Who—*what*—was she? She could be nothing to me, or I to her. And I said again, mechanically, "I love you."

"Oh, Phèdre." She turned away from me.

I said, "They told you what I was. That I've no use for men." She said nothing. I said, "I didn't have any use for anyone. Until you. I told you once, I'm under your spell."

She said again, softly, "Phèdre."

Her back was straight, and the nape of her neck, her shoulders, so glowing, like alabaster, the white porcelain of the rose lamp, with the flame inside.

I said, "I'm glad I killed him. What did I care before? He was nothing. But now. I robbed him of you. He didn't deserve you, Rherlotte. But you gave yourself. You gave yourself to him like any little lady's maid or girl from the dingy shops at St. Germain or Montmatre. And *I* don't deserve you. No one could in two centuries. Perhaps after that they'll be better. But you'll be dead by then."

I was moving towards her. By turning her back to me, somehow she enabled me to come close.

Now I could smell her hair, the scent of her supple body; so cool, so warm. Smell the velvet of her dress.

Around her body I slid my arms, crossing them, taking her breasts in my hands. I put my face down into her neck. Her pulse was against my mouth. I held her tight, trying to choke her, stop her breathing. Her neck was like silk. I wanted to bite through it and get at the flame in her lamp of alabaster, her red blood.

She was twisting. Coming around towards me. I saw the blur of her beauty, like an exquisite painting smeared, and had her mouth. For a moment I tasted her, the full lower lip and the sculpted upper one, the tongue's tip, and the edges of her animal teeth. And then she pulled back and slapped my face, stinging and hard, and her nails raked my cheek.

Then, like any Armand, baulked, not being able to accept, *believe,* I struggled to subdue her. Trying to hold her off, but also to tear her gown and spill her breasts, to have her skin in my mouth, to stop her clawing out my eyes.

She beat against me with a lioness's hands. Her hair came down in a hot waterfall, full of little, hooked pins.

I was crying her name. There were tears on my face and on her face. She struck me again and the force of her blow separated us. The wall met my back, struck my skull. She ran to the table and snatched up after all the sharp knife.

I laughed at her drunkenly. "But isn't this how *he* was? Stinking of wine, burning with his *ardour.* Don't you like me, Rherlotte? Am I too like him, that thing you say you loved?"

"Go away," she said. Her voice was hoarse, husky and quite low. The knife shone clear, the shade the rain had been. "Leave this house at once."

"And never return here? Of course not. An unnatural woman. A damned woman. How could you bear me?"

"Out, I said." She stood taller. Her face was that of a young king who can command ten legions.

Ridiculous, I knew I couldn't say another word. But I said, "Come here. Stick the knife in me. You want to. Why not? I won't resist."

At that she flung down the knife with a clatter. "I'll ring for Marthe," she said, "shall I? Will you like that? The *maid* to see you as you are?"

"What do I care. I wasn't brought up to tell lies to the servants, as you were, little bourgeois."

And so she crossed to the bell-pull and saw to it.

And then we stood there. She and I. Still and silent in the room which now fluttered with agitated wings of light and dark.

Perhaps the fire was only going out. Or else our rage had affected it.

Marthe came after a long time. She was plainly unused to being summoned so late. She looked bemused, half asleep, astonished. Seeing me, she looked afraid.

"Take Mademoiselle down and unlock the door for her," said Rherlotte.

I said to her, from the room's edge, "Goodnight, *Madame.*"

But that was all.

Marthe rustled hurriedly down the stairs. I followed her like a woman going to her own execution.

She undid the door with some difficulty, all thumbs. And let me out on to the street.

When the door had been shut, I stood below and looked up.

The lamp did not go out. Not for some while. Was she weeping? Let her. But Oh God, what had I done? Her pretty room I hadn't wanted to spoil. Her beauty, which I shouldn't have touched.

Do I fall still? Haven't I yet struck the bottom of the black abyss? No, for the street feels as if made of feathers. How close the sky is. And so cold, so cold.

I walked some way. Once a cab passed me. When I saluted it, the cabman leered at my disheveled, hatless hair, the scratches on my face.

The wheels ground over the streets like those of a tumbrel. But, fool that I was, I thought myself already dead.

CHAPTER NINE

When I reached my flat, I sat in an armchair, and dropped into a tindery, feverish doze. Sometimes I woke for a few moments, and saw the sky in the windows begin to lighten. Then I heard traffic strangely echoing in the street. The moans of the wind. At last I woke to a horrible cold that seemed to be miles inside my burning body. The window through the undrawn curtain was locked in a frigid whiteness.

I got up and, going to see, saw the almond trees were in blossom, solid white, with snow.

At that moment a carriage came with difficulty along the street. I paid it no attention. I went into my bedroom, and stood looking at myself in the pier-glass.

My face was pale, the eyes had half-moons of shadow. The scratches on my right cheek had bled. My clothes were creased and my hair tangled. I appeared like a beast that had escaped from the circus. I recognized this aspect of myself at once.

How long I stood, watching this creature that was me, I don't know. Presently there came a very loud knocking on my door.

I drifted into the hall. I opened the door, not concealing myself, for nothing was real, Indeed, it couldn't be, for there in her nets and robe stood my aggrieved concierge, and behind her, my aunts, Sophie and Susie, staring at me blindly with round blue, pebble eyes.

They were dressed identically in dark blue apparel, with round hats and unseasonal white gloves. Sophie had a muff of civet and Susie one of grey fox. These were the differences, aside from

Susie's darker hair. They had no bags, nothing with them but for identical small antique reticules, sewn with faded sequins.

Outlandish, they looked. As much so as I?

Between us humped the concierge, gesturing with her arms, her small eyes taking in everything with alarm.

"They said they'd come from the country to see you, mademoiselle. They say they're your—aunts."

"They are."

"Your face—mademoiselle, did you meet with an accident?"

"Thank you," I said.

Sophie said to me, "We should like chocolate now."

Susie said, "The train took a long time."

"There's no chocolate," I said. "When the restaurant opens."

Suddenly I laughed, and stood aside to let them in. Two demons, they passed me, bringing in the smells of girl-children who have been travelling on a train, cinders, old honey, tobacco, and the woody, vernal, mothball scents of O—.

I asked the concierge for things from the restaurant as soon as possible. It was all I had to deflect them. I closed the door in the woman's face.

"So you travelled on the train," I said.

"You said to."

"No I didn't. How did you manage it?" I think I was half interested. It was as if my outer skin, the part of me that was so cold, were interested. Inside, I smouldered, fumbling about, oblivious.

"It's not warm enough," said Susie. "When will you light the fire?"

"Oh, now, of course."

I made up the fire, but couldn't bring myself to perform the actions of making tea. My mouth was dry, but I wouldn't drink. I sat in the armchair, while Sophie and Susie prowled about, and when I heard them in my study and bedroom, pulling open drawers, I took no notice.

About eight or nine, the breakfast arrived. A child's breakfast of bread and butter, jam and chocolate.

They ate greedily, splashing the drink and smearing butter on their clothes.

Lying back in the chair, I watched them.

"Are you ill?" said Susie

"You look quite ill," said Sophie.

"Yes, I'm very ill, and you're liable to catch it."

"We stole money from mother," said Sophie, prudishly. "She doesn't know where we are."

"Paris is just all streets and walls," said Susie.

"And it's snowed," said Sophie.

"We like more chocolate," said Susie. She opened the pot to see where the fresh supply was.

I thought drearily, I should send Constance a telegram. But I hadn't the energy. Not yet.

"Who scratched your cheek?"

"A lioness at the zoological gardens."

"You could die of that," they said, almost smiling.

Just then, the door again. Sophie went at once, unbidden, to open it. "Who are you?" they asked Brunhilde, my cleaning woman, from whom I had stolen a hat when I went to poison Jean Viktor Pascet.

"An old witch," said Brunhilde.

She came stamping in. At the sight of them, the mess, of me, she said, "Christ on His cross, mademoiselle."

I'd brought her a new hat, all that time ago. She hadn't liked mine. I told her how I had searched and searched but couldn't find the original. In a street market, to which she had insisted we go for the purpose, she chose a black squashed thing with a knot of little, red, unsucculent cherries. She wore it even now.

Quite calmly I told her an hysterical friend had attacked me. She imagined her fiancé paid me too much attention, which might well have been true. As I thought nothing of him, I hadn't noticed until it was too late. I told her that I wasn't well. Meanwhile these children were a relative's daughters who had come here without her (Brunhilde had never met Constance, who christened her), lacking her knowledge or consent. I asked Brunhilde to send the telegram, posting her out again into the bitter streets. But she went at once.

Sophie and Susie lay down before the fire. They fell asleep. By day at O— they often slept. At night, for all I knew, they climbed on the roofs and used their catapults against the owls.

In the end I went to bathe my face. I washed, and put on my robe. I brushed my hair. Some came out on the bristles. Rherlotte must have torn it loose.

Rherlotte. Her name sounded at intervals in my head, meaningless and far away as some unacknowledged station on my aunts' route from O—.

Brunhilde stood over me.

"It's all to be arranged like you said, mademoiselle. They're to go back on the evening train. And serve them right, the naughty things. But you do look done in. Shall I take them off your hands for the day?"

Inside myself I struggled to understand what Brunhilde had said. From my lips, a stranger speaking for me, came the words, "Oh yes. That would be a relief. Please take some money from—"

"No, no, mademoiselle. We'll sort all that out another time. It's no trouble. My cousin's got two girls. I'll take them there first." My mind now struggled to grasp this notion, the two demons in some ordinary house. Probably they would murder the whole family. But perhaps not Brunhilde. "Put on your hats," she said to Sophie and Susie, as if they were only children. "Your coats aren't warm enough, but you'll do on the omnibus. Have you been on one before?"

"No," said my aunts.

"Time you did then. Now I'll take you to the pastry shop first. You can each choose a cake. The one you like best." Their avaricious eyes brightened. She held out her brown workwoman's hands to them, standing there in her battered cherry hat and split-seamed coat. "Come along now. I don't want to lose you."

To my outer self's amazement, Sophie and Susie came and took her hands. In the doorway I saw them look up at her. She was chattering out questions to them, which they answered. Their faces were blushed by the fire, which Brunhilde had assisted. She said, "You came to see the city. Well, you can see a bit of it. But it's a big city, this one, and old. Do you know why the river is called the Seine?"

When I went to the window, I saw them in the snowy street. She was pointing things out, still holding their hands, moving their arms like those of puppets. And they were still staring up at her, as if they'd never seen anyone like her, or anything, either, and conceivably they hadn't.

After they disappeared, so it seemed did I.

My mother once took me walking at O—, in the winter, when the snow was down. I was little, and the snow frightened me, it was so cold, and so tall—the trees enmeshed in it, and banks of it going up so high. Now and then as I trod, my feet sank deeply. Or I slid. I'd heard a story of a local boy, skating on the ice of a pool, which broke, so that he died in the freezing water, in two minutes, they said. My mother's admonitions to look at this view, or that bird bravely (bravely—what choice did it have?) pecking the buried berries, were lost on me.

She grew melancholy of course, she sat down on a fallen trunk in the woods, that was like a pole of iced iron. She held me by the hand and said that, if we sat here long enough, the cold would feel warm and we'd go to sleep.

I was frightened worse, not knowing why. I said nothing. I waited by her side until, sighing as if foregoing a great pleasure for my sake, she got up and led me home to Constance's Château.

In the afternoon, a mauve gloaming settled on the city. In every window burned the fatigued yellow lights that had had to be kept going all day.

Coming back to awareness, not knowing why, I recollect I glanced at the clock. It was just after three.

In a while, Brunhilde would return with her charges, if nothing had happened, if they hadn't done some great wickedness that brought Paris to a standstill.

By seven they must board the train. A faint, awful thought occurred to me. That the snow might delay their departure. And then I thought I might go back with them. Go back to my grandmother's house. I tried to find my reason for thinking this. I didn't wish to, but then, I wished to go nowhere. And yet—and yet I had the strangest urge, as on the other day, to flight.

But I couldn't run away—from her. Even there, *she* would pursue me. And if truly she had summoned the police, which I doubted, I was hardly at this moment concerned. I could deny what she would say I had said. I had no connection to Armand Blos. And Anne must keep silent. It was Rherlotte who would be unbalanced, liable to murder.

Or I could confess to them, as to her. If I died, that might be the only perfect method of eluding Rherlotte.

But then again, as with the black river, suppose it were not the perfect method? Suppose that in death, still, I should be haunted?

I'd tried to rape her. It *was* rape. To that I'd been reduced. No wonder she flung me off.

She had seemed, before, so full of candour, so soft, melting in the light. She'd said, "Your wonderful hair." She had said, "I indulged myself with you." She had said, "My *dear.*"

Wasn't there, or hadn't there been, in her, against all odds, some tenderness for me? I'd felt it lying lightly over her, like an extra colour, a quivering, wild scent. It was as if she claimed me, when I spoke of loving her.

Couldn't there be some chance, however slight—

But no. No. No chance at all.

Even so, all at once, just then, mentally, I saw her. At her desk in her room, behind the iris glass, writing to me, one of her notes, black on white. The gracious writing with its sudden little dashes, its ripples of something savage and lawless no longer allowing itself to be held in.

Was it possible? Did I somehow see her, penning me a letter. What could such a letter say—what *could* it say? *I was mistaken to send you away. What you offered me is something that, after all, I want.*

For she *had* wanted my love. She had. I saw it in her face, a smothered little flicker of fire, quickly hidden. Even after I confessed what I'd done to *him*. Even then. When I said, *I love you.*

Now, in memory, I saw her, and the glimmer of some acknowl-
edgement deep down in her eyes. Before she turned her back.

She had wanted my love. How then, not me? She was afraid.

But with Rherlotte, her fear might be itself distasteful to her.
That alone might be enough.

What was she writing? Was it written, now? Was she folding
the page? Was she sealing the letter?

I went to my bedroom in disgust, and taking up my traveler's
bags, began to put into them some things for O——. On the train,
perhaps marooned in the snow with the demon aunts, I might
go mad. But that madness must be away from her. Out of this
city which was hers. No longer close enough that I might run,
stumbling and sliding, through the dangerous snow, to reach her
door.

When Brunhilde returned, she brought with her by
the hand, two little girls. Their eyes and cheeks were
bright. They had pockets full of sweets, and were talking, jabbering. About this one and that, who they'd met. And how many
stairs there were. And a cathedral, and a river, and a toyshop, and
a market. They were prancing about. Susie had gained a red scarf
and Sophie a white muffler. Brunhilde smiled. I had come back
enough myself to be startled. She said, "They weren't any trouble.
Full of curiosity. And my cousin's cat, they loved it so." I thought
privately they might, if left alone, have tried to skin it. Perhaps
not, Perhaps they had only needed to be treated as children magically to become children.

"There was a man at the steps gave me this for you, mademoiselle."

All at once, the world stopped still. I took the letter and waited,
staring at it. A white letter, with black ink. The handwriting of
Rherlotte.

Brunhilde and the strange children drew far, far away. I went
into the bedroom, pushed to the door. Then again, I stood with
the letter closed fast in my hand.

Should I open it? Wasn't it better to let this moment remain alive? For, if opened, mightn't it say to me some message of revulsion, some added thrust of pain, and a lasting silence.

I tore it. The white leaf fluttered to the carpet. Not touching it, I bent to look. Something metallic had fallen with it. That didn't matter. It was the words, these black patterns, dancing and jostling.

> *Phèdre—Here is the front door key to my house on the Bld. Strauss.*
>
> *You must know, I've tried so hard to make you mine, to make you fall in love with me. It seems, does it not, that I was most skilful?*
>
> *Don't come to me today. Come tomorrow. Come at two o'clock in the afternoon. I shall dismiss my servants. Even Marthe. No one will be in the house, but for myself.*
>
> *And I shall be, Phèdre, defenseless before you.*

Brunhilde tapped at the door.

"Oh, was it bad news, mademoiselle?"

"No. I'll go to the station now."

To the station with Sophie and Susie. Putting them on the train to O—. Not seeing them. Seeing always the image: her hands seizing me, her face, her mouth crushed to mine, her fingers strong as cords about my neck—

I wouldn't be, myself, going to O—.

How many years would pass, before tomorrow? Let me revel in them all. Let me press them near and suck out from them their very essence.

CHAPTER TEN

My impulse is to make a long preamble. How I bathed and dressed. How I powdered over the scratch on my face, as if ashamed. And that I didn't sleep the night before. Of course I slept. Exhaustion, delirium. Miles deep. There were no dreams that I remember.

Did I say, I stood before the mirror once again. Naked. I looked, trying not to see myself—but Rherlotte.

That I wrote on the mirror, in rouge, *de Gillan* and *Diane,* which was almost anagrammatical. Save for this *G*, these two *L*'s.

But such things, these twitters of the bride before her wedding… I must go straight on. Let me speak, instead, of the marriage night.

At a little before two o'clock, the slow careful carriage left me in the Boulevard Strauss.

What a change there had been. The houses were now in Switzerland. How festive they looked, like cakes, with their toppings of cream.

When I came to her house, her tree was clad in white. The urn with the shrub. The railings. The pink of the walls, the dark green shutters, these looked scathed, almost desolate. The house seemed lean, as if snow had wounded it. Also, it was like a tower. In a fairy tale. I had to scale it, to come to her. But really, only go up the icy, slippery steps. And then the gift of the key in the lock.

The door opened, and for a moment, I was warm.

I glanced about. I had only seen her hall, the stair, that one room.

It was so inevitable to climb that stair, that for a minute, I held off. Had she heard me walk in? She wouldn't come out. She'd wait for me, behind iris doors. As before.

I was terrified as I went up. A band of steel encircled my ribs. Twice I had to stop, simply to breathe. My ears sang. Was I happy? To suffer so much—is this happiness? And I was anxious. When I saw her, would she be the one I remembered? Or another woman. Or the same, but less beautiful. Or more? I didn't mind it. She could be lying on the floor in a dirty shift, kicking her heels, drinking absinthe and laughing in the raucous way someone—Lilas?—had sometimes done.

It didn't, didn't matter at all. She would be Rherlotte. She might say to me, Both my breasts have been cut off. My left knee is made of wood.

Rherlotte.

As I came up the last two or three stairs I met an enormous wall of colossal cold. A window had been left open, most likely by some departing domestic. I must remember, and warn her. We'd go to close it, maybe laughing.

Then the doors were in front of me. She'd hung them with a light pale gauze. Perhaps these curtains had been drawn back before.

As I touched them, the doors, a piece of white curtain trembled, and fell down inside the room.

Entering another, a new, world, do you expect all things to be as you know them?

Even so, I gazed down the stair again, as if to ask someone what this peculiar phenomenon might mean.

But the house was silent. It was a fact, she had sent them all away, to be alone with me.

Turning back, I pushed one leaf of the doors with the iris glass. For a moment it resisted. And then, swung open wide.

This room—I don't know it. No, I've never been in this room.

Inside a glacier, fringes of frost and ice hang down. So they do, here. And the same grey-blue light.

On the mantelpiece, the Louis XVI clock is broken, its glass cracked away. And there, on the table laid for two, the nymph of yellow enamel in a crumble of pieces. And half one of the green glasses is detached, and bits like angelica scattered.

What's happened? Was she angry? Did she smash these things?

But it's the long window, wide open as a door. A blank of white sky, which must have houses outlined in it, and the garden trees under snow. And round the window-frame, icicles. Long and beautiful, pure crystal, pointing in all directions.

In the middle of this room of ice, Rherlotte sits, looking at me.

Much later, when I find the second letter, I still don't see what has been done. Perhaps I never will see. For although I've learnt your lesson, Rherlotte, I learnt it as a child learns speech. Before ever I could understand.

Her eyes, fixed on me, are now unearthly blue. Her face also, bluish. She's old. An old woman, her cheeks sunk in. Her parted lips are brown. Withered like leaves that are dead. Only her hair has any absolute colour, but it looks dry and—false. A wig.

Her white dress, yes she put on white for me as she did in my dream, her white dress is stained with russet marks. From her left wrist, a ruby bracelet, those pinkish rubies called *Amaranthe,* come undone. Dripping, yet quite still. A pond of this on the floor near her feet. And by that, a man's razor—his? Armand's? Probably. Something he left here for convenience. The razor she's used, in the Roman fashion, to slash her wrist so thoroughly that the left hand is almost severed.

She sat this way. Her window wide, the cold making her warm so she could go to sleep.

After some hours, I wanted to put my arms around her, put my head on her bosom. But she would be hard and stiff as a dead tree by now. Since three or four o'clock yesterday, perhaps.

Besides, she'd never wanted me to touch her. She'd fought me away. How could I do it, now?

The page with her writing, on the table, says only, *I don't want my life. I know this damns me. I know it is a sin. Only a sin is ever so easy.* And her signature: *Rherlotte de Gillan.*

This letter was for all the world, and not for me. Perhaps even to make sure I had no blame. For she wants me to be free. She made quite sure of me. When she was sure, she ended. I don't need her letter. *She* is her letter. This body.

She made me love her. When she knew I did, and when I told her that I'd killed him, then—this. She taught me her own lesson. To live without her, as she had been made to live without him.

I didn't need a letter.

The cold was like a jewel around her, and I only thought, going away, that they wouldn't see her beauty, and now, I'd never properly remember it. This frozen thing, drained of its blood, would get in the way.

What does one do? As with any injury, some foolish hope. Presently it will be better. In an hour I'll feel it less, or a week, a year, a decade.

And then at last, It never will be better. All days, all nights like this one, always.

And then. And then.

When I knew I loved her, when she was sure that I'd suffer, as she did. His razor was like her friend. Anything of his. After she lost him she didn't want her life, let alone me. She promised me she would have her revenge on me. She has. Rherlotte.

Virgile, the Widow

What thou seest when thou dost wake,
Do it for thy true-love take…
A Midsummer Night's Dream
William Shakespeare

Laure saw the woman one rainy morning in late autumn, walking along the bank of the canal, her reflection gliding beside her in the water among the still falling yellow and brown leaves of ashes and chestnuts.

Bois-la-Diane was famous for its woods, which kings had hunted even a hundred years ago. For little else. The town was small and winding. It had one church, one rather distanced château, and the usual primordial shops—the chemist, the baker and patisserie, and several cranky, sly dressmakers, where women, twisted out of shape by years of sewing, attempted, spider-like, to lure young girls to dooms of drapes and flounces ten years out of fashion.

The woman on the canal bank was certainly not dressed in this way. She had a timeless look, almost (Laure thought), Grecian—but less in the manner of a classical Greek *woman* than a Grecian *vase*—tall, slim, and amphorally curved. She was all in black, the deepest mourning. Not an instant's relief of any other shade. Even her gloves—black. And the umbrella—blacker. On the canal, the white swan had dipped its head and sailed away. As Laure got closer and closer, she noted the woman had the blackest hair, and long black eyebrows, cruel-arched like scimitars. Her eyes were also black, and they had the glassy obsidian surface of most very dark or pale eyes. So Laure couldn't tell if the woman saw her at all. Then Laure had the urge to speak. But Laure was oddly as timid as she was impulsive and arrogant. What could she say—

Who are you, madame? Where are you going? Are you new to this town I have lived in almost all my twenty years?

"She wasn't a Parisian," Laure pronounced later. "Oh no. Perhaps not from any city. Yet not provincial either. She seemed to belong nowhere at all. Of course not to this place."

"You could tell so much?" sneered Sophrine.

"Anyone could. Even you."

Sophrine tossed her head like the heroine of a (badly written) racy novel. She was herself dressed very simply in white, and her strawberry-brown hair partly up and partly down in an untidy style. Laure looked at her with contempt. Usually she felt contempt for Sophrine, as for many others, including her own aunt, Madame Deschampeigne (a vague, dim figure, restrictive yet inconclusive, like a frigid larva). Sometimes, this habit of contempt worried Laure. But she was young. There was a false unspoken sense that everything had time to change, and probably for the better.

"Well, but was she as elegant as Artemise Lejay?"

"Lejay? Good God, far more. What do you think?"

Sophrine shrugged. "To me, Artemise Lejay is the most fascinating woman we can boast at present in this town. Obviously it could have been la Reine, in her day. But now she's old. Even so, even so… One sees it sometimes. Her eyes. She's never lost them. Still so blue."

Laure turned her back on Sophrine and walked to the lace-shrouded window of the sitting room. Sophrine's father's house, and all its fellows, gave straight onto a cobbled thoroughfare of Bois-la-Diane. The street was narrow, in spots unpaved, really a track, with puddles, and the yellow tearful trees drooping here and there along it. Such streets, unlike the houses, pleased Laure, quite. They belonged—or seemed to—to earlier eras, which she preferred. Nothing offended Laure so much, she thought, as the present day. The single advantage of modernity was that no one had forcibly married her off—but even there she had stayed exempt mainly due to the aloofness of the Aunt. Others certainly were forcibly married, or at least acquiesced to the sham. Most notably that very Artemise Lejay from Sophrine's pedestal.

Now Sophrine stole up, slipping her hand around Laure's waist. They looked from the window at the rainy street and sighed in unison. *Oh this dreary provincial life.*

"Do you think you only imagined your Grecian mystery?"

"It's possible. Or she was a phantom. The ghost of a young woman who drowned herself in the canal, perhaps. In mourning for her own death." Laure thought, *Why am I saying this? She was as real as you are, real as the street. More real. Much.*

Every Wednesday, and sometimes Saturday, there would be a sort of unofficial Ladies Club held at the château of la Reine. It began around the hour of the bucolic four o'clock dinner, which la Reine had altered to a frugal luncheon. It drifted on through an evening, sometimes an ersatz dinner, with only the old Peridot to wait on them, on and on to midnight, and frequently past midnight. If the authoress of the function had been anyone other than la Reine—Sidonie Aubade-Valents—perhaps such a situation would not have been countenanced. But anyone could trace la Reine's provenance far back before the Revolution. She was one of those country aristocrats who had kept her credentials, and with them her sense of power. Besides, her marriage had been a grand one, and she had given birth to six sons, each of whom subsequently died, like the husband, of war or peace, in one way or another. To be admitted to her circle was not a favour bestowed lightly. Some that wished for it hadn't received it at all. And if the women, married or un, young, mature, middle-aged or older, wandered about her house, or the overgrown grounds in summer, their hair down, and smoking cigars, well, the town largely ignored it. What could women alone do, after all, that was so bad? They were only women. The circle admitted no male. Once only an irate husband had arrived, Monsieur Gauveille, whose wife Marguerite was just then seated at the piano in her chemise. As her agile hands struck off silver beads of Chopin, the long doors to the terrace, which stood open on the two o'clock summer morning, were filled by Maurice Gauveille, a revolver in his hand.

"There, you slut! I know what you're up to. You whore of Babylon—look at you—half naked."

"But Maurice, it's such a hot night—"

"Undressed for high jinks. You bitch—you little cunt."

The other women stood looking at him, Artemise Lejay, as Sophrine hinted, her breasts bare, and a clutch of cherries in her hand bleeding down her arm. And Maurice Gauveille raised the gun. But from her great chair la Reine stood up and looked levelly at him. Laure had not been there, at this time, she was only twelve, and Sophrine hadn't been there either, she got the story from others.

"Monsieur, do please come in and sit down. Shall I ring for cognac?" inquired la Reine.

Gauveille faltered, but then he barked, "I'll start with you—I'll blast off your head, you monstrous and unnatural woman!"

La Reine, who was as always, in public, impeccably clothed, with a fabulous diamond, an heirloom, on her collar, gazed at him. ("Like a stone," said Sophrine.)

"Monsieur, you forget yourself."

"I have been forgotten, yes. But here I am."

"I have no sons to defend me," said la Reine, "and my husband, that his regiment was used to call the King, lies in the cemetery at Pere Chasse. What is it you can fear, monsieur, in this house, save your own brutishness?"

Gauveille could not speak the words, only offer invective that in no true way approximated. He threw the gun down in the fireplace—where Artemise quickly darted to retrieve it—and fell at the feet of Marguerite, sobbing.

Told this story five years later, Laure had remained impervious to its danger. She was not shocked. Hadn't any proper sense of how close the roomful of women had come, and one day again might come, to maiming and retributory death.

Men had slight significance for Laure. Her father had been only a periphery figure, soon gone, and her mother hastened after him.

Besides, the story of the revolver might be only a legend of the tribe, the tribe that met in the château of Sidonie Aubade-Valents.

Sophrine first brought Laure to the house one other late summer evening. A year older than Laure, Sophrine had left the country school, and neatly set herself up typing letters and copying accounts for her father's grocer shop. He paid her little, but then she had all her board and lodging, and never went short (as she phrased it) of any small trifle she fancied. When her mother hinted at suitors or a trousseau, Sophrine would stroke her father's brow (he was now the shorter): "I shall only marry if I can find a man as excellent as papa!" As to the afternoons and nights at the château, "She is a great lady," Monsieur Papa would declare. "It shows she has a fine egalitarian awareness, Madame Aubade. And an honour for Sophie. Stories? What stories? What nonsense. Invented by jealous gossips. And besides, think ahead, madame," this to his wife, Sophrine's mama, "the old woman may leave our girl a little something when she dies. It can't be long now. She's seventy if she's a day."

As Sophrine led Laure up overgrown steps through an old garden, the cicadas fell suspiciously silent, then resumed once more. Laure was now fifteen or just sixteen—her birth-date unsure. She was nervous. She had only seen la Reine once or twice, driven about town in her carriage, which still carried an ancient crest on its doors. This visit tonight had arisen like smoke from a pair of afternoons' fire. Laure and Sophrine had gone into the woods, like children, gathering early mulberries, hazelnuts, and so on. "Oh now," exclaimed Sophrine, " a bird's nest's dropped into my hair." They struggled to free it, and Sophrine's hair fell down in a shining shower. They were pressed breast to breast, as Laure believed, quite pragmatically. She had become used to the sudden flashing feelings that happened at such times. Not sought to prolong or explain them to herself. An innocent.

But then Sophrine had laughingly leaned forward, her breath scented with cinnamon and fruit and her lips reddened by berries, and kissed Laure with a flicker of the tongue. "Do you like that? Can you taste mulberries or raspberries?" "Mulberries." "Let me do it again. See if you can taste the raspberries, too." Laure forgot about the raspberries. So did Sophrine, it seemed.

There was a tree with a convenient low, wide dry lap. It was densely warm, and the forest so still but for the birds and small animals that scattered through it, none of them minding. They dallied for hours, moaning with unbearable excitement—Laure had no inkling how to resolve the glorious torture, although the sight and feel of Sophrine's breast, Sophrine's investigation of her own, sent waves, almost convulsions, through her centre. Finally Sophrine grappled her quite roughly, until Sophrine's thigh between her own, her own between Sophrine's, produced an explosion of heat, and so a heavenly fit, during which they rolled right off the low chair of the tree, among the bracken and powdery dry mulch of last year's leaves.

Nothing much was said. Only Sophrine: "Do you love me now?" And Laure, slightly offended, "What? Why?" "Ungrateful little beast. After what I've shown you." Even so, presently, the experience was repeated, in Laure's bedroom at the Aunt's house (with muffled shrieks into pillows, but the Aunt was deaf).

Thereafter came the invitation to attend the château.

"But—you go there?"

"Of course. And so can you."

"But why?"

"Oh, Laure. What a simpleton you are. Why do you think? Oh don't sulk. It's because you like what we do."

Laure thought. She pivoted on one hip and stared.

"You mean *that's* what it's all about—all the women who go to the Aubade château?"

"Of course it is. What else?"

The walk to the château, half a mile from the town, had been at sunset along a lane overhung by glowing chestnut trees. The walls were high, in places unsafe. They climbed skittishly through at a break rather than use the gates or carriage drive.

In the grounds, the ancient woods had seeded new woods. Weird paths trickled off to strange little false temples, glimmering in half-light. Five feet high, an ivied Pan played the syrinx under an elm. In the old garden too, nettles, clovers and wild garlic:

docks grew like tall umbrellas and a cedar tree had torn its way through a terrace, shattering the stones with its roots.

It was dusk by then, altering to night. Stars littered the sky, growing ever brighter. An owl called, then swept out over the park on impossibly wide pale prehistoric-looking wings.

They emerged from the trees and fallen urns, and there were roses bursting over a broken wall, and the scent of stocks hung heavy as a velvet curtain. There was a lawn, with another statue on it, a stone girl, nude. And suddenly two other girls, not made of stone, ran out of the bushes, and away along one of the little paths. Their hair was down and although they were fully clothed, their feet were bare. They had a Bacchante wildness to them.

Sophrine began to hum Mendelssohn's musical setting of the Lullaby from *A Midsummer Night's Dream*. Oh yes, snakes with spotted skin—thorny hedgehogs—banks of wild thyme, too and flowers of purple dye—

Generally Sophrine's responses—Laure had always known, was well able to remember even after the pair of afternoons' fire—were trite. The responses, Laure's long-lost mother might have said, one would expect from a grocer's daughter. But the Mendelssohn was not at all of that type. That it was obvious only made it more perfect. Laure felt then a rush of freeing anticipation, and too desire.

"Shall we...?"

"Not yet."

Through the bushes, by a choked pool. Steps and one more terrace, and then the château rose in a ghostly shadow on the last of the twilight, pushing up and next falling away and away. It was very big. There were rounded towers with turrets which, by day, would show a steely blue, or black or green where decaying tiles had dropped out. Doves nested in eaves, but now a sparse hail of bats spun about. There were lights, here and there. Sophrine walked straight in at two long lit open windows—the very ones made infamous by Monsieur Maurice Gauveille.

It was a salon, with a grand piano resting on an Aubusson carpet. Laure also noticed paintings, mirrors and low sofas in a lemon brocade. But she noticed these things really only in retrospect, and then they were so apt, so fundamental to what she would have expected, she wondered at first if she had been mistaken, made them up. Perhaps the room was really empty.

No *person* was in the room. Then the old woman entered. This was not the château's mistress, but a creature la Reine called, scathingly, her "Jewel." Peridot, one of her remaining servants.

Peridot had been at the château apparently since her girlhood, which must have been in the eighteenth century, from her looks. She was very short and small, walnut brown, her head bound and tied by thick dark grey hair, and poked forward like a tortoise's.

"One, two," said Peridot, counting Sophrine and Laure off on the air with her right forefinger.

Sophrine only looked amused.

"Herself will see you at once," said Peridot.

She had an accent of the south, rounded and bronzy from the weather. Sometimes she used words and expressions Laure couldn't make sense of. Perhaps no one had ever fathomed them, only come to know what they meant, like all language, by repetitious application to apparent facts.

They followed Peridot from the room, along corridors papered with silk, in places marked by the damp, and up a marble stair with a gilded handrail. Lamps burned at junctures, enough to provide sufficient light for girls brought up in the country, beyond the River Styx.

Then they went down an awful little uncarpeted wooden stair in the almost dark. Laure hated this stair. She felt cold on it, and was sure someone had been murdered there. At its foot, a door was opened, and they were in the suite of la Reine, Sidonie Aubade-Valents. ("Her name is English," had said Sophrine earlier. "No one knows why.")

The rooms opened one from another. They blazed and burned with scores of lit candles. She sat by a low table in a carved mahogany chair. Laure was to find there seemed to be a chair like this in every room, and it was always hers. She wore (she always would) very elegant clothes, in grey silk, buttoned high at the throat and wrist. Her gowns were always out of, but also above and beyond, the fashion. Her hands were mediaeval, long and thin and transparent, with oval translucent tawny nails. One jeweled ring on each, a dark polished ruby and a dull facetted emerald. Heavy and tarnished gold wedding rings, two of them, were worn on her right hand. Her face was less effective. She had been beautiful once (they said). Now she had, as Sophrine *always* said, lost everything but her eyes. It was a fallen face, grown shapeless, or wrongly shaped. The nose had enlarged and spread. The jaw vanished in dewlaps. Even the eyes, of course, had become diluted, like waterlogged irises, and the lashes thinned. But you had to ignore it. You had to say, in common decency, *Oh, she still has her eyes. They are still beautiful.*

La Reine gazed up at them, and Laure was startled because Sophrine at once offered a staccato little curtsy. Just like a grocer's daughter—*but I won't,* thought Laure, and did not.

"Good evening, Sophrine."

"Good evening, dear majesty." (Laure had been prepared for sycophancy.) "May I present, Laure Deschampeigne, my friend."

"You're welcome, Mademoiselle Deschampeigne."

"Thank you, ma-madame," stammered Laure, angering herself by flushing at the omission of the other title.

La Reine didn't seem put out. She beckoned them over, and offered them a box of cigarettes (not the cheroots of the tales). Sophrine took one, and Peridot came and lit it for her, with a match.

"You don't smoke, Laure, my dear?"

"No, madame. My Aunt suffers with her chest. No one smokes in our house." *How provincial I sound,* had thought Laure. *How subservient and fawning even though I won't address her as a queen.*

"Do you mean then, she would otherwise allow you to smoke?"

"Oh—probably not."

"Well, never mind. Here, you may do as you wish."

Peridot then again came forward, now carrying a book. It was large, bound in leather, and gilded. The pages, coloured like sugar almonds, had names written all over them. The book was laid on the table, next to an inkwell and an old-fashioned pen. Sophrine at once bent forward, soused the pen in the ink, and signed her name with a silly schoolgirl flourish. Laure thought, *Is this what she does, to get us in her power!* For the names in the book were clearly evidence of their attendances. (Like school?) Laure didn't lean forward in turn to sign, and the book was left lying there. No one referred to it.

"Sophrine," said la Reine, "I mustn't keep you. Why don't you join the others? I *will* keep Laure, just until the dinner hour."

Laure felt almost frightened, since Sophrine instantly went out, and then the old Peridot too went out, moving rather sideways, like an old crab. And Laure was alone with la Reine. And beyond her shoulder, in the hazy blaze of candlelight, one could see right into a bedroom, to a bed canopied in tapestry.

"Please sit, Laure Deschampeigne."

Laure sat. Disgruntled, she said, "Thank you, madame."

"What is it?" asked la Reine. Claws glinted in a frail bony paw: "Do you think I'll demand *a favour* of you? In there, hmm? Well?"

Laure shrugged "It would be beneath you."

"Would it, indeed. But you're so young and fresh. Clear-eyed, and with such fine pretty hair. No? Are you sure I won't?"

Laure stood up.

The old woman laughed. "Sit, sit. You shan't be harmed. I don't rub my alligator flesh against little maidens. Good God in a Blue Sky, girl. I had to put up with my husband all those years. Do you think I want to inflict any of that on my own sex?"

Laure blushed furiously and scowled at her shoes—the best ones with rosettes, put on for the occasion, damn it.

"No," said la Reine, soothingly, lighting another cigarette for herself directly from a candle. "I should like to converse with you, for a little while." She had already slipped into the familiar form, the intimate rather than the formal "you." But she was old, seventy-eight, Sophrine had said. She looked a hundred to Laure.

Laure said, "It was kind of you to ask me to your house, madame."

"But you know why?"

"Not really."

"Because—and I'm certain you do, since Sophrine will have told you—you are of my own persuasion, like the other ladies who come here. Oh, it isn't to visit me, I assure you. Sometimes I'm not even to be seen, except perhaps at dinner in the evening. But I make free my house to you all. I give you liberty, my little birds. I like it, I confess, very much, to hear or to sense those foot-steps, the laughs and little cries. But more than that, to let you into a cage which makes you safe, at least for a few brief hours. Of course, when I'm gone, God in His sky knows what will become of you all. But at least you will have tasted happiness, to recognize it, or passion. Perhaps great passion, if you are very fortunate and very unlucky."

Laure stared at la Reine's face, her attention caught. Age and ugliness became only a mask. Behind it, this being spoke to her like a bell.

"The great passion," repeated la Reine. "Yes, why not. I have known it, very nearly. I doubt I shall know it again. For me it was only wonderful pain. The woman wasn't of our kind, but she was accommodating. One can only stand so much of that. The glory lay all in the pain, then. Not in the rather shabby fulfillments. But for you, Laure, I wonder. Not with little Sophrine, I think. Even if she was your tutor, for which you should always wear her like a rose in your heart and not forget."

Laure cast down her eyes. She found she had become aroused. This old woman had the power to arouse her, solely by her words.

And in this arousal, and this nameless surge of longing and ex-citement—oh, not for la Reine, but for the hallucination la Reine had seemed on the verge of conjuring—Sidonie Aubade-Valents abandoned her. Cunning as an old fox.

With silence, cigarette smoke and hot summer candlelight, they sat in stasis, until Peridot poked her tortoise head inside the door. "I have seen a repast laid. We are twenty-two tonight."

Laure noted Peridot did not call her mistress by any title at all.

It was the first of so many evenings, dinners. All different, all familiar. Finally all quite *ordinary*. Although later ones were often more dramatic, gross even, with scenes, lovers' quarrels carried on publicly as, elsewhere, they could hardly be, recriminations or—much worse—sinking into trivia. (As, for example, seeing the nearly exquisite Lejay discussing the price of coffee and soap. Expatiating upon it, her equine beauty growing banal, like any well-off young town matron, with the keys to the family cupboard). Laure expected too much of the château, naturally. It *was* her nature. She had the unfortunate and self-harming habit of sometimes seeing magic in persons and things, where it didn't exist. She herself busily constructed the glamour. Then, learning the perfectly obvious truth, disliking and castigating the offending object, with a feeling of betrayal.

At least, she had not been, and never was to be, guilty of that with Sophrine. Nor did she wear the grocer's daughter in her heart like a rose. This romantic ideal had appealed to Laure, its tincture of mediaeval love-courts, secret classical nostalgias. But— *Sophrine*? Ha!

The court of la Reine was, though, partly responsible for this particular englamourment and disillusion. The first approach having been through the twilight midsummer garden, then la Reine herself, the "conversation" (monologue) in her room, then that first dinner, at which she contrived to tell them all a story.

"This crest on the china, do you see? My own, not my husband's. Nevertheless, it belongs to the château. Do you see what it is? A bird? Yes. A crow—a jackdaw. Only some two hundred and fifty years old—a very immature crest. But you find him, my black bird, sometimes, worked into a corner of the tablecloths or napkins. Always the tableware. Oh, and in one picture from the 1760s, in the annex to the north tower—he's painted on a bough, holding a pomegranate in his beak. A detail of the work, but significant. It was a woman who had it painted, my husband's grandmother, the White Comtesse."

Laure had listened intently. This was just antique enough to interest her at once. And perhaps la Reine had chosen it on purpose, flatteringly. But then it was difficult to tell if the other women had ever heard it before, this historic myth. Some listened attentively, their chins on their hands, or toying with the moist rim of a chipped crystal vessel (most of the château glass was chipped). Others kept eyes downcast. Some silently flirted with each other.

A couple even stifled yawns. But then they might have been do-ing tiring things, at home, or here.

Twenty-two in number, as Peridot the tortoise-woman had said. They drifted into the meal from all over the château. (No rooms, as Laure would learn, were out-of-bounds, though many were vacant of furniture, or else stacked floor to ceiling with it, the haunt of mice and spiders. There were, Sophrine had assured her, priceless things everywhere, simply left lying about. You could go in and thieve the smaller ones, and who would know? La Reine never would. Laure thought perhaps *Peridot* would. Did Sophrine mean anyway that she herself had made off with items, against some parochial rainy day, and not been caught out?) Even the barefoot maenads entered the dining room with clean hands and brushed hair. None was bare-breasted, not even Artemise Lejay, although many of her blouse buttons were undone. Others, such as Clothilde Boulanger, wore rustic evening gowns. No one, though she knew most of them by sight, and had exchanged words with several, spoke to Laure during this first visit, beyond a *Good Evening* or *How do you go on?* None used her name. On her very next visit, all that changed. They addressed her familiarly, impertinently, and pulled her hair.

The table was heavily laid with silver, and incised goblets, yet everything was a little declined. The cloth, faintly stained and yellowed, the glass past its best, the silver brackish. Overhead a chandelier tinkled in the airs from the open windows. Cobwebs veiled its prisms and now and then floated down onto a bowl of apples, figs and peaches, many of which were bruised. It was a haphazard meal. Dishes of cold wood-pigeon, a cooling ragout, salad of rampion and radishes and bitter green things. Later Peridot mixed and cooked little flat sweet omelettes over a silver table-brazier. But there was a great deal of wine, blood-coloured, and liqueurs of all shades, that far outshone the story-teller's stagnant emerald and ruby.

"The story of the jackdaw is this: There were two aristocrats, an uncle and a nephew, both young, almost of an age through some vagary of the births. Don't suppose that they lived here, at the château. They resided some distance away, in another house twice the size. Their crimes and vices likewise, were gigantic, a marvel in an age when men of their station and wealth seldom behaved well. In short, they were a byword for depravity—worse indeed than that other, later, strange beast, known as the Marquis de Sade, who was also, it seems, a great liar. In the Revolution, these two men, the Comte de Valents-Blanches and his nephew, would no doubt have been torn to shreds by the people of their estates, long before they reached the ladder of the Guillotine. But it transpires they did not live in that mitigating era.

"One day these two were looking for a diversion. They presently hit upon something. One of them, the nephew, had chanced to see a young girl in the village, as he rode through. She was not much more than fourteen, but fully formed, as country maidens often are. She had long fair hair and a skin like damask, and lips as red as wine. What would have been usual with them, the men, was to have sent for the girl and raped her, turn by turn, until satisfied. Then, if she still lived, they would have sent her back with the normal jest, that they had prepared her for her husband. However, they'd done such a thing quite often, and by now found the experience almost enervating. It chanced they were dining as the topic was broached, and the nephew, picking up a fruit from the table, drew the uncle's attention to it. 'Just so is this demoiselle, uncle. Rounded and smooth, with the bloom ripely on her. One could bite into her, one could eat her up. What a feast she would be.' At this the comte narrowed his eyes. He had been handsome once, but already his methods had marked him, he was no longer so. 'Then let us,' said he. 'No, I don't mean our usual game. Not at all.' After which he outlined his plan.

"This château then, was in their possession, but slimly staffed—although doubtless they kept more people here than I do. All around the great woods, a wilderness of beech and chestnut, swept down, and this wonderful town of ours, Bois-la-Diane, was merely a well with two or three shacks leaning beside it. The comte ordered his preparations, and his terrified servants, whom fear had made as depraved as he, carried them out. The young girl was abducted. Brought to the château, she was drugged by a mixture of pink valerian and Indian opiates in brandy.

"Deep in the park, where the ancient forest then encroached, far more so than it does now, the comte's servants laid a table with the snowy moth-wing linen of Chinese looms, and falls of white lace, and over that scarves of purple so fine they were barely to be seen, only their fringes of leaden gold."

("*The Thousand Nights*," said Sophrine of this juncture afterwards. But Laure had only considered la Reine would not carelessly have omitted the extra *And One Night*, as Sophrine had.)

"On to the table then they heaped the best of the château's fruit, from its orchards and hothouses. Apples and plums like garnets and yellow Carrara marble, peaches and apricots, blue grapes, and grenadines, and by that time even pineapples, cut open and leaking their saffron juice like amber resin. There were also flowers. Every flower that grew here then. The green and fine blue plumes and red spikes of herbs, the bowl-faced wax white roses, the wolf-flowers from the forest's edge, the wild hyacinths, the monstrous striped orchids, and lilies bred under slices of glass. All these cast and scattered over the cloths and veils, among the fruit. And next there were sweets, made especially, bonbons brought from Paris and Versailles, in the shape of keys covered with edible gold-and-silver-leaf, or butterflies of sugar so thin you could see your own fingers through them. Lastly they placed the decanters of old, greenish glass, or those of gold and inlaid silver, some of which had precious stones for stoppers, and goblets of filigreed gold and coloured Venetian glass that Doges had drunk from. All this, on the table. Then they carried the girl out, unconscious. She had been stripped naked and shaved carefully of every hair, but for her lashes, eyebrows, and the gilt tresses of her head. She had been bathed and sponged with essences until she too smelled only of fruit and flowers and sweets and wine. And they had draped her with strings of round white pearls.

"They laid her at the centre of the table. They spread out her long hair and scattered a few more pearls—priceless—and exotic flowers into it. They arranged, the story goes, a bunch of grapes as cool as jade over her loins. And over her eyes they let fall a long lavender ribbon. And then, they put down the plates and the table knives."

La Reine paused here. Peridot, who hovered, refilled her mistress's glass. But la Reine did not touch it.

She said:

"Do you see? Even then they were driving there, the uncle and his nephew, driving very fast in their black carriage, towards the château. They were starving hungry and planning to eat her. Alive. Carve off pieces of her flesh, suck out her marrow, garnished by fruits and confectionery. The girl was to be their feast. Is that terrible enough?

"Now we come to the jackdaw.

"You can imagine, bees and wasps and flies by the swarm had been attracted to that table. Within ten minutes, every flower had a bee at its centre, while the wasps crawled over the girl's pure skin. Flies stood on the sweets, cleaning their faces like cats, with forefeet like black splinters. Perhaps he only came down for the insects, the jackdaw.

"He was ink black, with golden eyes, just as you can see him in the picture in the annex. He flew down, and maybe caught a bee or two in his beak. But then he flew up on to the girl's soft, curving breast. He stood and looked at her, lying there with the ribbon over her eyes. Right next to him, nestled in her side, was a cut pomegranate. The jackdaw pecked it, and the wine juice splashed the table-cloths. The girl slept on. When he left her, where he had stood, his claws too had made a fading pomegranate-coloured mark.

"Just then, the black carriage turned in to the lane and came rushing towards the château. How hungry they were, the two men, how they longed to dine.

"Then up flew the crow on his inky wings. He flew over the wood, over the wall, and over the lane, straight at the heads of the horses he flew. He must have looked, don't you think, like a bolt from heaven, the thunder-bolt that brings love or death?

"The horses reared. No surprise in that. The coachman rolled from his box, and broke his legs, and walked after with a limp, but he lived, they say. Then the horses dashed on, straight at the wall, until swerving, they broke their traces and were gone. But the carriage smashed headlong against the château gate-post of stone. The bird had vanished.

"They died those two, the comte and his nephew. They were broken into bits inside their skins, so that picked up, they *rattled.* It was too quick for them, but if we credit Hell, perhaps not."

La Reine took up her glass and drank.

She said, "The girl awoke and ate the fruit. She was cared for, or she went away. She lived happily and never knew what she had been spared. But the peasants knew. In the end it was the old Comtesse Valents-Blanches who adopted the jackdaw as her crest. And now, so too do I."

After the dinner, Sophrine took Laure through room after room, up and down stairs, along corridors of the château. Sophrine carried a lamp, and never, Laure thought, had she looked more like a pert little housekeeper. But also, night was there in the château, and Laure felt the enormity of night and of the house.

"You believed that tale, didn't you, Laure?"

"Yes."

"Swallowed it whole. She made it up."

"You think so."

"Well, how could it happen?"

"Easily enough. The mere facts. The art, Sophrine, is in putting them together to create a story which seems supernatural, yet isn't."

"Oh you. I can just see you on the table with all those melting sweets, stung all over by wasps and with grapes in your private place."

But again, just then, Sophrine undid a door, and there was a vast room, perhaps a ballroom, with huge windows and mirrors, and moonlight shimmering like water on the floor.

"The rooms in this house," whispered Sophrine, in awe, "seem always to shift about. I never know where I'll find them next."

To Laure this was a confession that Sophrine's house, and all those she knew or could imagine, and therefore all her horizons, were small. You knew where everything was. But the château was like a huge landscape. You could be lost in it.

She was about to make some remark, when Sophrine whispered even more softly, "Ssh. *Look.*"

There was a low sofa stranded under one of the windows. A woman lay on it, naked, white as a statue in the moonlight. A fall of dark hair going to the floor, the narrow lines of her body, revealed her as Artemise Lejay. Her left leg was bent at the knee, resting on the sole of her left foot, opening her centre where a second darkness, not grapes but also hair, blotted off the moonlight.

Another woman, Laure was not sure who, stood over her, but not touching her with her body. Instead the unknown woman was making a painting, stroking motion, over and over, on and on, just within the smoky cleft—and her instrument was like an incredibly long and curved finger—

"A feather," breathed Sophrine. "A *crow's* feather."

Over and over, and Artemise lay arched and still, tense as a bowstring, And now they heard her say harshly, "Oh!" and then, after a few moments, "Oh!"

But that was all.

They, and their lamp, went unseen, or unacknowledged.

Outside, Sophrine pressed Laure quickly against the wall, but a sour ache had begun in Laure where pleasure had been. She did not want Sophrine at all.

"She's my ideal," breathed Sophrine, "that Lejay. Isn't she a marvel? I've never before seen her like that, Oh, to be in that one's shoes—"

"Leave me alone."

"Oh, Laure, don't be a baby. Of course I like you too."

An uncomfortable rush of heat of a different sort, and a cramp at the base of her belly, made Laure push Sophrine away. "It's my little monthly enemy."

"You fool," cried Sophrine angrily, "it won't matter. I'm not some boy—"

Laure picked up the lamp Sophrine had put down, and walked briskly away. Sophrine soon came scurrying after her, afraid to be left in the dark with only the harsh peremptory "Oh! Oh!" to cling to.

In the salon with the piano, some of them were playing cards. La Reine had gone. Peridot had gone. Avid as chickens, the women craned forward, scrabbled and slapped down their cards with sharp clucks.

Laure's head ached, her womb ached. She presently walked along the carriage drive (past the killing gate-post), and back into the town of Bois-la-Diane, on the moonlit lane.

The chestnut trees were black as iron, with dry silver-wet edges. The trees were full of invisible rustlings, and only the town was silent, still warm, patrolled by cats.

After some four years, then, now nineteen or twenty, Laure walked the other way up to the château of Sidonie Aubade-Valents, on Wednesday, in autumn. The lane was soaked and full of brown leaves, and it was only three o'clock in the afternoon.

Four years had not altered so much. One or two women no longer attended, three or four had been added. The *magic* had run out almost at once, that first night even, with the menstrual blood.

The château was a destination to go to. As one went on with one's life.

"They called her Madame Death, in Paris, so I'm told."
"And in the south—"
"How mediaeval you sound, Clothilde, Marie. Or like something at least from the seventeenth century."
"I heard she was also in South America!"
"And she's a Jewess!"
"The *Wandering* Jew, perhaps," remarked Violette Charpentier. "Well I haven't seen the creature. Is she even in the town? What do you think, Laure?"

Five of the Club had gathered in the old parlour, which, like the salon, lay off a corridor from the château's cavernous Hall.

Violette, the scholar, would have explained, and once had, the Hall was the masculine place, the male core of the house, the hearth big enough to roast an ox, complete with rusty irons, beams that crossed like quarrels, war and dueling swords and pistols hung up, and mildewy heads of stags and bear that had once roamed the woods.

The parlour was, as its name conveyed, for talk—chatter—always a female spot.

Violette was doubtless forty, in town parlance "an old maid." Lack of looks had permitted her escape. But had she ever had a female lover? Perhaps. There was nothing virginal to her, thought Laure, even though she might be stoppered and sealed tight.

Now Violette looked at Laure, consideringly, along her long thin nose on which ready spectacles perched.

"Who?" said Laure. "What are you talking about?"

But her face flamed suddenly. She knew.

"Oh look," said annoying Marie-Louison. "This one's seen her. Tell us, Laure."

"I have not. That is, I did see a woman today, a stranger, probably. One knows everyone here, I suppose. So maybe it was—But what were you saying?"

"You don't know the story then?" asked Clothilde. "Ooh! Laure, Laure—it's quite frightful. Ghoulish."

"Really."

"Supposedly," said Violette, "this woman (if she is here) is a type of prostitute."

A chorus of admonition.

"No, no. She was *not.*"

"Any woman who marries could be called a whore," cried married Annette Mercier.

"True, in many cases," amended Violette. "In this case, if the *tale* is true, definitely. She certainly marries only for gain. And does it repeatedly."

Laure stood staring. Her heart thudded like a drum, hurting her a little as it struck the confining walls of flesh and corset. When agitated, the heart always wanted to get free.

But she had come here with some vague sense that she might hear something about the stranger glimpsed by the canal, the stranger she, Laure, had passed, unable to frame either a courtesy or a question. And yes, that face, those black eyes and black eyebrows—how truly *strange* she had been, that woman, that *stranger.*

Laure opened her mouth to interrogate them again, the silly or procrastinating women, but just then Peridot's head, more tortoise-like now, four years on, poked into the room.

"Luncheon, if you will take it."

They treated Peridot with scant politeness. This was mutual. Probably *her* attitude had come first, with all of them. The "Jewel" stood there as the wash of women swept around her. La Reine's guests were usually hungry, or likely to be. Dishes of sweets and fruit left about were always empty by the evening's end. Spoilt children, they expected to be cared for, and were cared for.

Laure was the last to go, not hungry at all, and something in Peridot's sharp old eye delayed her further.

"What?" demanded Laure.

"What? What? The genuine country Bourgeoise. No style."

"I never claimed to be an aristo!" Laure flashed back. She was amazed at the exchange. Normally Peridot insulted or challenged them in subtle ways only really noted afterwards. "What do you take me for?"

"A little girl," said Peridot. "Do you know what you were speaking of? No. Peridot knows. Knows it all. How not, when Peridot does the marketing and talks to the tradesmen and the laundry women."

Laure stood stunned. "Do you want me to tip you?"

Peridot's surface did not ripple. "Here's my hand."

With a most extraordinary feeling, dry mouthed, Laure took a coin from her little (bourgeois) bag and dropped it square on the tortoise's palm. Tortoise-shell closed over it.

"She's called Madame Corrot. That's the name, do you see, of her last husband-gone-to-God. She's a widow. But then, apparently, she's a widow some ten or twenty times over."

Laure pulled her lips together. They had slipped open, as if she knew she could hear better through her mouth than her ears. Her eyes, she knew, were as wide as a deer's

"Why? *How?*"

"Oh, she don't murder them, her husbands. She'd be in the jail, else, wouldn't she. Or sent to the blade."

"Then—they die—"

"She isn't bad luck, either." Peridot stopped speaking. *Does she want another bribe—I didn't give her enough—* But Peridot said one of her phrases, "The cock gets up afore the pinafore, and down again he goes, too." Then, "It turns out, if a man knows he's on his last legs, but wants a bit of fun before he leaves, he calls for this woman, with her black hair and her white legs. She won't do a thing, unless he weds her, and makes her a settlement. Then she'll do all that'll be done under the sun. She has a reputation and is reckoned beautiful. Else she couldn't make her terms."

Laure said, "And then he dies, and she's free again."

"And well-off. Which is the reason for it all. She's a professional widow, mademoiselle. And now she's called Corrot, but it used to be Duvalle, and last year, in the city, it was Lebonniére. Afore that I can't say."

Laure didn't reply, *Why have you chosen to tell me?* One is the heroine of one's own story. And besides, Peridot had exacted payment. Maybe she had done this with everyone here, all the younger and more gullible ones at least. Maybe it was anyway a lie.

So Laure straightened her face abruptly as if to iron it; and stalked past Peridot with a "Very well. That will do." Just as she had seen her Aunt do in her house, with her servants, although not recently. The Aunt was softer and deafer now, more like a slightly mad nun.

In the dining room they looked up with anticipation: they predicted Laure would continue to question them, would blush again, and so on. She didn't. And they stopped talking about the woman who was a professional widow (if she was). Wouldn't resume the chat.

Instead, Annette complained about her husband, the fat notary, and then Marie-Louison about hers (the draper's clerk). Clothilde Boulanger started on about her brothers, Rose and Honorine Éperve about their father. All classes mixed here. There was no caste system. And for now, too, they were only nagging, whining women, just the thing men joyed to despise. And Laure, glancing at them, thought proudly, *I am more like a man. I despise them too. I want them only for pleasure, the tickle, rush, gasp and explosion between my legs. I don't like them at all. Do I wish I wasn't a woman, even? Perhaps not. Men repel me another way. Or, they don't matter. Am I only ashamed of these women? Their awful littleness.*

La Reine wasn't at the table. Actually, Laure hadn't seen her, or at the dinners, for a month or more. Artemise Lejay too, was absent. Violette scraped up miserly portions of cheese sauce and bread, her long nose in a book. Lucide was flirting with Marie Jeanne. In a stupid, exclusive, irritating way.

Even Sophrine hadn't come, hard at work on papa's ledgers.

Rain streamed past the windows, and sometimes handfuls of leaves blew across the casements in a bad-tempered wind.

Is *she* like these women? Just the same? Oh, with some veneer of a city, maybe. Some coldness and coarseness too, because of what she's done? She looked—quite pure. Like black and white marble. Like Pygmalion's statue just come to life. They must like that in her, her *husbands*. Can it really be true? What a story. Where does she live? One of those large houses by the church, perhaps. Or a little picturesque cottage tucked behind the market? Why is she *here*? Perhaps no one will buy anymore. Fallen on hard times— *into a basket,* as that Peridot would say. A hovel then. One scruffy servant, and one meal a day. It didn't look like that. Her dress—it was silk, and fur on the jacket—but then, was it even her?

What is her name now?

The Aunt was seated at her own gloomy window in the large house on the rue Dalle. Yellowish light seeped through folds and pleats of lace. She had been reading one of her books (novels by men penned fifty or a hundred years before).

"Laure… I thought you had gone out."

"I did. I have a headache. I came back."

"I beg your pardon? Oh, your head… It's too late now for luncheon. Tell Ouelle to put you out some bread and butter. And hot coffee."

Not to prolong the interview—the Aunt had called her in to her sitting room—Laure nodded impatiently.

But, "You shall sit here," added the Aunt, putting down her book absently, its satin marker trailing. She spoke as if bestowing a treat on Laure. Laure felt every hair of her head pulling tight in a rigor of dismay.

The Aunt herself rang for Ouelle, and presently the woman came in. She was plump and untidy, always straightening her apron, rearranging pins in her mass of singeing light hair—to no avail. Her anxious pink moon face swung eagerly to them.

"Fetch coffee, Ouelle. Make sure it's hot. And some of the brioches, with butter and preserves."

"Yes, madame."

Outside the door, Laure knew, Ouelle would sigh and raise her eyes to God at the nuisance of these two women, the old one and the chit, pestering her away from more important tasks, such as the knitting of endless caps and mittens for her herd of nephews and nieces, or her canoodling with the wood-seller, or rabbit-man, over the garden wall. With the rabbit-man especially Ouelle had had a sort of understanding for years. Now the Aunt had grown fairly vague, Ouelle invited him often to the kitchen for a quick nip of something and perhaps herself. One always knew when it had occurred. There were for days rabbit stews and pâtés at every meal. Ouelle's look of eager anxiety with the Aunt was merely an act, carried on for so long that now it occurred spontaneously.

"Ah, Laure, Laure," sighed the Aunt. Then gazed into the shadows of the room. After some minutes she added, despondently, "Soon, winter."

"Yes, Aunt." Laure remembered to speak loudly, making her own ears ring.

"And we, like the poor birds, our heads beneath the wing."

She means, thought Laure, pitilessly, *she will soon be dead. She includes me in it, too. I suppose I shall be in twenty or thirty years.*

And Laure too inadvertently sighed.

"Where have you been, Laure?"

"To the château. It's Wednesday."

"Ah, yes. Madame la Comtesse Valents-Blanches. The Ladies Days." She never responded more than that to it now. In the first year, when she found out, although not from Laure (someone would always be willing to tattle), that Laure went to the château, the Aunt had drawn her up into the sanctum of her bedroom. At first she had seemed ready to burst out in a tirade, then deflated. "Do you know what you are at?" was all she had said. Laure stood and waited, not knowing what to say, if the château was worth fighting or even deceiving for, since, in the case of Laure, already she had found means to indulge herself, on the Aunt's very premises. But the Aunt, deflating even more, had then said, "Well, it will pass. These things. One day you'll meet someone. It will be for him to deal with." Laure, remembering this, today raised her eyebrows.

And the Aunt now said, "We shall be cozy together. Ouelle must light a fire." She felt the cold, the winter breathing on her neck. Because she was well-off, and could afford it, in winter the house was always too hot, and aromatic with new tonics, and tinctures of peppermint and clove for rheumatism. *How cruel it is,*

Laure thought, surprising herself a moment by her own compassion—or dread—*how we become old.*

But then the coffee came in and Ouelle lit the fire and a lamp, and the Aunt began a meandering reminiscence of her past triumphs—balls, suppers—in another town, and Laure's head began to ache in earnest.

She sat in a sort of stupor, promising herself that at four o'clock she would go up to her room. Now and then the Aunt fell asleep, and liberty seemed possible, but these sleeps lasted no more than a few seconds.

The fire, having roasted the room like a chestnut, sank low. Little golden eyes fleered among the charred sticks, spirits lurking in the grate, as Laure had believed, in childhood, they lurked in the chimney.

She had been a nervous child had she? Afraid of being left alone. Her mother had done so a great deal, only she couldn't recall any of that time. She had a horrible suspicion that, when she was nine or ten, she had wanted to stay always close to the Aunt, importunately. And that today's unwanted invitation was a resurrection of those earlier times, which only then would have comforted Laure.

She had slept with a low-burning lamp in her room, because of nightmares, until she was thirteen. What had the nightmares consisted of? She was afraid of ghosts, afraid of witches, of wolves in the woods, of things in chimneys—

"Oh, Laure," said the Aunt. "Laure."

"What?" Much too sharply. More mildly, "What is it?" Finally, mildly but also loudly: "What is it?"

"I wish I could be young again. How I wish I could."

Laure frowned. What could she say? The Aunt's face now was that of a child. A child afraid of ghosts, winter, and a black wolf named Death.

But then, "There now," said the Aunt. "You've had your tea. What a good girl. Run along, Laure. I must read a little."

"Ouelle, come here."

Ouelle came there. She *stood* there. Plainly interrupted.

"Ouelle, have you heard of a woman in the town, a Madame Corrot, a widow?"

Ouelle flung up her pink hands to her pink face-moon.

"There, m'mselle Laure! Fancy you should hear of *that*! Well I never."

"It's true?"

"What a woman. Do you know, those men—" she spoke proprietarily, as if all the men in the town were hers—"they're laying bets on it. Will it be the old mayor over at St Georges-du-Marais—or that old miser Boucher—he's got something put by, and he's an old lecher, he is—"

"Ouelle," said Laure sternly.

"Excuse me, m'mselle. But there. A woman like that. Of course," said Ouelle flouncingly, "it may *not* be true. A pack of lies. How could such a thing be possible here? In the city—even in Convienne—there they'll do anything. But then, it could be our Doctor St Romarin. He's an intellectual. The brainy ones are often the worst."

Laure shook herself as if dispelling water from her pelt.

"I do think it's all a lie. You're quite right, Ouelle. It would be impossible in this town. For example, where would she live—?"

"That," said Ouelle, "isn't *any* mystery. She's taken rooms in the Blue House. Three day-rooms, a bedroom, and the big drawing-room for visitors. Pelu told me." (Pelu was the wood-seller. They were still on comradely terms.)

"Perhaps you're right," repeated Laure vaguely. "My Aunt—"

Ouelle leaned forward. "The mistress," said Ouelle, "she's getting worse—can hardly hear a word unless I shout—forgets everything. Do you know, this morning she called me Susine again. Lay the fire, Susine, she says. And books in every room; she starts, then forgets and takes another one."

"I must go out," said Laure. She added, "She's sent me for some thread."

"She can't see to sew. How can she want thread? We need none—I'd know, I do the sewing."

"Thank you, Ouelle."

And Ouelle bobbed and sailed away, a cork afloat on other's lives.

Laure's head now pounded. She ran to fetch her outdoor things. As soon as she undid the door, a white flush of rainy wind slapped her face and the leaves dazzled up in a crazy dance.

She was almost running along the street. Not quite. Etiquette and the corset she wore combined to slow her down.

Pelu said…and it might be Doctor St Romarin—or all the way to St Georges, another dreary town… And it's lies. Or it's true.

Where am I going in this fine rush?

Laure stopped. She was between two muddy, cobbled lanes passing for streets. Small houses crowded together. She had come quite a way from the grander house of the Aunt, not noticing. Only the white wind and the leaves, everything bounding with her.

The light was fading, too. Presently old Jacques would be lighting the lamps in the church square…

Here and there already a lamplit window. Two women going by, stiffly nodded to her, the Aunt's niece. A black cat melted between the iron bars of a gate

Well. But I'm going to look at the Blue House, which all this while, as ever, overlooks the canal.

Is it Laure's head which pounds, or her heart? Are her hands cold, or too hot?

She walks briskly now, her pointed little chin held up and her eyes full of something that might even look like rage.

It stood there, timbered, blue once, now only a blue superimposed by memory, peeling, the boards threadbare. It must be damp. It reflected in the water, where the woods came entirely close, it reflected like a blue sun that wasn't any longer blue, or a sun. A ghost. A ghost house mirrored in a canal.

Laure had walked as far as the gates, and now she idled, looking in through the ironwork, which wasn't at all the same gate—

much larger, older, finer, rustier and less well-kept—than the gate in the town street that a black cat had melted through.

The Blue House, in its blue days, was said to have been visited by a dauphin, and by poets. Various eccentric or elderly people now rented the rooms.

The darkness was coming. The sky looked white, but everything below, but for the canal, which had turned to pewter, was filling up with shadow.

In the courtyard of the Blue House, a hawthorn tree grew. Its dying leaves were thick on the paving, sticky and slick from rain. On the gate pillars were two globes, pitted, old planets stuck there after they had dropped from the clockwork heavens.

No lights in the Blue House.

All shadows, so palpable, and the smell of damp and moss, of leaf-decay and water, of snails moving unseen, and stagnant lives, and something pleasingly sweet, like jam.

Loitering, Laure pretended to have lost a button from her glove. She searched about for it in the leaves at the threshold of the court. Now and then, as if hoping for help, she glanced up at the darkened windows.

Then, one window bloomed to gold. Laure gazed and saw, behind the now almost transparent loops of curtains, a female figure straightening from the lamp.

It was not the one, not the right figure. It was too angularly thin and bowed too low. It must be old Madame Belvard. Yes, of course. The upper floor.

And then the front door opened, and out came another figure, another woman, and it

and it

it was the Woman.

In the shadow of the fast-falling darkness, the black clothes of widowhood blended away, a charcoal drawing. Only the white face and throat were floating there a moment. One white ungloved hand, before the glove covered it. Ghosts—

Laure stepped back. She grazed against the gate-post with the dead planet on it. The Woman, the Widow, walked past her.

But now, the Woman turned and directed at her one unconditional glance.

Oh God, the face. It was like a blow.

The black rustling gown—another one, and another coat, and a hat on which sailed one ebony feather, a flicker of earrings like eyes…and the leaves, faintly disturbed by the footfall of her black boots with their slender muffs of black fur—

The face, disembodied still, hung in darkness, and the red mouth, almost as black as the eyes in darkness, parted.

"Good evening, mademoiselle."

Laure heard herself answer, far off, reasonably, as if she were a machine, "Good evening, madame."

And the white face nodded, or rather gracefully inclined, and everything, every weightless atom of the phantasmal presence, slid away, through the gate.

And then, on the path outside, Laure understood a carriage was waiting, with the door held open.

From dark to dark, night to night, the being glided. She was in the carriage. The door was secured. A man sprang on to the box. The horses, evolving from the nothingness that now all things were, invisible essences of motion, poured off like running silk.

Leaning on the gate pillar, Laure looked up and saw the stars had been lit in the sky by some doddering employee of heaven—some old Jacques God kept on a pension. And she laughed. Loudly and wildly enough that above her, Madame Belvard snapped to her heavier curtains, and the oblong of gold was gone, to leave black night supreme.

Somewhere in the woods, she was lying. Under two and a half centuries of mulch and roots, of flowers and trees. No one knew quite where, or whether to be sure.

Of course she had nourished the ground, and where the cornucopia of fruits had fallen, they had dropped their seeds, and the flowers too had left less visible flecks of propagation.

How long had it been before the suns of summer, the rains and snows of other seasons, had broken the table and its samite veilings? Even before it toppled or sank into the earth, things had been at her. Wild things from the woods—the foxes and rodents, wolves even, for there were wolves in the woods and the park then, and birds, things of the air, other crows.

The end of the story must always have been amorphous, because how could she have, that village girl scarcely more than a child, survived? She hadn't been fed poisons, or even copious amounts of opium—because, if they ate her, the comte and his nephew, they too would have to ingest these substances. But her frame, weakened by the terror of abduction, trepidation, perhaps by some inner flaw in its superficially perfect whole, had not withstood the potion and the table. Yes. She had died. Despite the helpful jackdaw, despite the miraculous accidental rescue. Died. What else could have happened?

At least it had been peaceful. Laure had thought, when Violette or Lucide or Marie-Louison, and the rest (growing ever more voluble), offered her an alternate outcome of la Reine's dinner story. The maiden hadn't died in pain, too drugged to struggle yet able to feel—their knives—their *teeth*. The creatures that ate her, did so when she was beyond feeling it, and also they did it because they had needed to eat her. She was devoured by life, not death.

"Somewhere in the woods," had said Violette Charpentier, raising her pale greyhound's face, "but no one can know where. Flowers and trees. Fruit trees. Bones, gold goblets, Venetian glass, pearls‚Äîsunk deep in the soil."

"Some of the bones would have been carried off," Laure had remarked with the asperity of fifteen.

"Oh yes. And no doubt jewels and trinkets too. Magpie's, foxes. Does it matter, Laure? An elegy resists such facts."

And there was a secret painting. (Not the other in the annex, which Laure had seen. That one was dulled by too much varnishing and by grime, the jackdaw on the bough only just decipherable as a blot, with one half circle of gold in its eye, like a sickle.) The *secret* painting lay in the apartment of la Reine herself. Sophrine said la Reine had it commissioned, when she was a girl‚Äîwhich, good God, was itself more than half a century ago.

Had Laure been shown *this* painting? Obviously not. La Reine never, after the first interview, invited Laure into her rooms below the horrible murderer's stair. None of them had seen the painting. They had heard it described‚Äîby whom? None would or could say. Laure calculated they had read about it in some book.

Laure herself, hearing it described, did see the secret painting‚Äî it evolved on her inner eyes, formed itself completely. Somewhat in the elaborate, classic style of a David‚Äîbut also more sensual, more merely lovely‚ÄîAlma-Tadema?

Now, in the trance state which precedes sleeping or waking, within her unencumbered mind, neither a vision, nor quite a dream‚ÄîLaure beheld this painting, and, for a second, entered it.

Ormolu hair, scarves, ribbons, tassels, streamlets of pearls, running everywhere, and down into the tall rough grass where poppies flamed. Fat flowers on the table, the fat, burnished fruits, the girl's succulent body. The ribbon masked all her face but for the delicacy of her nostrils and the shaped lips. Spires of precious goblets behind her head like towers of a cathedral. Insects. A bee, daintily painted, alighting now on the crimson rim of a glass.

And in the girl's out flung, open right hand, braceleted by white or discoloured pearls, and chains of metal, the red coal of an apple.

Laure stood in the hot grass. She heard the drizzling choir of the cicadas, the buzz of the bees and flies that she now saw freely roving over the table. Frogs croaked from some pool, a daylight nightingale sent its mechanical chirrups and flooding trills across the woods.

She could see the girl breathing, slow, shallow breaths. The jackdaw was nowhere to be seen. Only…expected?

Laure could almost feel the hardness of the table under her own shoulder-blades.

Wake up, Laure wanted to say. But surely, she was already awake. And, if she raised her eyelids, so petal-thin (mauve-stained) some inner light shone up through them—what would she see? What first sight?

And then Laure heard the sound of wings and woke totally with a start. A blown wood-pigeon on the windowsill of her bedroom in the house on the rue Dalle, glared at her with a pink-red eye.

I am awake. I have been brought to my senses.

It was more than the surfacing from dream or sleep. What had happened? Her last thought had been of the secret painting— and her first, too—but neither was quite a dream. Between these two images, her night-long experience had gone elsewhere, into some sumptuous purple darkness she couldn't at all remember, but which must have stained her eyes.

Laure got up. With a great fuss the pigeon flew away. It was Saturday. Market day. There was familiar noise in the town. Noise in the house, Ouelle and some other servant clattering with pots and cups, and then the insubstantial voice of the Aunt calling for something piteously, like a little girl.

What have I come to?
This place has nothing to do with me at all.

Laure had no intention of going to the château that Saturday. She lay about on a sofa, reading a book. That was her appearance. She saw none of the words. What did she see? Every so often, a bright window lit high up in the wall of her mind. Then she saw the shadows below, and someone came out of them, also a shadow.

Ouelle accused, "You haven't touched your dinner. This was a good dish, this rabbit pot-baked with herbs."

The Aunt had eaten everything put before her, but it made no impression. She looked sallow and unfed, and presently, in the sitting room, asked the girl who came in with wood for the fire, "Isn't dinner ready yet?" "Why—madame—you just now had it!" cried the girl. "Did I?" At once contrite. "Oh then, I did. So I did. Oh, then." But when the girl had gone, "Did we have our dinner, Laure?"

"Yes, Aunt."

The Aunt sighed.

Rain fell. In the garden behind the house, the ancient chestnut tree, the walnut and fig, were already almost bare, the wind had grown rough in the night. Clinging roses, the colour of parchment, had shed their petals everywhere. But now the wind fell away, pretending innocence.

"What are you writing, Laure?"

"A letter, Aunt."

"To whom?"

"Oh, no one important."

Laure, with her back to her Aunt, at a desk in the window, covered her drawing, half a tentative face. Then folded the paper over and over. "The raspberry canes have blown down," she reported flatly.

Darkness began to come, perhaps early. It was only four. Ouelle marched in with a tray of tea, with some fancy cakes from the patisserie. Not everyone kept this custom, but Ouelle had noticed the mistress seemed so hungry now, all the time, and indeed the Aunt started up, clapping her hands like a child.

"Did you bake these nice cakes, Ouelle?"

"Oh yes, madame."

"And with marzipan flowers," said Laure, "just the same as in the shop. How clever!"

Ouelle shot Laure a look of mild hatred.

The Aunt took a cake, and holding it, forgetting it, she said, "I'm so cold, Susine."

Just then the doorbell jangled, too loudly and for too long, as if some stupid boy were pulling at it before running away. Sophrine always rang the bell in this manner.

"That will be Mademoiselle Merault." Ouelle bustled out.

Laure moved swiftly to toss her drawing into the fire on the pretence of adding a piece of wood to it. (And noticed, unnoticingly, its heat; the room was quite hot enough.)

Five minutes late Sophrine and Laure had gone up to Laure's room.

"I've been all morning and afternoon again over papa's accounts. What a mess he gets them in. It's a good thing for him he has me, and not some clerk who'd cheat him."

"Yes, Sophrine, you're quite the little housewife."

"I am not. Why aren't you ready? Put on a proper dress. Papa offered me the pony-cart, but mama took it to visit one of her cousins. So we'll have to walk in the wet."

"You go alone."

"What now? Afraid of a drop of rain? You're sulking. What have I done?"

"I'm bored with that place."

Sophrine sat down. "How can you be bored?"

Laure cast her a withering glance. Sophrine never *was* bored. Her narrow tiny brain so quickly crammed and made busy.

But oh, the overwhelming temptation to speak—

"I went for a walk last Wednesday evening."

"In this weather? Was it sensible?"

"Then how do you propose to return from the château, *in this weather?*"

"Well, you know la Reine sometimes lends us her smaller carriage—"

"Or she doesn't bother. She cares nothing for us. We used to amuse her. What did she say—little giggles and cries. It's quite disgusting. I hope," said Laure, wondering why she was ranting all this nonsense, "at her age, I shall be past all that."

"Do you think you will? Men say women stay hot longer. If they have any heat to start with."

"Men. Which men?"

"Well, I overhear talk, you know. In the shop. Or when papa entertains his friends." Sophrine added, "But then, do you have any heat, Laure? You haven't even given me a kiss since last spring."

"It's what I say," said Laure, too strongly now, "just what I mean. What's the point of it all?"

"Pleasure," said Sophrine simply. "The joy of life."

Laure looked at her warily. Perhaps Sophrine wasn't such a shrewd little fool.

Laure said, baldly, "Would you do it with a man—enjoy it with a man?"

"If I had to. I may have to, one day. Marry. Bear children. It's what they make us do, isn't it, in the end. But that doesn't have to be the end of—other things. As to enjoying it, how can I know? I shouldn't think so. Their hairiness and smells—their noises. Oh, you've been spared a great deal, not living in a house with men, your *ears* finding out at seven years old the kind of things your papa gets up to with your mama behind a closed door—! Then again, I suppose I could dream of Artemise while it went on, the way I do when I'm—not in company. Or of you."

"*Me?* You think of *me?*"

"Yes, yes. What do you think? You're my darling. When you bent over me just now, and I could smell that scent you wear, and see that loop of hair moving on your neck—well, look how flushed I am."

"You're not saying you *love* me?" demanded Laure, in a sort of frightened scorn, "I remember that, the first time. You wanted or expected that from *me*. Just like some *man*."

Sophrine burst into merry laughter. "Of course I love you. I love all the ones I've had."

"You've *had* me, have you?"

"Yes, Gobbled you up like an apricot tart."

"And like the comte in the story of the girl on the table."

"Oh that. That's different. Oh Laure, you're always so serious. Don't you know what you're saying?"

"Pray tell me, since you're so very wise."

"Love, for you, mustn't be easy. Isn't natural. It has to be some tremendous, colossal—collision. The thunder bolt. So I don't mean a thing. None of us does. You're waiting for love to come, *that* kind of love, that smashes you to pieces—kills you—that's what you want."

"Rubbish. Rubbish."

"And you may not find it. Or if you do—"

"Be quiet, Sophie. That's enough. How dare you?"

"How dare I?" Aghast, "What have I said?"

"Leave me alone. Such impertinence."

"Laure—are you crying?"

"Of course not. I caught a chill on Wednesday. Yes, it wasn't sensible, going out. And I shan't, now."

Sophrine put her arm about Laure. Laure shuddered her away. Laure thought of Sophrine in the wood, the berries and kisses, and after, now and then. And Laure thought of Marie-Louison, in the château's summer garden, and Lucide, and Annette Mercier, who was thirty-two years old and had borne eight children, two of which had died. And of one or two, one or two others. Brief flickers of attention, culminations of greed. *Like a man, I'm like some man. I only want them for that*—these thoughts she had thought a trio of days ago. But by then, Laure had seen the Woman walking beside the canal.

The liaisons, affairs, momentary ignitions, they had faded. Laure hadn't tasted sexual pleasure, in any form, even when alone, for half a year. The riots of hunger so soon appeased, had they palled?

Did she prefer to go hungry? Did she want to *starve*?

But Sophrine was saying something, arch and infuriating.

"And so do come, Laure. If you don't want to walk, we could borrow the trap from your neighbour, that good—"

"I won't go, I tell you."

"But don't you want to hear what she has to say?"

"Who?"

Sophrine folded her hands and assumed a tolerant expression, making Laure long to strangle her.

It transpired that the previous Wednesday (Laure had by then left the château) la Reine had emerged from her seclusion at the dinner hour. "She said that by today she would have something to tell us. And—oh, Laure, she did look so odd."

"Really."

"And then she drew Annette aside. She spoke to her privately, and Annette turned quite pale. And then—she curtsied."

"You curtsy to her all the time."

"Yes, but Annette doesn't. We asked Annette—she wouldn't say a thing. But yesterday I saw her husband riding out that way— the notary."

"The old woman wants to sell something," said Laure. "You know how sometimes she does. A painting. Or those furs. And she sold her diamonds, she told us, all but that single one in the brooch, which Violette Charpentier says comes from the crown jewels of the Bourbons, and I don't believe a word of *that*."

Laure felt fresher. She glanced at the room and wanted to leave it. She thought of the château. It seemed still dull—yet all at once unknown. Perhaps dangerous.

She thought of the Blue-of-memory House.

The lit window.

The shadow.

Only three days ago. How have they passed?

If I don't go to the château, I'll have to go there. I'll loiter about like a stray dog or some no-good.

Laure snapped: "Very well. I'll go with you."

Sophrine said, "Papa told me la Reine had called Monsieur Mercier up to the big house on financial business. Papa said to me, Sophie, watch out. She's going to tell you about a little money coming your way."

Disgusted, Laure threw off her dress, as if Sophrine had now contaminated it. She drew into her arms a garment of faded ivory yellow, the colour of the storm-wrecked roses.

"Don't pull a face, Laure. You know quite well one day you'll have everything from your Aunt (God keep her well). Below la

Reine, yours is one of the best-lined families in the town. Better even than Lejay's, for all his airs. No worries for you. But papa—who can blame him if he wants a nest-egg for me."

And all those curtsies, thought spiteful Laure, *on account.*

The great dining room was well-lighted. The chandelier, which seemed to have been dusted, glittered and spangled as it moved slightly in the château's eddying draughts. Also there were candles blazing, squadrons of them, on the table.

She's extravagant tonight.

Despite the borrowed vehicle, mud had splashed the hem of Laure's dress. Why should she care?

All the women were there. There were twenty-five of them at present, including herself. She knew them all by sight and to exchange words with, only a few intimately. Artemise Lejay was splendid in a dinner-gown of dark blood red. At the moment her acolytes were Honorine Éperve and Douce Rochelet. (Had the constant Sophrine ever been enlisted? Laure didn't know—or had never noticed.)

When la Reine entered, which was after they had been served a Spanish wine for warmth, Laure looked up to see her, curiously.

Well it was true. She did look most odd. She was like—an animated waxwork. And as she advanced into the room, Peridot the Jewel hovering behind her, Laure's scathing pity changed to wonder, and then an instinctive fear.

All the women were the same, or similarly affected. Their glasses catching countless bright dots or sparks from hearth or candles, their wide eyes burning. A picture of suspense.

For Sidonie Aubade-Valents had put on a brocade gown, of a green fierce enough to rival Artemise Lejay's scarlets. And on her neck and in her ears were emeralds, large fine ones. Her hair was piled very high, and by its pagoda effect they saw she had grown very stooped. She leaned hard on her cane. Her head poked forward, rather as the tortoise head of Peridot had always done. But the seamed and flaccid breast of la Reine, her ploughed throat and furrowed face—were powdered. And on her cheeks, not in-artistically applied, but so unlikely as to seem hectic, some rouge.

Not a waxwork. No, she appeared now to be a beneficiary of the embalmer's art, made ready for the casket.

The room spun. Or in fact, not the room, but Laure herself, spun round, inside her body, which did not for a second move.

Everything, when she came back, was removed far off. And so she drifted to the table, miles away from all of them, and weightlessly stood there and waited. Not even looking now at la Reine. Not needing to look at her.

Only the terrible heartbeat, which made the candles seem massively to leap and sink, swell and diminish, and the tablecloth to pulse.

And stupid, stupid Sophrine, touching her arm an instant, seeming to think Laure's chill was after all bad, and had made her feverishly so white, and her eyes so black and rimmed with red.

She did not speak to them until the meal was mainly done. It was a substantial dinner, several courses, with small roasted fowls, glazed pheasant, a fricassee, sauces, a soup, pâtés, cherries in liqueur, hothouse oranges, sweets coloured like candlewax.

When she had drugged and sated them, for most of them ate heartily, maybe even desperately, and all but one of them drank the wines (Laure was the exception), la Reine began to talk. In her former way, generally, mildly, inexorably taking control of them.

At this point, in the past, she had told her stories, if she had one to tell. Legends of the house, like that of the Feast, or historical anecdotes. Or peculiar episodes of a childhood here, which seemed to be hers, although they knew she had not come to the château until she was a bride of eighteen.

Now she told them a story of her future.

She told it well, as she always had. Without undue involvement. And on her painted ruined face, as ever, the calm if not uninterested indifference to them and to herself, which might denote, after all, only a genuine sympathy. Ultimately, who can help themselves or anyone? The most we can give, perhaps, is our truth, and the ability to condone the truth of others.

"Well, my friends, our time together is drawing to its end. I'm going to die very shortly." (She didn't pause for expressions of grief or protest. There were none.) "I shall remain at the château for perhaps a month. Then I must go alone to Paris, to my house there. Peridot, my inexhaustible Jewel, will accompany me, to see to my needs, until it is finished. I regret, on my departure, the château will be shut up and presently assumed by my creditors. Like any proper aristo, I'm sadly in debt. They have waited, knowing they would get what I have quite soon, and now soon they will.

"I hope you've found some enjoyment here. I hope it's done you some good, as was my intention. I can leave you nothing. I have nothing left to leave you. I've used all I have entirely selfishly for myself, and my own wants. Peridot, of course, I've provided for; how else could I ask her service at last. A payment. But there is one other payment I shall make, a settlement, after my death, for something bought, also selfishly, to comfort my last month as a whole woman."

The awful words—awful in every possible way—for her, for them—dropped like cool stones.

"Tonight there's to be a slight affair, not a ceremony, more an adjustment to my life. It may startle you, or dismay you. You may be angry. But, my dear friends, at the door of death, and perhaps a horrible death, I must tell you I am unconcerned by your censure or malice. Even, I'm afraid, by your kindness. Should you wish to witness the event tonight, then you may. Or you may wish to go at once. While I remain at the château, you may come and go as you want, although after tonight, you will never again see me, or see this carcass which is all that's left of me. And in one month, a little less or more, the gates will be shut against you by my executors. Just as, only a little after, the gates of existence will slam upon my going out."

There was a pause, then. A silence. Perhaps the candles made their habitual soft hiss, or the fire, or rain sounded at the windows and in the chimney. Then, conceivably, they heard their own breathing. The sound of living circulating in their veins.

"During my last month, I shall entertain a companion here. She will stay, while I do. When I leave for Paris, she too will leave, although not to go with me. By then she will have done for me all that can be done, and will be free. There's always gossip in a town," said la Reine. "I think you'll have heard of her."

Then someone let out a shrill yipping cry. It was Clothilde, Laure thought. But then came the voice of Artemise Lejay, haughty yet strangely common, as when she had discussed the price of soap.

"Do you mean, grande dame, this arrangement you've made—That is, do you mean it's with this woman we've been hearing of? This—what is it? Madame Corrot?"

And then, equally appalling, apt and unforgivable, Violette Charpentier inquired, "But she serves men, does she not, that one? A *widow*, I thought."

Not a flicker disturbed la Reine.

"Oh, she'll serve a woman too, if the money suits her. How did I know? You must allow me to be reticent on that."

Then an outcry full of silly provincial women's' oaths. It came and went. Touched nothing.

Sidonie Aubade-Valents spoke to them once more. "She will be arriving presently. Annette's husband, Monsieur Mercier, is conducting her in a carriage, with all the proper papers. She'll be here in—oh, twenty minutes, by that clock on the mantelpiece. Naturally, she and I have already met, last Wednesday evening to be exact. Before dinner. But you are curious, perhaps?"

Clothilde Boulanger sprang up. She looked as if she surprised only herself. "My father wouldn't allow it—for me to be in the same room as such—Excuse me, grande dame."

And even as she hesitated still, dithering, others jumped up. Honorine and Rose, Lucide, compressing her mouth, which was always rather too small, Marie Jeanne, five or six more. But Artemise Lejay swept to her feet, without another word, and drove from the room, taking her redness with her, and the rest who meant to or thought they meant to, swirling like leaves in her wake down the drain. The doors shut, and Violette, sitting fast, let out her thin laughter, one cruel peal.

After which they heard the clock, as if only now had it come alive and begun to tick.

Of course Peridot had known so much because she had been told. She hadn't disapproved, that wasn't her place. Yet, did she despise, the way the slave so often despised the master? Peridot, to Laure, was an enigma.

Laure though was not thinking of this. Nailed down by her hammering heart, she continued to sit motionless, and then, once or twice, took a tiny sip of wine, as if she were normally thirsty.

Then they moved to another room.

Coffee was served the remaining women, in the salon with the piano. The yellow octogenarian curtains had been drawn, and this way, their heavy swags revealed discolouration and holes. The piano even had not been dusted, nor opened. Closed, it was like a coffin.

Laure discovered she stood now nailed in one spot again, this time near the fireplace. She held a translucent cup, and sometimes took a sip, but the cup never emptied, as the glass had not.

La Reine had not come in with them.

The clock along the passage, in the dining room, struck ten. Had the clock ever struck before? Laure couldn't remember that it had.

And had a carriage driven up? It must have done. Probably it had gone round to the old stables, as on Wednesday evening. (All the women agreed to this—in one of the mad rushes of chatter that followed their eviction from the other room. Otherwise they would have heard or seen the carriage that Wednesday. But what was she like, the creature who was coming here?) "Laure—didn't you say you saw the bitch—?" "*Marie!*" "Well, what would you call her?" "A slut, she's a true whore—" "Laure, Laure, come to, wake up! What's wrong with you? Tell us—didn't you catch a glimpse of that woman in the town?"

Laure, turning her head, staring as if at a pack of wolves run suddenly into the salon, pawing at her skirts and slavering.

And then, Peridot was in the doorway, pushing the doors wide and standing back. And the tap-tip-tap of Madame la Reine's

walking-stick on the wooden floor, tap-tip-tap. And the rustle
of her gown. And a soft step, like the footfall of a cat on ice. The
Queen enters the room and she is holding the arm of someone.
An arm in firm black velvet. An arm that tapers to a narrow wrist,
a long white hand without a ring, but a hand in a black mitten…
Widow's weeds.

In the salon, utter soundlessness.

The Queen glances round with—what is it? Complacency,
nearly ennui? She longs to be rid of them all, all but the one she
has chosen. In fact, was it her cranky courtesy to let them see
what had come to replace them—this symbol of her death.

Death stands there.

Death, the widow.

"Let me introduce my dear companion. You may know her as
Madame Corrot. But she tells me that the name is no longer hers,
as other names are no longer. She prefers to be known then by her
given name, Virgile."

People move about. There is a male presence, rarely to be spotted on Club days and nights. Two lackeys in an outmoded livery,
seeing to a table and chair. And then Monsieur Mercier, Annette's
buffoon-like, smiling husband, bustling to lay out a document—
presumably there have been others, now reduced to this single
item. A contract, like a marriage contract.

La Reine crosses to the table on the arm of her dear companion,
who is to be called only *Virgile*.

The Queen sits, and as she does so, lets go of the arm (the
strong arm), and one of the lackeys places her cane for her.

Beaming (and sweating), Monsieur Mercier bends forward to
indicate where the old comtesse must sign. And even in this extremity, Annette, about fifty paces away, is partly leaning forward
too, anxious that her husband do nothing amiss.

After all, there is scarcely anything so vulgar as an aristocrat.
Here in the presence of them all—this!

And by her chair, la Reine's carved chair of the salon, that one
stands. Not as if to make sure of her fee, her price, her profit. Not
as if, really, to do or be anything.

Laure sees her stand there.

What does Laure see?

A mask without a face behind it? A shell formed, perhaps only freakishly, in the shape of a woman about twenty-five or twenty-seven years old? Or one of those things from fairy tales of the cold north of Europe—an elf-maiden, whose back is hollow?

Laure is thinking, *Oh God, shall I run out?* She is thinking, *Hold me up, I can't fall.* She is thinking, *Will she look at me, let her not look at me, I must look at her, I must look away.*

But all these thoughts are only a background, like the scratching of candlewicks as they burn, or the sullen whisper of the autumn wind.

Virgile is quite tall, straight and slim, accentuated by her crow-black velvet gown, with its long sleeves, and high throat, where there are polished agate buttons. Her hair is nearly as black. It has that blued-copper sheen found on the fur of some black cats. There are quantities of it, wound and coiled, and culminating now not in a hat, but in an ebony comb, from which a bit of veiling, soft, like smoke, filters out as if to conceal the forehead and the eyes, but then skirts and only shades them. In her ears, two golden crescents, very small. Two little new moons, twinkling. Her neck is long, like her hands and waist and, it seems, her legs, under the stem of the dress. Like her white face, with its perfectly drawn nose and jaw, its cheekbones. Its effect of a shield cunningly quartered. The brows are very strongly marked. Masculine, in this face which is female. The mouth a little too large, as if infinitesimally stretched—although not in a smile. The mouth, nothing else, has been touched with artificial colour. The eyes are utterly black and totally still. Do they blink? Can she close them when either she sleeps or when she ceases to be awake—or when she pretends she is *not* awake? Lashes—like stiff fringes, the colour of tar—which makes it seem there is a black line drawn around her two long eyes.

There is to her—which could make you wonder if she has trained herself all these years, and done so because she has had to do so—this quality of complete immobility. If the autumn wind, rising again on the park and on the town, were to burst in, it would stir the folds of her dress, might dislodge her wisp of veil, might even undo the interwoven ropes of her Indian hair. But otherwise it would not move her. She is fixed. Immutable.

No sudden *other* movement in the room, no flutter or start, not even the angular jerk by which Violette Charpentier manages abruptly to drop her coffee cup with a frigid noise—*nothing* makes the black eyes look elsewhere.

But the contract has been signed. The notary has appended his signature, and Peridot, also, has made her mark.

Not one of the other women was included.

They're only the audience, at last.

Then a lackey comes in with a tray of crystal thimbles full of Armagnac, and each of them has to take one, and they do, even Laure does (and puts her full cup down on a table too, not knowing she does).

Following this bizarre marriage, there's to be a toast.

La Reine stands up. She is haggard in her slight paint.

"To our health, my friends," says la Reine, "yours and mine." Sparing them nothing.

Is *Virgile* included? Is the dear companion also the friend?

What can she do, this diseased stick that must *lean* on a stick, what in God's name is possible for her, even given the skills of a *Virgile*?

They drink. Everyone drinks.

Laure drinks.

It is Marie-Louison who chokes herself. And Violette, grim as a prison wardress, who slaps her between the shoulders.

"I wish you every happiness," says la Reine, clearly. And then she takes the arm of Virgile, flawlessly offered her at once. And Virgile at that moment finally moves her eyes, gazing round at them all. These eyes are so black they seem blind. They seem thoughtless and without either mind or soul. Laure for one second meets them as they pass. Then they are gone, and the old woman and the young woman, old age and death, the two eternal widows, stalk slowly out of the room.

Violette dropped her cup. Celine Marblon diligently smashes her glass to the ground, and breaks herself into sobs. Then Marie-

Louison starts, and runs over to her. They weep and howl. Others take it up, sniveling.

Everyone is very shocked.

Peridot has gone, so have the lackeys. Monsieur Mercier, abruptly paternal, is coaxing a shaky Annette to come away, come away. "Our little Georges is asking for you all the time. You know he never sleeps well when you're out late. He needs his mother, poor little fellow."

Douce Rochelet steps up to Laure and seizes her arm.

"What did you think of her? She had eyes like a *snake. A serpent.*"

"Oh."

"Oh, I suppose you'll say the old witch has the right to do it—and to throw us out. Why it's all that's kept us safe in this horrid little sty of a town. Her patronage. The château. The thought she might—might give us—a small remuneration—Good God, what would it have cost her, the old wretch? Less than this honeymonth with that vampire! I should have left when Artemise did. *She* had the right of it. Wouldn't lower herself to be part of it. The old wretch! Any one of us could do it for her—what she wants, and be paid, and run off and leave her to die alone in Paris. What can she stand any way, at her age, in her state—" Douce was shaking Laure by the arm, like a terrier.

Sophrine stepped between them, brisk, as if to attend an irate customer in the grocer's shop.

"Now, Douce. You know we couldn't have done it."

"What—do you think that *reptile* is more beautiful than Artemise Lejay?"

"I think this—what is she called?—Virgile—is a professional," said Sophrine, "and la Reine needs a professional. I shouldn't know how to begin. Should you? And Artemise is much too fine, one couldn't even consider it, for Artemise."

"But to *pay—her—*"

"To pay to have work well done? That's only just."

"And us? Haven't we earned something?"

"How?" asked Sophrine. "By enjoying ourselves at the old woman's expense all these years? Come along. I don't mind it. So what."

Douce had detached herself from Laure. She walked off. Sophrine said, "I suppose I should get home."

Laure said, "You say you don't mind it. I thought you'd mind it."

"Oh, papa will. He'll carry on. I've saved some sweets for him in a napkin. I'll feed him those and not tell him everything, just how ill she is. I'll say I don't care, not getting any money out of her. I so prefer to stay with him, so why do I need a nest-egg, and anyway I'm so proud of our own money, how he earned it so honestly through his hard work and self-sacrifice, and isn't he the hero. Well, Laure. I'll miss my times up here. But I'm grown up now. We have to put up with things, don't we."

"I thought you would mind. I did think so." Laure felt herself sway forward, and Sophrine drew her back, and then they stood in quite an ordinary way.

But again Laure said, "I thought you'd mind. Yes. I did."

"You don't know what you're saying," said Sophrine. "You've got a fever, I'm sure of it. I doubt we'll get a carriage now, either. Artemise's trap has gone. I'll take you home, dear. I'll take care of you, Laure. It isn't so far. The moment we get there I'll wake up that Ouelle, she must make some hot milk, and put a hot stone in the bed for you."

Laure laughed. Languidly she touched her own forehead, which felt burning hot to her icy hands. As they walked through the park, between the overgrown hedges of box, and along the carriage drive, the wind was low and the rain had stopped. Neither looked back.

Sophrine spoke calmly. "Such a grand place. Even now, all neglected. I can hardly believe I'll never see it again. But I don't think I'll come here anymore. I don't know if you will. Some of them may, until the house is shut up and sold. But how dreary. How awful too, poor old lady, dying. I thought she'd reach her nineties. And her Paris residence is some poky box, I've heard. We'll have to think of some other venue we can all go to. Artemise Lejay lives in that very large house, but her monsieur won't think of letting her have us visit there. Or, only her favourites, I suppose."

On the lane, the chestnuts held out their glistening boughs, more than half empty of leaves, and rainy stars shone between.

They walked slowly, Sophrine holding Laure's arm as if to steady her.

What am I to do?

If only Sophrine would stop jabbering. It echoed in Laure's swimming head. The roadway twisted uphill, and there was a young fallen tree at its edge, brought down by the winds three nights ago, unnoticed until now. They moved aside from it, as most of humanity does, from dead things.

She's there, in the château.

Don't think of it now.

Not yet.

When?

The day after the "marriage" of la Reine and Virgile the widow, summer returned to Bois-la-Diane. There came to be a light the colour of a pale wine from Xérés. On this, the last leaves were pinned like flags of peeled bronze, and garnet scales. And the leaves which had fallen, turning to a damson mush, lit with singular orange streaks, out of which thrust the purple splash of autumn crocus. More than half unveiled, the trees showed pockets of apples, pears, left stranded like glowing lamps, or showed the fruit smashed on the ground in bitter ciders. Grapes on the vine turned gold with sweetness. A final rose the wind had overlooked, yellow-amber like the afternoons, stood upright in the garden of the house on the rue Dalle, for thirteen days, before the head fell on the path, intact, brown as a cobnut.

Warm, so warm, and hot, at noon.

The birds, misled or only driven mad, sang wildly and opened their wings to gild them like the mask of a pharaoh, and keep death out.

The town shone.

On the street Laure, fetching (strange, perhaps misguided) purchases of the Aunt's from the leaning shops behind the church, met Rose and Honorine Éperve.

"How washed-out you are, Laure—is it the heat? Oh this weather! What it would have been, to be at the château. Do you remember the luncheons on the terrace, or when we had picnics under the great chestnut in summer?"

"And the little stream. Do you remember that scalding day we took off our dresses and bathed in the pool, and we were dry again in five minutes?"

Laure stood, quiet and solemn. Did she remember?

"Well," she said. "There."

Honorine leant forward, her hat with its cornflowers of cloth tilting to cut off the sun. "Lucide went back there. She did. With Marie-Jeanne. We were talking with them yesterday. And can you imagine, Laure. That woman. Oh! That woman."

Laure, standing, idle. "Whom, Honorine?"

"*That* one. *She!* You know who I mean."

"Ah."

"Yes, that depraved person who calls herself *Virgilie.*" Almost—just able to prevent her tongue tripping out the correction—*No, no, Honorine. Not Virgilie*—"As if *that* could be her proper given name. The effrontery. The cheek of it."

"And," said Rose, deceptively mild, "it seems she takes her lunch alone. Dines with la Reine only in the evening—so her days mostly are all her own."

"And there she sits. My goodness, queening it. Lucide said the lunch was very opulent. Better than we generally had. But then, oh yes. And in comes the woman, all in her black dress, and sits there. And there are two servants, the men, if you please, serving her. And Lucide and Marie-Jeanne, they can just serve themselves. And not a *word,* not a *word.*"

"And so," said Rose, deceptively urbane, "Marie-Jeanne says to the woman, 'Excuse me, but what lovely weather we're having.' And this woman, this *Virgilette,* she just nods—graciously, Jeanne said, as if she were the comtesse herself."

"When all the time she's from the gutters of Paris or Marseilles or the Lord knows where—"

"So, at last Lucide asks her to pass the coffee pot—"

"Seeing as how no one has bothered to put anything anywhere within their reach—"

"And Virgilette simply passes it."

"Just passes the pot!"

"Just that."

"And not a *word*."

Laure, who is trembling violently, her legs weak, as often now they are, suddenly puts her hand to her mouth but can't stifle the trembling liquid laugh that breaks from her.

Honorine is affronted. Rose only bemused (deceptively?).

"What's to laugh at? She is a monster. Didn't you think her just like a lizard?"

Laure nods.

"Oh, you would laugh, wouldn't you. What do you care, Laure Deschampeigne? The old lady was nothing to you. But we—we were attached to her. She betrayed us, Laure." And Honorine's eyes bulge, amazing Laure, with sunbright tears.

"Artemise Lejay," says Rose quietly, "has sunk into an indisposition. She's quite sick, Douce said."

"No," said Honorine brutishly, "she's in the family way. Yes, carrying a child. All this time and she's never fallen. Her maid was up with her half the night, with Artemise crying at what it will do to her figure and her teeth. And that fiend, Monsieur Lejay, he's complaining at the expense and nuisance of her lying in, and then of the baby. As if he'd had nothing to do with it, the brute."

"Perhaps," muttered Rose, "he didn't."

"What can you mean?"

"Well, she's had lovers, you know. Not only amongst us. She's had men."

"What do you know? That's nonsense."

Laure said, "I must go back. My Aunt's waiting for these things."

She hurried up the street to get away from them, hugging the ridiculous parcels—a single short length of silk—for what?—some ribbons, the kind that would trim a young girl's hat—a packet of some cosmetic whitening the Aunt had never, to Laure's knowledge, ever used—some digestive pills the Aunt had formerly said were useless to her. And so on.

Laure thinking. Or rather, words, pictures, racing through her head, like the shadows and lights flashing between the houses and the trees.

In fact, the ancient garden, consumed by its desuetude after the storm, did not seem so beautiful, even in the sherryed light of a false summer. The cedar had pulled out more of the paving, and leaned heavily towards the south-west. Mushrooms swelled, hideous frilled fungi like boils with poison. The docks had grown claws.

Was this the place where those Shakespearean lines had come to her, four years ago? The midsummer evening dreams of a fairy woman lying asleep, of the glamouring flower of love and seduction?

Over on that stone bench she had sat with Lucide, and once with Celine Marblon, kissing, fondling.

In the park, the tall statue of Pan had been overgrown sufficiently, she couldn't find him, or his guardian elm.

Jays and magpies yattered from the woods.

Laure stopped, staring up. High, high in an oak tree not yet bared of its crenulated leaves, something was caught and sparkling like a crimson star. But involuntarily, dizzy from bending back her head, she took one more step—and the star was gone. She could not find it again.

The long glass windows to the salon were shut. Laure walked about, and along the terrace. In the end she retreated among the sprawled hedges of box, and glancing round at it, seemed to view the château as it might soon come to be, high-roofed, curved with black balconies, deserted, a few sparrows dashing about rotted towers.

At the end of the walk, she crossed (familiar with it all), the dried bed of some antique outlet of the stream, and climbed some steps. From here, between two hazel trees, she might look across the longer diagonal face of the château. Out on the looped carriage drive, a red squirrel was busily foraging. And standing nearby, motionless:

On amber, ink.

But oh, so still. A lizard ? A lizard black as coal.

Laure stepped forward and walked through the high dry grass, and the squirrel, hearing her approach, fled for the trees beyond the drive. (To Virgile it had paid no attention, no more than it would to a tall dark stone.)

And she.

And:

There was something so curious. The way she stayed so still, yet turned her inky head, and then, the white face, shield-quartered with eyes and nose and lips.

Laure stumbled. Righted herself. She walked the rest of the way.

She stood.

She stood before Virgile.

Before Virgile on the carriage drive in broad sunlight.

The white face was tinted, very faintly, with daylight colours. The whites of the black eyes were nearly blue.

"Good day, madame."

She wouldn't respond, wouldn't speak. They had said, she didn't.

Virgile's eyes blinked, once, it seemed absurdly slowly. Her lips, parting. "And to you also, Mademoiselle Deschampeigne."

Laure caught her breath.

"I used to come here, every Wednesday. Almost every Wednesday and Saturday, you see," said Laure. "And today is Thursday. But I'm here, instead. It won't matter now, will it, the regular days. I hope I don't inconvenience you."

And at that, the face, some slight stretching of the lips, and of the eyes—already so long and wide. Mocking, of course. The idea that anyone could inconvenience a Virgile.

I want to say her—your—name.

It would be unthinkable to say it. *Though I have,* thought Laure, *been saying it.*

"I hope you're well," said Laure.

"I'm always well."

Again, like a blow, this voice. Like the blow of the face. I did think you'd talk to me. To *me*. Because you did before, outside the Blue House, in the dusk, the Azure Hour when all things change their shape.

Laure's own voice broke out of her. "I saw—the most curious thing just now. Has Madame la Comtesse—has she told you the story of the Feast? No…yes…? Oh, but I'm sure she will. And the girl's supposed to lie under the park somewhere—and all the pearls and Venetian goblets—they were put with her, you see—all these things. And just now, in an oak tree—I saw a narrow red glass goblet, caught there in the branches. Or—I thought I did."

Laure couldn't breathe. She had said such a lot, but hadn't meant to say so much. Or to say more, differently. She fell silent and pressed her hand to her waist.

It might have been insulting—was it insulting—to have spoken of la Reine, to Virgile? Or had it not been?

Virgile stood, looking at her. Laure lowered her eyes. "You make me so nervous, madame."

Virgile looked at her. Two black questions—or only black mirrors reflecting.

Laure: "This situation—is a strange one for me. I'm afraid, madame, of saying something to offend you. When I don't mean to do so."

Virgile half turned, half turned away

away

Don't go in—don't go—let me stay with—stay with me—

"Have I offended you, madame?" "No, Mademoiselle Deschampeigne." How does she know my name? Oh, from the old woman's book, naturally, the one in her rooms, where I wouldn't write my name like all the rest, but someone must have written it for me—Sophrine probably. Or the old woman mentioned me. "Laure Deschampeigne, from one of those well-to-do bourgeois families, which hang on to an aristocratic name as grimly as they hid it less than a hundred years ago."

Virgile had begun to move towards the house. She walked very smoothly, but it was just possible to see that she took steps. Yet, the image is a cobra, gliding upright on its tail.

Laure walked quickly, and caught her up. This took courage, too. Walked beside her.

"Would you prefer, oh, that I didn't come into the house?"

"Whatever you want, mademoiselle. It's of no consequence."

Obviously not, since I am not.

"But, to take lunch there, as I've done in the past."

"If you wish."

What else had la Reine said to Virgile about Laure? "She dresses well, as these families always do, quite well for a provincial. A poor education, thinks herself better-read and more modern than she is. A snappish little thing. Quick to take offence or suspicion, too cold or too frothy."

No, why would the old woman speak of Laure at all? She would only want to talk about herself—and about...

About Virgile.

Laure said boldly, as they went in at one of the smaller doors (under a great round balcony on the floor above, hanging over like a thunder cloud), "Is it true you come from Paris, madame?"

And Virgile didn't answer.

"I ask—because, because, because some books I had ordered just came to me from Paris, you see. How envious I am, if you came from Paris...but, well—"

In the passage, with its pale, damp-spotted silk walls, and then turning into another little parlour, which looked on to a walled rose garden.

A table was laid by a window, and sunlight fell on it and turned it to amber, as this sunlight turned everything to amber, except Virgile.

One place laid. Of course, only one. In a vase, two blowsy pink peonies—but the garden outside had no flowers. The rain had stripped them.

Virgile went directly to the carved sideboard, where a jug stood under a cover. From this she poured a glass of milk, drank it, with quick laps. She offered Laure nothing.

In a dreadful dissolution, as if she felt herself separating in small pieces, Laure stood by the table, pretending to admire the sodden wrecked flowerless garden. On their briars, rose-hips had formed, edged by the sun with blood.

A man servant entered.

Virgile spoke, distantly.

"Lay another place."

Laure's heart leapt in fire.

"Oh, thank you—" stammering. Ridiculous.

The man did as he had been told. Then went out.

Virgile crossed to the table and seated herself.

Laure sat down facing her.

How beautiful she is. How beautiful. And yet—no, I believe that she's quite ugly—the beauty is a sort of camouflage—or illusion—but I'm magnetized and pulled into it. Like tumbling into a tunnel. And her eyes. I look in her eyes and go insane.

What would it be to come close to her, that is, *physically* close?

Laure had naturally thought of this. At first stopped herself. Then, while the one yellow rose persisted in the Aunt's garden, thought of it and thought of it.

Laure felt, at her thoughts, no sexual frisson, no urgent tingling in the blood or quickening of her loins. Rather it was as if a whirlwind caught her up. She was flung through space and dashed against a stunning obduracy, and as she dropped from it, semi-conscious, it caught her and raised her, fainting, dying, to its lips.

And this ecstasy was, if anything, far more powerful than the flood of sex. Even of orgasm. It was an orgasm of another sort. Emotional, spiritual, deathly and divine. *Ceaseless.*

Then Laure had not been able to stop thinking of it. She had lain for thirteen days, mostly in chairs, imagining over and over, approaching Virgile, and Virgile, without touching her, creating the whirlwind, and being lost in the whirlwind until, at some last moment, when nothing was left of Laure, when all in her had been given over—Virgile seizing hold of her—and being dashed against Virgile, the swooning and collapse, helpless and without will, every thought extinguished.

Dying in her arms, her grip. Drowned. Smothered. Devoured?

(And today, the Aunt interrupting, staring at her own garden and killing that rose finally by exclaiming, "Oh this wonderful July weather!")

Laure's hands now trembled so much she could hardly take up the glass the servant must have filled with wine.

Someone had brought food, too, she saw.

Laure stared at the food. She had never seen food in her life before, and definitely didn't know what to do with it.

But Virgile was eating, in hard, quick bites. Laure wished she could put her hand between those narrow white teeth. Feel them close on her flesh and pierce to the bones beneath.

She shut her eyes. Dizzily she leaned her cheek into her unbitten hand.

Virgile, it appeared, failed to notice.

Why should she have any interest in me?

Blankly, Laure said, "How is the comtesse?"

Virgile touched her lips with a napkin.

She looked at Laure for a moment, but not long enough.

"The comtesse is, under the circumstances, quite well."

"Shouldn't I have asked you? You see—I don't know what I may say and what I simply shouldn't mention—"

What do you do for her? I longed to ask that. Or perhaps I couldn't bear to know.

The meal was somehow over. Laure found she had peeled an apple. She bit into its nakedness, could not swallow the mouthful, managed it only with a gulp of wine.

Virgile was rising.

Blackness, the snake's stem, the spread hood of the widow's veil across a snood of hair.

Laure looked up at her now in terror.

Don't leave me. Stay with me, stay—stay—it's all I ask. Nothing else—truly—nothing—

"Good afternoon, mademoiselle."

"I should like you—to call me by my name. My name is Laure."

Virgile gave a little nod. But did not pronounce the name. Half turning now, turning away.

Away.

"And I—may I—address you as Virgile?"

How false the name sounded, when Laure uttered it. An unreal name, improbable. Worse than Virgilie, even.

But she said, "If you wish."

Laure stood up. And Virgile walked from the room. And then Laure sat down again. Trembling so much, her eyes streaming suddenly with tears, of frustration and shame.

Later, eyes dried, she walked about the gardens. She glared up into the trees, where the white doves fluttered uneasily, sensing the treachery of the sunlight. There were no ropes of pearls, no magpie nest from which a crimson glass or silver platter or red carbuncle stopper protruded.

She went to the pool, it was choked with leaves. A tawny frog, just like a leaf, sat pulsing on a stone.

The light slanted. It browned like the last rose, began like the last rose, to fall.

When she returned, shadows hung in the rooms of the château, and between them now and then stole one of the servants. No lamps had been lit. None of the windows, from outside, showed any colour.

Laure thought of Virgile, descending the murderer's stair.

A servant came, a girl, and Laure said, "Does Madame Virgile take tea?"

"Oh, no, mademoiselle. She's with the comtesse now."

Her flat face, without a trace of any simper or snigger, was somehow prurient and disgusting.

Laure knew she must at once leave the château and its grounds.

She must never return.

Now, as she walked, she cried again. She leaned against a bare beech tree some distance from the vast old house, and wept, sobbing. Her gloves fell on the fallen leaves. She picked them up, turning dizzy again.

Oh God, what was the point of it all?

When she reached the lane, she forgot how she had come there. But the sky was grey.

Up the lane drove an old carter behind his shambling horse, the cart piled with incomprehensible jumble, which in the gathering of dusk, might even have been bodies, plague victims shambled in there for burning.

He saluted her politely. It was old Jacques, the lamp-lighter.

She allowed him to go by, and walked slowly after him and his plodding horse, towards the town.

ACT THREE

"She has had a slight fall. Nothing too serious. But I'm somewhat concerned." Doctor St Romarin stood in the Aunt's sitting room. His spectacles were grave.

"She seems," he elaborated, "very forgetful. I expect you've noted it, Mademoiselle Deschampeigne, perhaps put it down to the vagaries of old age. But this isn't quite normal. No indeed."

Ouelle, with her abominable bobbing, subsequently served him the large cognac Laure had omitted to offer.

"Thank you, my good lady! Who knows when these fine evenings will turn on us, like wild beasts, eh?"

"Will I fetch another, your honour?"

"No, no, I won't impose."

"Do, please," said Laure.

The nasty flicker of his joviality was soon swallowed by the alcohol.

"I dislike alarming you, mademoiselle. I understand your natural tenderness towards your aunt has blinded you in this matter. But it's my duty to remind you, I fear, that madame's father, and her elder sister, both perished in this way—of a softening of the brain."

Laure was, after all, shocked. Perhaps, it was more distaste than shock.

"There," said the doctor, seating Laure in a chair, his duty done, "fetch mademoiselle also a cognac, my good Ouelle."

"No, that isn't necessary."

"I insist, Mademoiselle Laure. Your pulse seems rather weak."

And here was Ouelle again, with a cognac for Laure, and yet another for the doctor.

"Now, now, Ouelle, my good woman. What shall we do with you? The best course, Mademoiselle Laure, will be to confine the old lady to her bed, and to watch her. I'm afraid I must stipulate a watch both day and night, for the present. I can recommend a woman from St Georges-du-Marais, who will assist your servants and yourself. And I shall call myself, every day. I think, mademoiselle, you must prepare yourself."

Laure said, confused by the cognac, "But for what?"

"My dear young woman! For what do you suppose?"

"You're saying that my Aunt will soon die."

"It's very likely. If her condition is what I fear it to be, then we must even hope so. Of course, there's the hospital at Convienne. But we won't think of that at present. However, I have a colleague there whom I think I may acquaint with madame's condition. He too may wish to visit madame, if at all possible in his busy work. Sometimes one is mistaken in these things, I should say, misled. There is always that."

Laure went up to see her Aunt. She felt she had to, was expected to, not only by Ouelle and the girl, and the doctor, but by convention itself. Worse, by some intransigent moral code of natural ethics she had never grasped.

The Aunt lay on her bank of pillows, they, and she in her night-gown, trimmed with dull lace. No one yet was watching her.

"Laure—is that you, Laure?"

Laure was struck by an awful doubt; the Aunt might now take Laure for Laure's own mother, the Aunt's younger sister. (Laure's mother had answered to the same name, although her given name was Laurente.)

"Yes, Aunt."

Was it callous to stress their correct relationship? If taken for her own mother, must Laure pretend to it as well?

But the Aunt didn't seem aware of any difficulty. She only beck-oned Laure closer to her, and then, reaching out, gripped Laure's hand with surprising, distressing strength.

"Something I ate," said the Aunt. "That veal, I suspect the veal. Too rich. I never liked it. And the sauce with brandy and sorrel. It doesn't suit me. Tell the cook, he's not to serve it again."

They had no cook but Ouelle, no man in the house.

"No, Aunt. I'll tell him."

(There, deception.)

"Oh, dear. I've so much to do. There are those frocks… I don't like this, having to lie up here."

"You'll soon be well," said Laure. (The second deception.) The voice of a deathshead, too. She wanted to tear away her hand. Death—should never come in such a guise. This creeping thief with his train of lies. In the mediaeval play he was a priestly knight on a pale horse. His sword was keen and bright.

"The mice are bad," said the Aunt. "Tell Susine. She must do something about the mice."

"Yes, Aunt. Yes, I will."

"I wish it were tomorrow," said the Aunt. And then, quite appallingly, "Or yesterday."

The door opened and the girl came in. She had a basket of darning and put it down by a chair. (For the first time Laure was struck by the way they lived, so carefully, as if things might not be thrown out and new ones purchased…) It seemed the girl was going to watch, Laure was not expected to, at least, not for the present.

But the hand still held her fast.

"Now, mistress," said the girl, coming up with some concoction in a spoon, "here's your medicine. That's right. Now this water with your drops in it."

The Aunt let go of Laure's hand to take the glass.

"Isn't the summer weather lovely. I saw the first rose today."

"Yes, mistress. That's right. Lie back and have a little sleep. It will do you good."

Laure's mind went completely running off, trying to escape. *I read only last week, in the collected letters of Madame de Drút…*

Oh, that Laure thinks herself educated and well-read.

"I shall be in my room," said Laure, "if I'm needed."

Needed. What in God's name can I do? Oh damn this awful horror.

And I'm so tired now, always. Or no, it's this savage energy which wears me out—

As she patrolled her room, the read words of Madame de Drút how death should always come in the fiftieth year, one night, after good food and wine with friends. But until then, no illness, no old age. And at the stroke, only a "blissful tumble" as if from "some height into a sea of cloud."

It was dark. The lamp had not been lit.

Laure recalled her arrival at her Aunt's house. That had been more than ten years before. It was in winter, in a gloomy carriage, with snow falling. The street had looked so vast, wet and black, and the town stared at her with its narrow lighted windows.

"Poor child, she's wet through. Heat some water, she must have a hot bath, and then to bed." Laure had felt ashamed. Why was that? None of it was her fault, her father's and next her mother's abandonment of her. But of course a child always believed it was some sin of hers that had caused everything, *her* wickedness, worthlessness.

An adult, Laure stood at the window. "She will die."

The Aunt would die.

Probably it would be quick. But she had heard, mostly from servants, terrible stories of the end of her grandfather, and older aunt—who had gone roaming about like Ophelia, in a ball gown, with weeds tangled in her hair. As if in search of a stream.

But the shock of the Aunt's fall, from which she was, said Ouelle, black and blue on one side, even that might see her off.

Laure stood at the window. Stood and stood, until the arches of her feet ached.

Beyond the garden of her Aunt's house, the wall and trees looked like black lace, the lit windows of Bois-la-Diane looked back at her.

Then reeled abruptly,

Then steadied.

She heard Sophrine's prim voice, "You know quite well one day you'll have everything from your Aunt."

Which would die first? The Aunt or the Comtesse Aubade-Valents.

Laure's heart began to pound. She turned about to evade it and saw the walls softly tumbling like a snow-bank of pillowed cloud or a balcony.

Ouelle presently found her lying on the carpet in the dark.

"There you go, m'mselle. You only fainted."

"What are you doing in here?"

"I heard you fall. Oh you needn't think because you're such a slight little thing the ceiling didn't shake. It's an old house, M'mselle Laure. I know it well enough, that sound. Just like your aunt. Poor old lady. But she managed it on the stair. A wonder she didn't break her poor old neck. She will, next time, if we're not careful."

"Open the window, Ouelle."

"At this time of year?"

"It's too hot. I can't breathe."

"Yes, you are feverish, m'mselle. We must ask his honour St Romarin to look at you, when he comes tomorrow. God help the cognac."

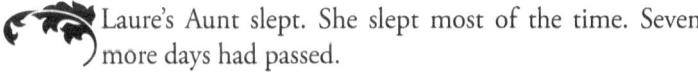Laure's Aunt slept. She slept most of the time. Seven more days had passed.

"Laudanum," said Ouelle. "Nice that she's so peaceful."

The woman had come from St Georges. She was big and strong and wore a white apron. (Ouelle said that she ate like a horse, both in quantity and gesture.)

Every day, about ten in the morning, the doctor appeared. He drank only one cognac on arrival, and only one on leaving. Ouelle had added water to the decanter, but he seemed not to notice.

Cursorily he glanced at Laure, who had not asked him to.

"Fainting, mademoiselle? We can't have that. No, no fever. Well. Perhaps just a little one. Your pulse is a little odd. Slow, then fast." Then, alone with her, "I expect you miss the patronage of the old comtesse." Laure stared at him. She didn't like the pudgy feel of his hands, his smell of cologne, antiseptic and liquor.

He peered into her eyes at the window, telling her to look now this way and now that way, impertinently fiddling with her eyelids. Then he said, leering, "Are your courses quite timely?"

Laure looked away. "There's nothing wrong with me."

"I think you may have a slight disorder of the blood, Mademoiselle Laure. You must eat more meat, and have plenty of that nourishing rabbit broth your fine Ouelle makes. And a glass of red wine, always take one with your supper. You don't smoke cigarettes? A filthy and bad habit for a woman. I know it was something of a fashion, at the château."

"Not at all," she said.

"Well, there were many stories told," said the doctor. "Some extraordinary things. Perhaps you'll have heard, Madame Lejay is being taken to Convienne by her husband. The anticipated death of the comtesse has upset her greatly. I've heard, by the by, the château might be converted into an asylum."

What a gossip.

"Well, well. I'm not quite happy with you. Not entirely happy." And pacing up and down before the fire, "What do I think of you? Well, you must take care of yourself. And I must take another look at you in a day or so." Most unlikely, she thought. And overhearing her thought, he added firmly, "I may be obliged to be more thorough. The good Ouelle can chaperone you, can't she, if you're shy."

Most unlikely.

Laure said crisply, "Pardon me now, I have letters to write."

That night, the seventh night, they roused Laure from bed. The house of the rue Dalle was full of fretful calling. The Aunt had got up, wandering from room to room with a dipping lighted candle in her hand. "Oh, m'mselle—she nearly set herself on fire!" When Laure came in, her Aunt clutched at her. "Mother—where is mother?" Laure and Ouelle led her back to bed, where the girl, who had dropped asleep on watch, was now guiltily crying.

Installed in her bed, the Aunt stared at them. She said, "They keep me prisoner here. They do."

Laure sat until first light in the sitting room, and the darkness was very cold, not like the endless unchanging warm yellow-amber days.

Is that to be my lot when I grow old?

How selfish I am.

How selfish. Despicable. I might have sat by her bed. But I won't face it.

She heard, once, twice, a disembodied voice calling anxiously, like a lost spirit, through the house, "Mother! Mother! Why don't you answer?"

And once a fox screamed at the edge of town.

At seven, Ouelle discovered Laure and scolded her. Laure said, "Be quiet." Ouelle stepped back and said, "Yes, mademoiselle. Excuse me."

Later, after Laure had dressed and forced down a few mouthfuls of chocolate, Sophrine came pulling on the doorbell in her rowdy way.

But her face was pale and diligent.

"No, Sophrine. No platitudes."

"You look so drawn, Laure. Have you slept?"

"Not very well."

"You look quite ill. Shall I come and stay with you? Papa said I might, seeing how things are—why are you laughing like that?"

"At you. I'm laughing at you. I don't want you, Sophrine. I'm sorry, but there it is. What can you do? You'll try to make me eat, or to cheer me up. You think I'm suffering because of this revolting thing which has happened to my Aunt. I'm not. I couldn't care less. I care only for myself. I hate how the house smells now, like a hospital—drugs and urine and peculiar soap. I hate this—this *indignity.* I hate life, I hate it, Sophrine, this trickery, this plot of God's to drag us all down."

Sophrine firmly said, "You must forget her, Laure."

"What? Forget what?"

"You know perfectly well."

"Oh, what are you talking about?"

"I warned you before. Don't you see, Laure, all this isn't some act worked against you. You have *connived* against yourself, and now, when everything seems to be fitting into place, forcing you to do only one thing—it's you *yourself*, Laure, who is forcing yourself to do it."

"Gibberish."

"Destiny—you think it's that, don't you? Your *fate*. Laure, you've sewn it together, a ball-dress, and now you only have to put it on. Do you think I'll help you?

"Get out, Sophrine. Return to your idiotic father and your fat mama. Go and grow fat and idiotic, too. You're nothing to me."

"Don't I know it. Any one of them was kinder to me, more appreciative, sweet. Even the Violette. Even the Lejay, although she never fancied me. But I won't let you throw yourself down into a pit of—of vipers. I knew from that night, of course I did. When you saw her in the candlelight, in that ghastly bridal ceremony that wasn't. And when we went home without a carriage, and you wouldn't let me come near this house with you. Oh, you were open as a book."

"Be quiet, Sophrine."

"I'll strike you if I must. I'll tie you to a chair or lock you in a cupboard. You were asleep, always sleeping. But then you woke up, that morning by the canal. And God help you, you saw that creature, all in her jackdaw black."

"Now you're speaking perhaps of the painting, the Feast. The secret one, nobody ever saw."

"Oh that. It was painted over. I've seen it—there's some other scene on top now. And she, that girl, she lies under layers of paint, just as her body's supposed to lie under layers of soil and roots. If she was ever there."

Laure felt the room spin quite softly, and where Sophrine stood so prissily embattled, for a moment Laure beheld only a gleaming globe, unless it was a golden cup—

Sophrine caught her arm. "Steady. Don't faint. You *mustn't* faint. You don't faint, Laure. You never have, as I haven't."

"Leave me alone."

"It isn't fate, Laure. Not yours or anyone's. You—*you*—have made it happen, and you can make it stop."

VIRGILE, THE WIDOW

Laure's vision cleared. She turned, slyly hiding, and said, level, resigned and slow, "Oh, all this fuss. Stay to dinner then. Do you want to see my Aunt?"

"I'd like to pay my respects to her," ruffled, no longer prophetic, her power lost in the natural ethics of incomprehensible morality.

"Sit down then. I'll tell Ouelle to fetch you some fresh chocolate. I suppose I must go up and see if the old lady's fit to receive you. Be prepared. She's in a sad way."

And going out, Laure shut the door gently. Then turned, opened another door, and stepped into the street.

Her dress, somewhat disordered. Hatless, her hair coming loose. Her eyes doubtless very wide and brilliant.

Ophelia, looking for her stream.

Fireworks of golden light burst between the trees, and the walk was done in a moment, as if Laure wore the Seven-League Boots.

At the front door, the formal door, with its flight of stone steps and two statues, she wondered if anyone would come to answer her.

Twenty days—or more—had gone by, since the night of the contract. Perhaps la Reine's "marriage" was already over, and Laure was too late.

How changed the château was, how changed. She had said she must never come back, and she had not, because this house was quite another one.

Someone opens the door. Some man in shirt-sleeves. And he lets her in, bored and as uninterested in her as she in him, because these demented women still have right-of-way, on the orders of the comtesse.

"Where is Madame Virgile?"

How strongly Laure speaks, although she stands there without a jacket, or a hat or gloves, and with half her hair undone—she heard pins striking the earth as she came along the lane.

The man, quite young, only points through at the great Hall, which lies across from this door.

"She's in the Hall?"

"Maybe," he says. He's being rude to her and Laure has the urge to slap his face, but then only laughs at him, and walks on, and hears more pins spring from her hair and drop now on the polished wood of the floor.

Her hair is all down and smoking round her. She sees from her eyes' corners how the sunlight catches and fires it up. Like the mad Aunt's candle.

The great hall also is ablaze from its windows, so the moth-eaten bears' heads and rusty swords look fierce, although more scabrous than ever.

No one is in the Hall.

Laure turns, angry and imperious, but the rude servant has vanished.

Then she simply crosses the Hall and goes into the passage, and so she reaches the various rooms which open from it, and at the door of the salon (which she could have come at quite easily from its open long glass windows), she hesitates, and sees (in one of those daylit chairs done up in dying lemon brocade) black night is sitting.

Laure leant on the door. She was suddenly so faint she could not get past it. Yet she must. She must faint only inside the room.

She swung giddily, jauntily, forward into the sunlight, and exclaimed, with the license of her faintness, like a drunk, "I should like to come in. Do you permit me to? I must."

Virgile—Virgile. Who sat looking at her. Virgile's black skirt swept the floor. And she spoke. "Must you?"

Laure felt the words go through her belly and her heart.

She staggered, half ran, across the room, catching pieces of furniture to help her, trying to reach the edge of the black skirt, not looking at the white face tipped, expressionless, towards her.

And Virgile interrupted. "Do sit down, mademoiselle. Sit in that chair. What's the matter with you?" *Playfully.*

Laure did sit down. It wasn't what she wanted, and yet, to have reached the black shore over this lake of light, she would have needed to have been a far stronger swimmer than she was.

So Laure laughed, and heard the laugh like violin notes, sitting in the chair, moving her hands, which somehow fascinated her, so flexed and white, so she increased their mannerisms.

"It seems," sang Laure, "I'm ill." Was it pride she detected in her own voice?

Virgile: nothing.

"You've heard of illness, of course, madame. But then, I'm for-getting, you allowed me the use of your first name. Virgile. And I—I asked you to use mine."

Virgile: silent.

"I can explain in a few moments," said Laure. Suddenly the wild trembling and sparkling left her. She sighed and spoke clearly and without any hurry, leaning back her head. "You know my name. My family, therefore. My Aunt, though she hasn't the noble birth of a comtesse, has her own modest fortune. I am about to inherit this, since she'll soon die." The faintness gathered to hold her. It was supportive and sensuous. It gave such liberty. "And I, as you can see, am also beginning to sink. I'm prepared to die. I want to die. But you know that. You recognized it in me, the mo-ment you saw me that morning, by the canal. Certainly that dusk outside the gate of the Blue House. That was why you spoke to me, Virgile. You spoke to my quite-costly clothes and the look of death in my face. Aren't I right?"

Virgile: still silent—and then a papery rustle, like the coils of a snake unwinding.

"And perhaps I could say," continued Laure, "I also recognized you. As my death. Is that too dramatic for you? Forgive me. I don't think I meant to say it. I want to make a bargain with you, Virgile. The usual one. If you made it with Sidonie Valents, why not with me?"

Laure had sounded arrogant. Why? Because this last of her in-dependence must flash up in the face of such utter self-negation? But now she listened, heard nothing. Virgile had not spoken in return—nor moved away. Laure had closed her eyes, and did not undo them.

"When I say my Aunt has a fortune, I do mean that she has. Oh, she doesn't have much recourse to it. But once it's mine, I could be extravagant. You wouldn't tell me if you came from any city, but I promise you, I and a companion could live in a city, even in Paris. I lived there, perhaps you know that too, when I was a child. There was a big apartment near the Tuileries. My mother used to keep a little shrine in her sitting room to Marie Antoinette. But I could engage an apartment twice that size. And there'd be money for all sorts of things. Indulgences. And afterwards, a very generous settlement, for a friend. Of course, I don't know how you wish it arranged. Probably I seem very gauche. We can use Mercier again, the notary, if you like. Was he sufficient? Or send to Convienne, if you prefer."

Virgile: has she stirred? Disappeared?

Laure says, "Obviously, you'll conclude your other contract first, the old woman here. But that work will soon be over, I should think. She said a month—that's almost finished. Or less."

Virgile: spoke. "It will be over tomorrow."

Triumph. Electric. Laure's eyes, still closed, dazzled.

The delicious luxury of giving way to this other, this shadow not even looked at—

"Then the notary must draw up a new contract," said Laure. "Mine. Ours. Do you agree?"

And Laure's eyes fly open, before she realizes they will. She is spent, half blind. Darkness still sits there, regarding her. She can just make it out.

"Of course I will agree, mademoiselle. Providing all this is quite real."

Exhausted. Disbelief.

Laure says, dully now, yet with an edge of fear, "What might not be real? What do you doubt? My proposal? My illness? My position?"

"Any of those things, mademoiselle. I shall need proof."

"But you *know*. You knew it before I knew myself. How can you need proof? But yes, yes, whatever is necessary. Call me by name."

"If you wish me to."

"Now, say it now."

But the voice did not say her name. It is a dark voice, a cello to Laure's violinish cries. And it says, "You're very insulting to me, mademoiselle. Is it because you've heard I am bought and sold?"

Laure lies in the chair, staring, shaking now with terror, her feet and hands like ice.

"You must think of me, mademoiselle, as a woman of business, then. Would you treat your dressmaker in this way? If you did, would she not spoil your gown?"

"What have I—forgive me—Madame Virgile—I only meant—"

"Addressing me as a mercenary, mademoiselle, you have treated me to a most careless display. You have cast your old aunt into her coffin and slammed the lid in order to pull me down on it. What's this talk of death? What do you think I am, the reaper himself, tricked out in a dress?" The voice is also deadly calm. "How dare you, mademoiselle. I have brought my clients comfort. For a fee, it's true. Most of us sell ourselves, in one way or another. Women and men both."

"Virgile—forgive me—oh God—you won't refuse me, will you?"

"No, mademoiselle. I won't refuse you. But I repeat, I shall need proof, and sureties, as I always do. You must permit me to know best. It's how I have survived this world."

Laure pushed herself from the chair. She kneeled on the floor. (If anyone had warned her this might occur, she would have struck them.) "I'll do whatever you say. I can write to you to-day—outlining what I think must be done. My condition will be verified by a doctor. All the arrangements, as you demand, when I myself know—will that suffice, I mean all this in writing, until I can present you with something more definite? You shall have it tomorrow, before you leave. Early in the morning. Is that…enough?"

"Very well. As you say. Then we shall see."

"Oh God—God—won't you even touch me—"

"I'll do everything you wish, if and when the time arrives."

Laure began to cry, without a sound. And even in this extremity, what agonized bliss it was to break on her black stone like water.

"But won't you say my name to me, just once?"

Virgile said nothing.

Then Virgile spoke Laure's name.

Golden splinterings passed through Laure.

"Say it once more—please, say my name once more."

"Laure. And Laure. Laure, and also Laure."

The shadow falls over her, a true shadow, cast from the amber windows and the dark figure before them.

"Get up, if you please."

Laure gets to her feet. She only wants to fall deep into the shadow.

But even now, Virgile has not touched her.

"Well, Mademoiselle Laure," says the Woman, "I'll give you something, as they say, on account. To receive it, you must be obedient."

"Yes."

"When I leave the room, you may follow me. Do you know the wooden stair that leads to the rooms of the grande dame, the comtesse?"

"Yes."

"There you'll stop still. You won't speak, or try to detain me."

"Yes."

"That's all."

Then Virgile goes out of the salon, and next Laure follows her. This is only like a dream.

After the corridors and the upper stair, the sunlight through the windows, the turning and the stair of wood, the murderer's stair.

Laure stops, as she was told. And Virgile by then is at the stair's bottom where the light scarcely penetrates.

Standing there, Virgile is divesting herself of her garments.

As the snake sheds its skin, painfully perhaps, quite slowly. Pushing and drawing itself through the needle's eye of its former life. Just so, the black bodice, its buttons of jet rimmed with silver, undone, the black skirt which drops in one piece like an inky leaf. The white underclothes, threaded with black ribbon, stitched with black embroideries, patterns, designs half seen. Then the body emerges, the renewed snake, alabaster white. A body like a

marble column, traced by the vague temporary scars of its enclo-
sure—fabric, stays—and more in shadow than in light.

It is a fearsome body, as Laure had formally thought, like that
of a statue, come to life. Nothing betrays it in those instants as
remotely human.

And yet it is now out of the black carapace of Death. It is a
woman's, even if the flesh is made of stone.

Virgile glances up at Laure, once only. And suddenly the faintest movement of a smile goes over the long mouth. There's no
kindness in it. Not even humour. What does the smile mean?

Forbidden to speak or move, Laure stares.

She feels no erotic sensation. No arousal. Not even (now), her
fear and terror.

And Virgile turns from her, gathers up her clothes, with the
swift efficiency of her own servant, and enters the outer door of
the apartments, without knocking. And, when the door shuts, is
gone.

Leaving Laure to turn back and go away, which she does, no
longer so giddy and volatile, but tired out.

There are a great many things to do. But Laure knows, as she
goes through the château (this different château; even the murderer's stair is no longer that, but simply a wooden stair, unim-
portant beside other matters), Laure knows what she must do
first.

Her first act was to come here, in the past. (Probably.) Then,
the Comtesse herself acted, taking to herself the Woman, who is
a serpent, and death, and yet neither, being mostly Virgile. The
third act is again to be Laure's act. Her action which, indeed, will
be passive. And yet, though passive, will be *active*.

The act of watching her Aunt die.

*I am going home to do that. Her death is my classroom. So that
when I too am dying, I'll know how to accomplish it.*

The château and its morning grounds have passed over and
around Laure like the folds of a dark gown. It *is* very dark. At one
point Laure has had a brief hallucination, just as she did once
in her adolescence, when she woke too quickly from sleep, and

saw an angel, with outspread wings, and faintly flushed by rose, levitating in one corner of her bedroom.

The hallucination now occurs at the edge of the château woods. Laure thinks for a second she sees two wolves, tearing apart between them a purple veil fringed with gold. But then the lens of sight slips or realigns itself. She beholds two squirrels playing through a bar of sun, the mauve shadow disturbed with a brilliant flicker of long grasses catching light...

But now the sun has gone in. The dark is nothing much, only an absence of that clear mellow fluorescence which, for twenty odd days, has hung over the town and country.

And Laure spares the sky a glance. Yes, the sky is changed. No longer opulent and glazed. Now it is a discreet sky, which does not disclose all its intentions.

Beyond the park, the lane, and then the town of Bois-la-Diane, where doubtless Laure, in her dishevelment, is stared at, even pointed out. These minutes are like the turned pages of a book, papers shuffled, which bring Laure to the house of her Aunt, in through the door, and find her confronting Ouelle in the sitting-room.

"M'mselle Merault has gone home."

"Sophrine. Oh. Yes."

"She was most put out."

Laure says, with a chilly authority, "I'm going up to change my clothes. Then I shall sit with my Aunt. Bring me up some hot coffee, will you, and a little wine. Not red. A white wine, and not too sweet."

"Yes, m'mselle."

"I shan't dine. Perhaps something later, on a tray."

"Yes, m'mselle."

"Has St Romarin come?"

"Come and gone. He had a long face on him. He said he might return, later."

"If he does, he may take a look at my Aunt. I won't see him. You may say I've decided to consult a doctor in Convienne, in my own case."

"Well, m'mselle, that *will* put him in a proper fuss."

"Then I hope he enjoys his proper fuss. Thank you, Ouelle."

Having washed her face and arms and put on a dress of grey material, Laure put up her hair, and powdered her face. This last necessitated looking in her mirror. The stranger who looked back both attracted Laure and discomposed her. She hurried before the mirror, and was soon finished.

Her Aunt's room was very hot, stuffy, smelling of medicine and, despite their best efforts, of slight incontinence. It could not be helped.

The woman the doctor had sent sat there, doing her tatting, her red bony hands moving deftly. She reminded Laure, this woman, of some hag who attended the Revolutionary Guillotine, one of those women who had never really existed as such, save in fiction.

Laure sent her out with a curt expression of gratitude.

No one would argue. It was Laure's "place" to sit here. That she had failed to take her turn, until now, had been surely frowned on. The woman only directed Laure in the intervals of medicines, and asked if she should come back to see to them.

"I shall do it."

Alone, Laure opened one window a crack, behind its lace. Outside the daylight was now the colour of her dress. A stillness had come, like a pause. She could hear nothing, not even in the house, or in this room, beyond her own movements and the intermittent crackle of the fire.

Lastly Laure went to look at her Aunt.

Her Aunt was very frail and lay there asleep, seeming in her contours almost flat, so little there was to her. Yet she breathed, and slightly moved her head. Her face was blushed by fever or the heat.

Also in fiction, Laure would have smothered her, of course, kindly terminating the Aunt's tribulations, and hastening her own ends. For this crime she might even then have become suspect, arrested, and taken to Convienne, tried and found guilty, executed. And Virgile—what would Virgile do in such a circumstance? Nothing, obviously.

Besides, it wasn't in her, in Laure, to murder this old lady. Let death take its own slow course. And she, Laure, would observe. How to place her head so and so. How to move her restless hands. But she must be decorous in her own dying, or Virgile would leave her. Virgile was not a nurse. That was not Virgile's role.

When she thought of Virgile now, Laure felt nothing. Or something so vast that, like God, it had become omnipresent, and could be ignored.

Laure seated herself at the bedside. In half an hour by the clock, she must wake her Aunt and insert into her mouth one spoonful from that bottle and two from that, and the drops in water which, the Guillotine-hag had warned, might have to be administered also by a spoon, as her Aunt had become so feeble.

She was only a doll now, the Aunt. Laure did not need to care for her, only charitably play at helping her, as custom demanded.

*I remember how...*when we roasted chestnuts, she would pour the syrup on them, and then put the plate into my hand. She wore a jade ring then, dark jade, like a bluish olive. That was only ten or twelve years ago, but how much younger she looked. Her hair had brown waves running through it and it curled on her forehead. And those earrings she used to wear, they intrigued me so—shaped like little kettles made of gold—and she let me wear them that time, when I was fourteen and my ears were ready. Then she gave them to me—I haven't worn them for ages—

Why do I remember that?

I remember the night-lamp in my bedroom, how she said it would be useful for me, because the house was still strange to me, as if I'd find my way about from it, and it wasn't there because of the bad dreams. Which stopped, anyway, quite soon, or happened less often.

Once I was here, in her house.

And how I didn't know which day was my birthday or if I was nine or ten, and she said nine *or* ten was perfectly good enough, and fixed my natal day for me in the spring, which she said suited me.

I remember running home here, with Sophrine, when we were children, out in the icy streets from school, when the town still looked quite large. Running into the glowing fire-lit house, and Sophrine would murmur, "What a grand lady she is, your auntie. Always so well-dressed."

My Aunt. She told me stories. She used to laugh.

She was pretty.

Look at her, look at her now.

Oh God, who would want to come to this. Life is the devil, not death. Doing such things to us.

Let me die young. It will be soon.

It's decided.

I have arranged it all.

And Sophrine says, "You have connived—"

Well, and if I have. This woman will die, and I'll die. We all do, in the end.

It was midnight by the clock. After the last doses of medicine, all of which Laure had had gently to push into the fleeting mouth, some of which only ran out again and stained the pillow pink and fawn…after that last dose at—what had it been?—nine o'clock—and then a bite of the bread and cheese, and the wine, Laure had fallen asleep.

But now the next pointless dosing was specified, she had woken on cue to the clock's soft chime.

"Aunt—wake up, wake up, dear." Laure's voice, which formerly had sounded grave and removed, now took on first an impatience, then an intimacy. This fragile debris was connected to Laure by blood. They had flowered, it and she, from one central stem. "Aunt—wake up, dear. Just for a moment."

And the eyes fluttered open. They were pale and cloudy, but a core of light appeared about the pupil suddenly.

"Laure…is it you?"

"Who else, Aunt? Can you try to swallow your medicine?"

"It tastes so bitter."

"I'm sorry. Yes, it's nasty, isn't it—"

When I was a child, and sick, and she gave me the medicine on a spoon, coaxingly, and then a spoon of honey or a sip of wine to take away the taste...

"Swallow the medicine, then take a sip of this wine. That's good. And here's the wine in the spoon—is that better, dear."

"Much nicer. Oh yes. Let me just have a spoonful more."

And a spoonful more of the wine.

Laure had put her hand behind the old woman's neck, to support it. Her hair, all grey and no longer strong, felt soft as the fur of a cat, and warm. Close to, the old woman smelled of nothing bad, only herbs, a little camphor, and a slight dustiness. The odour in the room was separate from her.

"Thank you, Laure. How good of you. How tired you must be, sitting here with me for so long."

Laure eased down her Aunt's thinly covered skull to the pillow. Laure sat back in her chair.

"I suppose," said her Aunt, "I have come to it, now."

"To—what?"

"To death. I suppose so."

Laure thought, *I must send for the priest.* I should have done that already. And then I shall write to Virgile.

"I'm not afraid," said the Aunt. Her lips quivered. "Only sad."

"Aunt, it isn't so serious as that."

Why am I lying? Coward, don't lie.

"Isn't it? I thought it was, I've been dreaming of it."

"Of what? Aunt, what *were* you dreaming?"

"Of leaving the world. I cried in the dream, but I wasn't myself any more. I was in the air."

"Don't think of it."

"Ah, my dear,' said her Aunt, smiling, "how can I not think of it?"

But she turned her head and her eyes closed.

Dear Madame, the letter would begin, *my Aunt died in the night, and now—*

And now I invite you to her funeral, your first proof. After this I will obtain a letter from the doctors at Convienne, concerning my own health. My second proof. And then we will make our legal and financial arrangement. We will go together to Paris.

Why is she sad to die? What possible pleasures has she here?

The clock ticked, and chimed the half hour.

The curtains had been drawn closed. Laure went to the windows and stared out at sleeping Bois-la-Diane. *Do I even remember Paris?* Only that awful, echoing flat, with its ghastly furniture that turned into bears at night, its draperies and bows, and the insipid shrine to that fool, Marie Antoinette. That poor brave fool...

We all die.

(I must sit down and write my letter. And send the boy with it at first light.)

And a park, trees and grass and a fountain, I recall those, and sitting crying there, because I had been left.

And then this place. And the old woman there, in the bed.

Laure turned abruptly, letting go of the curtains, the memory.

Have I really made this happen? Made her die so I can die, so I can have Virgile and languish in the arms of Virgile?

How absurd, such things don't happen. I must sit clown and write—

But if I had—

Stricken, as if by the striking clock which now tolls for one in the morning—half an hour elapsed only in a minute.

"I can't," said Laure. "I can't."

The murderer's stair.

I never went down it, that second time.

I won't. How can I?

She took me in. I was a stranger to her, and she made we welcome. Poor little wizened old child, poor little lost child left behind by me in the headlong rush—

Laure was weeping. The tears spilled down.

She ran to the bed, and knelt across it, taking up her Aunt's dry narrow hands, which felt as fragile as pastry, as if they might crumble in her grasp—"Don't die, Auntie—don't leave me—don't leave me—"

I can't let you die. I won't. What do I care for any of it, what does any of it matter? That woman in her black carapace, what can she be to me—I'll meet her in the end, not naked and white, but on a pale horse, with not one inch of skin visible, the only light the flash of the sweeping scimitar that cuts my neck in two pieces—

Virgile. Damn Virgile

"Aunt—can you hear me? You must live. I want you so much."

Yes, I sacrifice my death for you. My magnificent death in the arms of ebony and agate, I sacrifice my death for you.

The tears stopped, and Laure lay down beside her Aunt, holding the old woman lightly in one arm.

(So, at the beginning, she had fallen asleep beside her in this bed, a child of nine or ten.) And so now, Laure fell asleep, her head on the pillows stained with medicine and tears.

Sleeping she saw a carriage race away down a twilight avenue. Goodbye, goodbye.

I give it up. Didn't she show me anyway? Under her dark shell, she was only another woman, after all.

Dr St Romarin, when he called the next day, seemed not surprised to find Laure's Aunt so very much better. He praised his own prescribed medicines, the woman he selected from Convienne, indirectly himself. Never mentioned his gloomy diagnosis.

He found Laure, too, alert, an apron over her dress and her hair tied up in a cloth, overseeing the great tidying and cleaning of the house against her Aunt's return downstairs a week later.

"Some fever of the autumn, disturbing to the brain," said the doctor. "And you had a touch of it, too, I think, mademoiselle. But all gone now. A good thing you consulted me when you did."

But Ouelle sent up clouds of dust and brought down cobwebs on his intellectual head. She had hidden the cognac.

Later, that is, many years later, Laure regretted that she had not written to Virgile. This was not for Virgile's sake, for Virgile, Laure was certain, would not be concerned much, either way. It was for her own. It would not, of course, have been the letter Laure had planned and intended. It would have been a renunciation, an apology. An honourable farewell. But Laure hadn't written. Instead she had called Ouelle to heat some broth for her Aunt, then she had gone to dress, and tied the apron round her middle. *Let her go wanting,* Laure had thought of Virgile. *She's a woman of business. I'm nothing to her. Why debase myself further.*

And in the hours and days which followed, now and then, the thought would come of that dark carriage bolting away, carrying Virgile from the château, from the town, away and away, to some unknown town, city or land. Virgile, now lost forever.

Virgile was not death. That was too grand. Nor was she merely a business woman, a prostitute, the professional widow—too ordinary.

Had Virgile been love? No. Oh, no. Could Laure have let her go, if Virgile had been that?

Love was banal. It was affectionate, it shared memory, bickered and had arguments, and, in the case of the sexual lover, desire, the games of delight which ended in spasms not remotely deathlike. Love, Laure decided, despite all the poets had said, was more like the mad dance of life.

A storm broke on the town in the week after her Aunt's recovery. It brought down a great many trees and tore tiles from the roofs. In the midst of the tumult, Artemise Lejay miscarried in her husband's fine house, and Clothilde Boulanger accepted a proposal of marriage from Annette Mercier's eldest nephew, he on his knees and swearing his passion out-matched the weather. (These things happened, particularly in spots like Bois-la-Diane.)

I wish I had written to her. I feel ashamed when I remember that Virgile, if ever she recalls me, thinks I was only some hysterical and spoilt young hussy, who didn't know her own mind.

I wish, how I wish I had told her, that lady of business: I have given up everything for love. I have given up *you,* the tumult and the darkness, for the banal, mundane loyalty of a provincial family bond.

But I couldn't have said such things. She wouldn't have understood. She was nothing, was she, Virgile, but the creature I made her into? Perhaps that's always how she was—or is. The invention of others, and by that she survives and makes her way.

What Laure felt for Virgile, omnipresent as God, remained with her, but only like her shadow. She did not always see it, or notice it. Sometimes, when she did, it arrested her, astonished.

The Aunt lived a further five years in good health, rather forgetful of trifles, but no worse than that. She died in her sleep one Easter, after a pleasant dinner with wine, when her table had been crowded with her friends, and Laure sat at her side.

After that, Laure let the house on the rue Dalle, having, with part of her inheritance, bought the Lejays' fine large house, orchard and gardens. The Lejays themselves had long departed, not for Convienne, but Italy.

To Laure's new establishment, the women had begun to drift, on Wednesdays and Saturdays. The Ladies Club had reformed, and was again tolerated by the town, which, as years passed, whispered that Laure Deschampeigne was a wealthy woman, who, having no husband or children, might favour this or that young girl who visited there. Although others were sure that the Deschampeigne wealth would devolve in time on the daughter of Sophrine Le Brun, the wife of a substantial man often away on business.

The old château passed through many hands. No one came to live there. Its walls gave way, fell down, it became a picturesque ruin. Rats ate its furnishings. Fruit was thieved from its grounds, lovers lay together in its summer woods, unchallenged, uninvited.

There was, however, a story the old Comtesse had not died, but rallied, in Paris. They said she lived still in her miser's poky house, with only one servant (the tortoise Peridot), and was reckoned to be almost a hundred.

In that case, Virgile had brought her life, not death.

I still dream of Virgile, occasionally. Usually without warning or any reason at all. They are torrential throbbing dreams, from which I wake in a desolation of disappointment, and lie leadenly for several minutes, until a sort of relief brings me back.

As I become older, stouter and more stiff, no longer that Laure with lucent skin and fine bright hair, I return in my dreams to my youth, and put it on, and then she is there, Virgile. She is often standing on some pile of marble, like a plinth, but it is a stair or a hill, and she is all in black, and her face devoid of any mercy. I know I shall reach her and be dashed in fragments and she will catch me as I fall. And in a glorious agony I approach and approach this moment of complete annihilation—which I never ever reach.

Waking, I find Sophrine beside me, if she stayed the night, and it is perhaps her movements, brushing and pinning her hair, that have woken me. But even if she isn't there, or hasn't moved, never do I reach the moment, the crisis of my dream of Virgile. It is a dream of arriving, not arrival.

And Sophrine will crinkle her face at me, her face which, like mine, is showing the busy sewing and ruching of years, and she'll laugh and say, "There you are, my sleepy-head. Were you dreaming? Here's your chocolate. Drink it up, my love, before the children start clamoring for me. What a fine day! Just look at the sun."

The Umbrella

THE UMBRELLA

She sees the rain, and going into the hall, takes the umbrella. Outside the front door, she puts it up. It is big, black and shabby, a man's umbrella that she found on a train, where people usually lose them. At the time it was a godsend, because her own had just fallen to pieces and, having not much money and fewer prospects, every little helped.

Now, quite smart in her heavy, dark way, the umbrella is rather incongruous.

She walks slowly, calmly. The rain falls on the umbrella in quick mercury drops.

Living alone, she never has to explain. Explain why, so often, if the rain starts, she takes the opportunity to go out, with the umbrella.

The Sugar Girl had simply appeared one morning, out of the park.

She wore a floating amber dress, mid-calf length on her slim legs, and Roman sandals that showed gold-painted toenails. Her hair was fawn, long, silky, and her skin also fawn and silky. She was an image of honey brownness, with startling, contrastingly blue eyes. She had been doing a little shopping before going to work, presumably, for in one of those open doll's baskets that had come back into fashion, lay three peaches, two bananas, a bottle of white wine, and a pound bag of sugar.

Sarah had at once the idea that these items would be used to concoct a fragrant and sticky sweet, somewhere cool, at one o'clock. Perhaps to be eaten alone or, more likely—there was rather a lot for one—with a companion.

In those days especially, Sarah tended to make up lives for those she saw on the streets, in the buses. The elderly woman with a wicked mouth who had murdered her lover. The fidgety housewife who had a house crowded with rare plants and a husband who never spoke. The writer's mind, Sarah supposed. In those days too, Sarah was still a writer, even though she had to go to work in a damp little office, full of bombastic men and twittery small female clerks, who shared, all twelve of them, one ancient, smelly, unisex lavatory.

The Sugar Girl, the girl with the sugar in her basket, was more valuable to the writer's mind than most. She might be up to anything, she had such elusiveness. Not beautiful at all, yet there was something. A grace, a quality of animal movement. Was she a dancer? The slim strong legs, the high firm small breasts, the perfect slender muscles of the arms. Sarah studied her, and was sorry to see, after they had all waited at the bus stop the regulation fifteen to twenty-five minutes, that it was another bus than her own which the Sugar Girl stepped in to.

Next morning, however, the Girl appeared again. Again she waited, although this time with only a shoulder bag, and in a white jacket, for the day was much cooler.

Sarah watched surreptitiously the unbeautiful yet flawless profile. The Girl's nose was just a little too long. How wonderful. It was a face to paint or sketch in charcoal.

That evening Sarah attempted to draw the Girl, from memory; failed. Would she be there again the following day? She had appeared from nowhere. Perhaps a new job, or else a new route. Perhaps a new dancing tutor, a Madame Zinafskaya, with bracelets and memories of escaping something in the snow. "Now vee lifts zee left legs, zoh!"

The Girl appeared rather late, running down the park, her hair flying. She wore a blue skirt and a blue blouse, and big hoop earrings. Sarah, who had missed seeing her, felt her heart leap.

My God. I'm in love with her?

But if so, it was such a lovely love, so undemanding, not interfering with anything at all.

Two weeks passed, and every morning, the Sugar Girl arrived at the bus stop. Generally she stood, not in line, but to one side. Always, however, politely allowing those who had stood neatly in the queue to mount her bus before her. Two traits, then, a wish to non-conformity, a care of others.

She did not have a great many clothes, for there were quickly repetitions. The blue skirt and two or three tops, the amber dress and a grey one, the jacket, various transparent scarves. Sometimes her toenails were copper, sometimes gold or white. She wore no make-up but for a blue line drawn under her blue eyes, and what seemed to be dark blue mascara. Her lips were smooth as cream. She had short almond fingernails. Sarah told herself how the Girl had bitten her nails in adolescence, trained herself by willpower to stop. She was about twenty-two or three now, five years younger than Sarah then.

What was her name? Irene, with the last *e* properly pronounced? Julia, Laura, Isabel…, or something foreign—Sandrine, Natasha…

Perhaps it was something deliberately awkward and un-magical, in the manner of so many modern actors and dancers. Ginny Hinks. Trish Buckle.

Sarah broke into a second of audible laughter before she could prevent herself, and the man in front turned and glared at her. Sarah composed herself.

The Sugar Girl did not see. From her shoulder bag she had produced a plain book. Was it a novel? Something light, moronic, clever? Dance steps? Calculus? Sex?

The bus came, today Sarah's before the Girl's.

As Sarah rode towards her boring job, she thought, I could speak to her. The way people do. A cliché. *These buses!* or, *cooler/ hotter today, isn't it?* Why not?

Throughout the morning, filing impossible papers written in Martian in their normal mess, while one of the big men smashed bee after invasive bee—they had a nest under the roof—into Bee Nirvana, Sarah considered an opening gambit with the Sugar Girl.

And that evening, after her supper of cheese on toast, Sarah also thought about it. And in the bath. And in the bed. Suppose they spoke, suppose they made friends. They met for lunch. At the weekend they went on the river, Sarah rowing, and then the Girl, slimmer yet stronger, rowing better. And under a willow, as in the stories, sharing a bottle of Sauvignon, an apple, a sandwich. A kiss.

That smooth, pale, almost coffee-coloured mouth.

But there was no temptation, on her back in the bed, for a straying of the hands. Sarah would not abuse the Sugar Girl. About some now or past actress, Sarah might fantasize—she could not be the only one who had disrobed an almost-persuaded Vivien Leigh, in a Victorian bathroom scattered with real fur rugs, been slapped into happy submission by a suddenly gay Bette Davis, or, more modernly, become the dresser of Janet Suzman at the National Theatre. But Sarah did not want to fantasize to the sexual end about the Sugar Girl. The Sugar Girl was a private citizen. Even in a dream, she must retain most of her space.

The following day, the Sugar Girl was late again anyway. She almost missed the bus entirely. But not quite. So there was no opportunity for the cliché, and the next day was Saturday.

In the third week, on Monday, the Sugar Girl was at the bus stop, and only three other people were there, apart from Sarah. The morning was soothingly hot. It was an ideal day to go near, to speak. Perhaps even, "Do you have the time? My watch seems to have stopped."

Sarah stood in the queue, prickling with urgency. Sweat stippled out on her forehead and woke her deodorant to a sharp lemony rose scent.

But it was as impossible to go over to the Sugar Girl as to pull one's feet out of a sucking quagmire. Sarah could not move. And then the buses came, one behind the other. And there was the usual flurry as the driver behind tried to evade the passengers, driving by before they could get on or off.

In the unpleasant office lavatory, window wide, Sarah stood and thought about why she had not spoken to the Sugar Girl. Was it fear? The Girl might have a frightening accent, from Birmingham, say, or a raucous version of the East End, or—worse—the over educated Oxbridge set.

But surely, in her case, it would not matter. A rebuff then. Go away, piss off—but the Girl would not behave like that. Not to a simple comment on weather or query on time. If she sensed in Sarah something unwanted, she would be—what?—firm but gracious. That was all. Nothing embarrassing or alarming.

Tomorrow then. Definitely tomorrow.

But the tomorrow came, like Macbeth's, and several more to-morrows, and there was always now a reason not to speak. Too many people, an abnormal amount. A dangerous row going on across the road between two irate drivers. Finally, the Girl seemed deeply engrossed in another slim plain book, this one dark red: *The Secret of the Ukrainian Pirouette, The Beginner's Guide to Potato Peeling.*

It's absurd. Why not? Why not?

And now it was Friday again, and the Girl was late, rushing through the park under the green cauliflowers of the trees, in a new white broderie Anglaise top, and new white sandals.

Just in time for the bus. And Sarah almost stammered out, as the Girl ran by, "Just made it!" But that could be so annoying, somebody saying that, the obvious. She desisted.

The weekend passed in the ordinary way. Sarah did perfunctory cleaning, washing, shopping, read late in bed, listened to music, went out for dinner at the usual place, where they knew her.

On Sunday an attack of melancholy drove her up on to the heath. It was time she looked for another job. Preferably some-where with a café nearby and more than one toilet. She had walked up here, with Karen, last year. But that was then, this now. Sitting under a spreading chestnut tree, she thought about the Sugar Girl, and sadly beheld the littleness of the game. For game it was. She did not care to speak because to speak would, one way or the other, cause the game to end.

On Monday morning, the hot weather broke in a downpour, and Sarah took from its cracked vase the man's umbrella she had recently found on a train.

When she reached the bus stop, no one at all was there, and then, up through the rain, rain like a forest shutting all things away, walked the Sugar Girl. She wore her grey dress, now nearly black with wet, and over her head she balanced a cascading plastic carrier bag.

Sarah spoke at once.

"Will you share my umbrella? Its huge."

"Oh, thanks so much," said the Sugar Girl, and came in out of the forest of the water, and stood close to Sarah in the shadow.

The Girl smelled of rain, and Imprévu. Her hair was sprinkled with rain beads, and her blue mascara had smudged just a little, giving her the eyes of a feverish child that was also a were-albino-tiger.

"I thought it would," said the Girl. She had no accent of any kind, like the very best sort of actress. "And then I left mine behind." She meant, it seemed, her own umbrella.

"I expect that's the summer gone," said Sarah.

"Yes. Once it rains that's always it, isn't it."

There was fresh mint on her breath, conceivably, from a Polo. She had the doll's basket again, but inside everything had been covered by the wet plastic bag now crushed there.

"I love the rain though," said the Sugar Girl.

"Yes, it's very clean. Even though it isn't."

They laughed as one. Shiny crystals spangled under the umbrella. Then through the forest of the rain, the Girl's bus manifested.

"Thank you again—you saved me from drowning!"

And she was gone.

But I did. I spoke to her, sheltered her.

And now—

On Tuesday, the Sugar Girl did not appear at the bus stop.

Sarah felt an odd compunction. Had the Girl caught a chill? Well, she was young and strong.

The days passed. The Sugar Girl did not come back. After ten days, Sarah stopped worrying. Stopped thinking, with a dry mouth, of accidents, violence, abrupt death. Because there was no way she could learn a thing, she would never know. She could do nothing.

For the next four weeks, as Sarah worked out her notice, she looked every morning still, half imagined she saw her moving through the park, or her shape among the crowd about the bus stop. But it was never her. The Sugar Girl never came back.

It was like wanting to cry, but the tears would not come. They could not get out, because you could not weep at a loss like this. There had been nothing at all to lose.

Now in the rain, walking, Sarah keeps the incongruous, unsightly umbrella over her head. Crystals no longer dance in the air. The Sugar Girl does not walk beside her.

It is only that, now and then, when the rain starts, she takes the umbrella, and walks under the umbrella alone in the rain.

Green Iris

She thought: After a certain age, most women are with a man. She thought this on the night after she met Helen. She thought it philosophically. (Resignedly.)

Of course, war had changed things a little. Those droves of men, young and old (whom the gods loved died young or old) greedily swept away in the fire and mud of the trenches. But even so, even when a woman wasn't, now, in any physical actuality of marriage or relationship, still, generally, she *was* with one or other of them. She was planning how he might be had. Yearning after him—even if he was only a memory. The inconsolable widows in their black, broke suddenly out of the chrysalis and were dancing again, in their bright dresses. Cinderellas among the princes.

But this was worse, anyway. Helen was married, and Helen's husband had survived the war, was alive and still youngish, and extremely there.

March

Sabia Cobb met Helen Driver at a party in Wootton Street. Who was giving the party Sabia was unsure. She hadn't very much wanted to go, but a young man had asked her to. Usually, if she thought him harmless, she tried to go about with the occasional young man. It was only prudent. Or so Sabia believed.

This young man was called Marcus, and he drove Sabia to a tall house, folded in a grey March evening mist. Upstairs the party raged. Someone was always winding up the gramophone, and dance tunes came bleating out of it. Glasses and people clinked and glittered.

"Oh look, there's Driver," said Marcus, sounding contemptuous, which might mean he was impressed.

"Whose driver is that?" asked Sabia, annoyingly.

"No, Edmund Driver, the writer. He's not bad, they say. I've not read him. But an absolute swine, I've heard. He only comes to a party to make clever remarks, and then turns everyone into caricatures in some book." (Marcus himself was at the edges of the publishing business. No doubt such nasty caricatures, or similar ones, were of indirect benefit to him.)

Sabia was not interested. She drank her sticky blue cocktail slowly, and looked round under her eyelids.

Marcus had been too young for the war. Surely it wasn't this that made him look so unfinished—like a half-boiled egg. If so, that did not apply to Sabia, who had also been too young, properly to understand. Now in her twenties, she might herself be wise enough, yet still felt she understood very little.

Why, for example, was she really here at this party?

Then she saw, with her serpent's gaze, Helen.

"Who's that woman?"

"Which? Oh—don't know."

"Her dress is wonderful."

"Is it?" he said. "The rest of her is pretty good too, I'd say. But no, she isn't young. Well over thirty. Still, modern enough. And well off."

Sabia, who hadn't really noticed at all Helen's long, slender green stalk of a dress, did now see the flash of a wife's slave rings on her left hand.

Then Marcus wanted to dance, so Sabia said she was too tired. And in a while, he went off somewhere or other.

And then Sabia glided, as she herself amusedly thought, like a panther through the thickets, and arrived where Helen was. Helen was not drinking a cocktail. Someone had found some whisky, and she was drinking that. Three men had surrounded her, and Sabia wondered which was the husband, for how alike these men all were, in their black and white. Sabia eased herself between two of them, who good-naturedly allowed her to do so.

Sabia said brightly, "Oh Daphne, how are you?"

The four of them turned, and looked at her, blank.

"Oh, dear," said Sabia, her face falling. "Am I mistaken?"

Helen laughed. She didn't seem put out. She didn't really look, Sabia thought, as if anything could ever irritate her very much. Nor would she take much notice of it. Her face was so smooth, only the tiny faint pencil-sketched lines to either side of her mouth, and at the edges of her eyes.

No one however was going to enlighten Sabia. Or draw her in. Of course, she was not really in their class. She had a foreign-ness, an exotic quality that, carefully smother it as she did, was still somehow audible to certain people across great distances of money, accent and clothing.

Sabia pretended confusion. She slunk away as she was sup-posed to.

Presently, sitting on a couch with some others, she watched Helen drift out of the room. She was now on the arm of another man entirely. But Sabia paid him little attention.

"I love that woman's dress," she tried again, more successfully with these female companions.

"Yes, it's *gorgeous*, isn't it? From Paris, probably. That's Helen Driver."

"Oh—her husband's the writer, isn't he?"

"Edmund Driver. He's divine."

Edmund Driver, the Divine Swine.

And Helen, perhaps late of Troy.

A few days later, Sabia saw the most recent of Edmund Driver's books for sale. She walked into the shop and bought it, thinking there went her wine-and-cigarette money for the week.

The novel was called *The Last of Us*, a strange title. "Clever," presumably, as Marcus had said.

Sabia read it slowly in the dull March light, or beneath the rosy lamp, trying to find traces of Helen. But it was a book, of course, about men, their preoccupations and dilemmas, their masculine values. One woman did dominate the book, but she was an object, a Being, not really a person, remote, unreasonable, unfathomable and cruel. (Sabia supposed, if she herself had written a book, the male characters would be like this Woman in Driver's novel. Sabia didn't understand men, or rather, they didn't interest her enough for her to try to understand them. And so, she could only display them as empty icons, just as the Woman-being was. But also didn't this imply that Edmund Driver, along with most men, probably, had no grasp of—therefore no true interest in—women?) But anyway, the Woman was *not* Helen. Not physically—nor surely in any form. The Woman was in her twenties, her hair was (foreignly) black, she was voluptuous and impossibly beautiful.

Helen was tall and slender, white-skinned and fair-haired, the hair short, with what seemed a natural wave. She was in her thirties. She *was* beautiful—but not like the creature in the book.

Helen was beautiful like—well…like what?

Sabia began to try to think what Helen was like. Jokingly to herself, Sabia called her Helen of Troy, but Helen's looks weren't classical either.

I suppose, thought Sabia reluctantly, she has a Helen-beauty.

So it was quite serious, then. Oh, yes.

The following week, Marcus telephoned.

"You still type, don't you, Sabie?"

She said she did. Marcus asked if she would be willing to type up some stories a pet aunt of his had written.

"Is her writing readable?"

"Horribly so," said Marcus gloomily. "She wants to publish, but I don't think it'll be on somehow. But she'll pay you."

He said this bluntly. Marcus knew Sabia often supplemented her precarious finances with typing work.

Sabia agreed, and three days after received a large and ominous package. A glance at the stories filled her with nearly insane despair.

She pulled the cover off her typewriter and placed the machine on the dining table of her flat, arranged the ribbons, the manuscript, pens and pencils, then decided she must at once go out.

In flight down the street, she knew she would now waste the day, wandering about in escape; anything rather than return to the threatening machine and the pile of auntly stories.

She had always been this way. Always confronting her duty and promptly running away from it.

Sometimes she even did what must be done—eventually. As, eventually she might dust the flat, or cook herself a Proper Meal.

Walking through the drizzle, between the wet-newspaper of the buildings and glistening, dead-looking trees, Sabia thought of Helen.

On the dust jacket of Edmund Driver's book, there had been a tiny fragment of information about the author, written small, like a secret. He had been born in Buckinghamshire, fought in the war, survived, and was married. There were no children, or not apparently. Now he lived in London.

Sabia began to see that really the Drivers were quite traceable. They were perhaps even in the telephone book. It was often surprising who was.

In the afternoon, following a cheap English lunch at the Corner House, Sabia went home. She pointedly ignored the typewriter and waiting stack of manuscript, and instead began to seek the Drivers' number.

"The Driver Residence," finally announced a maid on the other end of the line.

"Yes," said Sabia. "Is Mrs Driver there?"

"Who may I say?"

Sabia invented a name. The name didn't matter, after all she wasn't going to speak.

Soon Helen picked up the receiver. "Hello… This is Helen Driver. Hello?"

Sabia smiled, and cut them both off from each other.

You are a bad woman, Sabia Cobb. Playing games on the telephone. What silly moments of spurious control—but it was no good chiding herself now.

"Hello," said the voice all the way from Troy, on and on in Sabia's brain. "Hello, hello." And what shall Sabia do now?

It was no longer a chore. Sabia's fingers skimmed over the clacketing keys, typing out the Aunt's Tales, a kind of failed Jane Austenesquerie set in Cheltenham.

"Good lord—that was quick," said Marcus, when she told him, also over the telephone.

"I do type quite fast. I'm quite a good typist."

"I know. She'll be ecstatic. Expect the cheque soon."

"Yes, thank you."

"Well, I owe you a lunch as well, Sabie." Drifting apart from her now, since seeing he had no "chance" with her, the rewarding lunch was offered with the correct amount of aloof patronage.

"That would be lovely, Marcus. Actually, what I'd really like—"

"I'm not buying you a hat," squeaked Marcus.

(Sabia wondered which girl it was—or was it another aunt?—who had reduced him to such curious apprehension.)

"No, I've got some hats, thank you. What I'd like would be a lot more work. I mean, something more steady."

"Well, I hear offices are still wanting—"

"I don't want an office job, Marcus. I just need something to pay the rent. I was thinking—you've seen I can type all right. Would it be possible to get me introduced to some authors who need a quick, efficient typist?"

"Most of them already have long-established typists, Sabie, little old ladies with cobwebby buns—and they won't trust anyone else with their precious junk. Or they type their own manuscripts— and a very dreadful mess they make of it, most of them, too. Odd animals, writers."

"Actually," said Sabia coolly, "at that party the other night…that author—who was it—Edmund Something—Drover—"

"Driver. Edmund Driver."

"Oh yes. Well I heard someone mention Mr *Driver?* wanted a typist. At the time, it didn't occur to me, and of course, I don't know him. But if someone could introduce me—"

Marcus said stuffily he wasn't sure. He had heard Driver was, as well as being "clever," stand-offish and arrogant.

"I've met him myself a couple of times. He wasn't too bad really, but it depends how he's feeling, it seems. They're very temperamental, I find, writers. Worse than the theatrical profession, I'd say."

From what she had seen of him, Sabia had gauged that Marcus liked to do favours. They gave him a sense of power. For everything he was able to grant, one day he believed he would reap a return. He seemed to forget how feckless and ungrateful everybody was.

"I'd be so grateful, Marcus."

"I'll tell you what. A chap I know—Conranne—he knows Driver a bit. I'll get him to have a word."

Sabia, obviously, had no reason whatever to think that Edmund Driver was in sudden need of a typist. No one had said anything of the sort at the party. But intuitively, she wished to approach her goal (Helen) through the auspices of Helen's husband. The male ruled in any household he occupied. To try to circumvent him would be madness, and all approaches must first be sanctioned by him. Her only real hope, however, had been to meet Driver and try to persuade him she might be useful. Sabia, from long experience of these men she did not ever understand, or try to understand, knew even so that she was often adept at persuading them to things. Perhaps her very distance helped her, or her, as she thought, serpentine silences. She had seldom gone far wrong. She had never even truly been accused of being what she was—a woman fascinated only by women.

Now, she also knew she must be quiet, and not insist, to Marcus, on meeting Driver. She would have to settle for the outside chance that:

1) Marcus would remember to ask this Conranne.

2) Conranne would remember to speak to Driver.

3) Driver coincidentally might need, against all odds, someone to type his work.

"Thanks, Marcus. I *do* appreciate it." Sabia put the telephone receiver back on its cradle, and walked to the window. Across the dingy street and the roofs, she could see the tops of Manorcourt Park. The mists were clearing, and by a stretch of the imagination, narrowing her eyes, the bare trees already had a look about them of new green.

APRIL

The weather changed, and April weather came, just as it was meant to. Pale limpid greens overran the watercolour surfaces of London, glimmers of iridescent turquoise shot through shadows in flashes of glassy rain, while the March sky shed its skin like a snake to reveal a body as blue as an eye.

Sabia stood looking at all this, now, and knew, as the month swelled, something was sure to happen, as nearly always one does in spring (usually quite wrongly).

When the telephone rang, she wasn't surprised. Not surprised when she heard the deep, unknown masculine voice, which said, "Miss Cobb? This is Edmund Driver. I've been led to understand you're a first class typist."

Sabia laughed. That shouldn't matter. He would think her elated at getting the work.

He said that his accustomed typist had a bad cold. It had apparently happened before and laid her up for a month or more, and he had a book for which the publishers were waiting.

He would be very pleased if Miss Cobb could come to see him at the house in St Giles Grove. Then perhaps they could arrange something to suit them both. "Bring your own machine, will you," he said, "we don't have one here. Take a taxi. I'll cover any expense."

He had a musical voice. He was Being Charming. She recognized it infallibly, for she was Being Charming too. They both wanted something.

They agreed this afternoon would be best.

When she put down the receiver, Sabia felt at once as if she had just gulped a glass of good champagne too fast. The Angel of April had smiled upon her, the saint of women in love.

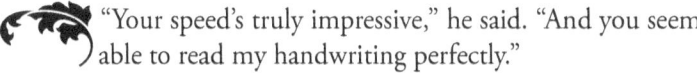 "Your speed's truly impressive," he said. "And you seem able to read my handwriting perfectly."

"It's very readable handwriting," she said.

"Yes. I don't know why. I'm pretty careless with everything else."

Sabia glanced at him quickly, and away. Her gambit was to look lucidly composed, yet impressed, and a little shy. She was very effective at this stance, having mastered it years before.

The room they were in was entirely pleasant, as was the whole house.

She had known, from the address, that this was a wealthy mildly historical area. St Giles Grove lay beyond Regents Park and driving through the greening avenues, and out among gracious high garden walls, with their floods of incipient laburnum, and the dove-coloured buildings sheltering half-seen in waking coppices, Sabia felt an ancient nostalgia for the beauty of architecture, the illusion of pagan woods. One expected a blue thread of offering smoke to rise any second between the trees.

The Driver Residence stood in Aspersedge Road, tucked away behind its walls, and surrounded by a garden of massive limbs and leafy boughs. Birds were springing everywhere, singing wild madrigals. The house was a creamy faded pink, and had also-faded bluish shutters by the windows, as if it thought it were in France.

Sabia was shown up at once to Edmund's study.

"Here, let me take that," he said, coming over to lift the heavy typewriter from her clutch. "They should have got someone to carry it up for you." He meant his servants, the parlourmaid who had opened the door.

On the first floor, the study had long, open windows to a little balustraded balcony that overlooked the garden below. Sunlight drenched the garden, the busy electrified birds, and showed a gardener with his assistant, tying off daffodils and attending to shrubs.

Ice-yellow curtains fluttered at the long glass doors. You could smell hyacinths still persisting in pots, and the aroma of fresh coffee another maid had just brought for Sabia.

He drank some of the coffee too.

"I can't stand tea," he said, "even in the afternoon. Wretched stuff, it works on me like cocaine. Coffee never does anything much at all. I suppose I'm perverse."

Sabia smiled. Admiring him, as he would expect to be admired. On the shelves, his seven novels in their Emblem editions, and then in various other foreign forms, made a dazzling display. Sabia, dazzled. Presently she was able to admit, "I'm afraid I've only read one of your books. The latest. *The Last of Us.*" And to his uneasily off-hand and studied, "Oh. What did you think of it?" she replied, "I don't think I understood it all. But I think it was one of the most interesting books I've ever read."

He was good-looking. She hadn't noticed at the party, barely did so now. But looks were also a reference point, and might not be ignored. They too would temper how he was, and what he might expect or demand in the way of female homage.

He was between—what?—thirty-four and thirty-six, thirty-seven. She couldn't be quite sure, for from some angles he looked older, nearly severe, with the strokes of grey that were beginning just above his ears in the dark brown thickness of his hair. His eyes were blue. Nothing unusual there. Rather dark blue, perhaps. He was well-dressed in a casual, almost untidy way. Not enough to be insulting or slovenly, more an attempt (maybe deliberate) at the carelessness he had boasted, the perverseness. Did he equate these things with vanishing youth? When he looked up like *that,* yes, just now, he did look much younger.

His hands were well cared for, but stained with ink. He saw her see this, and told her that his pen had begun to leak, but it was the pen he must always have, to write with, wasn't that childish? But that was how he was, so he used the pen still, and it ruined his hands and his clothes.

"But I thought you'd finished your book."

"Yes, *that* book is finished. But when I can, I always start another one fairly soon after." And then he sat on the side of the desk and said, thoughtfully, "It's as if I can't stop. The writing. I rather resent it, in a way. Is it a gift or a curse? Does it enslave me?—Yes. And if I'm not writing, Miss Cobb, I'm unlivable with."

When she positioned herself at the typewriter to demonstrate her ability, Sabia was for a moment nervous. But he might like that. So she said, "I feel very nervous."

"But this is just a formality. George Conranne already sang your praises to high heaven. He said you'd typed up something for one of Marcus's authors, and a more perfect typescript he had never seen."

Sabia stared an instant. She thought: What now would she owe Conranne—who she had never met—let alone Marcus the half-cooked egg.

But she began to type, and passed the test anyway; tapping fluently and exactly, covering several pages before Driver said to her, "I'm sorry, do stop now. I was frankly mesmerized, I think, watching you. I have to say, you're much quicker than Agatha." Then, reaching out for what she had typed, and reading it, "And no mistakes. None."

Sabia didn't make mistakes. She had learned in many ways never to make mistakes. She trusted herself, mostly, to excel in every public area of her precarious and skill requiring existence.

Then she heard Helen's voice (Helen of the Hello, the Trojan telephone with Sabia concealed inside it), talking softly through the bird trills in the garden.

"That's my wife."

"Oh, yes," said Sabia, politely interested.

Driver moved to the balcony windows. He called down to invisible, omnipresent Helen, "Darling, I've magically found a wonderful typist. Aren't I lucky."

"Yes, darling," called Helen. "But you always are."

How false the exchange sounded. What a stage-husband said to a stage-wife. And back again.

Most women talked like this to the men in their lives. Most women were stage-wives, stage-girlfriends, stage-lovers. It began, Sabia thought, when they were stage-daughters of five or six.

Driver started to moot Sabia's fee. This was soon agreed. He said, "Do you prefer to work at home, or here?" I'd really prefer you to be here. Agatha can't stand it, mind you, typing on the premises. I think I make her jittery, but also I keep bothering her with corrections, and changes I want to make. Would that worry you?"

"No, not at all. That's what I'm there for, isn't it, Mr Driver."

"Oh, Miss Cobb." Playful. "You really are heaven sent." Flirting with her. She flirted back just a very little, only with her eyes and the corners of her mouth. He was irresistible, of course.

Outside, Helen was telling her gardener that something wasn't right with that bush, it must be seen to.

It was arranged Sabia would come to the house every day at ten o'clock, and work through until about five. When she said, in answer to his question, that she would take the tube, he told her she would do no such thing. She must have a taxi every day, both arriving and departing. Also, she must lunch here.

He said, "Helen will see to it."

It kept seeming she was about to meet Helen. But this didn't happen. Nor did he want Sabia to begin work that day. He sent her away soon after that (by taxi, in accordance with his Word). He had lost interest, Sabia thought, quite suddenly. She wished she'd had an excuse to go into the garden, where Helen was, but that was stupid, there was none. Opportunities could be made later. So much had already been achieved.

Taxied back across London to her flat, Sabia found herself unaccountably annoyed with Edmund Driver. A reaction no doubt to making up to him, or to his wealth, or to his ridiculous poses and his Charm.

Sabia came to the house in Aspersedge Road each day except Sunday. On Saturdays she finished work at noon, and left, lunchless, presumably to get on with her life. At weekends the Drivers Did Things. They went away quite often, too, even in the week. He still kept a house in Buckinghamshire, "by a river," a large house with sloping lawns, where people stayed, and Edmund held court and Helen moved about in ice-cream coloured dresses. All this Sabia deduced, from shards of conversation that broke off the Drivers' main stem and fell into Sabia's ears, to the accompanying clacket of her typewriter.

She hardly saw him after the first interview, although she was told (the maid) that he checked her work each night. (Sabia had wondered who disturbed it.) He was also apparently out a lot, and when in, closeted in his study. The maid had showed her, the first day, into what had been allocated as a Typing Room, another pleasant chamber, but downstairs, and rather tucked away. It had pale walls and a high white fireplace shut by an old-fashioned screen. One narrow French door gave onto a corner of the garden, but it was closed off by a pine tree and a laurel, and no one seemed to come there. Instead, voices floated from far off, both out of the house and in off the shrubberies.

Helen was endlessly visited by friends, women, and one elderly man, some relation it seemed; she referred to him as Frederick. These people, burnished of voice, the women red-lipped and in tulip frocks of yellow and crimson, flitted or stalked across distant vistas of the wide house. Sabia glimpsed them over a sweep of hall or dining room. Glass winked, both in hands and paned across the eyes of the mummifying Frederick. Helen too was endlessly seen—for a moment here, a moment there.

Helen looked like no one else. She did not even resemble her handsome husband, as handsome women sometimes did, let alone grace him with a feminine opposite.

Helen seemed to Sabia to belong to none of this, not to the big house, nor the larger one in Buckinghamshire. That was her main quality, perhaps, her unbelonging. This, and her removedness from all things. She had a wealthy woman's slight manners, far less courteous than Driver. She was uninvolved, always. Listening to the chatter of others, her eyes slightly lidded over, like a cat that watches a bird, and can't be bothered with it really—an instinct that no longer means very much, even should the cat spring and the spring end in someone's death.

Was she dangerous, then? That was, carelessly and uninterestedly and uninvolvedly dangerous?

To Sabia, seeing her an instant, now here, now there, over and over, peculiarly Helen came to seem a normal part of life. (As one even partly gets used to the moon.)

But Helen and she had not, in this house, exchanged a single word.

And there really hadn't been any chance of "opportunities."

Like an awful little cog that ran round and round unheeded, barely needed, in the middle of the mechanism of the house, Sabia was left outside—or more correctly inside—everything else. Inside, yet totally left out.

At lunchtime, Sabia would get up and walk across to the other room the maid had shown her. And here she would find quite a nice lunch laid for her—eggs on spinach, or a cutlet, or sole in lemon sauce—even cheese and a sweet, and always coffee. It was as if the Least They Could Do was make sure this poor downtrodden little creature had a decent meal.

But Sabia, who could go for days on toast, a sardine, or some apples, pitched in greedily to the lunches. She had the instincts of a squirrel, to store against an always-approaching winter.

It was still spring, however.

Though April was almost gone.

One morning, typing diligently Edmund's latest clever, Helenless novel, Sabia heard a slight sound behind her, and thought the maid had come in for something. But Sabia's instinct, also, was usually to look behind her.

There in a shaft of the eleven o'clock sunshine, stood Helen. Sabia noticed incongruously that Helen's frock had a neckline cut like sharp petals. That, and the sun on her dark gold hair, and her eyes—an April blue. Nothing else.

"Hello," said Helen of the Hello. "It's Miss Cobb, isn't it?"

"Yes, Mrs Driver."

"Look, I wonder if you could do me a great favour. Mr Laudelay wanted me to copy out something from this book," (she held the book in her hand), "and I haven't time. But I don't want him to feel let down." (Mr Laudelay was Frederick.) "They get these fancies, don't they, the old," she added. "I suppose I'll be just the same. So, could you? I mean type it? You seem to work so fast, it should only take you a few minutes. Am I asking too much?"

Sabia wanted to smile at Helen's smiling mask, her uncaring diffidence-that-was-a-lie. Her ideas of not having time in that timeless state of the rich and looked-after.

Sabia wanted to say, "Fuck his book. I'll type out the Bible for you if you like."

She said, "Of course that's all right. It won't take long."

Then Helen came and set the book beside her, directly on the growing pile of her husband's manuscript. She opened the book and showed Sabia the requested page. The text was a poem.

Helen smelled of cologne and sandalwood, and the linen of her dress. She was warm, yet cool. Her shadow fell across Sabia and eclipsed everything. Then she moved away. (Naturally, Helen didn't appear to recall "meeting" Sabia before.)

Sabia finished the page she had in the typewriter, removed it and put it aside. She typed out the poem from the book.

This was a sort of fake ballad, meant to be perhaps of mediaeval aspect. The kind of thing Keats and Tennyson did much better.

It began:

I would I were with Edmund now
That summer leaves are green,
I would I lay in Edmund's bower
And Edmund's arms between.

The curiousness of the name, that it was the same as Driver's Christian name, alerted Sabia. But to what, though?

As she typed the rest of the despairing ballad-poem, she remembered meeting Edmund Driver on his driveway, pun unintended, the previous Thursday evening. He had just been driven (again, pun redundant) from Richmond, where he had lunched with some editor or other for some reason or other.

As with his typing, Edmund had to have his driving done for him. It was Helen who could drive, not he, Helen who swept them off in the dusk, or on Saturdays, manoeuvring the large silvery car as if it were only one more exactly fitting garment. But now, Helen elsewhere, the chauffeur managed the car.

"Miss Cobb," Edmund said, getting out.

He stood there in the April evening, smiling at her as Helen did not ever smile, male and decided: Sabia was yet one more of his (minor) possessions. He knew, obviously, she thought him impressive, liked him, did her very best to please him.

"About the book," he said—there could be only one, his—"I haven't been worrying you over any alterations, because you just don't make any mistakes."

Sabia beamed, became shy, looked away.

"I've begun to feel," he said, "it was only poor old Agatha's bad typing that made me think I ever had to alter what I'd written. I must be insecure. Where my work's concerned, I thought I was rather the opposite, a boor, actually, too sure of himself."

He meant, of course, *only* in his work. "Now I'm wondering in fact, no doubt also arrogantly, how many things I've mucked about with simply because they looked awry with Agatha's purple pencil typing corrections all over them."

Then he'd gone into the house, and Sabia had walked out to find her waiting taxi panting at the kerb.

Having finished the poem, it took less than five minutes, Sabia got up and went to the cloakroom to wash her hands before lunch.

As she was walking back across to the Lunch Room, Helen appeared again, in her petal-cut dress—the hem of the skirt echoed the notching of the neckline.

"I left the copy you asked for in the typing room, Mrs Driver."

"Yes, thanks," said Helen. Dismissive. "Oh, is that where we put you for your lunch, all on your own?" As if much went on in her house that Helen never knew about, as very likely it did.

"Why don't you come and have lunch with me?" said Helen. "For a change. Madge was coming over but she's cried off. Come on, I hate eating alone."

There was a lot of well-cooked solid food. Sabia, now, didn't eat very much. She was concentrating on Helen Driver.

They had wine, a very good white, and then a red that was of quality but which Sabia found too heavy.

Helen talked to Sabia. This was unlike what generally seemed to happen, all those views of compulsively chattering women, and old glassy Frederick maundering on in a pontifical way, as Helen sat cat-like, lazy-lidded, listening.

"How do you pronounce your first name, Miss Cobb?"

People seldom asked this, they made their own decisions. Sabia had been called, variously, Sabb-yah, *Saarb*-ya, Sub-*bee*-ah, and Sa-buyer.

She told Helen how she herself pronounced her first name.

"It's unusual," said Helen. "How did it come about?"

"I don't know," said Sabia.

"Really? Don't you?" Helen, quizzical, not believing her, waiting an instant to see if she would change her mind and own up, then saying, "Freddie would love your name. I must tell him. I mean Frederick Laudelay. Did you know he was a poet?"

"I'm afraid I didn't."

"Oh yes. Out of fashion now, poor old thing. Hasn't published anything for years. He probably never will now. He's very bitter about it, but pretends not to be, which isn't good for him. That poem you kindly typed out—that was by one of Frederick's former lovers. He found it by chance in the library, but the book's Edmund's, and he refused to let Freddie have it. Edmund isn't mean, of course. Just unrealistic sometimes. Sometimes one must give things up. Don't you find that's so?"

Sabia looked straight into Helen's eyes. They had altered their colour and were now grey. Just as her hair altered, a fair blonde in electric light, gold in the sun, almost bronze in shadow. A metamorphosing woman, Helen.

"I've only really talked to Mr Driver once, when he gave me the job."

"Oh, did I mean Edmund?" said Helen, rather confusingly. She looked quizzical again. "But you've talked more often than that, surely. He always wants to fuss with the typescript."

Sabia quickened slightly, as she had when Helen said her husband was "unrealistic." She didn't like him? No, she did not. Although she *loved* him, was *proud* of owing him. This was often the case.

"No, he seems quite happy with this book."

"Does he? Well, that's good." Helen lit a cigarette. Then pushed the box across to Sabia. "Help yourself. May I call you Sabia?"

"Please."

Helen said, "What do you think of Edmund's books?"

"I've only read one. I thought that very fine."

"Yes. Which one?"

"*The Last of Us.*"

"Yes," said Helen again. "Would you like to read more?"

"Oh, yes," said Sabia, looking calmly inspired. "I intend to."

"He's got several spare copies of most of them. Why don't you ask him? The bookshops charge far too much and libraries are hopeless."

"I will, if you think that would be all right."

"He'll soon tell you if it isn't," Helen said. "Frankly, he can't stand Freddie. He lets me have him to visit, but on tolerance only. I feel sorry for Freddie. You remember what I said about his lover? A man, of course. Freddie's a pansy. Which I suppose is all right when you're young and beautiful, but can be rather dire when you're over sixty, as Freddie now is."

Sabia found that now she was watching Helen. That was, *watching.*

Helen said, "I can never understand it, myself. Oh, I have nothing against it, not like Edmund, providing they're discreet. But to desire one of your own kind. It's beyond me."

Sabia said, quietly, "I remember a man once saying that a woman should find it easier to understand how one man might have feelings for another man, since women themselves fall in love with men."

"Oh. That's rather clever. But not true. *I* don't understand at all."

Sabia thought: Does this mean your feelings for men are also false? Or does all this mean you sense from me something, and are really saying: I can't understand a man fancying a man, let alone a woman fancying a woman?

Sabia said, "Well, you're very nice to him."

"To Freddie or to Edmund?"

"I meant Mr Laudelay."

"Yes. I said, I feel sorry for him. But I don't feel sorry for Edmund at all. Does this mean I'm not nice to *him*? Do you think that?"

Sabia felt her eyes widen, the deer in the presence of the predator.

She said, "Mrs Driver—"

"Helen. Try that."

"Thank you. Helen, I really can't know anything about how you are with Mr Driver."

"But you seem to know so much. Oh yes, my dear Sabia. I've seen you. As you go by all the doors. Glancing, looking in, like a lovely little lost waif astray in the forest, and every one of our rooms becomes a lighted cot, attracting your wondering eyes."

She is dangerous, Sabia thought, *just as I suspected.*

But what is she really saying? Keep off—come in?

"It's a very beautiful house, Mrs Driver—"

"Helen."

"And I can't help admiring it. Or your elegant friends. Or you. But I hadn't realized I was staring, or you thought I was impertinent in my interest, and I apologize. I'll try in future not to look at anything."

Helen laughed. A platinum voice, clean and modern.

"Oh dear. Will you arrive in blinkers?"

"If necessary. I need the work. I don't want to offend you. You've been kindness itself."

"Have I? Surely not. Relegating you to that little room for your lonely little lunches, never even speaking to you until to-day." Helen paused. She drank off her glass of Vichy water, and stubbed out her cigarette in an aquamarine ashtray.

"We must do this again."

Sabia got up.

Helen got up. They were nearly the same height, across the breadth of the table. Though not quite the same build, Sabia's figure was a little fuller.

Helen said, "What did you think of the poem?"

"The—oh. I'm sorry. I hardly took it in. I'm afraid I'm like that when I type. It seems to use another part of my mind. It isn't like reading, for me."

"I see. But did you notice the name?"

Sabia waited. She said, "You mean the man addressed in the poem, Edmund?"

"The fact that it's the same name as my husband's," Helen explained carefully.

Sabia recoiled. Suddenly she had seen what was going on. It was quite funny, in a disgusting and awkward way.

"Well, yes. Is that significant?" asked Sabia, balancing on this new inrushing tide.

"I don't know," said Helen, "is it?"

"I suppose," said Sabia, reasonable, "it's an old name. Mediaeval, perhaps."

"It goes back at least to the tenth century," said Helen coldly.

The parlourmaid came in. "The car's been brought round, madam."

"Oh fuck," said Helen.

No one batted an eyelash. She walked straight out, only saying to the maid in passing, "Tell him he needn't wait, I'll drive myself."

Helen Driver thought, so much was now obvious, that Sabia had wormed her way into the house because of Edmund.

It was Edmund Sabia was interested in, *inclined* to. And any of her subsidiary interests, in the furniture, the friends, or the wife, were dependent on her main theme. Which was that of a spare woman in rabid pursuit of another woman's husband.

Sabia was both cunning and naïve, as she herself had always known. Now she had been naïve, of course.

She could see it plainly enough, since Helen had virtually spelled it out. (Probably the poem was a ruse.)

Helen perhaps even *had* recalled meeting Sabia at the party in Wootton Street. That then had been Sabia's ploy, pretending to know Helen, in order to ingratiate herself and so approach her true goal. (Did Helen also recollect the voiceless telephone caller?)

Failed in first attempts, the wretched little bitch (Sabia) had somehow got some crony or still-malleable ex-swain (Marcus, Conranne) to put her case as a needy typist to Edmund himself.

Now here she was. And Helen had finally called her in, to show her her game was known, to warn her, frighten her. If such a little monster (Sabia) were capable of being warned or frightened, let alone forbidden.

Sabia considered how she came here always alluringly well-dressed and deliriously groomed. Sabia thought about how she always behaved towards Edmund. Her intent displays of admiration, and shyness. Her flirting eyes. Even that meeting on the drive, on Thursday—had Helen somehow glimpsed it from an upstairs window?—must have seemed quite coquettish.

In order to obtain Helen's proximity, Sabia had played up to Driver as a matter of course, and now Helen took the wrong play for earnest.

What else would she have said, if a servant hadn't walked in and the car been ready?

In other circumstances, it might have been an opening for Sabia's real suit. "But Helen, I don't want *him*—I want *you*—" But there too a barrier had already been firmly placed, of obscuration if not utter veto. Helen couldn't "understand" male mutual desire. And this might well mean (usually it did), to Helen, a woman who liked women was, as most of English society thought, an outcaste, whose persona ranged from the hysterically ludicrous, to the status of seventeenth century witch—for whom burning was too good.

So again Sabia, what now, what now?

If I had any sense I'd run. Make some excuse perhaps, a sick relative, or a chance-of-a-lifetime trip somewhere. Anything. Just get out.

Certainly, she didn't care about finishing his bloody book.

And the money had been all right, and the lunches useful—but cash and food could be gained elsewhere. She had managed adequately up until now.

But Helen.

Yes, that was the problem.

This itch now, not only of lust, but of ethical frustration.

Then again, one knew the dangers of casting oneself at an unwilling target.

However, not every possibility had yet been tried.

May

"Yes."

"Mrs Driver—May I explain? I'm so *sorry* I wasn't there last week. A friend of mine was taken ill very suddenly. She doesn't have anyone—so I've sort of had to step into the breach. I didn't have the chance to telephone you before—my friend isn't on the telephone. But I'm at home now."

A silence.

Helen said, "I see."

Sabia thought: She really believed she'd got rid of me. Is that why she agreed to take this call? Couldn't believe it could be me?

Then:

"Edmund is very angry, you know," said Helen, icy, remote.

"I'm sure Mr Driver's furious. And I'd understand if he didn't want me to come back. I feel very bad about this, even though it wasn't my fault exactly."

"A whole week," said Helen.

"Yes. But Mr Driver may have seen, I've only a small section of the manuscript left to type. I could do that in one or two days, if I came up a little earlier, and left a little later. I can work right through—lunch isn't necessary."

"My God. How quick you are, aren't you," said Helen, with the lightest contempt.

"Yes, I'm very quick, Mrs Driver. And under the circumstances, I shall of course want to reduce my fee."

Helen said, "You'd better wait. I'll go and ask him what he wants you to do."

Sabia waited. They made her do this quite a while.

Then the voice, when it came on, was no longer Helen's, but again the maid's. The maid told Sabia to come in tomorrow; the taxi would be at her flat at around nine-fifteen, the usual time.

Sabia wore a dark grey dress and coat, at odds with the season, which rampaged in all sparkling directions through Regents Park and over the sacred hills and woods of St Giles Grove.

Her face was powdered pale, the bright mouth like a bright beacon. She looked tired, delightful, young.

Luck was in (or out—it would depend). Helen was breakfasting still, alone in the almond-pink and scarlet morning-room, and through the open French windows came a squeak of birds and the scent of roses.

Helen wore a dressing-gown of greyish satin. She was already bathed and exquisitely made up.

"Sit down," said Helen.

Sabia took one of the striped chairs.

Helen was pouring herself more coffee, offering none.

"I asked to see you, because I wanted to thank you," Sabia said.

"Don't bother."

"I must. I really do feel bad about letting your husband down."

"Oh."

Sabia thought: What she's really saying is: I thought you'd had the sense to stay away. What do you want now, you little horror?

And I am saying: He is nothing to me. Look into and through me and see.

"Well," said Helen.

Sabia lowered her eyes. She said, "May I confide something to you Mrs Driver?" Mrs Driver (no correction back to Helen now, it seemed) gazed out of her windows.

Is she truly so indifferent? So untroubled… If she were, would she have run up her colours last week?

"My friend," said Sabia, with a little proper difficulty, "her name is Albertine… I've known her years. What happened was—pretty awful. She wasn't ill, exactly. I'm afraid I lied about that. She got hold of some pills. She took an overdose."

Helen after all glanced at Sabia. Not herself looking up, Sabia felt the white flash of that face upon her, the visiting moon.

"It was a failed love-affair," admitted Sabia, solemnly.

"That happens." Perhaps to reinforce earlier matters, Helen added, "Men let women down."

"I expect they do," said Sabia. "But Albertine wasn't let down by a man. Her lover was another woman."

The silence then—went on. And eventually Sabia looked up, and Helen was still staring at her, her lips slightly parted, her eyes gleaming—with what? Surprise? Derision?

Sabia said, "I've found all this rather unbearable. I'm sorry I didn't telephone sooner, but I wasn't in a fit state myself, really. I was having to look after her, and in a way, I couldn't think what on earth to say to you, let alone your husband. I hate lying," said Sabia, all desperation. "And yet, to tell you the truth—that I have that sort of friend—"

Helen was raising her eyebrows, her expression changing. For a moment she looked amused. Then sombre.

"Well," she said, "*I* have a friend like that, too, don't I. Frederick. But I begin to comprehend how trying all this was for you."

Sabia lowered her eyes again.

To pretend her heart was racing with nerves was now unneedful. It was. These were normally crucial moments.

She sat dumb, letting Helen speculate. Sabia dared say nothing else. But she had left the entry point she intended, the chance. To go further would be stupid.

When she once more looked up, Helen had, once more, turned away.

Not Helen, but Helen's hands, seemed a little uneasy. They fluttered here and there, to the cigarette box, the coffee-pot, the revers of her dressing-gown. *She,* the rest of her, seemed what Sabia had hoped for—thoughtful. But thought might lead anywhere, of course.

(Then again, Sabia was practiced. She had played part of her hand, yet knew that allegations based on such a slender thread as Albertine would be simple enough, usually, to evade. How terrible it was, however, Sabia thought, with a strange sudden shock of overview, always to be aware the object of love might, at any moment, become the instigator of your doom.)

"Well, Sabia, don't worry about this. Let's put it behind us. In which case, maybe you should go along now. I'm sure your type-writing machine has been missing you."

A tiny imp leapt in Sabia's brain. People who spoke to her like this always caused the imp to leap. But that was about all the imp could do.

Love though, does not always forgive. *Besides, I'm not in love with her.* In fact, I don't even like her much.

It's only *her.* That turn of her head, for example, what she's do-ing now. The altering colour on her hair. And oh, her skin.

She isn't going to take me up on what I've shown and offered. Her reaction would have been something quite other, if she were at all interested. (Like the others who have been.) Or interested in me, or the chance I've placed there on her plate, with the toast crumbs and the smears of butter.

Sabia left the morning-room and went along to the Typewriting Room. The sight of the machine and piles of manuscript, both to do and completed, appalled her. What was she still doing here? Of course, not to be suspected, she must now affect the agreed end. Hurry up and finish then. And after that be off, shaking away the dust of her shoes upon the groves of St Giles.

Sabia thought about Albertine as she typed. She had used Albertine so often before, that this being had become almost real. What a life she'd led too!

Sometimes Albertine (as recounted to Sabia's women) was en-tangled with another woman who drove her mad. Sometimes she was herself desperately obsessed with a woman. Now and then she attempted suicide—never successfully, of course. Even in her fictive state, Sabia found her too handy, ethically to be able to see her off.

By raising up the spirit of Albertine, a Lesbian, in conversa-tions, Sabia had now and then brought her own affairs to fruitful concordance. As in the reply, "Oh, the poor woman. Yes, Sabia, I see, I see. Well, you know, these things between women hap-pen, don't they? Even I…" etc:—etc: Or, the dialogue, spurred by Albertine, might take a nastier turn, always the risk: "Good

God—you associate with this person?" And once or twice, even: "Does this mean, Sabia, that you yourself—?" At which, naturally, a prompt denial had to be made. Sabia? Heavens, no. She too had been alarmed to discover Albertine's true nature. Indeed, the friendship would have to be curtailed. But one felt so dreadfully sorry for her, the wretched outcaste, totally beyond one's mental grasp, condemned and damned to her peculiar life.

Sabia realized she had mistyped a line.

This rarely happened.

It didn't disturb her too much. She ripped out the paper and threw it in the basket.

Helen hadn't responded, and would not.

Sabia put a new sheet of paper in the machine, and returned to her automaton-like task.

A week passed. Sabia was still typing at the house in Aspersedge Road.

Something irritating had happened. After all this while, the mostly unseen Edmund had suddenly appeared in the Typing Room during Sabia's occupancy, late one evening, about six, his hands full of paper.

"Miss Cobb—I'm glad I caught you. Look, you'll think me diabolical—but could you possibly add these two chapters in? And this. I realize it will mean some re-typing…but you did say you wouldn't mind it. I've been too lax with myself, and quite frankly the other day I had to face up to it. The book needs those extra elements. Am I asking too much?"

Sabia smiled, she was aware, rather unwillingly.

"Yes, of course, that's quite all right. It's what you're paying me to do, Mr Driver."

There were two long chapters. And three more now had to have revisions, which would mean typing them completely all over again. Sabia had an image of being trapped here forever as this man continually re-vamped his work. No wonder Agatha fell prey to prolonged colds.

"But, one thing, Mr Driver—your original typist—isn't she well again by now, and won't she—"

"Agatha? God preserve me from Agatha. No, Miss Cobb, I've been meaning to speak to you, in fact. Agatha has—I've been rather unkind and put her out to grass."

"Really."

"I don't mean to be a beast, but when I think what I've suffered with her, and her purple pencil, over the years. But you are perfect."

She must respond. The air grew heavy with the requirement. "Thank you, Mr Driver."

He was sitting on the corner of the table by then, looking at her. Charming her, determined to have his way.

"Try Edmund," he said. As his wife had done. "And may I call you Sabia?" He said it the same way Sabia herself did. Helen must have told him. And what else?

Sabia felt a strong if momentary wave of fear. She didn't know what to do, and had a sense of being—literally—*caught.* This was idiotic. If she didn't want to say No directly, then she could merely abscond, as she had before, and this time for good.

During the days since her return, she had seen nothing of Helen at all. Helen had been out all day, at her dressmakers, buying a hat, lunching with friends. (For the pieces of servant-talk still dropped around Sabia.)

Now Edmund Driver, holding her eyes with his dark blue ones, that had a look of summer thunder, angry behind the blaze of evening, put an envelope on the pile of new manuscript.

"It's a bribe," he said. "Please take it."

"That isn't-"

"Yes it is. I'm difficult, and I know it. To please me?"

She was so accustomed to it, with him, and with others, she Gave In, lowering her gaze. Probably he thought she blushed, but it was only the westering sun touching her face.

After he had gone, she reviewed why she had to stay.

Helen had deduced there was something "odd" about Sabia—the sort of oddity that meant Sabia wouldn't be trying to scale the walls of Edmund. And so Helen felt free to resume her external life. But also, Helen could not be sure Sabia was anything more than a young woman with her earning to make—unless, of course, Sabia, having failed to inveigle Helen, immediately abandoned such a lucrative job.

I will give it another week. That should make it safe, see all these revisions done for him, and anything else he dreams up. On this occasion, when I leave, I will take my typewriter home with me. Smuggle it out, if I must, disguised as a baby.

And if he still wants to go on after that, I'll say I have to go abroad. A cousin's marriage. Something.

During the remainder of the week, Helen was often in the house again. She was always poised, like an actress on a stage, inside the "lighted cots" of her rooms—the drawing room with yellow curtains, the striped morning-room and plush dining room. Once there was a scattered, chattery garden party out on the lawns, the noises of whose tea cups and female laughters splashed over into the Typing Room and clashed with the rhythm of the typewriter.

Coming out that evening, at half past six (she had frequently stayed later, striving to finish, like a person in the Greek Hell, her apparently unfinishable chore—Edmund had added yet another stack of handwritten pages) Sabia met a young woman in a costly, short-sleeved dress and flattened crescent-moon of a hat, weeping into her gloves.

"Oh," said the young woman, as if meeting Sabia were the last straw. Probably it was. She fled away along the hall, and then Frederick Laudelay emerged down the staircase, with half his hand closed into a book.

"Good evening," said Frederick. "*You* must be Sabia Cobb." His glasses glowed, hiding his weak old eyes. "That was Sissy Fairsmith. I mean Niobe-All-Tears."

Sabia nodded.

"She is upset," said Frederick.

Sabia made a move toward the distant door.

"Helen," said Frederick, removing his hand from the book, and looking at it in surprise, as if he had just retrieved it from a lion's jaws, "she can be so very bitchy."

Sabia stood there, erecting a porcelain face at him.

"She accused Sissy of making up to Edmund. Sissy's always had a thing for him of course."

He moved slightly and the light left his glasses. She saw plainly he was old and wilting and cindery, and unusually malevolent.

"It's not as if," said Frederick, "Helen cares. A soulless woman, really. I like your name, Sabia," he said, fixing his magnified eyes on her. "Is *that* how you say it?"

"Yes."

"You're a foreigner, aren't you," said Frederick, leering now with unrewarding teeth.

"Excuse me, Mr Laudelay, I must go and get my taxi."

Not disappointed a moment, he refused to be put off.

"And what do you think of Edmund then, Sabia?"

She said nothing, already moving away.

"He has such a way with women," said Frederick Laudelay. "And I'd say you were rather his type."

"Goodnight," called Sabia from miles off, obviously not hearing what he said.

When she reached the front door, she thought: *I'll come in to-morrow, and that's the end of all this.*

She was glad to see the taxi was waiting for her. Since her return, it was often late (and in the morning too early, as if maliciously misdirected.) She had been afraid the taxi would not be there and Frederick would come crawling after her along the drive.

As she was carried homewards, she thought of the heroine in *The Last of Us*, and of the half-glimpsed heroine of the book still being typed. Dark-haired, unboyish. So unlike fair, slender Helen of Troy.

It was hot for May, and getting indoors, Sabia pushed up her windows. There was nothing much to eat. She found a bottle of wine and opened it, and sat in the window seat.

A reddish-golden heat-light hung down on the street below, and through the folds of it she saw another taxi pulling round and stopping, and then Edmund Driver getting out.

Sabia rose and stepped back from the window.

She stood in the middle of the room, motionless, until she heard the sound of the bell.

It would be best not to answer. That was what would be best. Pretending not to be in. Or, if he had seen her *come* in, pretending to be in the bath, or asleep. Or deaf. The bell rang, and rang.

Sabia went to the door, not knowing why she must, really, so much pretense perhaps, play-acting, in the end you just couldn't any more decide which role you had taken on.

The man who stood there was tall and dark but not Edmund Driver, although he did bear a slight resemblance to him.

"Oh—I'm sorry. I must have the wrong flat. Mr Dickens—"

"One floor up," said Sabia.

The next day was Saturday. Only half a day. The last. The last of us.

As Sabia was typing the final page, Edmund Driver walked into the room. His hands were empty of paper.

Sabia sat straight up like a performing dog.

"Mr Driver. I was coming up to see you before I left."

"And you are. Seeing me, I mean. Also, my name is Edmund. For a wonderful typist you do have an awfully bad memory."

Sabia did not lower her eyes. She looked directly into his face. And she thought: Now suddenly I see, the women in his books—no, they're not remotely like me—they are the female physical counterparts of *him*—of Edmund Driver—his anima in written form.

"Everything is done now, Mr Driver. Including the last batch of changes, which is good, because this morning I received a letter from my cousin. She has a house in the south of Italy—she wants me to go over, some family thing. But I do want to. And I really can't say no, any way, you see."

Edmund Driver looked at her.

Sabia found she must say something more.

"I've enjoyed working on your book so much. Edmund. And your wife has been very kind. And I regret letting you down that week when—when my friend was taken ill."

"Stop lying," he said. "It won't work."

Sabia sat there. She said, "I beg your pardon?"

"I can tell," he said. "After all, that's my trade. Think about it, Sabia. I study and observe people. I know you're lying. Do you even have a sick friend, let alone a cousin in Italy?"

She knew better than to bristle with affront. She stayed still and unspeaking, letting him play out his song.

He sat down on a chair across the room. Not once did he take his eyes off her, as if she might vanish in a puff of smoke if he did.

"I realize this is my fault, Sabia. I've expected too much and been a damned nuisance. Wanting to change this, that, and then change it again. But perhaps you could see the improvement? I hope so."

She said flatly, "I don't really read what I'm typing when I type. It's a different process."

"Yes, Helen told me something like that."

Oh, they really had discussed her then. What *else* had Helen said?

Driver said, "If you'll consent to stay on, do a bit more for me, I'll pay double. Will that be any use?" Sabia kept *very* still. "Well," he said, "a bit more than double, then."

"No, Mr Driver. It isn't that."

"Edmund. And of course," he said, "you must have more time off, more time to yourself. Take a holiday. But not for a day or so, perhaps."

She thought, ridiculously: *He isn't at all like the man who got out of the taxi.* And then: *Is that man upstairs called Charles Dickens?*

But then she pulled herself together, seeing how her brain was trying to escape in the only way it could, over its own wooded hills, and leave her witless to deal with this.

"Perhaps," Sabia said, "we can come to some arrangement. But I do need time off."

"Of course you do. You've been working like a slave, for God's sake. And I am impossible, and a monster not to have seen."

The near noon light came in from the garden, slimly, Mayishly green today, although May, like March and April, was sliding off into the past. It would be June tomorrow, summer. Thick jade leaves and lingering blue-white mornings, and the longest day when, as late as eleven o'clock, sometimes even at midnight, faint rifts and traces of light still lingered in the dark.

She could see her now. The woman behind Driver's immaculately masculine face. The woman smiled at Sabia, courting her with indomitable and demanding eyes.

Sabia felt shaken. It was because she had tried to resist the blast, had not merely, comfortably, given in to it. Sway, bend, bow, don't break. That was the advice you gave a young tree. Till now.

She thought: I will have to escape. Perhaps I will have to move to another flat. All right, I shall move. That's easy.

She thought: *What has Helen said about me?*

Edmund Driver said, "But you've finished everything? That's marvelous. Look, why don't you come and have some lunch. I'm having it on the terrace. Beautiful weather. Come on, and we'll sort out a new arrangement.

Sway and bow. Give in, quick!

"Thank you, " she said.

She sounded cold and resistant

But he laughed, probably at the uselessness of any protest, and they walked out of the single French door, past the secluding pine, into the luxuriant vistas of the garden.

JUNE

London burned in the green flame of June.

Sabia and Edmund walked by the Serpentine.

She vaguely thought: How did this happen? How am I here?

But there was too much noise—the cries of children, the traffic from the roads, the loud glitter and breakage of sun on water and the roar of leaves at a sudden gust of fiery air.

In the tea-shop, they made him coffee. So, thought Sabia, astonished, have I.

"Would you like strawberries?" he asked. "Yes, you would."

She had strawberries.

Afterwards they strolled along the smoking pavements. Paused in some other place of trees.

"I'd better be getting back," he said.

"Yes."

"Wish I didn't have to, but there's this bloody awful dinner we're going to. Helen's idea."

"Yes."

"You look sad. Is that because I have to leave you now?"

No, Sabia said, it's because I have left me already. She didn't say this aloud.

She smiled at him, and said, "What do you think?"

"I think you've been tremendously good about all of this. And I am very sorry. You must be one of the nicest girls on earth."

"You make me sound cheap," she heard herself say. "And as if you're tired of me."

"No—I didn't mean anything like that. My God, you know I didn't. Don't you, Sabia?"

"Yes."

"Oh hell, I've upset you. I'd do anything not to."

"No, I'm not upset."

"Monday," he said. "Can I see you then? I can't till then."

"What do you think?" she said again.

"I think I must kiss you. At once."

And there in the shadow of the tree, the flare of sunny lawns far off, another country, and this one hidden, his mouth on hers. How decorous he was, still. She had been kissed once or twice, importunately, by men, crushed and penetrated by their mouths. Edmund didn't do this. Even so, even so, he *kissed*.

"I wish I was younger," he said.

"Then I'd be too young."

"I'd have waited for you."

"But you didn't."

"I hadn't met you then."

"Are you sure?" she asked.

"Christ, Sabia. Yes I'm sure."

Back on the terra firma of cement, he found her a taxi, and put her into it, the fare already accommodated.

Driving away, she thought: *Well then.* As if something had been achieved, like finishing typing something or dusting the flat. Or leaving school. Except she hadn't left anywhere or anything. It wasn't "done." It was still there, all about her.

She would dream of him tonight. She always did, now. Curious dreams in which he was striding along in half darkness and she was running after him, but only because she wished to get past. Or else they were riding on a bus, and it was out of control, and no one—the dream bus was always full of people—no one at all minded the mad career or anticipated the crash. No, not even Sabia.

When they'd had lunch on the terrace, that May Saturday, above the garden in St Giles Grove, the talk between them had been rather stilted, or rather, organized. And Sabia was reminded of that stage-husband-and-wife exchange between Edmund and Helen, which she had first heard when she arrived there.

Now it was stage-employer-and-servant.

But no, not really. It was more the stage-king who noticed the stage-commoner, singled her out—before the orchestra had quite launched into its best tunes.

She considered afterwards that perhaps she had been prepared to say and promise anything, since she was intending to escape so soon, and so thoroughly, with the hostage, her typewriter.

Edmund swiftly arranged an extravagant fee for her continued services as his typist. He had reassured her that really, now, the typing of that particular novel was concluded. He hoped, when she finally read it, she would see that it had benefited from his extra care, and her patience. As if it had been a joint venture. As if she hadn't merely typed the manuscript. Then he said to look at the laburnum beginning to come alive, wasn't it glorious, and exotic in its own way. And Helen didn't like it, never had. Helen liked more space in a garden. She was always prepared to chop something down, and they had argued over that, especially over her attempts to "open the views" in Buckinghamshire—great oaks which had stood for hundreds of years. But they did anyway. Argue, he meant.

No one was about. The maids had seen to the food, a hot-weather lunch with salad and cold meats and icy Hock, then left them to it. To what?

"I expect you regret not having a garden," he said, "now summer's coming. Or don't you care about gardens?"

"I like them," she said. "Other people's."

"You're lazy," he said. "I suspected as much. Industrious women always are, in every other area but the one in which they excel."

"You're saying a woman will only really do what comes easily to her."

"Am I? Yes, probably. Is it true? You tell me."

"I expect so."

He said, "Helen is a genius at running a house, or a party, that sort of thing. This includes how she herself looks, and what she says. She can wind anyone round her wrist and wear him for the evening or the weekend." He stopped there, having given Sabia the list of what Helen could do easily and well and therefore did, and leaving unsaid and gargantuan all those other things which (by one's own inference) one must assume she couldn't, didn't and wouldn't.

And Sabia thought: Yes. Helen has told him that I am Not As Other Women. And he's thought: I don't believe that. Or, if she is, this young woman will be different with me.

That was it, wasn't it?

Helen now believed Sabia to be quite safe, and decidedly to be avoided. And Edmund believed Sabia either nothing of the sort, or a challenge to his maleness. Now either way he must do more than Charm, he must Conquer.

Nothing like this had ever happened to her before. Not exactly like this. Somehow, it had been eluded.

It didn't matter, Sabia thought rigidly, sipping the cold Hock. Soon I'll be gone.

They had also discussed her Holiday. She must take at least a week off, even though he had been preparing a collection of short stories all this while, and would be enormously pleased if Sabia would, after her week of peace, come back and type them. Of course, he would pay her during the Holiday as well, as if she were still coming in. Sabia said he would not need to do this. Edmund said he would need to do this.

He said that Helen had gone up to Buckinghamshire for the weekend—to fell more oaks? He himself wasn't going. He had to meet someone from Emblem on Sunday, but really anyway, this weekend they'd invited all the most bloody boring people in the world (friends of Helen), including the brainless Cicily Fairsmith and Laudelay, whom he simply couldn't stand.

"I don't mind what he is," Edmund said, watching a brand-new butterfly flicker through his laburnum tree like a fleeting glance. "It's his eternal parasitic self-pity that I loathe."

Then Edmund looked away from the butterfly, and Helen and the weekend, and his loathing, and said, "What I'd like, Sabia, this evening, is to meet you and take you to dinner somewhere."

"That isn't necessary," said Sabia.

"No, perhaps not. Or only necessary to me. Will you?"

She turned and looked at him again.

The light was harsh along one side of his face, showing every crease and crack, scarring him forty years of age and more. The other side of his face, more dimly lit, was nineteen.

His eyes were very beautiful. Maybe the most beautiful eyes Sabia had ever seen in either sex. Glimpsing, like the butterfly, the Anima looking out at her.

She had to make out she was susceptible, but not too much so. After all, the excuse stood ready to hand.

"Mr Driver—Edmund—you are married."

"And you're not the kind that goes about with married men."

"No I'm not."

"But, with men at all?"

This habit of directness, a writer's wicked and dangerous gambit. How dare he.

But he had cornered her, had he not?

"What do you mean, Mr Driver?"

"Edmund. What I mean is, are you repelled by men?"

"Sometimes."

"I don't mean that, Sabia."

"Then no, of course not."

"No, I didn't think you were that type. My wife got the impression that you didn't take to men, much. But I think she was trying to put me off. Something she's usually keen to do."

"I told her about a friend of mine," said Sabia firmly, "and obviously I shouldn't have done so. My friend is not me."

"Good."

"However, Mr Driver, I do think we should end this conversation now. Yes, I will type up your work. But no, I don't want to go to dinner with you."

"Although you aren't repelled by men."

"If you were free it would be different."

"Free," he said. "As in Free of Chains."

"If you want to put it like that."

"I'll arrive by taxi to fetch you," he said. "Seven o'clock?"

"No."

"Seven-thirty then."

What was she to do? (He was on his set course, and would take no notice of denials from the one she must pretend to be.) Should she rush home and lock herself in her flat—even run away to some acquaintance, begging for shelter? (Who, precisely?) Sabia recalled how, seeing the man she'd taken for Edmund emerge from the taxi, she had finally opened her door.

If she managed to refuse him, whatever the perfect excuse of his marriage, he would begin to think like Helen, because naturally he had taken women, as he wanted them, often, often. He could always do it. He could do it now. Unless Sabia was—and he knew she was not, for she was not that "type," he had seen how she looked at him—an outcaste witch who must be burned or drowned.

"All right," she said.

Sabia knew she was not sensibly giving in. No longer bending, bowing. No, now she broke. She snapped in half, and one piece of her fell away. She saw it falling, as if from a high window.

She took the typewriter home with her quite openly. She told him she had promised a friend (not Albertine) she would type up some letters. She would, of course, do this at her flat.

Then, when she was indoors, Sabia wondered if she should just go out and walk about the city until nine o'clock say, or ten. Surely, he wouldn't hang about that long, lying in wait by the front door.

But all the while she played with this fantasy of avoidance, Sabia was taking a bath, dressing herself in an evening frock, powdering her face and colouring her lips, brushing her hair.

She stood looking at herself critically in a long mirror. The long, low-backed dress of silky green reminded her a moment of Helen's dress, that night at Wootton Street. But the dresses weren't really alike. Helen's of course, had cost a lot of money.

They would dine together. Then what? He would expect to sleep with her. That was inevitable, if she allowed herself this first leap from grace. Then, again, she would refuse. Her grounds were much safer here. She would see him—how could she resist—but nothing else. To give more was beyond her. Then there might come to be a row, and in the end he would tire of her.

Sabia was certain not many had put him off. Was he so predatory and unscrupulous?

Sabia caught herself thinking this: That it would be pleasant enough to go somewhere opulent on this summer night, escorted by a well-off, handsome and attentive man. It would be delightful to fit, for once, into the uneasy scheme of life. For even that evil sorceress, who tried to steal another woman's husband, was not ultimately unforgivable, by a male world.

And Sabia sank her head in shame and despair. And put on her silky jacket and high-heels, and sat smoking a cigarette waiting for the bell to ring.

There was an anecdote in his book, the one she had just typed for him. Sabia lied when she told people she couldn't read what she typed as she typed, a convenient lie, since it made her unanswerable to their delusions, or some of them. Sometimes—quite often—she could and did read the text before her. Only boredom and aversion clouded it from sight. The substance of Edmund Driver's novel had been lost on Sabia accordingly. But certain passages stood out like burning flambeaux.

One of these was the episode of the Doll.

It was recounted very tidily, almost as a short story inside the bulk of the book. No doubt it had a bearing on later sections of the novel, but missing so much and so much, Sabia had found no connection.

A character, his name had been William, met a woman at a dance and found her ravishingly beautiful. In the facile way of such stories, this vision consented at once to William's courtship, and indeed, the next morning he and she were breakfasting together in a room of a lavish hotel. Thus, across the eggs and coffee, he saw the mirage of the night was gone. Unbathed, her hair a mess, make-up-less and wrapped in a sheet, he found her reprehensible and actually revolting. William's response to the shock was romantic and masculine. Having evaded his Nemesis, and flying homeward on the train, he formulated the idea that the woman he had woken up in bed with had no longer been the woman of the night before. What he had first met had been a *doll* (as in the ballet, *Coppélia*), formed in the woman's idealized image, and sent out to lure men in her stead.

This tale of an unmasked Cinderella presided over Sabia's last cigarette.

Where Edmund took her was discreet—it would be essential that no one meet them there who knew him with Helen. But he was practiced. The restaurant gave all that away, as future venues would do also, lost in its glamorous mellow haze of candlelight.

She danced with him on the little space of floor. He said the floor was rotten, too polished. The irony of that missed him, this cunning user of words.

Afterwards, going home to her flat in another taxi, he took her hand, the first physical intimacy, everything else had been only phrases, looks.

"I want to come in with you, Sabia. To talk. I promise, nothing else. Will you trust me?"

"No," she said. But he gave a low laugh. And undoing and pulling back the hand of her glove, he kissed her palm.

She thought: He expects solely flirtation from me now, so any protest I make will be useless.

Sabia was light-headed, from the hot, tindery London darkness, from the small amount of wine she had drunk, from the terrible, even horrible, silliness of this interesting adventure.

She had no idea how to keep him out now, of her flat, her life.

But when they were standing outside her door, he took both her hands and looked into her face. "Poor angel. You really are a sweet girl. You do know I'll behave myself, don't you?"

And, as always now, she saw the Woman behind his eyes, the Woman saying to her, "You *really* know, my dear, the moment we get inside the room, I shall throw you to the earth and spring upon you." But irritably Sabia thought: *Oh, the hell with it all. Let him then.* And pushed open her door.

However, Edmund did not insist on anything. Once inside he simply walked about her sitting-room, staring at her pictures and picking up her books, apparently puzzled that she had an existence beyond him. He drank the coffee she made and told her it was very good, wherever she had got it. Helen never managed to get coffee he really liked. And then he talked for an hour about a play someone he knew had written, and then he said it was "on" and would she like to go and see it with him.

"You know I can't," said Sabia.

Ah, how implausible it now sounded, her denial. She almost laughed herself.

He didn't laugh. He said, "You must. Christ, Sabia, if you knew how miserable I've been all year, until you came along."

"Don't you say this to everyone you woo?" she said.

She savoured the words, and thought, pleased with herself— yes, *pleased*—How much like a Real Woman I sound.

And Edmund said, "I'm no saint. But I'm not a total bastard either. I'm not, Sabia. But you—you just shattered my defenses."

"Did I throw a stone? The first one, perhaps."

He smiled. "And that little sharpness only disarms me more."

Then he crossed the room—they had been decorous in how they sat, so far apart—and he drew her up, and kissed her with the first of his intent and impassioned, sensual yet courteous kisses.

Hanging there backward (it seemed to her) over his arm like a spent garment, focussed solely on the mouth moving upon hers, Sabia was indifferent, not even afraid, not even ready to fight, let alone pretend anymore. Yet her heart escalated, if only from smotheration, she clung to him, if only to keep her balance.

When he'd gone, she emptied the ashtray and rinsed the coffee cups routinely, took off her make-up and cleaned her teeth. Naked, as she preferred, she got into her bed, and lay looking up at the ceiling, hearing London settling to its black early morning half-sleep, like a fretful lion.

Soon it was daylight, and then it was other daylights, days and evenings, and they met for lunches, and walked in the park, and Edmund and she went to see the play. They ate dinner together; sometimes he came up to her flat, and he would kiss and kiss her there, kiss her until she sleepily forgot whom they both were. Until she thought they were an ordinary pair of lovers, chaste, mostly indifferent, she heterosexual and he unmarried.

She couldn't think why this happened. But again, possibly, it was just the make-believe she had always had to perpetuate, viciously catching her up at last.

How do I get out of this? she wondered sluggishly, sometimes when she was with him, often when alone.

I must really do it.

She was like a fly caught in a web, drowsy with the spider's venomous cocktails. Not uncomfortable. Nothing, really. She couldn't be bothered to escape.

And she didn't.

She kept on with it.

And so did he, unflagging, not tired yet of her Moral Objection to gratifying him fully. So she asked herself if, finally, the only course to take would be to give herself up to him sexually.

Then he would possess her, and so, victory won, become inevitably bored, as he must have done so many times before. Unless that particular boredom were only a myth invented in novels, and in all stories ever told or written.

Then, to her utter amazement, Sabia found herself seeking advice, in a clean little partly-hidden clinic, in the matter of contraception, pretending now she was married, and that her spouse had been prevented from claiming her as yet due to strange circumstances of his work, and journeys abroad, and stressing the complete unsuitability of her becoming pregnant at this time. She wore, for this charade, a wedding ring, having long ago bought herself a second-hand one, for other, quite unlike, purposes of illusion. However, the advice and help were duly forthcoming. Sabia went home with Safety in her bag. But naturally, she was still not ready, still not ready yet to face what she would have to.

All this while she hadn't, of course, returned to the house in St Giles Grove. She had foreseen that Edmund would say what he had, that Sabia would, after all, be better typing his manuscripts at her flat (away from Helen and all her works). Sabia had gone along with this, since she must have had no interest in Helen, Edmund being her only reason for hanging on at the house.

In fact, she *hadn't* now any interest in Helen. The idea of Helen filled Sabia with alarmed disgust. Discovering Helen had been the cause—of all *this*.

Meanwhile, he did not give Sabia any work, although he continued to pay her…as his typist.

One evening, Sabia had at last nerved herself to it. She spoke to Edmund, from their embrace.

"This must be unbearable for you. Let me make you happy."

He let her go then, and regarded her for some while. Then he told her again how very sweet she was. Then he suggested they go away. "Let me take you to Italy. That was where you wanted to go before."

His generosity in rewarding hers—as if canceling it (barter)—enraged her.

"No," she said. "Let's just—why not here?"

"Oh, darling," he said. "Every reason. This is your home. And this is London."

He's mad, she thought. Deranged. He is afraid that making love to me in London, even in England, perhaps even anywhere in Britain or her provinces—India, say—will be like having sex together in Helen's drawing-room under the eyes of the servants.

She wanted the sexual act achieved and over with. But it was no use saying that.

She wanted him to be bored and herself abandoned. And must not say that, either.

"Where in Italy?" she asked. She sounded sternly brisk, she thought. Then heard herself over. She had sounded—dazzled— again.

Sabia was turning out of Oxford Street when she bumped, literally, the crowd forcing a collision, into Frederick Laudelay.

"How lovely," said Frederick, maleficently happy. "Sabia! Most fortuitous. Do let me take you to tea at this dainty quaint place I know."

Sabia said she was late for an appointment, and so, must decline.

Frederick would have none of this. (Like Edmund?) Limpetesque, he attached himself to her, taking her arm, walking her along through a succession of less crowded streets, until they were in a square with gardens and some shops.

"Mr Laudelay—I really must get on."

"Just a little tea—do say yes. I'm at a loose end. Been stood up by some bloody editor who promised me lunch and never remembered to come. *That's* how they value me, now," he added bitterly, his eyes moist with self-pity.

"But my—someone is waiting," Sabia said. No one was.

"And who's that?" inquired Frederick, refocusing alertly on her like a rather priestly praying mantis.

Sabia said, "Someone I'm typing for now."

"*Male,* or *female?*" asked Frederick, with two distinct emphases, showing Sabia was snared either way. A female must now apparently imply a Lesbian, a male—Edmund Driver.

She had left Edmund only half an hour ago, refusing a taxi, having some shopping to do. Could Laudelay detect Edmund's expensive smell on her?

"Helen told me," said Frederick, standing with her as if they might never move apart, "you'd fled Aspersedge Road. Whatever happened?"

"I'd finished typing the book."

"Really? I thought one never could, with Edmund. He's always redoing it, like Penelope unpicking her embroidery. Peculiar name isn't it. *Aspersedge*— Oh, the aspersedge is withered from the lake, and no birds sing. Did you find that?" Sabia, disturbed by these weird flights, compressed her lips. "It is a *withered,* dreadful marriage they have. Dreadful. Poor Helen, she has so much to regret. But also, of course, she does nothing to help herself, and really she doesn't deserve any help. A barren, acid woman. A cruel and spiteful woman." He glanced idly at the facade of a shop—a tea-shop—perhaps the very one with which he had threatened Sabia. "Probably they suit each other, she and Edmund. Would you say?"

"They seem all right."

"All right? *Right,* Sabia—they are entirely unright. Come, now."

Sabia said, "I'm sorry, Mr Laudelay, I have to go—"

He looked at her, bleakly. "Lucky you. Somewhere to go *to.*"

She wondered if anyone, *ever,* had been seduced into a moment's fatal pity for him.

She thanked him (for what?) and walked quickly away.

When she glanced back, from the entrance to the tube, there he still stood, brooding and alone, desiccated under heartless sunlight.

"You see, you may have to travel without me. I wish to God it didn't have to be like that. Maybe it won't. If you do, I'll join you in a couple of days at the most."

She looked at the collection of papers and money Edmund had given her—like some dossier—dazed.

"You'll be all right, Sabia, won't you? You said you'd travelled before."

"Yes."

Not like this, she thought.

"It's Helen," he said. "She is being difficult. She wants to go to Nice. She wants to fly to France. I hate flying, all that noise—I'll get out of it somehow, and then I'll come on. And we'll be together, without interruptions, at last."

Sabia smiled, a facial reflex, thinking of the train journey across the edge of Europe. Mountains, lakes, towns, tunnels. And with regular meals in the dining car, with a sleeper. With everything paid for.

But she thought: If I go, I may not ever come back. He doesn't realize—or does he? Better than setting me up in a flat in London, to establish me in a ruinous old house in Tuscany?

He had told her, it was Conranne's house. A villa, with gardens, on a hill among hills.

"Have you stayed there before?"

"Once. With Helen. When we were first married. It's pleasant. No amenities, of course, but lots of olive trees, and wonderful local wine."

Sabia didn't know if she were glad. Was it a Holiday? She thought, probably, despite the proviso of his missing the train, and his giving over the dossier to her, he would meet her at the station, and travel with her, and then it wouldn't be a Holiday. In the sleeper they would act out the first scenes of the last pretense, which would set her free.

She dreamed she was on the train, galloping through the Pyrenees or Alps or God knew where, and Edmund, now a chic, black-haired woman, sat beside her, holding her firmly in place with both hands. The carriage was otherwise empty, and perhaps the train, which also lacked maybe even a driver.

Edmund had told her to allow for an absence of a month at least. Sabia organized her rent and her flat, and told a succession of recommendeds she wasn't going to be available to type their manuscripts, with the result that Marcus rang her up, complaining that he had tried to help and she'd "let him down."

"You *have* helped. I'm so busy now, that's why I can't take on any more."

"Is that all?"

"What else would it be?"

"You're not—seeing someone? Someone you shouldn't?"

"I'm not seeing anyone, Marcus."

Marcus grunted.

"You should be careful."

"Of what?"

"I don't know."

"Then why say it?"

"Well—I do know, Sabie. I mean, you're treading quite a dangerous path."

"Which means?"

"This is difficult."

"It must be."

"Driver," blurted Marcus.

She was tempted to say again, "Whose driver?" But instead, said, "What do you mean?"

"Be careful," said Marcus.

"Of what, and why?"

"Oh stop it, Sabie!" barked Marcus.

She put down the receiver.

Sabia asked herself if possibly she liked this "treading dangerously" in a normal danger. But she wasn't sure if she liked it. Actually she thought she would prefer all types of things to the absurd scenario which now went on. And yet, she was powerless (wasn't she?) to end it, till it had run its course.

Therefore, she prepared as she must, and at the end of June, she was waiting at the station, in a dress and jacket for which Edmund had given her the money, and with some small pieces of luggage for which he had also found the money, and with the dossier of papers that gave her access to other lands. With too, her contraceptive protection, and her irrational decision to do what Edmund would like. It seemed not that important to her. She thought she wouldn't mind it that much. Less than she had once or twice minded an assault by some unwanted lover of her own gender, one who had been real for her.

And yet too, she had the recurring image, as she waited for Edmund to come striding across the station forecourt, late but imminent, that in Italy she might simply run away, and lose herself among the sunburned, shadowy groves. However, she had entertained such fantasies before, usually when she was entirely trapped. And she looked round and round for her traveling companion, like any anxious, urgent woman, standing alone before the prospect of several great black snorting trains, with a boat to Bologne somehow inserted between them.

The heat was extraordinary. At first one thought it wasn't to be borne. But then you got used to it, and opened like a sunflower.

The house lay at the top of a flight of hills, like steps. From it fell away valleys dustily gleaming with silvery yellow olive trees, and dark garlands of figs, with farms that had russet roofs and crushed amber walls just like the villa. Hills rose again beyond all the valleys. After sunset, in each brief luminous dusk, they became a dark blue more convincing than the sky.

A balcony opened off the main bedroom, which seemed to hang in space over the unquiet valley, out of which rose up the scent of oil and tamarisk and thyme, and the bleating of goats.

No one at the villa could speak English, or only a word or two. Sabia had no Italian. They communicated, she and the people there, by signs and wordless calls and exclamations. Restful.

Instead of English food, there came spaghettis and heaps of glistening rice beaded by olives, sausage, ducks' eggs and terra cotta kraters of dark Chianti.

Sabia walked along dusty roads, railed with poplars, that led up and down through the valleys, with the villa nearly always in sight, but high up and far away. She lay in the garden arbour and slept after lunch, tranced by the rasp of crickets.

Sometimes she did wonder why she was there, and then, inevitably, when Edmund would turn up. (She could remember times like this in childhood—the adult guardian—relative or teacher—delayed or absent, and so being at liberty. Precarious, borrowed hours.)

For he hadn't arrived at the station, and in the end she had boarded the train avidly alone, as he had warned her she might have to. Rushed away then, through sea-divided landscapes, which soon altered to a larger more theatrical backdrop that never seemed to her quite believable, Sabia gazed into forested chasms and at sunlit lake surfaces, and forgot Edmund Driver. She became very good at forgetting him. Even sleeping on the train, in the starched, harsh, initialed sheets, even pushing out into the swirl of other stations, where finally someone pre-arranged met her with a large black car, even during all this, or because of all this, Sabia slipped further and further away from everything which had caused her to be there.

She had so often (always?) acted out a role, and now, framed by such magnificent and almost convincing scenery, here was simply another role for her. That of a pampered woman cut adrift and quite alone, a rich woman in a romantic villa, a Tuscan mansion, whose ceilings rose half a mile above her head, whose cool blue and blazing yellow rooms might at any moment summon up the ghost of a Dante or a Medici.

It was very easy to let go of all responsibility. After all, Edmund *would* eventually arrive, and then she would have to do whatever had to be done. So why not eat the emerald figs, and drink the wine. Why not watch the young kitchen girl, brown as a deer, washing her firm rounded arms in a bucket by the outdoor pump. And the two white dogs from the farm, playing, and the turpentine-blue lizard that lightened over the red wall.

At night, stars littered the sky like white embers carelessly dropped, but it never caught fire until next morning. Let that be a lesson to her. There was always time.

JULY

Sabia was sitting in the garden of the villa in Tuscany. It was about four o'clock in the afternoon, the summer furnace of the sun swinging slowly on across the hills, leaving a long ash of shadow in its wake.

Sabia sat quite mindlessly, as she sometimes found that she did. This would be how an animal would exist, she would think, a cat, even one of the villa lizards. In an indifferent awareness of all things, the sky, the sun, the garden with its crimson roses and tenuous vine, the smell of the pasta left over from lunch, caught in pockets among the flowers and herbs. Aware of faint movement in the house, the fat cook, and the maid, and the boy making a slight unthreatening clatter from the yard—and below, vast spaces down the hill beyond the plant-pierced wall, a car creeping round continually on the pale splits of the roads.

She watched the car through her serpent's eyes, unblinking.

She watched the car a great while, and it meant absolutely nothing to her.

And then, gradually, one flimsy filament at a time, she came to understand what a car was, and that this one was the very one which had brought her up to the house on the hill. And now, here it was again, and it must be Edmund who was now in the car.

Sabia stood up. She shook back her hair and smoothed the skirt of her frock across her hips, and licked her unpainted mouth. She picked up the hat she had brought out to protect her from the sun and didn't bother with, and held it. As if she, not he, was now to go somewhere.

Then, the oddest idea. That when the car reached the gateway, which she could see quite clearly through the tangled roses, it would draw up. And out of it would step, not Edmund, but Helen.

Why Helen? Also, *if* Helen, would this be fascinating, a second chance? Or only a deep embarrassment? Or a worrying scene of some kind… But it wouldn't be Helen.

Then the car drove in through the gateway, and kept on up towards the house.

Sabia thought she would lie down again in the arbour, and make out she was asleep.

It was her way of putting off the inevitable. After all, let Edmund come into the garden, kiss her awake like the Sleeping Beauty. She wondered, the over-turning afternoon deep purple on her closed lids, if she would remember Edmund, or be startled at how he had changed during the week or so she hadn't seen him.

Then she heard a man's footsteps on the path.

A darker shadow fell across her. Nothing else. There was to be no kiss, then. Sabia pretended to wake.

Shading her eyes, and looking up, she saw she had indeed totally misremembered Edmund, who was no longer like Edmund at all, but like another man she'd never met in her life.

"Miss Cobb? I'm George Conranne."

"Oh," she said. "Are you?"

"Yes."

"Your house here is very lovely."

He blinked at her.

"I know you were expecting Edmund," he said. She waited. "Edmund told me—something about it. You're not going to have to mind."

He was about Edmund's age. He did have a look of Edmund too, as if they might be distantly related, and perhaps they were.

The garden was now blurred by its combined dimness and brightness. A bird fluted and burst across from tree to tree, like a hurled weapon.

"I think we should go inside," Conranne said.

"Why?" said Sabia.

"I have to tell you something. I think I'll manage it better in the house. Please, do come in."

Sabia got up again. She walked back along the picturesque and broken path with him, between the tan flowerpots, and where the small statue was, of a nymph, she thought, wet now with shade.

Inside the house at once a chill fell, but it was a sensory illusion—in a few moments the marbled room would seem as hot, or worse, than outside.

Conranne poured her a drink. Of course, these were his drinks, just as it was his house.

She wondered if she had also become Conranne's, sold on by Edmund, who wasn't there.

What had happened? He'd got cold feet, he'd changed his mind, flown in the roar of engines to France with Helen, and sent this man to explain and buy—or coerce—Sabia off.

No, it wasn't that.

Sabia sat down on the carved wooden chair by the window. She looked at the paved stone segments of the floor, but didn't slip off her shoes.

Conranne also looked at the floor.

"You and Edmund," he said. And then, nothing.

After a while, Sabia said, carefully, "Can't he get away?"

"No, he can't get away. Oh, shit," said Conranne, with anger. "I thought I could manage this. I can't. I'll just have to tell you. Did you love him?"

As if it were pre-arranged, Sabia knew.

She said quietly, from a circle she seemed suddenly to have risen up into, about three feet below the ceiling, "*Did* I love him?"

"He's not—able to be loved anymore," said Conranne. He downed his drink. "He's dead. I'm sorry. There it is. He's dead and she is, and there you have it."

Sabia couldn't move.

She said, "Do you mean Helen?"

"Yes, yes. Edmund and Helen."

The boy appeared in the doorway (an actor mistaking his cue?), stared at them and swiveled, hurrying away.

Conranne took no notice.

He poured another drink. Sabia considered what she should do. What *did* one do? Think.

I have to be stricken, shocked—but I needn't cry—not everyone cries. I want another drink of this nasty sweetish whisky—or no, I still have most of the one he gave me.

She sipped the whisky. But wait, she hadn't sipped it—she could not move yet. The slightest effort, and the glass would slip out of her nerveless fingers. They felt nerveless. Perhaps that was the best thing to do, it would speak volumes, and louder than words—

But Sabia found her nerveless hand had grown into the glass which it couldn't lift to her lips, nor let go, either.

Conranne was bending over her.

"Do you want to hear what happened?"

No.

"Yes," Sabia said. Or the part of her still fastened up towards the ceiling, that said it.

Conranne nodded, so she must have said the right thing.

"Helen shot him," said Conranne.

He may have said something else before, which she hadn't caught. Then he was saying other things.

Sabia thought: *Is he lying?*

She thought of Helen, showing always the reverse of her own coin, cool, indifferent, uninvolved—and yet crazily on guard and jealous. Sabia thought of herself, flirting, not with a lover but with Normalcy—more dangerous than any man—and being swept up by the normalcy-that-was-so-dangerous and run away with, everything out of control.

Was that it?

"Walked up to him and shot him point blank," said Conranne, really rather a *bad* actor (worse than the cue-mistaking boy). But then the dialogue was awful. So trite and melodramatic.

"Why?" Sabia's voice. (It must be, no other woman was in the room.)

"She made it clear. Helen. She left a letter. I think the gun—that was from the war. She killed him, then herself. Women don't do that. English women like Helen, don't do that. Not like here. They're always doing it, here. But not Helen. But she did."

Sabia found her head had drooped over. Now her hand brought the whisky kindly, sympathetically to her mouth.

She drank the whisky. How sweet and thick it was.

What had Helen's suicide letter said? *You have betrayed me again, and I have had enough of it—all these women. Or this one woman.*

Sabia thought perhaps Conranne had told her some of what the letter had said, but she didn't take it in.

Then he was saying something along the lines of she must stay here as long as she wanted. It would be better if she didn't go back to London, not for a little while. The police were involved, naturally. Various people had guessed, linked her name to Edmund's. Not too difficult, Conranne supposed bleakly. Conranne mentioned in turn the names of the guessers, which included Marcus, and Frederick Laudelay.

"That one," said Conranne. "Laudelay, bloody queer—I think he made damn sure he drove Helen mad with it all. But Laudelay was—well, her official spy, if you like. He was always on the case. Every time Edmund started something—even if he hadn't—oh, I'm sorry, Miss Cobb, but I expect you knew you weren't the first."

"Yes," Sabia said.

She got up, surprising herself, and dropped the glass on the stone floor as an afterthought. Or only a clumsiness. Something.

Conranne glanced at it. Oh dear, she'd smashed his glass.

Sabia said, "When did it happen?"

He told her but she didn't hear, and she knew she couldn't ask him to repeat it, not then, nor later, at the dinner they attempted in the twilight (when moths came to the candles), or later still, when she had packed her bags and asked him instead about the express which would return her towards England.

"Really, you *mustn't* travel yet. He wouldn't have wanted you caught up in—"

"Yes, I must. I won't get caught up."

"You've been awfully brave."

"No."

"I'm so sorry," he said. "Can I help—in any way—are you all right for money?"

No, she said. But then realized she had said *Yes*.

At midnight she stood on the bedroom balcony, and looked at the stars wobbling, obviously insecurely pinned to the night sky. Breezes brought drugged almond scents from the valley, and distant song from the worlds of other lives.

What do I feel? What shall I do? Who was he? Who am I? Has something happened? *What?*

Sabia thought of Helen, in one of her ice-cream gowns, marching in on Edmund, in the study—perhaps the dining-room or garden, shooting him point-blank with the service revolver, as in a film, then herself—but it was not convincing. Sabia knew they were still alive, unless of course she had, in the first place, simply imagined them into existence, and all the rest of it.

Winter

A girl with curly, mousy-blonde hair sat down, in a great flailing of gloves, scarf, coat, in the seat opposite.

Sacha looked at her. The girl was no stranger, but Phyllis Wanderton, who shared the little office with her at Drye and Lewis.

"I ordered us the welsh rarebit," said Sacha. "Is that all right?"

"Yes, that sounds nice and hot."

"It's nice and *cheap*."

They smiled, complicit, young women on a budget.

Outside, on no budget at all, the first generous snows of this northwards country town were fluttering down and down.

"Old Bert says it'll last until Christmas," said Phyllis, of the fey Greek-mythological name. "And then vanish just in time to stop there being a white Christmas day. Isn't that mean." Perhaps she meant God, or only the weather, or Old Bert even, the doorman, who also saw to the coal fires kept meagerly and smokily alight in every office.

Phyllis had been shopping, so Sacha had come on ahead to the *Kettle on the Hob,* where they "perched" for lunch.

Phyllis suddenly produced a horrifying doll from a box. It had pink plastic skin and distressing eyes that opened and closed maniacally. It looked like a religious fanatic.

"I got this for my niece. What do you think?"

"Yes," said Sacha.

"I think she'll like it."

"I'm sure she will."

"The dress is satin, or a bit like that."

"Yes."

"But I've still got a lot of shopping to do. You're so lucky, not having anyone. Oh! What am I saying? Sorry."

The doll was put away and they relapsed into a domestic silence, waiting for the food, staring out, chins on hands, into the Antarctic beyond the window.

They shared two rooms, a kitchen and bathroom, at the top of Gate House, once gracious but now all in flats. When Sacha had appeared, Phyllis had been trying for several weeks to find someone to share and help her with the rent, after the previous sharer had secured a husband and "gone off." Both Phyllis and Sacha maintained thereafter a fiction of frugality, which sometimes was abandoned in an orgy of chocolates or expensive tea. "This is the room you'd have," had said Phyllis, that day still in her dressing-gown and slippers, showing Sacha the big front room, past which the traffic would start to veer at six in the morning.

But also Phyllis…had a certain look. Without being pretty, she was succulent, strong, with plump muscled arms from tennis. "Oh, the men in this house," she soon said, "I can't stand them. I wish they weren't allowed to live here, I really do." And later on, when Sacha remarked that she would have to write and tell her friend Albertine, in London, about the lucky find of the room, and how Albertine herself was having so much trouble with her close woman companion, Phyllis had said, "Oh, you mean…like *that?*" "I'm afraid so." "Oh," had said Phyllis. "Well, I don't mind that, you know. I mean, it's innocent enough, isn't it. Not like what *men* get up to. Do have another biscuit." And Sacha had smiled, as if it *were* quite innocent, correctly predicting naughty little games ahead, such as might be played in a school, late night exchanges of confidences, and cuddles that could, and indeed would, lead anywhere.

Phyllis was part of that oblivious underground of women who thought what they did was nothing, that their distaste for men sprang from maidenly virtue not sexual antipathy. Usually a day evolved when abruptly they woke up, and hastily married some unfortunate male, whom they then scorned, bullied and nagged into enormous distance, and so enjoyed the unmolested and Perfectly Normal remainder of their lives.

Knowing exactly what she was *not,* and that she was "innocent," Phyllis didn't get jealous either.

So, it was quite all right for Sacha to go on looking under her lids at the woman in the corner, whose clothes she must be admiring.

She was definitely not the *Kettle*'s usual customer, wrapped in furs and smoking cigarettes that left a faint costly marker on the air. And surely those were pearls that were her earrings.

Her hair, short and severely combed, was a very dark brown, almost black. And her eyes a dark, leadenly-glowing blue. She had drunk a cup of coffee. She seemed to be waiting for someone, or something. But nothing had happened.

She was like Edmund, Edmund's Anima, who had stalked fatally through his novels, at least the two Sacha had read when she was still called Sabia Cobb.

It had been curious really, the newspapers, where they knew of and mentioned her, always got her name quite wrong. She'd been called, variously, Sabine Colbourne and Sabina Court, and, more nearly apposite to one of Sabia's true, even then, former names, Sabina Cohen. But she had merited only a small splinter on the whole. The crime of passion was firmly centered upon Edmund and Helen, the glamorous and the damned.

"Helen gave him enough rope," Frederick Laudelay was reported to have said. "She asked him endlessly to stop, and he promised her he would. But he was like an opium addict. He couldn't. So then she let him go as far as he wished. He was planning to run off with this girl to France. To Helen that was the last straw. That was when her nerve snapped." (Such a lot of clichés—and the destination wrong—had Frederick really said all this?)

There dashed over Sacha (who had altered her name to Sacha Cope on the train from London) a wave, a shudder of horror.

"What's up? Is it the rarebit?" asked Phyllis, in her schoolgirly-motherly tone.

"No, just chilly."

The woman who was Edmund Driver's Anima got up abruptly and walked out through the room, out into the white storm of the day. The snowflakes consumed her.

Sacha wondered if she had imagined the woman, or if Edmund were haunting her. For she had seen the Anima, in human form, once or twice. Yes, even on the boat from Bologne, gliding back over the calm sea, when the Anima had stood on the deck, a tall, powerfully-svelte figure, with Edmund's hair minus any grey, and Edmund's eyes.

Perhaps they did haunt you, the ones you didn't care about, the ones you were most likely, otherwise, to forget.

"What's up?" Phyllis, again.

"Nothing. I think I've got a cold."

"Oh poor you. Let's get some whisky—hot drink tonight. Oh, but I was going to say, just come across to the florist's for a minute."

It had been easy to get out of London. Sacha-still-Sabia took what she needed, in the suitcases Edmund had bought her for

Italy, and her typewriter in its case. She sold her paintings, some clothes, and the books she couldn't lug with her. She left the rent unsettled, and no notice given, no forwarding address. She was, at this, already adept enough. This sort of thing.

When they had paid for their lunch, Sacha and Phyllis walked, arm in arm (innocent), across the square, and peered in at the florist's window.

"I just fancied those," said Phyllis, "to brighten up my room. In this weather. Something that'll last." She had forgotten, standing there, evaluating, that Sacha might have a cold. Phyllis usually quickly forgot things.

Sacha stared in at the icy glass. Past the Christmas tree and holly, and the model sleighs, a heap of funeral wreathes lay waiting on the floor.

"What do you think?"

Did Phyllis want to buy a funeral wreathe? If so, for whom? Stop it Sacha.

"I don't see—"

"No, look there. That's it."

It was a stone bowl of irises, evidently fake, made from waxed paper, Sacha thought, coloured a rich unlikely violet indigo, with wild yellow eyes of flame, like the Jabberwocky.

"*Egyptian Iris,*" read out Phyllis. "I wonder what that means. But—oh, look at that. Just look." She pointed.

Sacha gradually saw that one of the unreal irises had become even more unusual, and was turning a curious acidulous lime-green at the edges of its petals—obviously *turning,* because the one behind it, now she *did* look, was bright green all over, even its fiery eyes, which were now the shade of unripe lemons.

"That can't be meant to be like that," said Phyllis. "It gives the game away, doesn't it? Something must have gone wrong. Something in the dye, or where they've put it. And how could you be sure? No, I don't like that then after all. I mean, if that happens, it won't look real, will it. Not like the others. I mean it looks impossible."

Femme Fatale

❧✣❧

For M.H. and J.R.

FEMME FATALE

The woman stood in the middle of the street, and cried. Her cloud of black hair was coming loose from the upswept style in which she had earlier, presumably, confined it. She wore a dark blue costume with a white blouse. She had no hat, but gloves she *had* brought with her. These she pressed to her eyes, not to staunch but to mitigate the avalanche of her tears.

Carts drawn by donkeys, and occasionally a frustrated old horse, now and then maneuvered around her. It was one of the more important Roman avenues, left over in the old town and quite wide, paved by bubble-like cobbles. Even a car might arrive on it, with a belch of blue infuriated fumes. One nearly squashed the woman. Yet she seemed not to notice. No one, so far as I could see, had attempted to help, or at least question her, let alone lead her away.

"Bloody fool should be in an asylum," said my companion.

"But why should she? Perhaps somebody's died."

"Oh, Esther, you are such a wet creature. You drape yourself over everything in astonishment—then recoil when it makes a grab at you."

"Not always," I replied. I meant, conceivably, I hadn't recoiled when she herself had done so.

"Oh, rubbish. Come on. Let's get to Les Alyses and have a drink."

My companion, whom I shall call Munne for want of anything better, also had a little car. And in this being we had been driving, or *she* had been driving us—or the *car* had, it possessed a dark soul of its own—across the swooping plains of the region, littered with enormous rocks, and flayed by unsparing sunlight the color of bleached Sauterne.

Munne now hooked my arm, and was in the act of dragging me into one of the narrow cobbled side streets, above which house-tops leant close enough to conspire. Exactly then, however, the madwoman in the middle of the road let out a wild soprano wail. It contained syntax.

"What does *la folle* say?" quacked Munne.

"I—couldn't hear."

But I had.

The woman in the street had called to the heartless stones of the town, to the sky, to any ears able to absorb her words: "Where is she? Where is my friend? What has become of her? Will no one listen to me?"

We drank wine in the little hotel. Munne had ordered a cocktail, a *sac bleu,* but they had no notion here what she meant. Her strident efforts to enlighten them resulted in the serene waiter leaving us unserved entirely. At last I had walked to the counter and gained a bottle of red. It was rough and ordinary and tasty enough, with the flint of the yard, as they say, in its belly.

So, the wet little leech did the work at which the dominant Munne had failed.

I loathed her. She was an awful mistake.

Stinking of a priceless English version of French scent, swathed in expense and stupidity. I should have known. Have I ever known? Ah, yes. Always. Once it is over.

But we spoke quietly of what we might have for lunch, and then how we would walk up to the Roman baths, and then to the ampitheatre, and how, after a light aperitif, perhaps sit in the oval arena, where hundreds or thousands of years before gladiators had slain each other, and there we would watch the open-air cinema. They were showing an epic Biblical romance from America. Was it *Ben-Hur*? I forget, or half remember.

The town ached with heat. The room ached with it. Once or twice a customer came in to eat his lunch in the dining room.

They were all men, but of different sorts. A business official with some slim ledgers to take out and look at, a couple of bakers—they spoke of business. Even a very clean, respectful farmer, who chatted with the waiter about the cartload of produce he had just brought to market.

Munne ordered our lunch. As usual she persisted in selecting for me things I "should eat," but did not much like. This time a ragout of hare.

All the while I watched the second door to the dining room, the one by which we had entered and that opened on the narrow street.

Perhaps I had guessed she must come here. After all, it was the best of the town's three hotels. But that was a spurious reason. The crying woman would come to the hotel dining room because I was curious about her. Perhaps my nosiness would draw her in, like a strange odor, partly alluring, mostly repellent—yet irresistible. Or else maybe she had been conscious that I alone paid any proper attention to her. Yes, it would be that. She would struggle to the hotel and sink down at my feet, clasping my ankle, a supplicant. Did I mention—I think I didn't—as well as distraught she had been beautiful?

Then she came in. Just like that.

Munne didn't even notice. She was gobbling up a plate of some delicate toasted entrails resembling the tails of mice.

But the woman, she moved directly—not to me, of course—but to a corner table just below the staircase. I saw then the table had been reserved. For her? Certainly she put the reservation aside, lifted the cloth from the carafe of water and poured herself a glass. She seemed now in control of her emotions, but less calm than drooping, lax. She looked like someone who has exposed their very last savings on a bid to win the national lottery, and not won, and so lost everything—yet it is no surprise to them, oh no: they expected nothing else.

Her eyes were a vivid green, elaborated by the darkness of her lashes. Also probably by weeping.

Now though, dry-eyed, when the waiter went up to her—rather cautiously I judged—she gave some order in a low voice. It might have been anything, but was doubtless only what she would take for lunch. The waiter nodded, a type of wary bow, and went away. She sat there, and began to pleat the table napkin into tiny precise folds. As if this were essential. If properly done, it would hold the world together for a few days more.

"Stop staring, Esther." Munne had uttered. "*Mon dieu,* what is the matter with you? You're like some awful child, my vile little niece in London. How I hate that brat. Gawps at everyone like a fish from a slab. But you are worse. What is it? Oh, *I* see. *La Folle.* Why don't you go over and sit with her, then, if you're so intrigued."

"I am intrigued. But I shan't sit with her."

"Oh *bouf!* Sit where you please. Be damned to you, you bloody Jewess. I should have known better."

Despite her words, Munne herself remained quite cool, her voice only flirtatiously spiteful. Did she want from me a more impassioned response? But I hadn't time. I was now, veiling my greedy gaze behind my little traveling mirror, staring once more at the woman who had cried. Should I therefore christen her Niobe? Or Maguerite... Somehow that name seemed suitable. However the waiter was coming back, and standing by her table under the stair he spoke quite audibly, "M'mselle Irén. I'm afraid it is all gone."

"Well, then...I will have the omelet, thank you."

Her voice was plaintive and sweet.

Was it we, the awful Munne, and I, more *awful,* bad as the dead fish English niece, who robbed poor Irén of her desired lunch— the hare? She could have my portion. I didn't want it certainly. I, as Irén now did, would have taken an omelet.

I said nothing.

Munne though cranked her black coiffured head about on her smooth and thinly pearl-strung neck, and herself stared blatantly.

"My God, quite a beauty after all. I hadn't spotted it when she was blubbing."

This might be genuine appreciation, or only Munne attempting to provoking me. Really I knew nothing about her, and now cared less.

The hare arrived in a hot, oval, clay serving-dish. The poor dark-pale remnants were in heavy gravy with vegetables and other stuff.

Munne ate with satisfaction. For a brief while her general attention would be diverted.

Noon had passed by then, but seen outside the glass of the door, the ancient stones of the town pulsed white, or dissolved in stone-cast bronze shadows. The place had been young in Mediaeval times, but parts much older, young only in the days of the Caesars. What were we doing here, wandering about, future ghosts like fireflies that would be dead and done with in five minutes.

The waiter came back to our table with the new bottle of wine Munne had ordered. Undoing it, adjusting its bib and pouring for us, he muttered, "It is very tedious. That woman. Why doesn't she go away—go home? Surely she has one."

Her mouth full, Munne goggled at him with bulging eyes.

I said, "Which woman?"

"She—over there—the corner table. She came to stay here only two days, but then started this business of her missing friend—and now she has reinvested herself in the hotel for an entire week. She goes about searching for the friend, sobbing and accosting people. Twice the police have brought her back here, as if *we* are her guardians. They have threatened her with jail. It does no good."

"And her friend is missing?" I inquired.

Bending low above us like an onerous tree in an apron, he sighed, "She *has* no friend. She arrives alone. There is only her name in the book of our guests, no other. I will show you if you wish."

"So she's truly insane?" asked Munne, after an audible gulp to shift the hare from mouth to stomach.

The waiter made a shrugging and wafting gesture.

"Perhaps."

"Did she seem so from the first?" I said.

He shrugged once more. "It is on the second morning," he whispered, so distinctly I suspected Irén might hear every word, even over there under the stairway. "Down she rushes, her hair undone, shouting that this other and non-existent woman is unexplainably gone. They supposedly share a room, you understand." He glanced at me and winked solemnly. It seemed he deduced Irén and her non-existent and invisible companion were of a certain inclination. Apparently he had *not* deduced that so were Munne and I. Or else he had.

"What happened?" asked Munne, avidly wiping her lips.

"Such a scene is made, the manager must come out. Reason is tried. But the young woman is screaming we have to fetch the police. We all assure her they are unnecessary, since she entered the hotel quite alone, signed the register alone, dined alone in her room—although admittedly enough dinner had been ordered for two ladies—and that the chambermaid now is quite sure only one person had occupied the bed. But the pandemonium does not abate. So next the doctor is summoned. He suggests perhaps M'mselle has had a falling out with some female companion before ever she came to us, and this shock has slightly confused her, so now she thinks still she and the other lady—"

The waiter broke off because the two bakers had suddenly set up a raucous barking noise to summon him. With a whisk of the wine bib he turned instantly and hurried over to them.

"Well!" gloated Munne. "*What* a strange business."

She and I now both hungrily glared across at the corner table—but how peculiar. It was empty. At some point during the waiter's loud sotto voce monologue, Irén must have risen, thrown down her napkin by her half-finished plate, and slipped away. But how, where? She had surely not gone upstairs, nor had she—had she?—passed across the dining room. This bizarre sleight-of-hand heightened our joint sense, Munne's and mine, for at this instant unfortunately we were at one, of the unforeseen. Despite the fact that it must have a rational explanation, it seemed to us that once again, someone had mysteriously "vanished." Into thin air.

An awful afternoon.

We plodded up and down the alley-like plaits of streets. We found a square, where trees mutely hung down their flags of leaden green in bored surrender to the heat. The market was busy. Horse and donkey dung ornamented the thoroughfare.

Munne determined furiously to buy a cheese. Eventually she got it, almost flung at her, after she had paid far too much. Clutching the prize thereafter, and in the manner of the best such cheeses it reeked, we toiled to the Roman baths. Here were fragmented stems and sinks, partly now the colour of walnuts, and clambered by ivy and moss. And so at last we fetched up in a small bar, near the arena, which kept its cinema sheltered in a large circus tent. In fact it was not an arena either. It was a stadium, once the site of volatile and murderous chariot races. How suitable that *Ben-Hur* was to be shown there, if it was, with its redoubtable chariot race, while a piano, stranded on the tent-darkened track below the screen, would thunder out the memory of grinding wheels, pounding hoofs, shrieks, curses, and the audible splash of blood.

We drank absinthe, with water and sugar. The drink was the colour of emeralds.

"My car's safe enough," remarked Munne. "Shall we stay a night here, then? Would you like that?"

"If you want."

"Well, I was thinking, then you could go on following that girl about, that mad woman with the vanished friend."

I had hardly followed Irén. Irén, if anything, had followed me into the hotel—if not quite in the fantastical way I'd visualized.

Naturally I had not stopped thinking about her. I had wondered all afternoon what Irén was doing. Staggering through the town once more? Or lying prone and limp and weeping upon the hotel bed, in which "only one person" had slept.

Was it all some unconscionable plot? Had the female companion of Irén truly existed yet been abducted? Or had she run away and next bribed everyone in the hotel, perhaps the entire town, to lie to Irén: *No, no, you were alone from the start. No one was with you.* In order to drive her mad?

"I know that look," said Munne. "You don't want to see a film, do you? You want to go back and moon about the hotel...find out her room number...go and knock on the door—"

I yawned. It was a reflex. Animals do this sometimes, when disturbed or uneasy.

But Munne snapped like the teeth of a steel purse, "Oh, you Jewess! I begin to hate you! Finish your drink. I'm going for a walk. Don't try to come with me."

Nor did I.

In the dusk the sky and town went blue, and dim smoky lamplights appeared in slender windows, where also you could see the perched forms of static people. They never moved. Perhaps they were stuffed, or mannequins.

While I had finished my drink, I had overheard, as if purposefully the two men sat near in order that I might, another swift conversation regarding *La fille folle.*

"Oh, I saw her arrive, too. She was on foot. She was *definitely* alone. I thought, what is a smart little dove like that doing walking, and alone?"

"And did she—how shall I say?—talk aloud to the air, as if another person were with her?"

"Ah no. She was most demure. I approached and offered to carry the two big bags she had with her. But politely she refused."

"Did she seem distressed?"

"No, not at all."

"But she is a stranger here—she can't have walked here from Perville, can she? Incredible! Somebody must have brought her, then abandoned her."

"I don't know, can't say. I first saw her by the hotel, you understand."

After which, they both glanced slyly at me. The idea of a perverse plot again stirred in my mind. But why did they need to convince, of all people, myself? I counted for nothing. More likely their glance was only one more figment of a universal dislike of women alone in provincial bars, at least if they were not properly in their place as whores.

Presently it occurred to me, quite without worry, that I was in the grip of what Munne, and others, would term *one of my obsessions*. That being the case, might I myself be imagining all kinds of false dialogue everywhere about, especially in a foreign tongue? Not that this had ever happened, that I had been aware of before. But I was often accused, by lovers or enemies—how often they became the same thing—of such trances and misconceptions. No doubt they were all quite right.

Not Irén therefore, but Esther, was the madwoman.

Munne didn't return, and by then, judging by faint rumblings and tinklings from the direction of the arena-stadium, the film was well-advanced. The sun began sinking with a reddish ambivalence behind the town's highest peak. This was a fortress, I thought, commenced in Roman times and augmented during many others until virtually a compendium, an architecture of mixed blood.

I meandered down the coils of streets. They seemed designed to disorientate. Some were so thin, and massively overhung by upper storeys, I suspected mechanisms would abruptly clank into position, slamming fast slabs of masonry at either end of the passage, so it would become shut. Now a prisoner, I would scurry about, unable to scale the walls or find any alternative exit point. I should also learn no one else dwelled there. The shops and houses would all be void of people, and thus of sustenance. And that particular street would stay closed, until, my howls unheard, I had perished in it of starvation or fear.

By the time the lights were being lit, however, I had somehow escape this fate and gained the hotel.

Going in, I checked to see if Munne had returned to arrange a room for the night. She had not. That didn't greatly astound me, let alone dismay. She would come back. She had no pleasure driving after dark, where one was constantly bumping, as she insisted, into animals and stray peasants on the roads. It was possible she might, of course, take a room and exclude me, but I had slept in hotel lobbies before.

Instead I ordered another drink, and sat in one of the chairs. Not much was yet going on, although the lamps were all burning in the restaurant. The electricity was somewhat erratic as I had seen in other towns of the region that possessed it. The light fluttered and sometimes winked. As if the very weight of time and bygone things kept cavorting distractingly across its clean modern path, laughing and pulling faces.

Not long after I had sat down, a hotel page of some sort ran up to the desk and began to gabble. The clerk reacted dramatically. "Oh! Room so-and-so! Oh, it's *that* one! *Her!*"

I knew immediately, and without moving an inch part of me rose to its feet.

There was from the desk a little further frothing. After which several customers, on this occasion gentlemen with their wives, began to flock to the counter. From their elaborate dress and attitudes, I guessed there was some party or celebration due to take place in the dining room.

Sure enough all the hotel staff soon became engaged in racing to and fro. Bottles and goblets swirled by, as fluidly as if borne by skaters on a pond of glass. In the dining room rows of orange candles were being kindled, their nervous blinking backing up the frequent electric winks, to form an entire conspiracy: *Ah, but we could tell you, ah, if we wished to, we could...*

I rose and went up the main staircase, which was of dark wood. It had wooden banisters carved with shields and briars.

An oil lamp burned on each landing, of which there were two and a half. Her room, of whose number I had been inadvertently informed by the desk clerk, lay around a bend of the upper corridor. I stood outside, my emerald drink in my hand. With enormous diffidence I knocked on the door. I had pursued and run her to earth, and I was abashed.

"I brought you this."

I offered her the untouched glass of absinthe.

She was the same height as me, but in all other ways unlike. She was heavier in build, voluptuous. The deep green of her eyes made mine into—so Munne had been right—a pallid Piscean icy grey. Her hair was a black cloud.

"Why?" she said, looking only at me.

"Why not? Perhaps you might be thirsty."

Behind her a side-lamp burned. Unlike all the other electric lights it didn't seem inclined to wink. Was it *in* on the conspiracy? Or did it just not want to miss a moment by blinking?

She took the glass, and hesitantly sipped it.

"I don't know who you are," she said. "This might be drugged, or poisoned."

"I'm Esther. It isn't."

"My name is Claire," she said. Ah, not Irén—of course not, that was her surname. Claire. *Light.* No wonder the lamp had to keep up with her. But Munne would have told me Claire did not mean that as a name, not at all. It came from some Latin context and meant *well-known.* "Come in," she went on. "The room's a mess. You see, it was the way she left it..."

"Your friend."

"My friend."

The room was actually not in a mess. Perhaps the chambermaid, she who had sworn the bed had facilitated only a single occupant, had tidied up. The bed itself was made in the hotel way. On the dressing-table before the mirror stood a small array of cosmetics and potions. One could not fail to see, there were many duplicates, and these twins were unlike each other. There were two sorts of powder, one far more opulent, and darker. There were two dissimilar combs and two brushes. The second brush had some pale glittering hairs caught in it, not matching the black cloud of Claire Irén. Only one lipstick, standing by itself in a gilt holder. And a solitary stick of kohl, such as an actress might use, lay prone. Up against the glass stood a bottle of cologne, only doubled by its reflection. It had a Paris label. But further off there was a contrary bottle of some tonic, sticky red, with its cap imperfectly replaced. Some stockings reclined over the back of a chair, six of them, and two pairs of a slightly variant shade. While over there the wardrobe stood ajar, and a couple of dresses could be seen. Were they of different sizes? No doubt, no doubt, just like that pair of shoes, now spotted lying under that other chair. The shoes looked very small. Claire's pretty peasant feet would require a wider fitting.

The chambermaid too, I assumed, had seen all or some of this. Maybe she concluded everything belonged to Claire. Or that Claire had brought it with her as part of her mad make-believe. Which might well be true.

"Do you see?" Claire said nevertheless, in a quiet, flat voice. "Her things—she simply left them all. She must have—oh I don't understand it—she must have gone out in her nightgown. That was all that was missing. Not even her bag—At first, when I woke up, I thought she'd had to visit the bathroom. But when she didn't come back I went to see, and she wasn't there. So then I put on the light and looked all round this room—stupidly—as if she was still here and only the darkness must have hidden her. But she was gone. Quite...gone away. I opened the window and looked out even. But it's twenty feet or more to the alleyway. Could someone have come in, soundlessly, and—oh God—chloroformed her, say, and dragged her out that way?" For a second Claire's eyes became deranged and terrible. Then they filled with tears. And then the tears drained back into her and she tiredly said, "I put on my clothes and went out and searched for her all through the hotel. There was nobody about. Only a young girl in one of the passages, who ran away when I spoke to her. I suppose I looked rather wild. The man downstairs at the desk had gone somewhere, perhaps to bed. And I couldn't find—*her*. I've looked ever since, all over the town. Everywhere. I've been to the police. I've begged them to help me. But they all say there was never anyone with me. They all insist I came here alone—only it was *she*, my friend, who wrote both our names. And the writing in the book isn't hers—but it isn't mine, either. Not really. I don't think so. Oh, why would they do this, Mademoiselle? Why would they be so cruel? Have they taken her and murdered her, do you think? Oh, you hear of these awful things. She was so young and slender and little. She was like a *spirit*. No one could hurt her. Do you think she just suddenly began to hate me—she just suddenly woke up in the night and thought, *I hate this Claire*—and was so horrified by me that she couldn't even tell me, she just ran away at once? We'd known each other for several months, more than seven. I never treated her unfairly—why would I? I loved her. And she—she was…she was my friend."

We stood in the room, gazing at each other.

Then she raised the last of the absinthe and drank it down, and put the glass on the table by the bed.

"She even left her handbag," said Claire, and turning she pulled fully open the wardrobe door, to reveal four dresses and two coats, and little things, hats and gloves and handkerchiefs, lying about loose inside. And there was a bag there certainly, and Claire drew it out and put it on the bed, handling it like a damaged bird. "It has our tickets for the train in it—the train at Vienne, to go back. Only we didn't catch that train. And there's her journal, look, and her pencil. Oh there's no clue there. I looked. She stopped writing three days ago. She often did that, missed whole weeks— See, this powder compact I bought her—"

I stared obediently at all the articles, as Claire carefully delivered them from the womb of the bag, and laid them before me on the bed.

Claire's arms dropped to her sides. She stood over the bag and the journal, her head bowed. I thought of a mother by her dead child, in the moment before everything splits asunder and she ceases to be human anymore.

Did I believe any of it?

I didn't know.

And yet, I did believe her. The world is vast and primal, pretend as we try to. Anything might happen. And does. That ancient toothless crone was, a second ago in the previous century, a rose-cheeked lass with golden tresses. That innocent pink baby will grow up to begin a world war. If we credit such real villanies, why not also that a thin young woman with silvery-blonde hair and tiny feet, might well fade away in a single night hour, melted down like a candle by moonlight, or some rare acid of the ether.

Now Claire didn't cry. As if she were beginning to see that tears did no good, that remonstrance achieved nothing.

Very softly, with no inflection at all, she added simply a coda. "I don't know why they would do it. I don't know why they would lie to me." Then she sat leadenly on the bed. "But I would kill them all for a cigarette."

"Oh," I said. And produced my own case—Munne's gift. I smoked only ever one or two cigarettes in a week. And Munne didn't like that brand. There were plenty left.

So then I sat beside Claire Irén and we smoked for a while. Neither of us spoke.

Below, vaguely and from the dining room presumably, there gradually rose a clotted imbecilic noise. The party was in full swing it appeared, and in a while too the random phrases of a small band began to be audible, a violin, an accordion, and so on.

"They're playing *Le Rouge de ma Rose*," she remarked at last.

"Yes. They seem not to play it very well."

"Oh, I expect it's all right, downstairs."

"It sounds as if people are dancing."

She sighed. "I wonder if I shall ever dance again."

I took her hand, and she held my hand. Hers was cold and still, as if lacking a pulse. I wasn't making an advance to her. I didn't want to at all. It would have been like trying to seduce that mother with the sick bird or the dead child on the bed beside us.

There was nothing I could say. To protest I believed her and vow I would help her search the town again, question everyone there, hammer on the doors of the police house, would be foolish and meaningless—worse, false. I could not do that. I did not *know* if I believed her. Besides, the whole place seemed set firm against what she had said, whether by illusion or in reality.

In the end the music had dispersed, and somewhere I heard an old clock offendedly stutter out nine times.

Then she sighed again. "You've been kind," she said.

"No. I wish—"

"Don't wish," she said. And she drew her hand from mine and laid one smooth cool finger on my lips. I could smell her scent, both her perfume and her personal aroma. And it came to me at that instant, inside this room it was in fact possible to detect, faintly lingering, another feminine flavour also. A scent not hers, not mine, but that of another woman, younger than us both, and fairer of hair and skin. I swear I didn't imagine this. But then, how can I be sure. It might have been the tincture of the wretched chambermaid after all, the tidier and insistent adversarial witness. Or something wafted in from the outer night. Or nothing. One more lie.

"Goodnight, Claire," I said at the door. "I hope—"

"Don't hope," she said. "Goodnight—" and she said my name in a curious way, with an accent I had not heard before in her voice: *Eztre*.

And after this she lay back on the bed, and drew the empty bag towards her and held it, and from outside I shut the door.

Below, the lobby was filled by a merry overflow from the dining room. Women in huge decorated dresses, like a sort of confectionary, repeatedly skeined across the area. Gentlemen stood fuming pipes and cigars beside an impromptu table laid with decanters. Some glanced askance at me, a stray female alien beyond their purlieus, or laughed.

At the desk I was informed my "companion," Munne, had manifested and taken the best double room, and supper had been ordered for us there. Which was apparently a great nuisance, due to the catering needs of the dining room party.

Reluctantly I returned upstairs, now to the first floor, and found the room, which was an entire suite, with internal double glass doors and iris-purple draperies. The windows looked curiously through an odd gap in buildings, perhaps knocked out for this purpose, to the chariot stadium, now flooded by light from a late-rising full moon.

Munne was in a temper. She accused me of a hundred crimes, some of which were true but not in this particular instance, and several of which were physically impossible.

Finally the supper arrived. It was sketchy enough, but improved by a magnum of Champagne.

"Such bad taste to drink this with a meal, but I know you have no care for that!"

Throughout the meal, between her phases of concentrated eating, when silence beautifully reigned, she reviled me. I was a parasite, a leech. I was a common slut and heartbreaker who paid no attention to the tendernesses she lavished on me. She should get shot of me. She should have me shot. She might do it herself. Was I aware her uncle had taught her, in earliest girlhood, how to employ a revolver?

I nibbled paté and some cheese and grapes, and drank the Champagne. I thought of how I had left my last cigarettes for Claire Irén, and that I wished I might have done something more concrete to assist her, but was too spineless, too much a coward, a parasite, a leech, indeed worthy only of shooting. Not worthy enough of it, frankly.

At last the food and drink churned Munne out of her vitriolic bad mood into a lascivious one.

"Oh, hang it all," she said gallantly, "you know I love you, you bitch. Get some of your clothes off, *ma belette,* and let's screw all over that lovely big bed."

Presently she raised her head from me, much as she did from a dish of food.

"I see tonight I must break you to my will."

She did so. After all, I was spineless. What was there to break?

I woke because I heard, or so it seemed to me, a thousand clocks all chiming the hour of three in the morning. I was drunk, no doubt. Precisely the way vision might double or treble, my hearing had. Wanting water I left the bed and fumbled for the carafe, but it was empty. I should have to seek the bathroom. Despite the elegance of the suite, the bathroom was outside its walls, lying just along the corridor. Accordingly I got dressed, for know my luck, if I attempted my foray déshabille, I would inevitably meet some indiscriminate, amorous male, whose response would be worse even than the excesses of Munne.

Having dressed, I took my bag with me, nurturing some vague idea of locating new cigarettes somewhere or other in the town. A properly irrational thought. What could be open?

The hotel was quiet as a deserted ruin. It might have been those Roman baths I had strayed into, uncannily closed over and altered in looks. Perhaps these corridors were catacombs rather.

Perhaps the dead lay mummified and neatly parceled behind all those granite slabs that were doors. I paused only to drink a little water from a tap. Then I went on.

When I reached the lobby, the desk was deserted, just as Claire Irén had described it, and all electricity switched off, it seemed. An isolated lamp burned dully yellow, casting webbed shadows over walls and floor.

When I tried the outer door it was adamant. But in the dining room, now cleared and hollow, haunted by phantoms of the dinner party and the band, the street door mystically yielded to my touch. I let myself out, and shut it softly behind me. Up the cobbled street I went, under the heavy, nodded-over heads of the upper storeys.

Naturally I found no tobacconist ready to sell me cigarettes or aniseed cashews. But when the dry sun lifted over the plain beyond the walls, enflaming the white stone of the town to amber, a man came by with a cart. For a couple of francs he agreed to take me where I asked to go. This was not the Hell reserved for Ineffectuals, those whose sins are of omission, and for which, sometimes, they blame themselves worse than for robbery, violence or slaughter. It was merely another town of Roman stones.

As for Munne, I never saw her again, though her type, sometimes. Probably her curse rests on me still. But occasionally I do entertain a surreal and cartoonish vision of her, descending to the lobby in disarray that following morning. I hear her bellowing not through tears but peevish rage, that her friend has disappeared, her friend has vanished in the night. And do they tell her then that no one had ever seen me, nobody at all? I had never been there anyway. I had never existed.

Le Jardin

L E J A R D I N

The telephone call was brief, brittle and bright. Mr Dryne was free on Wednesday and would like to arrive at one p.m. Rachel thought of the French term: *arrive*—the sexual connotation. But she said, quietly, "Yes, I see."

"Please don't trouble about lunch. Mr Dryne will bring something."

"Yes. How nice."

The assistant thanked her and rang off. Her fate was now sealed. She would have to let Julian Dryne and all his works into her flat, complete with the lunch he had promised her, when she said she preferred not to visit the local bistros at lunchtime.

Rachel sighed, and looked about her. The shabby, comfortable flat, with its old garden, that was in summer almost tropical in abundance, crimson roses in the trees, plumes of fern, waterfalls of laburnum, everything kept just at bay from the house by the short terrace. But which in winter, as today, and as it would be on Wednesday, was sere and spare, the bare branches revealing the ugly block of flats, a puddle caught for ever in the cracked terrace flags.

Julian Dryne was impossible to resist. He had written her seven letters, finally somehow found her ex-directory number, had his assistant call her, called her himself nine, ten, eleven times.

Jokingly he had said to her, "I'm never going to give up, you know. This means a lot to me. Please don't think of it as an intrusion. I'm such a wild fan of hers. I'm sure you can understand. You *met* her. Can you guess what that does to me?"

"Haven't you discovered anyone else who met her?" Rachel had asked, irritated, as if by a series of stabs from a pin, into talking.

"Well, yes. But she became such a recluse. You, your family, were almost the last people. And he's dead, of course."

Rachel thought, and if he wasn't, he would never let you near him. That house in the suburbs of Cairo, with its mastiffs, and armed Scandinavian guards in dull black suits.

But Rachel had no protection except her anonymity, which Julian Dryne had pierced and did not now believe in.

She had given in, to have it end. As one said to the school bully, do it then, punch me and make me bleed. Then it will be over.

He *arrived,* of course, twenty-five minutes late. When she had opened the street door for him, she heard him come into the hall with a male assistant. Then he sent the assistant away and rang her bell.

She opened the door to her flat, and looked up and up at him. He was about six foot three, and thin, and leatherily tanned. Maybe forty-nine, fifty-one, about seven years her junior. But with that not-always male thing of vigorously imposed youthful fitness, so harsh, as if to be a Lesson to Us All. She was almost relieved to see his teeth had a faint tin burnish from smoking.

"Julian," he said, holding out his thin brown hand with its expensive nails and gold signet. "And may I call you Rachel?"

"Why not?" said Rachel.

He had brought a lunch hamper from Fortnums, divine absurd things that should be for young lovers, who had no time to cook, between explosions of lust—truffles, salmon, clotted cream, walnuts—and two bottles of Dom Perignon, in two coolers.

"I hope you like it?"

"Oh, I like champagne."

She had set the table, and now he opened the wine expertly—one prayed he would make a hash of it, but obviously not—and filled the two glasses.

"Let's drink to her, shall we? To Avrilenne?"

"Yes," said Rachel.

He said the champagne wasn't cold enough. You couldn't beat old-fashioned ice, could you. Trying to make her a co-conspirator?—in *their* young day—trying to get her to do *something* hospitable.

She filled a large saucepan with ice and cold water, and let him stand both bottles in it.

The bare garden was outside this room. It stood at her back as she faced him along the ancient table, polished, and scattered with what looked like bullet-holes.

He said, almost at once, "*That* explains all those singing birds, the scent—roses? How do you start them so early?"

"I don't," she said. Then, "It must be air freshener."

"How disappointing. It smells wonderful."

He began to tell her about the books he had written, and about the book he wanted to write on Avrilenne Kissei. "She's so much more fascinating than the other women who worked with gardens. I mean, the European and Eastern elements she combined in her designs. She lived in Cairo. I think she did? Is that right?"

"For some years, with her husband."

"But you didn't meet her there."

Rachel took a breath. Although they were still eating, or he was still eating, she took out her cigarettes. She did not care if he minded. In fact he did not. He came at once to light her up with a platinum lozenge, then went back to his place and drew a long, grey cigarette for himself from a case. He did not ask for an ashtray, used the plate. She suspected him of threatening her with this, an intentional boorishness. But again, she did not care.

"I met her once there, when I was a child. I'm afraid I don't remember anything about it. I was told I had, that's all. The meeting I recall was when I was about twenty."

"In the fifties," he said, "fifty-seven, fifty-eight—"

"Yes."

"That was at your father's house in Suffolk."

"One of the houses. It must have been Suffolk, I suppose."

"Was that when—" he hesitated. She knew what he had been about to say, but did not respond. He said, "But I want you to tell me."

"There isn't much to tell. My father decided to meet Kissei on business. He came to the house with his wife."

"Did you know she was so important?"

"I knew about her. But she wasn't, you see, so famous or important then. Professional women were still dismissed. It was a pretty hobby for her, designing gardens."

"No one realized she was a genius," he said. "That's so typical. Only after her death—how old were you when she died?"

"I was in my thirties. I'm afraid I didn't know. I'm still not sure of the date."

"1969." Julian Dryne crushed out his cigarette, and lit another. "Please do drink your champagne, Rachel."

He sounded like a strict nanny from her childhood. She laughed. He said defensively, misunderstanding, "I'm afraid I'm a hundred-a-day man, left to myself."

Rachel made no comment. She smoked four or five cigarettes a day. She drank her champagne, and let him refill the glass. It was a fine old glass, embroidered by design, but with a little chip out of it. He knew she had no money. The fortune, if there had ever really been one, had vanished with her father. Dryne had gauged the flat, of course, damp patches, dark areas. A sitting room with a dining table, a bedroom, a small study, a bathroom and a kitchenette. But then he meant to offer her a large sum. It must be reassuring to him, all this.

"Well, Rachel. Tell me something about Avrilenne Kissei. What did you think of her?"

"I thought she was unusual."

"Yes, yes. That's right. What a perfect description. She looks beautiful in some of her photographs. Plain, almost dumpy, in others."

He waited, his eyes stretched wide, mouth devouring another cigarette, a biscuit with Stilton lying untouched, because he needed the drug so much more than the food.

"She was beautiful," said Rachel. "She had beautiful eyes. Dark green, with a slight cast in the right one. She wore glasses for drawing." As she had known, she did not want to speak to him about Avrilenne. But the bully had forced her to the bushes. The beating must begin and go on.

"Did you talk a lot, she and you, Rachel?"

"No. Not really. She spent most of her time in her room. She'd had a horrible journey, and then 'flu. Kissei was always running away from things that had gone wrong for him. He sorted out some deal with my father. She came downstairs for the last three days. She sat with the other women. She didn't say much."

"But you must have spent some time alone with her."

Rachel looked at him. "Are you asking if she was my lover?"

Julian Dryne smiled, magnanimous, oily, "*You* must tell me that, Rachel."

"Must I? Then no."

"She was in her forties and you were only twenty."

"That wasn't the reason."

"But I've seen your own photo, Rachel. You were a lovely young woman. And Avrilenne—liked women."

"The only time we spent alone was one afternoon after lunch. We walked in the garden. It was a very big garden. It had the usual things, topiary, a little maze, a rose arbour, sunken garden, pool, water-steps." He was reacting like some awful sort of word-eating plant, expanding greedily to every phrase. Rachel said, "We just talked about the garden. There were things she said she would have liked to suggest."

"Was that when she—" he could hardly contain himself now, "when she told you about the château at Narbelle?"

"No, she never told me about the château."

"But the drawing—" he cried. It was out.

Rachel lowered her eyes. "What drawing, Mr Dryne?"

Her clothes smelled of Egypt, that was what Rachel had thought, a yellow—sandy—pink—ochre smell of dust and the river and the invoked spices of mummy. There had been a yearning to question her about the city. And then an aversion. Avrilenne was plump, her skin carefully preserved, her sable hair perhaps artificially free of any grey. She wore no make-up except for the red lipstick and eyebrow pencil that women affected then.

Her eyes were sleepy, droopy, the colour of the Nile in stories and not in fact.

That afternoon Rachel had met her on the terrace, the long, wide, white terrace with a statue of Apollo, turning his harp towards the descending Steppes of the vast garden.

"Will you walk with me, Rachel?" asked Avrilenne Kissei in her weary husky voice, that had lost all accent of anywhere and sounded only utterly foreign, presumably to every race. It was by the lily pond that Avrilenne stopped. She said abruptly, "Do you ever think about death?"

Rachel said, truthfully, "Yes."

"Does it frighten you?"

"Yes."

"But isn't life more terrifying?"

Between the flat sallow lilies, their reflections gradually appeared, some vagary of the hot still afternoon sky. They had a look of each other, and gazing down, Avrilenne had laughed.

"There we are. But in a moment, gone."

Rachel had not minded this strange conversation. The people in her father's house spoke of Cricket and cars, social functions, taxes, investments, politics (the Suez crisis in honour of Kissei), clothes and food.

Avrilenne and Rachel sat in the rose arbour. "I would pull this dreadful garden apart," Avrilenne said. "It is all *things*. I would make it whole. Like an operation. Everything would be healed, and better afterwards."

Then she had gone to sleep, snoring a little, very softly, as if she were unable to rest when alone or with her husband. Rachel sat by her side, smelling her Egyptian smell and some tindery French perfume that she wore, and half closing her eyes, watched the dragonflies dance on the water of the pond.

Avrilenne woke about four, in time for the ritual English tea no one, save the most voracious, ever wanted.

She made no apology, seemed unruffled by her lapse. She put out her fine, veined hand, and stroked Rachel's cheek. It was not a lover's caress, only very proper, the touch of a familiar aunt.

"I was once your age, Rachel. One day you will be mine. The horrible wars are all over. I shall send you something, one day. A drawing. May I do that?"

Rachel had, at that time, never seen the drawings of Avrilenne Kissei. Did not think they would matter much, that is, not in pecuniary terms, or in the way of fame, but simply in the scheme of life. But the drowsy eyes of the fictional Nile made her say, "I'd like that. Thank you. But you won't remember."

"Yes. I should have liked to know you better. If you'd been older. Somewhere else."

"I might go back to Egypt," Rachel had said, boldly.

"Don't. Your heart will be broken."

"I might break it anyway," said Rachel. "I sometimes drop things."

Avrilenne laughed loudly now, her green eyes turned up to the Sun, flashing gold.

Then some servant came, and called them in like naughty children to tea.

The next day Kissei and his wife left for London.

"Those birds," said Julian Dryne, "they sing so loudly. I didn't think that happened at this time of the year."

"A few fine days deceive them," Rachel said. "The weather's odd now, isn't it."

"That's true. My God. I've fallen into that thing where childhood summers are always hot. Does that happen to you?"

"They were," she said.

"But they can't have been."

Rachel smiled. "I was in Egypt, remember. And then in France."

"Of course. France—I'm almost hearing cicadas now…"

"The central heating does that."

"Yes… But you say she never spoke to you about the château and the garden she planned there."

"She didn't, no."

"I'll swear that's a nightingale," he said suddenly, craning from his chair, scanning Rachel's garden. "But not here, not in England. Not on a winter's day."

Rachel said, calmly, because she could hear the nightingale too, "one of my neighbours thinks he hears it. It's strange. Perhaps it's escaped from somewhere."

"You do hear them in France, of course," he said, "in summer. All day long. And they mimic the other birds. There—is that a lark—my God, what a chorus—and now it's stopped."

Rachel said, "My neighbour suspects someone has a CD of birdsong, and is playing it, with the window ajar." This was true. The neighbour suspected Rachel of the crime.

"Well, the rain's stopped them. Or stopped the CD."

"Yes, it has."

How effective were his matt little eyes? Could he see, although it was just audible, there was no rain falling on her garden of bare branches, no rain needling at the stagnant puddle on the terrace?

He was refilling their glasses from the second bottle.

"Tell me about the drawing," he said, throwing caution to the winds. "*Please.*"

"I asked you before, which drawing?"

"The drawing for the garden at the château of Narbelle. Which was never finished—neither drawing nor garden. And of course, we know what the Germans did to the garden when they occupied the château."

"I'm afraid not."

"The drawing Avrilenne gave you, Rachel."

Rachel looked up. She met his eyes. "I think you've been misled, Mr Dryne."

"Sorry, Rachel, no. I have an impeccable—let me say, source. And my source assures me that some time before her death, Avrilenne Kissei sent you the signed but unfinished drawing which she made for the garden at Narbelle in 1936."

Rachel found it simple now to look right through him. She said steadily, "This is really why you wanted to see me, isn't it, Mr

Dryne. Because you think I have a priceless signed work by an architectural floral artist who's come into sudden fashion."

"I'm—interested, yes, Rachel. Of course I am."

"You'd like to buy it from me."

"That's blunt. Yes. I would like to."

"You brought your chequebook. Do you have that much in your account?"

Julian Dryne blinked, then grinned his fouled teeth at her. "You're a deceiver, Rachel. I have certain documents that will show you I can pay you very handsomely. Will that do?"

"Don't you want to see the drawing?"

"Oh Rachel, I'm faint with wanting to see the drawing."

"Pen and ink, with colour wash, actually," she said. "Quite small. Twenty inches by sixteen, without frame."

"Oh God, Rachel—" He was like a man longing to fuck her, desperate, pleading, grinning, almost dribbling, and on her white plate the cigarette smearing to its black death in a pond of weeping Stilton.

"This is very embarrassing," said Rachel. "Worse for me, in fact. I could have done with the money."

"What—" His face, acid pallor, dim teeth and eyes. "What do you mean?"

"You see, Mr Dryne, had I appreciated what you wanted, I could have told you before. Yes, I did have the drawing, of the garden—Narbelle, you say?—but I've been short of cash for years. I'm afraid I sold it long ago."

"When—oh when—where—Rachel, *where?*"

"Fifteen years ago. I took it to a flea-market near Highgate. He gave me—you'll curse me, Mr Dryne—fifty pounds."

"Fifty—fifty—Rachel, it's worth thousands—it's *priceless,* Rachel."

"Oh dear. If only I'd waited. I didn't know—"

"Tell me the place, Rachel."

A Filofax, a pen, things pushed aside, the lighter toppling in the Stilton.

"They closed, Mr Dryne. I know because I went back with an old chair I wanted to sell. I can give you the address, but it's a Chinese restaurant now."

"Give it me anyway, Rachel."

She gave him the address of the restaurant that had taken over the flea market where once she had sold a few items. The drawing not being one of them.

She had been told, by her own "source," that even if he ceased later to believe her, he would not send men to break into the flat, to search. He had his ethics, apparently, and she had clearly seen his eyes go round and round the walls of this room. He had made the guest's excuse to visit the bathroom. She had sensed he had, during this excursion, looked into the bedroom, into her study, the doors of both of which she had left wide. Even the kitchenette had been over-run by Julian Dryne, helping her with the ice-bucket saucepan.

"I'm so sorry," she said. "Its a catastrophe for both of us."

"Yes," he said. "Can I make a phone call?"

She told him he could. He went out into the hall, and she heard him telling another assistant to go straight to the restaurant.

The scent of roses, tamarind, orange trees, flooded the room in a deluge, and when he came in again, he reeled at it—"That scent…"

"Yes… I think the Stay Fresh is leaking in the kitchen. Of course, those smells aren't real, are they, all chemicals."

His eyes bulged. Like a small boy cheated of Christmas, he said, "Isn't there anything…?"

"I didn't know her well. I don't know why she sent me the drawing. I never appreciated her fame, or the fame she'd come to have. I feel as if I dreamed the lottery numbers and didn't buy a ticket."

"Yes, yes." He brushed her grief aside. He drank the last of the champagne. He looked so ill she suspected she had hastened his death.

Inside twenty minutes more he left her, and when she saw him to the door, the young blond assistant heaving out the hamper, which she had not earned the right to keep, she said to them, "I regret you had a wasted journey."

The drawing of the garden at the château Narbelle had come through the post one morning when Rachel was in her thirties, just before, it now seems to her, Avrilenne Kissei had died, there in the enormous stuccoed house at Cairo, under the shadow of the spider-like fans, the red carpets bleeding on the walls, the mastiffs baying in the courtyard, Kissei pacing below, unable to go up to her, unable to touch her or hold her hand.

There was a note. It said only,

> *For you, Rachel. You said I would forget, but I have not. This, perhaps my very best, even though unfinished. And the garden itself now rubble. The German soldiers raped women there, and tortured men. Later the Resistance burned it all. The wisest thing. So, only here, Le jardin. And now I too am stuck in the ground. But you go free.*
> *Allez, ma Chère.*
> *Avrilenne*

Rachel took down the picture she had hung that morning where normally *Le Jardin de la Narbelle* depended on her study wall, a picture of the same size, to hide the mark and give it cause, if checked.

She now leaned this picture on the desk, and held Avrilenne's Garden in her hands.

The inks, the colours, were just a little damp, after the shower. A mistiness hung over the architectural paths, the grey slenderness of a statue. On the roses, the hints of droplets, drying. The tamarind opened like a fan.

The glorious odour of flowers was faint at last, its wave dying back, and the birds were only the faintest twittering, mingled in the violin-scraping of the cicadas.

The garden had grown, since she had first received it. Initially, Rachel thought she imagined each new bloom, the statue of Pan that appeared beside the wall, the greener leaves on the wall the creepers climbed, and where the jacaranda spread its spicery. But she was not much given to doubt. Rachel lived always in the moment, glancing ahead, behind, aside. She watched as the garden expanded, filling up the paper to its edges. It exuded sounds, warmth, scents, and times of day, and in its dusk, sometimes she had vaguely glimpsed, behind the glorious wreaths of the trees, a passing, girl-shining Moon.

Avrilenne had been afraid of death, and gone to death, as most things fear and must go. But this she left.

Such a thing was not for a Julian Dryne, nor for anyone. Rachel did not consider it hers. One day it would be done, and no new rose would open, no more rain would fall, the cicadas would crumble to silence and the nightingale be dumb. There was no rational reason for its being, there would be no definite reason for its ending. As with all love, as with all life.

She hung the picture, shut the study door. In the sitting-room she cleared the plates and glasses, threw the monstrous, over-assertive bottles in the bin. Then, standing at her long window, looked into her stripped city garden, over the bare branches, to the block of flats, and the winter, and the world.

by Mavis Haut

When Tanith Lee writes as Esther Garber, we hear a voice that belongs to a well-defined personality. Though we are aware that Lee is still there behind the scenes, Garber does not serve purely decorative purposes. This new writer-in-residence sets Lee free from her better known writing past and opens the way to new directions. The preternatural characters and the strange worlds they inhabit in Lee's science fiction and fantasy can be put to one side while the two women explore the world as she/they know it. A new set of fingerprints have added themselves to Lee's new venture.

The collection of novellas and stories that constitutes *Fatal Women* examines the changes in values, social structures and attitudes toward gender and sexuality and love. It considers how women have adapted to these changes as they have entered into the modern era with its increasingly less segregated and differently delineated gender roles and learned to play their parts in it. Naturally, this diminished separation between categories spreads far beyond matters of gender. It causes considerable alterations in the way the world is perceived. Geography too has shrunk, history has become instantly perceivable, and change has flooded through the whole social spectrum. And of course literary conventions and boundaries have been blurring as rapidly as social or class divisions. Magic realism, for example, has become such a frequent feature of the novel that fantastic elements no longer signal that a work belongs in the category of genre. When she writes as Garber, although Lee is enveloping herself in a realism that is largely unprecedented in her work, she continues to grant herself the odd unbridled detour into the surreal and fantastic territories of imagination that her former readers will associate with her writing. However, the anomalies that appear in this book are fairly small and inconspicuous.

Lee's companion and accomplice arrives with her own detailed history and an unshakeable determination to be nothing but herself. (Lee's own, pleasantly conversational introduction to Garber and her siblings too, appears in Lethe Press's recent edition of *Disturbed by Her Song*.) And so it is Garber-in-herself who becomes the main repository of the fantastic even as she is key to a writing which contemporary literary convention would not term fantasy. The most notable peculiarity of Garber's "real" world is that it spans an impossibly long period, stretching from the mid-nineteenth century up to the here and now of the twenty-first. As we might expect from Lee, the representation of these more literal and immediately historical realities is scrupulous—but her attention to exact detail has always been meticulous and even the most exorbitant of her fantasy worlds has come equipped with a full range of material and cultural furnishings and references, and with characters whose observations and behavior are appropriate to their time, place and culture.

Esther Garber is explicitly homosexual. Her homoerotic disposition is of particular significance in relation to Lee's new writing persona insofar as it allows the merged writerly identities of Lee and Garber to inhabit a feminine awareness that is unadulterated by masculine concerns. Garber is an aspect of Lee and as Lee's alter-ego, it would be almost impossible to include a male perspective without relinquishing the special closeness and vitality that exist when new elements can be fully integrated and internalized into an identity. If Garber were to have been heterosexual, she would not have been able to occupy the intimate space in which a feminine identity can reflect upon itself in uninterrupted privacy. She would have to be more wary, more distant, and would probably become a little lost in the crowd of Lee's more turbulent characters. Lee describes the content of these co-authored works as consisting of "varnished truth and gloves-off lies." As always—and Lee is at all times the novelist, even when scrutinizing her own authorial identity—philosophical and psychological questions are phrased through manifestations of human nature. The medium is narrative, not analysis, which means that there are no very clearly demarcated conclusions to be drawn. Readers must supply their own explanations for the behaviors and the quirks.

The title of this book, *Fatal Women*, is used in two senses. It can mean either sexually or lethally fatal. In some instances the word encompasses both meanings. There are three fatal women who become intimate with death; one (in *Rherlotte*) is a serial murderess; another (Laure in *Virgile, the Widow*) is a romantic, death-obsessed adolescent, and the third (Sabia in *Green Iris*) acts with such empty carelessness that deaths follow in her wake more or less inadvertently.[1] The remaining three stories (*The Umbrella, Femme Fatale, Le Jardin*) do not involve death in an immediate sense but they continue to center on women's negotiations with desire, loss and the urge to protect love and creativity from greed, venality and ridicule.

In this Garber-Lee collection, the strong focus on the cultural and historical aspects of the real outer world suggests that perhaps the impossible longevity of the Garber siblings is needed if the sweeping changes in the zeitgeist that occurred between the mid-nineteenth and the early twenty-first centuries are to be represented as a continuous, developing, and meaningful sequence. Lee's concern with the meaning and effects of historical progression is evident throughout. The experiences of women looking for ways to come to terms with the social order, particularly in matters of love, identity and the indissoluble connections between them, are shown in all their relentless fluctuations. Set in more than one century, the pieces in this collection illustrate the evolution of feminine perceptions and personas as they adjusted themselves to the culture vicissitudes to which they were exposed.

Rherlotte is a true woman of the nineteenth century. She exists in an era when it is possible to experience grand passion without questioning it. Phédre, although too young to have become fully self-aware, already seems to be feeling premonitions of the increas-

---

[1] I discussed these three novellas in greater detail in *21st Century Gothic*, ed. Daniel Olson, Scarecrow Press, Inc. 2011.

ing emotional reticence that will overtake women in the twentieth century. Brought up by her grandmother, a former courtesan, Phédre is surrounded by considerable luxury but inhabits an emotional desert. She is indoctrinated with the idea that sex is a lucrative commodity which any woman of sense learns to exploit. The hypocrisy of the era regarding sex, money and class leaves her tainted and excluded from respectable society. Although she does her best to appear unsentimental and to avoid emotional indulgence, when Phédre undertakes to murder men who have abused other women, she behaves as if she is responding to a true calling and refuses to accept payment for her services. We suspect that, even if she is acting without being aware of her own motives, she is avenging her mother's suicide following the desertion of a faithless lover. All this begins to change when Phédre is approached by Rherlotte, the bereaved mistress of a man whom Phédre has poisoned at the behest of his betrayed wife. Rherlotte embarks on an elaborate seduction and succeeds in gradually awakening Phédre to the experience of grand passion. She then leaves Phédre to experience the same devastating loss she has endured. The opposing polarities of passion and reason have been fighting a long battle for possession of Phédre. Finally, her defenses give way and the unconditional and potentially fatal value her mother gave to love overcomes the grandmother's unwavering preference for money. This novella makes use of a series of striking and theatrical scenes to tell the story of homoerotic passion and a very feminine revenge that is effected solely through the emotional inner life. The structure is especially appropriate to a period when representations of female psychology, women's self-perceptions, and even the simplest portrayal of women were often made in very dramatic terms.

Set in the late nineteenth century, *Virgile, the Widow* is presented as a drama in three acts, even though in this period the female melodrama with its motifs of death and passion had already begun to wane. We first meet the protagonist, Laure, as provincial adolescent, much given to day-dreaming and poetry. The elderly aunt in whose care she's growing up is kindly in a vague, middle-class sort of way and Laure is left free to do much as she pleases. Her friend from the village school takes her to a soirée at the château—such events are held for the benefit of local girls who feel oppressed by husbands, convention or provincial life—and initiates her into homosexual pleasures. But Laure is inhibited by sensibilities steeped in romantic literature and soon becomes obsessed with the funereal beauty of a black-clad and sophisticated stranger in the village. She hears that Virgile is a professional widow who can be hired at a price to ease the last months of the very old or terminally ill. Her services are said to be unlimited. The villagers regard her with narrow-minded disfavor, though, when the chatelaine befriends her, their snobbery and opportunistic hopes prompt them to overlook her morals. Laure is further captivated by Virgile's clear contempt for bourgeois prejudice. She perceives her through a romantic fantasy that fuses love and death and is soon stalking the beautiful widow. When her aunt falls seriously ill, Laure almost wishes she would die and so leave her free to experience passion and her own death in Virgile's arms. However, when the widow strips herself naked in front of Laure, revealing that she is nothing more than a fleshly woman, Laure's fantasy melts away. She solicitously nurses her aunt and we catch a last glimpse of the mature Laure in comfortable intimacy with the friend of her schooldays. It is evident that, so near the turn of the century, grand passion has become more difficult to entertain outside the contexts of history or literature. Or the romantic imagination.

The third novella in which death appears, *Green Iris*, also deals with fantasies of pleasure, though this time it ends in disaster. A pervasive sense of alienation stems partly from the period—shortly after World War I—and partly from the personality of the protagonist, Sabia, while the motif of green iris conveys dissimulation and false appearances. Sabia is skilled in two things, typing and deception. Where Laure and Phédre had been in the grip of sincere or least imagined desire, Sabia experiences nothing more than irresponsible whim and caprice. Her emotional emptiness leads to boredom. Offering to work as a typist, she insinuates herself into the household of a woman she imagines it might be interesting to seduce, but instead becomes inadvertently embroiled with the woman's writer-husband. Sabia's emotional involvement is faked and her lies spiral out of control. The affair leads to the death of the couple with whom she has been meddling so pointlessly and she ends up in a dreary provincial town, living out an empty unreality. Her experience has taught her nothing. She has felt nothing, learnt nothing, understood nothing and sacrificed whatever personal integrity she had to self-deception and avoidance. Out in the larger world it is the period between two world wars. Sabia's duplicity mirrors an era of escapism when senseless celebration struggled to drown out thoughts of so much senseless death and lessons that might have been had from confronting the truth were lost in the noise of the performance.

The women of the remaining three pieces should perhaps be described more as keenly conscious of woman's fate than fatal. In no way is any of them a femme fatale in the style of temptresses and hard-headed destroyers of men who feature feature in hard-boiled crime fiction written by and for men and who in their essence resemble men in drag. These stories treat of women in themselves, women as they perceive other women, women interested in sharing a feminine understanding of their particular situations and the predicament of women in general with other women. In all three narratives, sexual desire and, even more importantly, sexual objectives are subordinated to a desire to support and avoid any harassment of the other. They respond to each other unintrusively, restrained by consideration and sympathy. With their quiet thoughtful demeanor they contrast with other more assertive and less self-aware characters. These women take few active steps to alter the flow of outward events. However, they never for an instant cease to take note.

The young woman at the center of *The Umbrella* has the workings of "the writer's mind." But, though she indulges in the slightly frivolous habit of making up stories about passing strangers, in reality she would never intrude upon the private lives of others. This slender and gracefully constructed story balances on the fine point where emotional delicacy and sexual attraction meet. Little happens. What minimal action there is all takes place at a bus stop. On her way to work every morning over a period of several

weeks, she watches a girl who comes to the stop at the same time
as she does. The woman is strongly drawn to the girl, who is quite
possibly oblivious to the reaction she is eliciting. The woman is
diffident and hesitates to start a conversation but eventually they
exchange a few words when rain provides a pretext to offer the
girl shelter under an umbrella. The girl never reappears at the bus
stop. The woman never discards the umbrella. Years later, she is
still taking solitary walks beneath it in the rain. This is a story
about love that does not demand or even need to be requited,
where respect for personal integrity prevents putting even the
slightest pressure upon the other. This uncluttered stillness ex-
presses the aesthetics rather than the dynamics of love. No physical or material climax comes to bring this story to a close. We are
left listening to the resonances of undispersed emotions—and
the patter of rain.

Femme Fatale takes us to another extreme. Told in the first
person, it recounts the experiences of a very young Esther when
she finds herself in the clutches of a dictatorial sexual predator.
Munne, who seems to be driving at random through Provence,
has picked Esther up somewhere along the way. She is the type
of homosexual woman who displays all the characteristics of a
dominating male, bullying and criticizing Esther. As they enter
an ancient town, they pass a woman who is weeping uncontrolla-
bly in the middle of the main road. Esther is rudely reprimanded
for failing to concede that the woman must be mad. At lunch
the same woman is sitting at a nearby table. The waiter informs
them she has been making hysterical scenes in the hotel about a
companion she claims has disappeared, whereas in fact everyone
else is certain the companion never existed. Later, Munne, irritated, leaves Esther to her own devices. Esther seeks out the
"mad" woman in her room and is shown a collection of personal
effects the companion supposedly left behind when she disappeared without explanation during the night. As they talk together, Esther never discredits the woman's story and keeps an
open mind even in her private thoughts.

When Esther goes downstairs, Munne has ordered supper in
their room. Following much ill temper and even more cham-

pagne, she tells Esther, "I see I must break you to my will." Esther merely comments, "She did so. After all, I was spineless. What was there to break?" Waking in the night, she goes to find a drink of water. On impulse and entirely without forethought, she leaves, also without explanation, leaving behind everything but the clothes she is wearing.

The true center of this narrative is not a masculine kind of sexual bullying—the bully is anyway a woman. It pivots on the kind of support women need and can offer to one another, even where it does not stem from an established friendship. Social regulation is imposed and maintained by men and will therefore obliviously disadvantage or even threaten women. This is especially true in relation to women whose views or dispositions emerge from a feminine consciousness that fails to conform with social norms. Esther is guarded. She shrewdly keeps her opinions to herself. Only the reader hears her unspoken asides. She is aware that she too would probably be considered "mad" if she were to openly expose what she observes, and so, though Munne often calls her stupid, she has not been branded mad. Her reluctance to voice or act upon her observations sometimes give Esther a slightly contradictory appearance but though she may not like Munne anymore than Munne likes her, at least she is perfectly aware of how she feels. Even so, she offers no outward resistance to Munne's criticisms or domination and when she finally takes action it is less through decision than impulse. Her brief expression of self-disgust and her subsequent departure seem to have been triggered by sexual coercion which is particularly disruptive because it involves involuntary participation in an unwanted physical act. The fragility of feminine self-belief is remarked here from several angles. It is seen both through a woman who is regarded as "mad" and a "nuisance" and whose experience is consequently discredited by everyone, and through a woman who is demeaned and bullied by a person who cares nothing for her, but who nevertheless finds a way to make use of her experiences. Esther's nocturnal departure creates a parallel which mimics that of the lost companion of the so-called mad woman. Unexpectedly, it also rounds off the

narrative with a sudden light burst of humor which suggests that
worldly wisdom is already on the way.

In several respects, *Le Jardin* has resemblances to *The Umbrella*.
Both stories center on an experience of beauty and love in which
desire that remains intact in itself may come to seem more poi-
gnant and perhaps have a more lasting meaning than desire which
quickly expends itself in sexual satisfaction. Lee's depictions of
deliberately unrealized desire demonstrate that to internalize love
does not mean to renounce it and that prolonged pleasures of the
imagination can be found in desire-in-itself. To dismiss this turning away from sexual activity as simple as sublimation continues
to focus on the goal of an end product, the forms of love that Lee
portrays here have no instinctual drives to reproduce. Because
they can exist more or less in secret and remain as invisible and
internal as female sexual organs, they do not need to adapt to
personal and social norms that are frequently unreceptive, pre-
dominately masculine, and invariably action-based.

In *Le Jardin*, the element of sexual desire never goes beyond the
suggestion that a woman artist had once expressed her love and
desire in the gift of a drawing. She leaves this unfinished drawing
of a garden to a woman who was only an adolescent on the single
occasion when they met and walked together around a garden,
but Rachel recognizes the dead artist's love in the unexpected
legacy. The drawing has magical properties. Like a real garden, it
continues to grow and elaborate itself; it also produces the natural effects that belong to physical reality, such as birdsong, the
scent of flowers, the sound of rain. The artist's immersion in and
identification with Nature and its magical continuation in this
work underline the feminine character of an aesthetic founded in
the natural world. Emphasis on the fact that, as a woman, it has
been harder for the artist to achieve the reputation she deserved
also conveys the lesser value often given to a feminine aesthetic.

The story is taken up when Rachel has reached middle age and
the dead artist has gradually become famous. When an art col-
lector continues to press her for an interview, she is well aware
that he is avidly hoping to get possession of the drawing. She
hides it away carefully before he arrives and attributes the un-

seasonable sounds and scents that leak from it to such mundane sources as air freshener or a neighbor's CD player. She provides cool and minimal answers to his salacious questions about her girlhood relations with the artist. Although he suspects her honesty, when she tells him that, unfortunately, she sold the drawing to a junk shop years before the artist's work came into fashion, he finally gives up and leaves her to return to her calm, unruffled life. The intrusions of commercial greed and the fickle insincerities of fashion have been averted and the drawing can continue in its posthumous work undisturbed. This story speaks of the particular character of feminine creativity and the difficulties of its interactions with the outside world.

Esther Garber supplies a space in which Lee's narratives find it perfectly natural to resolve themselves by means of introspection rather than through external activity or interaction. In this collection, the tempo has grown slower. Colors and sounds seem softer and more muted than in much of her earlier work. There is a quiet luminosity in this space. Lee's writing persona is more meditative and some ways seems more solitary in its internalized privacy. This work has a reflective intimacy which creates the slightly shimmering effect of images as they fall across very slowly moving water...

TANITH LEE was born in 1947, in London, England. She received a grammar school education, and thereafter worked in various jobs, including restaurants and libraries.

The publication, in 1975, of her first fantasy novel *The Birthgrave*, liberated her into full-time professional writing. Since then she has produced ninety-four novels and collections, and over three hundred short stories; written for TV, and BBC Radio.

She is married to the artist and writer, John Kaiine. They live with cats on the south coast.

Tanith Lee has won several Fantasy Awards.

ESTHER GARBER is apparently a European Jewess, very orientated towards Paris, and with memories of a strange childhood in Egypt (around the 1930s, probably, but, as with all Garber's timeframes, dates are hard to fix).

Her body of work is so far quite small, as she only came to serious writing in her fifties.

Many of her life experiences appear to have been detailed in her work...but one can never be sure what is fact.

MAVIS HAUT lives in London. She is the author of *The Hidden Library of Tanith Lee* (2001), various book reviews and a chapter on Lee writing as Esther Garber in the 2011 collection *21st Century Gothic*. She is currently working on a study of ideas that have contributed to contemporary feminism, along with some less usual interpretations and applications of her materials.

www.ingramcontent.com/pod-product-compliance
Lightning Source LLC
Chambersburg PA
CBHW031106030726
47496CB00002BA/410